MW00333073

Betrayal in the Casbah

by Ted Kissel

© Copyright 2022 Ted Kissel

ISBN 978-1-64663-567-2

Published by

≤ köehlerbooks™

3705 Shore Drive
Virginia Beach, VA 23455
800-435-4811
www.koehlerbooks.com

BETRAYAL

IN THE

CASBAH

TED KISSEL

VIRGINIA BEACH
CAPE CHARLES

1

MAY 2000, ALGIERS

Mitch never enjoyed attending the diplomatic receptions and dinners night after night. The fake smiles. The air kisses. The small talk. And of course, the lavishly decorated embassies. It all felt like a pile of artificialities among people whom, in the real world, he wouldn't give the time of day. He had been a defense attaché for almost three years, following a career as a fighter pilot. Transitioning from that high-stress, in-your-face, no-bullshit environment to this courtly, finger-food, double-talk world was difficult. But he played the role, hiding his dissatisfaction behind smiles and handshakes.

Ambassadors and senior members of the State Department had called him an outstanding diplomat. He protested, but they recommended to the secretary of defense that he be promoted to brigadier general. He didn't want the promotion. Becoming a general officer would lock him into this diplomatic prison for another five years. He couldn't see his life going down that avenue. He shuddered at the thought of struggling, on a daily basis, to be a combination of

James Bond, Emily Post, Julia Child, and Walter Cronkite. Even if he pulled that off, his liver would never survive the nightly baths of alcohol.

Nevertheless, one warm spring evening in 2000, he left his office at the US Embassy in Algiers and rendezvoused with the American ambassador outside the building.

"Good evening, Mr. Ambassador. How has your day been?"

"Fine, Colonel Ross, except for this reception we're heading to," the ambassador replied, shaking his hand. "I don't dislike the Hungarian ambassador, but his wife . . . She's such a pain in the ass. Always asking questions about Dallas and what to see when she visits this summer. Hell, I've never been to Dallas."

Mitch wasn't sure how to respond, so he just agreed with the typical "Is that right, Mr. Ambassador?"

The ambassador's massive black Cadillac pulled up. Mitch climbed in, following his years of protocol training and taking the secondary VIP position behind the driver. Four security "gorillas" piled into a vehicle that looked more like an armored car than a Ford Crown Vic. With all their guns, radios, and body weight, he was in awe that their vehicle could even move.

The two vehicles flew through the narrow streets of Algiers, the ambassador's driver sticking close to the security vehicle's back bumper. Mitch could never relax in these situations, often nervous that a cataclysmic pileup between the two vehicles would kill him rather than a terrorist's bullet. He sat back and tried to keep cool, but he was thankful when they neared the gates of the Hungarian embassy and the waiting reception line.

Mitch quickly adjusted his uniform and made sure that the badges and ribbons had not been dislodged. Then he ran his hands through his hair and checked his shoes for scuffs.

"Oh God, Colonel," the ambassador groaned. "There she is, waiting for me in the reception line. Just follow me, and when she begins to talk, try to distract her by saying something nice about her dress. That'll give me a window to find the drinks—I need a stiff one to get through this evening!"

Mitch glanced at the other man when the vehicle doors opened. "Don't forget our plan," the ambassador whispered as they climbed out.

As predicted, the Hungarian ambassador's wife was not shy with her questions. When she asked if Dallas had great shopping, Mitch felt a sharp pain as the desperate ambassador stepped on his foot.

Mitch examined her, trying to think up a compliment. Actually, her dress was quite nice. Its spaghetti straps lightly touched her shoulders, while the neckline gently exposed the cleavage of her well-proportioned breasts. She looked lovely. A sharp elbow from the ambassador snapped Mitch out of his trance.

"Ahhh, Mrs. Kovacs," he sputtered. "Your dress is simply beautiful! Was it made in Hungary?"

This seemed to break her hypnotic lock on the US ambassador. Her head jerked toward Mitch. There was a cold stare, and she said, "Thank you, Colonel, but it was made in Paris, not Budapest!"

Turning away, Mitch saw that the ambassador had already distanced himself from the reception line and secured a whiskey sour. Now a Russian political officer seemed to have him trapped in an intense conversation. Scanning the reception, Mitch noticed a group of military attachés clustered in the corner of the garden, near a fountain that looked more like a swimming pool than a work of art.

"Good evening, Colonel. How is America doing today?" The soft female voice caught him off guard. Mitch was immediately angry at himself for not noticing this woman approach.

"America is A-OK today. And you?" he replied, looking her up and down.

"Excuse me for surprising you, but I noticed your arrival and hoped to take a few minutes of your time."

Instantly his Defense Intelligence Agency training took over. Mitch mentally evaluated her accent, clothes, mannerisms, and facial color. One thing was clear—she was drop-dead gorgeous. There was nothing second rate about her appearance, with her long, silky, black hair, enticing dark-red gown, and delicate golden teardrop earrings. Rather embarrassed by his senseless initial comment, Mitch wondered if she thought that he was a complete jerk.

But she smiled and mused, "'A-OK.' I love that about you Americans: you just get right to the point without a lot of extraneous words."

Mitch laughed, "Yes, but sometimes it comes across as being extremely rude."

"Oh no, Colonel, I don't think anything you say could be considered rude, but I do have another question." She reached out slowly and touched his hand. "Would you please help me obtain an American visa? Believe me, I'd make it well worth your while!" She looked deep into his eyes as she asked. It moved his soul.

He had been confronted with many visa requests in the past, but never by someone so exquisitely beautiful. And her offer was something that only his libido could envision. Of course, helping her would be illegal. He wondered if she was playing a game and attempting to set him up in a diplomatic sting. Mitch tried to change the subject.

"I'm sorry, I didn't catch your name. Are you from Algeria?" His eyes slowly undressed her.

She laughed, shaking her head. "I'm so sorry, Colonel. Usually I'm not this direct, but I jumped at the opportunity. My name is Fatima Pahlavi. Public affairs officer, Iranian embassy."

His blood froze. *This must be a trap.* She was probably an Iranian intelligence agent. Mitch thought of the US military attachés who had been fooled by beautiful agents and photographed in bed after supplying the ladies with classified information. It was usually a ploy to embarrass the United States and, of course, ruin a military attaché's career and life. As he prepared to respond to the femme fatal, he heard a familiar voice behind him.

"Bonjour, Mitch. It doesn't surprise me that you're with such a beautiful woman."

He turned to find a very tall, slim French Army colonel reaching for his hand. It was Yves Dureau, Mitch's best friend in this unnatural world of diplomacy and intrigue.

Mitch had warned him that most American men didn't like the French custom of kissing other men during a greeting, so Yves grabbed his hand, shook it rapidly, and leaned in close. "Mitch," he whispered, "we must distance ourselves from the lady. She's poison!"

Mitch nodded and then turned to the Iranian. "Ms. Pahlavi," he said, "I'm terribly sorry, but Colonel Dureau has just informed me that the US ambassador requests my immediate presence."

Mitch attempted to avoid her piercing stare, but she knew his response was bullshit. In this strange diplomatic world, though, she also recognized that he had just been rescued by his savvy French friend.

"Colonel Ross, don't forget my offer. I will call you next week," she curtly responded.

Mitch smiled weakly and touched her hand as Yves pulled him toward the edge of the garden. Here the Mediterranean gently washed its warm waters over the fine sand.

"Thanks for getting me out of that shitty situation, Yves," Mitch said, shaking his head. "She was really intoxicating."

"I could tell from a distance that you needed help. It appears that the French cavalry rescued the defenseless American in the nick of time."

Mitch laughed and looked up at the Frenchman, whose rugged good looks in his legionnaire-style uniform reminded Mitch of Harrison Ford. Yves was smooth in his movements, never hesitating as he smiled while taking a glass of red wine from a passing waiter.

"Mitch, I do have something to discuss," he said, quietly. "It has to do with an Algerian submarine."

Mitch looked around, knowing that the conversation was shifting to classified territory.

"Yves, perhaps we should walk along the beach. There are too many ears listening here," he said, eyeing the Hungarian security guards, waiters, and guests standing just a few feet away in the garden.

"I suspect you're correct," Yves agreed.

They turned and meandered toward the darkness of the beach,

leaving the security of the Hungarian embassy behind. Soon Mitch could barely hear the reception's classical music over the pounding waves.

"Mitch, there was a damaged Algerian submarine in the commercial harbor. It had a gaping hole on its starboard side near the stern. Do you know anything about it?"

Mitch was somewhat surprised at how much Yves knew, but considering the French embassy had a population four times the size of the US Embassy in Algeria, Mitch should have assumed as much.

"Yes, Yves, I knew that the sub had been damaged and had to surface or else it would have been lost at sea."

"How do you know that, Mitch?"

"I have my sources at the embassy, but I can confirm to you that the submarine was rammed by another sub while playing a deadly cat-and-mouse game."

That was all Mitch could reveal. The embassy's CIA chief of station had explained the situation to him earlier in the day. US surveillance had detected a Chinese attack submarine intentionally ramming the Algerian boat. Over the past few months, there had been a breakdown of relations between the Chinese and Algerian governments over the price of oil. That was followed by an embarrassing speech made by Algerian delegates at the United Nations. The delegates condemned China for its childish reaction over a few dollars more per barrel of oil. But for the Chinese the situation represented a loss of face, and they wanted revenge.

Even among friends and allies, not all classified information could be exchanged, so Mitch looked at Yves and shrugged.

"Sorry, Yves, that's about all I know."

No doubt Yves knew he had more information but realized that by pressing the issue, he would be stepping over the diplomatic line.

They continued along the beach, never imagining that with each step in the dark, moonless evening, their lives became increasingly at risk. How could they know that just ahead, hiding partially submerged along the shore, a terrorist had noticed them approaching?

Within the protective blackness of the sea and the night, he had been waiting for a lucrative target from the diplomatic reception. Two unsuspecting infidel military officers were more than he had hoped for. Crazed by the teachings of al-Qaeda and Osama bin Laden, he was willing to sacrifice all for his beliefs. His heart pounded in his chest as his muscles tightened, anticipating the impending attack.

They couldn't hear him whispering, "Allahu Akbar, Allahu Akbar, Allahu Akbar," praising God's greatness as he pulled the stiletto from his belt, slowly emerged from the sea, and prepared himself like a panther ready to strike his prey. They had no idea that this extremist could almost taste their blood.

Walking beside Yves, Mitch heard the sudden sound of splashing water. A force like a freight train hit the left side of his body, slamming him onto the wet sand. A knife ripped through his uniform and sent a flash of burning pain through him as the blade sliced into his stomach. Mitch screamed when the attacker put his full weight on top of the knife, as if trying to push the blade completely through Mitch's body.

Mitch struggled to understand what the hell was going on. He grabbed at the man's wet, bearded face, seeking eyes and a target for his thumbs. But then there was another violent impact as Yves slammed the attacker off of him.

Yves began to scream, and Mitch thought he had been hurt, but he was desperately yelling for the embassy guards.

Just as the bearded man gathered his footing, a Hungarian security guard arrived and smashed the attacker's head with a metal rod. Mitch heard a sickening crunch as the rod dug deep into the man's skull and felt a splatter of liquid as if a ripened melon had been ripped apart.

"Mitch, Mitch, you're covered with blood!" Yves yelled as he realized that his friend had been stabbed.

Mitch lay back on the soft, wet sand and reached for the handle of the knife sticking out of his body. His mind, thoughts, and movements became a blur as he lost his grip on reality. So many voices yelling, people chaotically running, and the taste of salt on his lips from the sea. His world became surreal.

"Don't pull it. Leave it in or you'll bleed out," cried the US ambassador, appearing next to him.

Mitch tried to get up, but the pain forced him back to the sand. The knife dug deeper. As he lost consciousness, he felt hands of a professional examining his body and directing security guards to carry the stretcher to the embassy.

He heard Yves's voice trying to reassure him. "Mitch, you must hold on. Don't slip away. Remember, my apartment in Paris is yours. I'm sure that you'll find a good wine and a lovely lady to share it with you!"

Mitch slowly closed his eyes and felt his soul drift away.

— • — •

The beach became a distant shadow, and Mitch no longer felt the pain or heard the chaos. He was floating, floating between the huge, billowing clouds. He reached for the controls of the jet, but there were none. He was adrift amid the beauty of the brilliant sun, crystal-blue sky, and soft cotton clouds. It was warm, and he was content with the silence and security. This was where he wanted to remain, this was his nirvana, but it was not to be.

Slowly yet inexorably, a powerful force guided him back to that time and place where he had felt pain and seen death. He didn't want to return. He wanted to forget the ugliness of reality. The attack, the knife, the blood all rushed back to his consciousness, and he knew that he was not to remain in this heavenly paradise.

No longer adrift, he felt again the ripping pain in his side. A distant voice pierced the silence,

"Colonel Ross, *vous voudrais un verre d'eau?*"

He slowly focused and saw a young, attractive woman in white with a red crescent on her collar. "Are you an angel?" he asked.

"No, Colonel. *Je suis Abella, et vous êtes dans un hôpital algérien.*" She pointed to a plaque attached to the inside of his closed door which read, *The People's National Army Hospital of Algeria.*

She didn't say anything else. But he knew that in time everything was going to be just fine. Abella seemed to notice his slight smile as he thought of Paris and Yves's promise.

2

As the days turned into weeks, Mitch's French improved. Each morning he anxiously awaited Abella's arrival and her smiling face. This was more than just a patient–nurse relationship; Abella was becoming his reason to freshen up in the morning and attempt to comb his hair despite the pain. Yves had told him many times that the best way to learn a language was by using a long-haired dictionary. Mitch had never truly understood what he meant until now.

"*Bonjour, mon colonel, comment ça va?*"

"I'm doing very well, Abella, and you?"

Abella frowned, shaking her head in disappointment.

"*En français, en français,*" she scolded and then smiled and winked.

"Okay, Abella, *je vais bien, et vous?*" he responded.

She laughed at his terrible accent, but also because the back of his gown was wide open, exposing a portion of his butt. Mitch hadn't noticed the untied gown. In his eagerness to move closer to her, he leaned beyond the edge of the bed to catch the scent of her perfume. His hands lost their grip on the mattress, and he awkwardly fell forward.

He landed hard on his knees, the impact ripping the stitches from his wound. Pain shot through his body as if he had impaled himself on a picket fence.

"Shit!" he yelled, grabbing his side and moaning loudly as he collapsed on the floor. Warm blood oozed from the reopened wound.

Abella dropped the flowers she had brought and flung herself toward him. She held him tight, pressing her hand against his bloody fingers. He had dreamed of being close to her, but never like this.

"Mitch, you're hurt!" she cried.

He was stunned by her response—not only had she spoken English, but she'd done so in a perfect American accent.

"What . . . what was that, Abella?" he whispered, each word emerging painfully through clenched teeth.

She ignored his question and pulled him nearer. His head pressed against her breasts. He heard the rhythmic drumbeat of her heart increasing as she tried to lift him.

Abella had a strong, athletic build despite her medium height. Still, lifting Mitch's full weight was a challenge for her. She steadied herself, then pulled and dragged him to the bed. He reached up and grabbed the bed's side rail as Abella struggled to lift him to his feet. Once on the edge of the mattress, he rolled onto his back, welcoming the soft support of the bed.

"Abella, you speak American!" he said, trying to catch his breath.

She ran from the room without responding. Reaching down, he gathered a fistful of bedsheet and pushed it against the wound to stem the bleeding. He stared at the blank ceiling as questions overwhelmed his mind. *How was she able to speak American so freely? What is she hiding from me? Who is Abella, and is that her real name?* He had only known Abella to speak French, though he assumed she was also fluent in Arabic as all Algerians seemed to be.

His thoughts were soon interrupted by her angry voice just outside his room. Abella reentered as quickly as she'd left, pulling a doctor by the sleeve. There was intensity in her voice as she pointed to the bloody sheet, commanding the doctor in Arabic to examine Mitch. It was an unusual sight in an Islamic country. In this culture, demanding and directing a man of authority as a woman could be very dangerous.

"I'm sorry, Mitch, but now is not the time or place for me to answer your questions," Abella blurted out. "This asinine doctor refuses to help you because he says, 'I do not assist infidels!' But I'll see that he helps you. I will remind him that my girlfriend and I saw him groping a nurse last week, and I know his wife very well!"

Turning back to the doctor, she spoke to him again in Arabic. She kept her voice quiet this time but maintained her authoritative tone. Abella again pointed to the saturated sheet Mitch was clutching. It was no longer able to absorb his blood. She pushed the doctor toward him.

"Abella," Mitch whispered, "you'll put yourself in danger, speaking to him this way."

"I cannot be diplomatic at the moment, Mitch, so please shut up, and let me take care of you!"

Her forceful attitude was stunning. As she looked at him from time to time while prepping his wound to be re-stitched, she felt a new closeness between them.

"The doctor seems to have had a change of heart."

"His wife is a strong woman and quite influential in our government," Abella said. "She is the vice president of the Council of the Nation. She also happens to be the cousin of President Bouteflika. If I told her what I had witnessed, and it was confirmed, the doctor would disappear from this earth."

Mitch was shocked. Abella might be someone much more significant than just an attractive nurse he'd grown fond of. Obviously she was a skilled nurse, but her language skills, connections to the highest governmental officials, and her swagger astounded him.

She noticed that he was staring at her. Abella glanced at the doctor. He had turned away to wash his hands before re-stitching the American's wound. She seemed worried. Mitch wondered if she had slipped and revealed more about herself than intended.

Keeping her eye on the doctor as he washed his hands, Abella leaned close to Mitch. He felt her lips against his cheek as she grasped his hand and whispered, "All of this will become clearer to you, but you must trust me."

- • -•

Mitch had mixed feelings the day he finally was allowed to leave the hospital. He hadn't slept well the night before and was up early, knowing that the shower would be quite a challenge with all the bandages on his abdomen. But he successfully completed that task and then moved on to the chore of stuffing his torn and bloodstained uniform into the small hospital travel bag.

That damn hospital gown had opened up and revealed his ass to strangers for the last time. The casual civilian clothes he wore now had been delivered from his embassy residence. They felt clean and refreshing. He wanted out of this surgically sterilized prison, but he didn't want to say goodbye to Abella.

The US ambassador had notified Mitch that he was sending his chauffeur and a US State Department special agent to pick the colonel up at noon. The ambassador also mentioned that he wanted Mitch to attend an important meeting at 3 p.m. in the bubble.

Mitch was fascinated by the embassy's bubble. An acoustic conference room, the bubble resembled a huge, transparent, walk-in egg and was equipped with many layers of anti-bugging technology. He always enjoyed meetings there, primarily because it meant that the subject was of a very sensitive, classified nature. Plus, the bubble provided the best air-conditioning one could find in the embassy compound. That meant escaping the stiflingly humid Mediterranean weather for at least an hour.

At exactly 12 p.m., Mitch received a phone call from the hospital operator informing him that he had visitors waiting in the lobby. Abella insisted that she push his wheelchair to the corridor where the two embassy men were waiting.

"Abella, you know I'm perfectly able to walk to the lobby," Mitch said as she gestured to the wheelchair. "I'm sure you have other duties to attend to."

"Policy dictates that you must be in a wheelchair when being discharged from the hospital, Colonel," Abella responded authoritatively. She laughed and softly touched his cheek with her hand.

"Can I be perfectly honest with you, Abella? I hate the thought of not seeing you. Perhaps it sounds childish, but it's like that old song says." He cleared his throat. "'I was serenely independent and content before we met. Surely, I could always be that way again, and yet, I've grown accustomed to your look. Accustomed to your voice. Accustomed to your face.'"

Abella gazed at him and her cheeks flushed. "You flatter me and say things that I have never heard from a man," she said. After a pause she insisted, "We must go before your embassy visitors become angry."

He settled into the wheelchair and let Abella push. Reflecting on what he had just said to her, he didn't regret it.

His thoughts turned to the traffic accident that had taken his wife. It seemed a lifetime ago, though in reality only six years had passed. It always troubled Mitch that they had argued that morning. Because of his stubbornness, he didn't tell her that he loved her before they parted ways. He had vowed that if ever he felt close to another woman, he would tell her daily, in many different ways, exactly how his heart felt for her.

As they approached the lobby, he wanted to share one last word with Abella before anyone noticed them. Before he could, the wheelchair lurched to the right. Abella abruptly pushed the chair toward the wall, and Mitch had to yank back his foot as they slammed toward a swinging door and into a linen closet. The door closed with barely enough room for the two of them.

Although there was no light in the small room, the light seeping around the doorframe revealed the outline of Abella's body. Her hands softly cradled his face, and her warm, moist lips passionately pressed against his. Instinctively their lips parted and tongues intertwined. Mitch had dreamed of this but thought it would never happen.

He wrapped his arms around her and slowly rose from the wheelchair, pulling her closer as their tongues continued their dance. She pushed her body against his, and what started as a flame became a raging fire. His hand slid down to her buttocks, gently squeezing and massaging. He wished she were no longer clothed. Abella let out a soft moan. This tiny closet had become a paradise, and any inhibitions they'd brought into it melted away.

An abrupt pounding on the closet door snapped them out of their euphoria. He sat quickly in the wheelchair, and Abella adjusted her dress. She slowly opened the door, both anticipating an embarrassing situation. Then Abella began to laugh. He peered out and followed her gaze to an elderly cleaning lady walking along the corridor, pushing a broom and hitting every wall and door as she swept.

"Thank God," Abella whispered, exhaling loudly.

He breathed deeply, feeling the same wave of relief. Then, looking down the hallway again, he noticed the US special agent talking to hospital security.

"Abella," he hissed, "we have to get to the lobby ASAP. I'm sure security knew when we left my room."

"Okay, Mitch, but when we are together again, I need to refresh my American-language skills because I'm not sure what ASAP means?"

"You bet. Would there be an opportunity to perhaps continue our linen-closet research?"

Abella rapidly pushed him toward the lobby. "Absolutely," she replied, "but let's find a bigger closet!"

The chauffeur and special agent turned as they entered the lobby and Mitch stood from the wheelchair.

"*Merci beaucoup, mademoiselle,*" he said, giving Abella a clandestine wink.

"*Faire attention, Colonel,*" Abella cautioned. Then, with a smile, they parted.

3

Mitch felt empty as the embassy vehicle departed the hospital. The special agent attempted some small talk, but the colonel was not really paying attention.

"Colonel Ross, I bet you're ecstatic to get out of that damn germ-infested hospital," the agent said. "It's been, what, a little over a month? Must've been boring as hell. Just sitting in that shithole room without American TV channels, eating that Algerian crap food. Christ—goat, couscous, and dates? Give me a burger and fries anytime over that shit."

Mitch tried to ignore him, but the cultural insults were too much.

"You know, your opinion is like an asshole—everyone has one, but some smell worse than others," Mitch replied, trying to stay calm.

The agent said nothing to him for the rest of the trip to the embassy. The colonel was glad he didn't have to think about anything other than Abella. As the chauffer radioed in their position and they rounded the last turn, the twelve-foot steel embassy gates slowly opened, and they drove into the compound.

Mitch had become complacent about the routine of entering the compound, having experienced it hundreds of times. But for someone new, it would be rather frightening. As their vehicle came to a rapid stop, security guards pointed machine guns and sawed-off shotguns at their car. The guards were partially hidden in their firing positions along the wall, behind a couple of palm trees, and inside a small guard shack.

Checking his watch, Mitch saw he had approximately two hours before the meeting in the bubble. He opened his door and waved to the guards. Jake Davis, chief of security, lowered his shotgun and approached. He gave Mitch a big smile and a bigger handshake that rattled the fillings in the colonel's teeth.

"It's damned good to see you again, Colonel," he said. "We were afraid you were going to be medevac'd out of country and permanently sent back to the States."

Jake was a good old boy from Kentucky who had spent his entire career as a special agent for the US State Department after graduating from the University of Louisville. Most people took note of his size first. He could have played tackle for the Chicago Bears. But Jake was a unique man and always up for a challenge. Mitch had been told that he was the first African American to enter the State Department as a special agent. He had a great sense of humor and frequently provided a welcome comic relief in this environment of long hours and extreme political stress. Mitch liked him a lot.

"Jake, it feels like I've been away for ages," Mitch replied with a smile and a pat on his back. "But I'm almost one hundred percent. I figure I'm just about ready to kick your butt in a game of darts for a round of beers."

"You're on, Colonel! Just name the time and the place," Jake replied, pulling a well-chewed cigar from his mouth.

As Mitch grabbed his bag from the trunk of the car, a wave of fatigue hit. He thought about coffee from the cafeteria but dismissed that thought; he felt filthy. He headed for his embassy residence and a well-deserved shower.

The Algerian gardener seemed ecstatic to see him when Mitch made his way through the embassy gardens. An elderly man who grew roses as passionately as Baskin and Robbins created ice cream, his roses were of all different colors, each one with a dynamic fragrance.

Out of appreciation for his skills, Mitch had given him a special gift—his cherished LA Dodgers ball cap. Mitch loved that cap, but when he wore it the gardener always commented on how wonderful it was. Since giving it to him, Mitch had never seen the man without it covering his balding head. Still, Mitch was surprised when the man rushed over and hugged him.

"*Bonjour, bonjour, bonjour, mon colonel,*" he exclaimed joyfully.

"*Bonjour, mon ami, ça va?*" the colonel replied, asking about his health.

"*Oui, je vais bien, mon colonel,*" he replied.

As Mitch escaped his grip, an embassy staff member approached. "Colonel, welcome back," the staffer said. "I'm sorry to inform you that the ambassador has pushed up the meeting on his calendar. He wants to see you in the bubble now."

"Damn, I wanted to shower!" he groaned. "Okay, tell the boss I'm on my way."

He picked up his bag from where it had dropped when the gardener pulled him into a bear hug. Gazing over the beautiful roses one more time, Mitch took a deep breath and proceeded to the chancery building and the bubble.

Five minutes later, he reached the chancery. This large, white, ornate building looked more like a fortress than a diplomat's working residence. Inside, Mitch showed an identification card to the US Marine on duty. The Marine looked beyond the card and immediately stepped out from behind the secure entry. Mitch marveled at how Marines always resembled a photograph from a recruiting poster. Every aspect of their appearance, from uniforms to haircuts, was perfect.

The Marine's boot heels thudded together, and he stood ramrod straight with a perfect salute.

"Sir, it's an outstanding day today because you have returned to the embassy compound!" he rattled off with flawless precision.

Although Mitch was not in uniform, he dropped his bag, stood straight, and returned his salute. "I'm very happy to be back, Gunny, and it's good to see you again." He dropped his salute and the Marine lowered his.

In his time at the embassy, Mitch had learned that US Marines showed the utmost respect to officers. They waited for the officer to take the lead on all actions, to include shaking hands. So Mitch stuck out his hand, and the gunny sergeant grabbed it with gusto and a big smile.

"Sir, there was talk here at the embassy that you might not survive that stabbing. Our Marine detachment went into a morale tailspin when we heard that. It's just been in the past week that we finally got the good news. We all made a special toast in your honor at the Marine bar!"

"Well, thanks, Gunny, and please pass on my heartfelt appreciation to the rest of the Marines in the detachment. But to be honest with you, if I don't get my butt to the bubble ASAP, the ambassador might finish what that terrorist tried to do." Mitch grabbed his bag and ran into the chancery.

As he approached the bubble, a US special agent standing at the entry motioned for him to hurry. Inside the see-through structure, he saw the ambassador sitting at a table with the chief of station.

Ah, shit, Mitch thought at seeing those two government heavyweights. This was not going to be a routine meeting. *Damn it! I can handle the ambassador, but compounding it with the top CIA official at the embassy is not going to be a cakewalk.* He swallowed hard just before entering, stomach acid rising into his throat.

"Sorry, Mr. Ambassador," he said once inside. "I was detained upon my arrival to the embassy."

"Mitch, it's not your fault. I'm the one that changed the meeting schedule. Besides, the last time we were together, you were lying on the beach, struggling to stay alive. Thank God you're here. Sit down, please."

Pulling up a chair, Mitch nodded at the chief of station. He felt a slight pain from his wound and a burning in his throat.

"You know Greg Cain, don't you, Mitch?" the ambassador asked.

"Yes sir, we usually grab a coffee at the cafeteria in the morning and compare notes," Mitch responded.

"Great. Greg, why don't you take the meeting and explain the details." The ambassador leaned forward and clasped his hands on the table.

"Damn good to see you, Mitch. Glad everything seems to have turned out okay," Greg said, bending over the table to shake his hand.

Having gotten the formalities out of the way, Greg got down to business.

"Mitch, I understand from researching your background that you flew combat missions in Desert Storm. On January 20, 1991, during one of those missions, you came very close to getting shot down over Baghdad. You were hit by antiaircraft artillery, the left engine exploded, the jet was on fire, and your back-seater, Bags, was wounded. I also discovered that you were awarded the Distinguished Flying Cross for heroism by the vice president of the United States for your actions during that mission."

Greg stared at Mitch without expression. Although everything he'd said was completely true, Mitch felt the warmth of embarrassment rise on his face.

Greg continued, "Your task was to suppress enemy air defenses and protect Air Force and Navy bombers and strikers going to downtown Baghdad. Their mission was to take out communication systems and command-and-control centers. You carried four high-speed anti-radiation missiles, commonly known as HARMs. You used them quite effectively that day, taking out an SA-2, SA-6, and a radar-guided 57 mm antiaircraft artillery, otherwise known as AAA. From your post-mission debrief to intel, you stated that during your final attack, your last HARM went ballistic. That seemed rather unfortunate for you, because the SAM site that you were attempting to kill launched a missile that exploded near your jet. As you stated during your debrief, it drove you down to a vulnerable altitude, resulting in your aircraft being hit by 23 mm AAA and subsequently catching fire."

Greg paused and took a long drink from his bottled water. "So, why am I telling you all of this? You lived it, and perhaps from time to time, you're haunted by it." He stood, placed his hands on the table, and leaned toward the colonel like a prosecuting attorney ready to drop some damning evidence. "But you didn't tell the intelligence officer the actual story concerning that mission, did you?"

"Greg, what the hell are you saying?" Mitch asked, looking at him and then the ambassador. "Do I need to contact a lawyer? Am I being accused of something?" The bubble wasn't as pleasant as he'd remembered. He felt trapped in this see-through capsule.

The ambassador reached out and placed his hand on Mitch's shoulder. "Relax," he said. "You're not being accused of anything. But there is a purpose to this. Please, sit back and listen."

Mitch's heart beat like a snare drum at a rock concert as he tried to collect himself.

"Sorry, Mitch," Greg continued. "I didn't intend to be so dramatic, but this is where your recollection of the mission seems to have become somewhat blurred. Since the war, US intelligence agencies have obtained new information indicating that it was not a SAM that forced you to lose altitude and then subsequently get hit by antiaircraft artillery. In fact, a MiG-29 fighter hit your jet with an air-to-air missile."

Mitch squirmed in his chair and glanced at the ambassador. "Sir, let me explain the situation during that portion of the mission." The ambassador did not reply but raised his left hand, stopping Mitch from continuing.

Greg broke the silence. "I'll continue, Mr. Ambassador. Mitch, you broke off your attack on the remaining SAM site when your back-seater, Bags, saw the MiG-29 converging on a flight of four F-16s. From debriefing the F-16 pilots and telemetry data from an AWACS jet and satellite information, the MiG was descending through twenty-eight thousand feet at 0.95 Mach, lining up for a kill. You knowingly had no air-to-air missiles on board your F-4G Wild Weasel that day. We know that information because you had ground-aborted your primary jet, and then you and Bags ran to the spare. The crew chief reported that they had not loaded air-to-air missiles on the spare that morning."

Again, Greg grabbed his water bottle. After draining it, he went on. "You were at twelve thousand feet, setting up to attack another SAM site, when you came hard right and began an immediate climb. You knew that you were not carrying offensive air-to-air missiles, but you continued toward the merge with the MiG-29. Just out of curiosity, what were you thinking?"

Mitch no longer felt embarrassed at what Greg had revealed. He was ready to tell the truth. Glaring at Greg, his jaw tightened as he attempted to control his anger. "You're right, Greg," he responded, with attitude. "I knew I didn't have air-to-air missiles, but I didn't want to see Americans die. The MiG was obviously using his passive systems because there was no defensive maneuvering by the 16s. I could tell that the Iraqi was positioning his jet to fire heat-seekers at the Vipers."

"Vipers? I thought the F-16 was called the Fighting Falcon?" the ambassador broke in.

"It's the name that the Air Force–fighter community gave the F-16. We felt that it was much more of an aggressive name than Falcon," Mitch answered, trying to be diplomatic. Then he turned back toward Greg, his brashness returning.

"I had one remaining HARM onboard, and I knew that it was useless against the MiG. But I thought there was a chance it would scare the shit out of the pilot when he saw it coming off my rail. The HARM's contrail resembles an old steam locomotive belching out vapor and gas. At times the thrust can be massive and significant. I've had an engine flameout from the distorted flow of air caused by the HARM launch. It's an impressive missile to launch, and it has a remarkably unique flight path. That's why I didn't hesitate to use it."

The ambassador seemed absorbed by Mitch's description of the mission. But Greg continued downplaying everything the colonel said.

"So, you were wasting the HARM purely to distract the Iraqi pilot?" Greg asked. "Plus, you really had no clue what he was thinking. It was only your assumption that he would be scared. There is one thing that we can agree upon. He definitely wanted to kill Americans, and he had the missiles to do it!"

Mitch's pulse pounded, and he attempted to maintain decorum. "You might be right in some of your conclusions, Greg, but let me say this: My mission during Desert Storm was to kill or distract the enemy from shooting down our bombers and strikers. That meant putting my body in the firing line of the enemy so that our bombers could accomplish their mission without losses. That's what Wild Weasels have been doing ever since Nam, and we continue to do it. If the only thing I had to distract that MiG from shooting down our strike package was my aircraft, then so be it!"

"Greg, ease up on Mitch and let him continue. I want to hear more about the HARM," the ambassador said.

Mitch gathered his thoughts and then resumed. "The HARM, when launched, drops off the rail and then its engine ignites. But the unique aspect of the missile is its flight path of pitching up fifty to sixty degrees. To me, that was the significant factor because we would launch at approximately five thousand feet below and less than a mile separation from the MiG. I told Bags to lock up the MiG with our radar because I wanted the Iraqi to realize there was another fighter in the area. I also wanted him to think that he would die within seconds if he didn't break off the attack on the Vipers. Once Bags locked him up, the MiG pilot was no longer interested in the F-16s. He immediately broke left and began to descend toward my jet. I maintained a five-thousand-foot altitude separation between us. I wanted to optimize the use of the HARM pitch-up flight path, and to increase the pucker factor of the enemy pilot."

"So, you knowingly put yourself and your back-seater in a dangerous situation, just to attempt to scare the enemy pilot," Greg said, staring at him.

"Yes, I did, but every time I strap on the F-4, regardless of whether it's a combat mission or just training, it's inherently dangerous."

"Mitch, you mentioned that you wanted to increase the pucker factor of the enemy pilot. What does that mean?" the ambassador asked, furrowing his brow.

"Sir, that's fighter-pilot jargon meaning to increase his fear factor."

The ambassador nodded. "Continue, Mitch."

"As soon as the MiG turned away from the Vipers, he locked us up," the colonel went on. "I immediately smashed the pickle button on the stick. At that point, we were within a mile of the merge. I paused to make sure that the missile had cleared our jet and then broke right, pulling seven to eight Gs in anticipation of the MiG's missile launch. In the meantime, Bags dispensed chaff and flares, not knowing what missile would be coming our way."

"Did you know or possibly see the outcome of your HARM shot?" Greg asked rather nonchalantly.

"Hell no," Mitch said. "I knew that we'd been locked up, and our radar-warning receiver was blaring that a missile was inbound. All I could do was maneuver and hope like hell to over-G his missile."

"But you weren't completely successful, were you?" Greg interrupted, looking at him and then the ambassador. Mitch was stunned by Greg's question. *How does Greg know about the outcome of the missile?*

He tried to put that thought aside. "The MiG's missile detonated approximately twenty feet from the left intake of my jet. The explosion caused catastrophic damage to the left engine. The engine exploded, causing fire to spread throughout the left side of the fuselage and the entire wing. I immediately cut fuel flow to that engine and had difficulty controlling the adverse yaw effect from the right engine. I initially throttled back on the right engine but realized that we were losing too much altitude, so I plugged the burner back in. That resumed the extreme yaw effect from the good engine, pushing the jet violently to the left. I attempted to counter that by holding full right rudder, but I was too exhausted to maintain that rudder position. I yelled out to Bags to get his damn foot on the rudder pedal."

"Did you get a response from Bags?" Greg inquired.

Again, Mitch was surprised by Greg's question. *Why would he ask that question? Does he know Bags's communications cord was damaged? I know Bags didn't tell anyone about the MiG attack.*

"Bags couldn't respond because his com cord had been damaged during the explosion," Mitch said. "I felt him immediately get on the rudder pedal, which helped to counter the yaw and allow me to concentrate on keeping the jet in the air."

"What about the fire? Was it still burning on the left side of your jet?" the ambassador asked.

The colonel shook his head. "No sir, when I cut the fuel flow to the left engine, the fire was extinguished and was no longer a factor."

He continued, "I realized that we had lost too much altitude, and I was having difficulty recovering with only one engine. Unfortunately, we were at five thousand feet when the 23 mm AAA opened up on us. We were too low and slow when the tracers began to pass over my canopy, and then I felt the jet being hit again on the left side. The artillery shells ripped into what remained of the dead engine, causing further damage. If the rudder had been hit, our only alternative would have been to eject."

"Is that when your back-seater, Bags, was wounded? Was he still able to keep pressure on the rudder pedal?" Greg interrupted.

"Bag's canopy was damaged during the explosion of the engine," Mitch said. "When we were hit by the AAA, fragments of its shells or pieces of what remained of the engine entered through large cracks in his canopy. I was not aware that he had been hit in the chest until later in the flight when he began to moan."

"Weren't you worried about the MiG taking another shot at you?" the ambassador inquired.

Mitch glanced at the ambassador, not entirely sure what to tell him. After a moment, he spoke. "To be honest with you, sir, as we say in the fighter business, I was assholes and elbows at that point and not really thinking about the MiG. I could only hope and pray that the F-4 would slowly climb out of the range of the AAA."

"The term 'assholes and elbows' means exactly what?" the ambassador asked. "Am I to assume you were overwhelmed in the cockpit with all that was going on at the time?"

"A brain overload might be a better term for what I was experiencing in the cockpit," Mitch said. "There was a point, while we were passing ten thousand feet, when I wondered why the AAA stopped and when the MiG was going to attack again. But nothing happened, and we continued to slowly climb and turn toward our escape, Saudi Arabia."

He was drained physically and mentally from all the stress and cross-examination. He wished he were back in his embassy residence with a stiff drink. A bourbon straight up was just what he needed to wash this afternoon away—like a late-summer rainfall in a parched desert.

Greg pushed his chair from the table and stood. "Mitch, I've been rather hard on you this afternoon, but there's a reason, which will be explained to you. Bottom line—I honestly don't want this to ruin our friendship. This will all make sense to you at the end of the day when we leave this damn crystal bubble egg."

To Mitch's surprise, Greg said this in a heartfelt manner.

"When you fired your HARM at the MiG-29, it must have momentarily picked up the radar emissions of the Iraqi jet and detonated with its proximity fuse. Or you were damn lucky, and it slammed into the enemy jet. How do we know this? When Desert Storm ended, an investigative team was in the area. They found the wreckage of the MiG and parts of your HARM among the debris. As I stated earlier this afternoon, AWACS and satellite telemetry had observed your desperate struggle to stop the MiG, survive the missile attack, and finally overcome the AAA. You questioned why the AAA stopped abruptly while you struggled to climb out of its range of fire. Actually, the AAA had not stopped firing but was directing its fire on an F-16. One of the Vipers in the four-ship you attempted to protect must have noticed the MiG. He broke off his ground attack to help you out. Unfortunately, the AAA shot the 16 down."

He took a breath before continuing. "I'm also aware that you knowingly violated a major general's direct orders by leaving your primary target area to chase the MiG, descending below the minimum briefed altitude of fifteen thousand feet, and attacking an enemy aircraft without air-to-air weapons. Those were court-martial offenses for violating the general's orders! That's why you stated in your intelligence debrief of the mission that you had been driven down in altitude by a SAM launch and then hit by AAA fire. The scenario that you gave to the intel debriefers was not a court-martial offense. But it seems clear that the truth would have ruined your career, and your future, had you reported it. Remember, none of what I am saying will ever leave this bubble. Please try to relax, Mitch."

Now Mitch was really stunned. He stole a quick look at the ambassador, then turned back to Greg. *How can they know this? I don't trust them!* Perplexing thoughts raced through his mind.

Greg continued, "We're still not sure how you and Bags kept your jet in the air and flew it to Al Kharj Air Base in Saudi Arabia. Frankly, it seems miraculous. Plus, you were almost smoked by a couple of US F-15 Eagles that scrambled from Al Kharj. AWACS had picked up an unidentified aircraft that was not squawking IFF while crossing the border. That jet was you. Luckily, the Eagles were instructed to get visual recognition. The Eagle drivers debriefed that when they saw your F-4, what was left of your engine was just a huge, smoking hole. They also said that most of your left wing had been burnt and blown away. They didn't expect you to make it to Al Kharj and requested a SAR-team launch in anticipation of your ejection."

The ambassador shifted in his chair and then interjected, "Greg, before you continue, I'm a little slow with your military jargon. What are IFF and SAR?"

"Sorry, sir, I get carried away once I get going," Greg responded. "IFF is an identification system that I can brief to you later. But simply put, it is a system on aircraft to quickly identify a friend or foe. SAR means search and rescue. Usually, at a minimum, an MH53 helicopter would be launched to pick up downed aviators."

"Got it, thanks," the ambassador replied.

Greg continued, "Then you had an issue with your left main gear collapsing at touchdown at Al Kharj. This shouldn't have been a real surprise, considering the status of the left side of your jet. Therefore, to complicate matters even further, this was a crash landing. But by the grace of God, you and Bags survived again!"

"Okay, okay, but I know all of this. So why am I here?" Mitch blurted desperately.

The ambassador moved his chair slightly away from the table, stretching his legs and crossing them. "Mitch, we know you have experienced a lot in your time, from combat in the desert to fighting with a terrorist here in Algiers. But the intelligence community conjectured, without actual testimony, many things about your mission on January 20, 1991. Greg and I wanted to hear the story from you to confirm what we thought we knew. Unfortunately, the only way to do that was to be very direct and sometimes harsh. We don't want to destroy your military career. Therefore, as we've said, none of this will leave this bubble. Now, let me ask you a question. Did you see the F-16 in your immediate area before it got shot down?"

"No, sir," Mitch replied, still somewhat puzzled.

The ambassador continued, "That American Air Force pilot, Captain Seth Hunt, ejected and was subsequently captured. We know this because we identified him in Iraqi propaganda videos found by coalition forces during and after the war. Evidently, Captain Hunt was passed from the Iraqi Republican Guard to terrorist groups throughout the Mideast. There have been eyewitnesses that claim, to this day, that they have seen an American matching Hunt's description."

The colonel couldn't believe it. "Mr. Ambassador, that's almost impossible. He was shot down in January 1991, almost ten years ago. How can we be sure that he's still alive, or know where he is now?"

"I'm sure you realize, Mitch, Captain Hunt saved your life by taking that AAA off of you and onto him," said the ambassador in a solemn tone. "I honestly don't think I would be speaking to you today if he hadn't done what he did. You should be very grateful."

"Sir, you make it sound as though I should thank him personally," Mitch replied.

The ambassador took a long silent look at him and then smiled. "Perhaps you'll get that opportunity if the CIA and State Department have accurate intelligence."

"So, Hunt is alive?" Mitch asked.

"It appears he is. The last known whereabouts of Captain Hunt were reported by French intelligence to the CIA two weeks ago. A Libyan terrorist organization known as the Libyan Islamic Fighting Group, or LIFG, imprisoned Hunt for several years. The French had information from an informant that the LIFG paid an Iraqi terrorist group handsomely for Hunt in 1996. However, the LIFG has recently fallen on hard times. They're being pressured by Gaddafi and banned worldwide as an affiliate of al-Qaeda by UN Security Council Resolution 1267."

Still reeling from the thought that Hunt was alive, the colonel's train of thought burst out. "Does that mean Greg and I are traveling to Libya? Why can't the US Embassy in Tunisia handle this situation? They're closer!"

The ambassador gave him a stern gaze. Maybe he understood Mitch's confusion, but he could not ignore the diplomatic faux pas of being interrupted. "May I continue, please? You and Greg will be going nowhere, and I believe the answer to the second part of your question will be forthcoming."

The ambassador glanced at Greg, then uncrossed his legs and slowly stood. "An Algerian terrorist was recently captured at the Port of Algiers while attempting to board a ferry to Marseille, France. The terrorist, Omar Abdul Hamady, informed French interrogators that Captain Hunt had been released by the LIFG and given to the

Salafist Group for Preaching and Combat, or GSPC. Hamady was a member of the GSPC, an extremely dangerous Algerian terrorist organization aligned with al-Qaeda. Hamady told the interrogators that before his capture, he and a GSPC colleague had traveled to Tripoli and received a captured American pilot. Hamady had been instructed by GSPC leaders to return to Algiers with the American.

"This new intelligence information has been briefed to President Bush, and the likelihood of an American POW in Algiers is being factored into US policy toward future relations with this country. The president and the Senate Intelligence Committee have agreed that the investigation and whereabouts of Captain Seth Hunt must be kept at the highest classified level.

"The White House, through State Department channels, has instructed me to work with US intelligence agencies to find Captain Hunt. That means I will be relying on you two to accomplish this task successfully. I don't want fanfare or casualties. You can use all means available to rescue him, but I have also been instructed that no special ops will be a part of this mission. We cannot afford the political fallout if Navy Seals were sent in to rescue Hunt and there were US losses. Again, I must emphasize, I don't want to see anything on the front pages of Algerian newspapers or *The New York Times* about what we are doing! I want that American pilot. As the president said to the secretary of state last week, 'This has been going on too damn long. Get him back to the States now, alive!'"

4

Mitch never got his bourbon that evening after the verbal beating he took in the bubble. Greg attempted to make amends by offering to buy the first couple rounds at the embassy Marine bar, but the Marine bar was the last place Mitch wanted to be—he needed to distance himself from anyone that even smelled of the US State Department. He dragged his bag through the rose garden once again. He waved at a security guard standing on a platform overlooking the embassy wall and felt his mind gradually shut down from all the fatigue and stress. He followed his feet along the well-worn path to the door of his embassy residence. Fumbling as he attempted to find the lock in the dark of the moonless evening, Mitch stabbed at it, missed, and inadvertently dropped the key.

He got down on his hands and knees to find the key and noticed a small, folded note partially tucked under the mat. He shoved the note into his pocket.

"Screw it, I'm going to bed!" he said to no one as he dropped his bag in the entryway and proceeded up the dimly lit staircase. Entering his bedroom, he collapsed on the bed fully clothed. His mind spun like a jet out of control as Greg's questions echoed. Mitch tried to force his eyes to close, but it was no good. Sleep would not be a part of this night.

He lay like a corpse, staring at the dark ceiling, his mind refusing to quiet down. *God, I'm beat. I'm not sure I can trust the ambassador or Greg. To hell with it, I need that drink, and I need it now!*

He sat up on the edge of the bed and looked across the room toward the small cache of booze tucked away in his closet. Just as he stood, the phone rang loud, piercing the darkness and scaring the hell out of him. He clenched his fists and glanced at the illuminated clock near the bed. *Who the hell is calling me at 11:30 on a Friday night?* The phone rang again, but he hesitated. He didn't want to talk to anyone. He waited for the third ring and grabbed the phone. Jaw tightening, he sternly said, "Colonel Ross speaking."

There was silence on the phone, and he was ready to slam it down when a timid, soft voice responded, "Mitch? Mitch, is that you?" The fragile tenderness in her words quickly erased his anger. "Did you get my note? I asked an embassy guard to place it near your door."

Mitch stuffed his hand into his pocket and pulled out the note. It said simply, *I will call you this evening. Abella.*

"Abella!" His weary mind and excited emotions collided.

"I'm sorry to bother you," she said, "but I couldn't resist hearing your voice again. I felt so alone when you departed the hospital, and I thought that we may never have an opportunity to talk or see each other again. We didn't have time to make any plans—I was hoping you wanted to see me again."

"Believe me, Abella, I would love for us to spend much more time together. But I've had one hell of a day, and I need to get some rest." He paused. "Out of curiosity, how did you get my number?"

"It was very easy," Abella laughed. "I contacted the embassy operator and told her I was your physician at the hospital. I made sure to sound very authoritative and she didn't hesitate. She probably would have given me a key to your residence had I pressed her!"

"Abella, would you come to my residence tomorrow evening for dinner? I'm invited to a reception at the Spanish embassy, but I'm going to blow it off since I was nearly killed at the last reception I attended. I'm sure the ambassador will understand."

"I would love to come, Mitch. That sounds wonderful!"

"Great!" he said, thinking through the details. "I'll take care of the security paperwork allowing you to enter the embassy and my residence. I'll be waiting for you near the embassy security building. That's where you'll enter the gated compound. Can you come at 7 p.m.?"

"I'll be there. Sleep well, Mitch."

"You do the same, Abella, and thank you for being my angel."

He held the phone to his ear long after she had hung up. He wished they were still talking, even though he knew phone conversations were monitored by the Algerian military. Mitch was used to hearing a second phone hanging up after any call.

- • - •

The next morning was bright with anticipation that he would finally be alone with Abella. He finally took the shower he'd been waiting for, put on a clean uniform, grabbed some fruit, and departed for his office in the chancery building.

An embassy office was not as glamorous inside as most folks might imagine. In fact, the chancery was rather dusty and in need of an interior decorator. This was not a location where foreign diplomats gathered but rather the working heart of this small, busy US embassy.

Mitch's military attaché office was located down a flight of stairs and behind a cipher-locked, thick metal door. When he arrived, he went through the routine he typically did three to four times a day. He pulled his identification card and swiped it over the lock, then punched in the coded numbers that allowed entry. His office was oversized and a bit ridiculous with its sofas and gigantic leather chairs that were used by no one. Two nine-foot shelves adjacent to his desk were full of intimidating-looking documents and books that he had never reviewed nor had the desire to read. The wooden desk was massive. He often thought that the lumber would have made an ideal sport canoe.

It was obvious to him as a fighter pilot that the previous attachés had been ground pounders and not aviators. Their interests centered on decorations and creature comforts rather than on accomplishing the mission. The entire office was belowground, so there were no windows. Mitch had no complaints about the lack of natural light; the subterranean location provided natural air-conditioning. And during those long, hot, humid North African days, this was a precious thing indeed.

Mitch didn't have much of a staff because of the likelihood of a radical Islamic terrorist attack on the embassy. The State Department had reduced the embassy staff to essential personnel only, which meant the colonel commanded very few individuals but had a tremendous amount of responsibility. He enjoyed the fact that with fewer folks to worry about, he had more time to concentrate.

His assistant was a US Navy commander who flew in from the embassy in Tunisia for a few days each month. Then there was Dave, the US Army warrant officer who seemed to devote most of his time to planning his post-military life. Even though Mitch's rank was much higher, he could never get Dave to perform his administrative duties while the colonel was out of the office. And he was always out of the office.

"Dave, how have you been?" Mitch yelled from his office. He hadn't yet seen Dave, but given the time of day, he should have been at his desk. "Give me a rundown of what's been going on in the office while I was recovering in the hospital." Mitch sat in his oversized cave, waiting for the initial response. After a few moments he repeated himself, but with an abbreviated military approach: "Hey, Warrant, get your ass into my office right now, and that's an order!"

Still no response. He stood and walked around his desk to the door, proceeding down the hallway to enter Dave's small office. Dave was not there, but the colonel found a note taped to the back of the computer monitor. It read, *Sir, I noticed that you had entered the office, and I was going to say hello, but I realized I had a meeting with the embassy building-maintenance manager. My residence kitchen is overrun with roaches, and it needs to be fumigated. So I'm scheduling a time when that can be accomplished. By the way, is there any chance that I can stay in one of your extra bedrooms for approximately five days? I would need the room tonight and over the weekend.*

Mitch ripped the note from his monitor and wrote a response with a large, black permanent marker: *About your request... not only no, but hell no, especially this evening. We need to talk!*

He was fuming and seriously thinking of calling DIA headquarters in DC to have Dave relieved of duty and shipped back to the States. He probably should have done that long ago. But then the phone back in Mitch's office rang, snapping him out of his rage. He sprinted to his office and snapped the phone to his ear in hopes he hadn't missed whoever was calling.

"*Bonjour, mon colonel Ross*, it is that dastardly Frenchman, Yves, that should have visited or at least called while you recovered in the hospital."

Mitch chuckled when he heard the voice. Yves Dureau had that unique ability to add levity to a terrible situation.

"Unfortunately," Yves continued, "the Ministry of Defense in Paris requested my presence. I love Paris, but I detest that puzzle palace my country calls our military headquarters. I had to leave Algiers the morning after you were attacked. I truly hope that I find you well and recovering as each day passes."

Mitch struggled to respond without laughing at Yves's description of the French Ministry of Defense. "I'm actually feeling great, and to be honest, this is my first day back in the office."

"That is wonderful to hear, but I have one request of my American friend. You must join me for lunch today. I am completely out of diplomatic protocol to request at such late notice, but I must make amends for my lack of courtesy while you were recovering."

Mitch considered giving some excuse because of dinner with Abella. But seeing Yves would afford him the perfect opportunity to probe his French military colleague concerning Captain Hunt. Any information Yves might disclose could help.

"Yves, I would be more than happy to have lunch with you. But I must apologize now for the limited amount of food I will consume. I have planned a dinner this evening with a beautiful nurse that I met in the hospital."

Yves laughed. "Why am I not surprised to hear about you and beautiful women? If I recall correctly, it was a beautiful woman at the Hungarian reception who was attempting to entrap you. But as long as the nurse is not Iranian, I suppose I will accept your apology."

"No, I can guarantee that she is completely Algerian, but with an interestingly rebellious personality that I find quite fascinating." Mitch was surprised to find himself responding from his heart and not his head. He assumed Abella was completely Algerian, but he had no proof of this. And then there was the matter of her perfect American accent.

Yves was no dummy, and he picked up on his friend's tone immediately. "Well, Mitch, I must say that I believe you find the lady more than fascinating. But that conversation is for another day. Does twelve noon sound acceptable to you?"

"Absolutely," Mitch quickly replied, eager to change the subject in light of the Algerians who were surely listening to their conversation.

"Then twelve it is. See you soon, my friend. I will uncork a fine French wine to celebrate your recovery."

As the call ended, Mitch heard the familiar click of a second phone hanging up. Irritated with the Algerian military for recording everything Yves and he had discussed, he realized he shouldn't have told the truth about his dinner plans. He should have made up a bullshit story about having dinner with the US ambassador and his staff.

He quickly headed for security to arrange for a protection detail to accompany him to the French embassy. Arranging for protection each and every time he left the embassy was frustrating but necessary, given the hypothetical target emblazoned on his forehead, just waiting for a terrorist's lead sedative.

After finishing with security, he stopped by his residence to change into civilian clothes. He wanted to adhere to the unwritten rule Yves and he had established: if it was just the two of them, then it was max relax and casual all the way.

There were a lot of rules, both written and unwritten, surrounding diplomatic appointments. One of the most important was to be on time—even if the other attendees were your friends. Mitch had learned that one the hard way. Therefore, at 11:30 a.m. he joined a two-man Algerian security detail—a driver and an armed guard— inside a bulletproof Toyota Land Cruiser.

He buckled up and braced himself for a ride that he knew from experience would feel like an attempt to break the land-speed record. Fighter pilots liked to say, "Speed is life." This saying also applied to security details chauffeuring diplomats around foreign countries. Of course, security workers had plenty of good reasons to speed through hostile territory. They had to assume that anyone walking the street might be an armed terrorist.

As soon as the massive embassy gates opened, the security guard in the front passenger seat adjusted his grip on the machine gun he lovingly cradled. The SUV leaped forward, rear tires squealing, and the driver immediately wrenched into a left turn. Mitch felt as though he had just been launched off an aircraft carrier deck in the Persian Gulf. The buildings opposite the embassy compound became a blur as they shot through the broad boulevard.

This street had once been a main artery of this former French colony. Yves had told him about how dreadful it was when France lost Algeria in the early 1960s during the Algerian War—a painful loss that still lingered in French society. He told Mitch to imagine the

US losing Texas and all its resources. That, he said, would represent a similar impact as the one France sustained with the loss of Algeria.

As they rounded another corner, the former colony's grandeur was on full display. Powder-blue balconies adorned the beautiful, tall white buildings built by the French in the nineteenth and twentieth centuries. This sight meant that they were nearing the French embassy. A moment later he felt the rapid deceleration of the SUV as they approached the entry gate.

The French embassy was the largest diplomatic compound in this capital city. The steel walls loomed invincibly, topped off with concertina wire bundles. An Olympic pole vaulter might be able to surmount them, but then he or she would have to contend with ten to fifteen heavily armed guards on platforms overlooking the compound.

Mitch's vehicle slowly turned into the entrance and faced a twelve-foot steel wall. They waited for a moment. He glanced at the guard peering over the wall and aiming a very large automatic weapon directly at the passenger window. Mitch tried to act normal, but his survival instinct made him lean toward the opposite side of the vehicle, away from the window. His seat belt protested, digging into his right shoulder and abdomen. A speaker adjacent to the wall broke the silence as a voice requested their identity and business at the embassy. Mitch's driver slowly rolled down his bulletproof window and announced them.

There was no reply, but a moment later the large metal wall lowered into the ground. They were instructed to move forward to the second identical wall facing their vehicle. The first metal wall rose again, wedging their vehicle inside. Ten-foot brick walls flanked them on either side, each one almost scraping the SUV's side-view mirrors. More French guards aimed their machine guns down from their vantage points atop the walls. Mitch's driver slid each of their passports through a small metal slot. He then rolled the window up, and they sat in silence. A few minutes later the guards disappeared and the wall in front of them lowered.

Now the stress faded and Mitch's breathing became relaxed. He thought now, as he often did when entering the French embassy compound, of the biblical passage that mentioned something about passing from darkness into light. The arduous entry procedure was a price well worth paying for the end result.

Once inside, he gazed out the vehicle window. It was truly the closest thing to paradise in all of Algiers. He no longer needed the bulletproof vehicle or his security guards. He didn't wait for the formality of his driver opening the door. He quickly moved away from the embassy vehicle and stood, taking in all the magnificence, finally feeling free.

He ignored the bland embassy buildings and even the large, stunning park beside them. What existed to the left of the park— that was truly breathtaking, as if Monet himself had painted the scene, with all the bright colors of a summer day in a small French village during the latter half of the nineteenth century. Mitch's eyes took in the radiant hues of the flowers lining the path through the park to the quaint cottages. The French flag flew majestically from a large pole in the middle of the park. Children rode their bicycles and played with a small dog. Young French mothers shaded themselves with parasols while pushing their strollers and taking in the warm Mediterranean breezes.

As he walked along the path, where no vehicles were allowed, he encountered more beautiful gardens. People sat at small tables surrounded by flowers and trees, eating lunch served by Algerian servants. The small but elegant old-world cottages were nestled amongst trees and a few grape arbores. It was a glimpse of what it must have been like when Algeria was the jewel of France's colonial empire. Yves's voice snapped him out of his time travel.

"Colonel Ross, please join me in my garden for lunch."

Mitch looked over to find the tall Frenchman waving and looking as if he were on vacation in Marseille. He wore light-khaki trousers, a blue long-sleeve shirt, tan loafers minus the socks, and, of course, sunglasses.

"Yves, you look Hollywood," Mitch responded, heading toward Yves's garden and cottage.

The French diplomats having lunch in their gardens glanced in his direction and laughed quietly. Yves had a reputation among the defense attaché community for being a suave bachelor. Obviously, his fellow diplomats were also quite aware of his status.

"It's so good to see you, Mitch, walking upright with your usual bright smile!" Yves exclaimed as he grabbed his friend's upper arms and leaned over to give him the traditional French kiss on each cheek. He must have felt the stiff recoil and remembered that American men generally did not greet each other in that manner, because he stood upright, laughed, and shook Mitch's hand.

"Thanks, Yves, for inviting me to lunch. It's always good to spend a little time in this nirvana you call an embassy."

"Please sit, Mitch, and taste the best wine in the world. Or perhaps I should say, the best wine this side of Napa Valley." He smiled and raised his glass.

Lunch in Yves's garden was made even more exquisite by his gourmet cook. Each course seemed to be the best until the next was placed before them. Mitch finally had to remind him that he could eat no more because of his dinner plans.

The conversation stayed casual during lunch, primarily revolving around Mitch's recovery, with a few details about Abella coming to the surface. Mitch grew anxious as lunch came to an end. He didn't want to abruptly change the subject, but he needed to know if Yves knew anything about the captured American pilot.

"Let's stop talking about me. I want to know the real reason you had to fly off to Paris on such short notice. Was there a damsel in distress? Perhaps the Miss France bathing-suit competition needed your judging expertise?" Mitch hoped that his lighthearted comment didn't sound too ridiculous, but he needed the transition.

"No, no, my friend, I can only wish that my trip to Paris was so pleasant. Actually, I spent most of my days at the Ministry of

Defense, briefing generals on the situation here in Algeria and receiving updates from our intelligence community."

It appeared Mitch's casual approach had failed, so he went straight for the jugular. "Yves, I hate to be so bold, but I must ask a direct question about your intel updates. Was there anything about an American pilot shot down during Desert Storm and possibly imprisoned here in Algiers?" The question was extremely direct and risky, but he was running out of time.

Yves leaned back, grabbed his wine, and drained the glass. Lowering the glass to the table, he took a deep breath and stared at Mitch. The colonel had not only tiptoed over the forbidden diplomatic line but leaped over it with both feet.

"What I wish someday is that I can be as bold as you, Mitch. Being French, it would take me numerous meetings and many more glasses of wine to ask a question such as yours. Your directness is so American. I suspect that is why France is no longer a real world power and the United States carries the big stick."

The sun burned the back of Mitch's neck as beads of sweat formed on his brow. His heartbeat had jumped to a deafening cadence. He braced for disappointment as Yves philosophized about their cultural differences.

"You amaze me with your ability to read my thoughts," Yves continued. "Yes, the intelligence briefings included details about your pilot. I had intended to discuss this matter with you, but I was not sure whether you were aware of the subject or wanted to bring it up this afternoon." He smiled, then grabbed the bottle of wine and refilled their glasses.

"Mitch, you must promise me that you'll hold this information very close. If it got out that the French were disclosing this information to the Americans, many French covert operatives in Algiers would be eliminated. Also, I would most likely be removed from my position here and permanently sent back to France. It would mean the end of my military career and the loss of a potential assignment as the military advisor to the French ambassador at the United Nations. But most importantly, I would lose the opportunity to fulfill my youthful dream of living in New York City."

Yves raised his glass and softly touched it to the colonel's.

"Let us proceed quickly because I know that your mind will be transitioning to dinner and your nurse."

"Thank you, Yves. I owe you so much!"

"Perhaps someday you can repay me with dinner at the exquisite Daniel restaurant in Manhattan." Yves laughed and then took a last sip of wine.

Realizing that time was of the essence, Mitch jumped in before the Frenchman could start in on the classified details. "Yves, before you begin, I was briefed yesterday at the embassy concerning Captain Seth Hunt. From what we know, thanks to French intelligence agencies, the American pilot seems to be somewhere here in Algiers."

"Precisely." Yves nodded. "From what I learned in Paris during your recovery, the former terrorist Omar Abdul Hamady is the key to the information we need. The problem we face is that Hamady escaped from French custody. Although he said he is no longer a member of the GSPC, I find it difficult to believe that he has severed his relationship with them. We must find Hamady. He told the French that once he handed the American off to superiors within the GSPC, his work was done. He said he could not continue the story beyond Hunt's return to Algiers."

Yves stopped talking as his chef approached the table with another bottle of wine. Mitch found it rather curious that while they had not been interrupted during their entire lunch, once their demeanor became more serious, the chef appeared. Yves waved him off, saying there was no need for more wine as Mitch would be leaving soon.

As the chef disappeared into the cottage, Yves turned back to him. "Mitch, we must be very careful. GSPC has members working here in the embassy. Dealing with Hamady will be very dangerous. Tomorrow I will talk to embassy intelligence about him."

Yves glanced at his watch, then looked at Mitch with a devilish smile. "You have something much more important to attend to than sitting in the hot sun, sipping wine with an old French colonel. I believe we have done well this afternoon!"

Standing, Mitch shook Yves's hand. "You're the best. Yes, I do need to get going. This evening will be very interesting."

Just before Mitch turned to head back to his security detail, Yves gave one more warning.

"Mitch, remember this is very risky. You must assume that anyone you encounter could be linked to the GSPC and Hamady. Their modus operandi is to decapitate anyone that they suspect is against them—especially infidels."

"I'll keep that in mind, even this evening."

"Yes, Mitch, especially this evening!"

Turning away, Mitch saw in the distance his driver and security guard leaning against the SUV and smoking cigarettes. He headed in their direction, winding back through the beautiful, serene park. He tried to prepare himself for the harsh world waiting outside the French embassy gate.

"Sorry for keeping you waiting," he told the guards as he approached the SUV. "I hadn't seen my friend in a long time, and it's so peaceful here."

His driver said nothing as he took one last drag from his cigarette. He flicked the smoldering butt to the ground, gave Mitch a long, intense stare, and then entered the vehicle. The security guard was already sitting in the SUV. He completely ignored the colonel, instead concentrating intently on his machine gun. He didn't seem to care whether Mitch was securely inside the vehicle. Mitch's sense of tension grew as he opened the door and slid into the back seat. The two Algerians were making him uncomfortable.

Leaving the embassy was much easier than entering. The French security guards returned their passports, smiling as they bid them *au revoir*. The guards lowered the dual gates, and the SUV made its departure.

No one spoke during the return trip to the US embassy, except for a quick exchange in Arabic between the driver and guard. Mitch wasn't in the mood to talk as he wanted to mentally transition to his evening dinner with Abella. But the demeanor of the two Algerians unnerved him. It was almost as if they knew what Yves and he had been discussing.

As usual, the driver radioed in their position when they neared the US embassy. Everything proceeded normally as they rounded the corner and approached the gate offset to the right of the road. But they weren't slowing down. In fact, the driver accelerated. The security guard dropped his machine gun and grabbed the dash with one hand and the handgrip above the window with the other. The gate slowly opened as the driver pointed the vehicle as if to ram the entrance.

Mitch tried to wedge himself in the footwell just behind the security guard's seat. Bracing for the sudden impact, he had no time to whisper to his maker. The vehicle slammed through the partially opened gate, shearing off the front bumper and side-view mirrors. As they cleared the gate, the rear bumper was caught and torn from the SUV. The vehicle fishtailed and spun to the right, crashing against a coconut tree just within the embassy walls.

Sitting up as quickly as he could, Mitch saw flames along the seams of the hood. Embassy security guards should have been behind trees and buildings, ready in their firing positions in case of a terrorist vehicle attack, but now they were running chaotically. The ruined SUV finally slid to a halt. As the cloud of dirt and smoke settled, Mitch noticed the front-seat airbags had done their job and protected the two Algerians, but both men seemed to be unconscious.

He wanted to exit the vehicle and run. A voice within him yelled to stay put. Considering the chaos outside and the number of guards running around with loaded weapons, he might just be safer in a burning SUV. Suddenly his door flew open, and a meaty hand reached in, yanked him out, and threw him clear of the vehicle.

He rolled through the dirt in a state of shock and confusion. In a flash two security guards were there. One held him down with a knee to the chest, and they both pointed automatic weapons at him. Mitch couldn't speak. His heart pounded in fear as he stared up at the guards and their weapons. Then a voice bellowed out incoherently, coming from a huge figure moving through the smoke. It scared the living shit out of Mitch, and he braced himself.

Finally, the words began to make sense.

"Colonel, how the hell are you? You seem to attract this type of bullshit." The giant of a man looked down at Mitch and called the guards off. He reached down and easily picked the colonel up with one hand as if he weighed nothing.

The chaos was finally subsiding. The fire had been extinguished, and the driver and security guard taken to the embassy medical clinic. Mitch could think clearly again, although his head pounded with pain. He strained his eyes, trying to focus on the people around him. He stared at the big man who had pulled him from the vehicle and recognized his buddy Jake Davis. Immediately, the tension disappeared from the back of Mitch's neck. He reached out and grabbed Jake's huge paw.

"Jake, you're my hero! Thanks for looking out for me, buddy. I guess I was incoherent for most of that." Mitch was almost surprised to hear himself put together a complete sentence.

"The least I could do, Colonel," Jake said. He handed a fire extinguisher to an embassy staff member.

"I need to discuss that driver with you, Jake. That crash was intentional." He kept his voice low, not wanting others to overhear.

"Colonel, as we took the driver to the clinic he stated that your vehicle was being followed," Jake responded firmly. "He claimed an unlicensed car pulled out of a side street shortly after you departed the French embassy. He said that he briefly spoke Arabic to the security guard in your vehicle about the situation so as not to alarm you. The car following you continued at a very close distance. He claimed that a gunman from the car took aim just as your vehicle crashed through the embassy gate. His belief was that he had no other recourse but to take that evasive action."

"Do you believe him?"

"I'm not sure, Colonel. I've had my eye on that Algerian for some time. Not sure what side of the road he walks on. His initial background check came back clean. But that doesn't necessarily mean much in this country. He could've paid off folks to have his record scrubbed."

Mitch glanced at his watch. He was running short on time. "Jake, I gotta get going. I've got a dinner rendezvous this evening. Perhaps we can talk tomorrow. And I still owe you that game of darts!"

"Not a problem, Colonel. We can discuss this at your convenience. About that dart game, I've been practicing, and honestly, you don't have a lick of chance. Yes, it'll be a sweet day when I take your money and your beer."

Jake had a unique ability to de-stress a serious situation. Mitch always welcomed the big-Jake effect—especially today.

"Keep practicing, Jake. You'll need it."

The big man laughed and waved as Mitch headed for his dwelling. Normally his next move would have been a direct report to the ambassador, who would need the colonel's perception of the crash, followed by a written report. Fortunately for Mitch, the ambassador was attending a reception at the Jordanian embassy. The reports could wait. Mitch had a much more important matter to take care of.

5

Mitch almost bodychecked the front door as he flew into the living room and then headed for the kitchen. It was quite a nice kitchen, with all the conveniences of a modern American home. Unlike most homes, it had a small balcony with a breathtaking view of the Mediterranean Sea and the Bay of Algiers. Unfortunately, his long days in the office and nights of playing diplomatic games meant the balcony went largely unused. Perhaps tonight he would take Abella out on the balcony and enjoy the view—the gentle sea and Abella's beauty.

The house was filled with the succulent aroma of meat, vegetables, and baked bread. Mitch had been stumped on choosing a menu. In the end he asked his cook, Djamila, to fix a traditional North African meal, deciding this was the safest option.

He entered the kitchen and found Djamila completely in her glory. She wore her usual white dress with the added color of a flower-printed apron. Commanding that galley like a general in combat, she was a master chef, and what's more, she enjoyed the work. He never worried about the outcome of a meal with Djamila in charge.

To watch her move quickly through the hot kitchen, tending to multiple dishes simultaneously, was mesmerizing. Even in the hot kitchen, with sweat dripping off her nose, Djamila was an attractive woman. She was of medium height and slim and wore her long, dark-brown hair in a ponytail that extended to the middle of her back. Her family was a beautiful blend of cultures and countries that had conquered the Algerian region throughout history—Roman, Phoenician, and Spanish.

"Colonel Mitch," she asked, "please sample the couscous and lamb. I need to know if they are ready or need further preparation."

He had given up trying to convince Djamila to drop "Colonel" when addressing him. She insisted that he was the boss and deserved the respect. So, as usual, she got her way. He discovered early in this diplomatic lifestyle that the keys to success were good wine and a great cook. He had shipped many bottles of great Napa Valley wine to Algeria, and when he hired Djamila, he had the perfect combination.

"Okay, Djamila, my taste buds are primed and ready to go," Mitch responded, knowing that she didn't understand all the American slang.

But instead of giving him a bite of couscous, Djamila wiped his forehead with a damp cloth. He gave her a quizzical look, and she placed a fist on her hip as she shook her head.

"What? Did I do something wrong?" he laughed.

"No, but have you looked in a mirror? I know you didn't leave the house like this today. You are completely filthy!"

Mitch realized that he had completely forgotten about the crash.

"I've gotta get upstairs and take a shower," he said, shaking his head. "But first, let's taste that delicious-looking food."

Djamila plated a small portion of the couscous and topped it with little chunks of lamb and steamed vegetables. Before he could touch the plate, she covered it all with her special gravy. He watched hungrily as steam wafted toward the ceiling fan.

She handed him the plate and a fork. He softly blew on the hot food, then took a bite.

It was truly fit for the gods. It was a familiar dish, but Djamila had a magical ability to turn something commonplace into an extraordinary meal.

"Djamila, you have truly outdone yourself. This is amazing!"

She smiled proudly, taking his plate and fork, then gave him a thumbs-up and pointed to the entrance of the kitchen.

He nodded, knowing better than to linger in the general's kitchen. "By the way," he asked as he turned for the door, "did you happen to get the flowers, candles, and set up the music for soft jazz?" He immediately felt stupid; Djamila never forgot anything.

She looked at him, rolled her eyes, then grabbed his arm and led him out into the formal dining area. Everything was perfectly arranged. The pink roses were magnificent and filled the room with a sublime aroma. Two ornate candles were impeccably placed, just off the center of the small white cloth that covered the table. Djamila lowered the lights with the dimmer switch, which automatically filled the room with the soft jazz Mitch had envisioned. Somehow, she had taken this large, formal room and transformed it into an intimate getaway.

He looked at Djamila and bowed. "I'm not worthy. I'm not worthy. You are the best!"

She laughed and pushed him toward the staircase.

As the shower melted dirt off his body, he inspected himself for wear and tear from the crash. He had been fortunate. There were a few minor abrasions, but he had escaped broken bones and a potential bullet.

He stepped out of the shower and went to the closet. Abella had only seen him in a uniform and a hospital gown, so anything would look great in comparison. *I hope she comes casual and not dressed to the nines just because she'll be entering the US embassy*, he thought, remembering their phone conversation. *I didn't tell her anything about what to wear. I really want tonight to be max relaxed.*

He grabbed a pair of khaki trousers, a blue polo shirt, and light-brown loafers. He slipped the clothes and shoes on minus socks and ran a comb through his hair. Looking in the mirror, he thought of his dad. Although he had passed away a decade ago, Mitch could still see him in the color of his own eyes and slight waves in his hair. In any other region in the world, having thick blond hair, medium build, and light-blue eyes could be an advantage. But here in North Africa, it made blending into a crowd difficult and dangerous.

Mitch glanced at the time while putting on his watch and ran downstairs. He had thirty minutes before Abella was due to arrive at the security building, and he wanted to make sure Djamila was aware of the timing of the evening.

"Djamila, how are things going?" he asked.

"Colonel Mitch, you look so refreshed and casual. I so rarely see you dressed this way. It is usually a uniform or a suit, but now you remind me of a golfer."

"Well, I'll take that as a compliment. I just wanted to review the timing of this evening."

"Okay, Colonel Mitch. If I recall, you are to pick up the lady at the security building at seven and escort her to your residence. In the meantime, I will be pouring the wine before your arrival and place the glasses adjacent to the couch in the formal living room. I will dim the lights, light the candles, and the music will be softly playing as you enter your home."

"Djamila, you're amazing, and I'm stupid. I should have assumed that you had everything timed and arranged perfectly."

Mitch now had ten minutes to walk across the embassy grounds. Djamila disappeared into the kitchen, and he headed out the front door.

It was a perfect evening with a crescent moon, billions of stars, and a crystal-clear sky. The embassy was strangely quiet. The only movement he noted was a security guard lighting a cigarette while standing at his post near the ambassador's residence. Mitch quickly passed the roses, taking in their superb fragrance. Then he turned on the dirt path and noticed lights from within the security building. He made it to the building with a few minutes to spare.

The room had the stale smell of cigarettes and body odor. The ashtrays overflowed, and used paper coffee cups littered the tables. It was obvious Abella had not arrived because the embassy entry guards were sitting around and talking about the World Cup and Algeria's chances to advance. If she were here, the scene would have been very different—these young men would be sitting silently, staring and mentally undressing her.

Mitch walked to the secured metal door that led to the main street running adjacent to the US embassy. As it was one of the few entry and exit points within the embassy, he knew Abella would enter here. A small bulletproof window in the door allowed for visual recognition. He peered through the window and into the darkness of the night and noticed a taxi pulling up. From the back seat, a beautiful woman stepped out of the car, dressed in a well-tailored black suit and heels. Abella paid the driver and then turned toward the door. Her hair was as black as night and flowed like water onto her shoulders. She looked absolutely stunning. Mitch stood awestruck and open-mouthed as she approached the door.

A security guard snapped him out of his trance as he keyed a special microphone and requested that Abella slide her passport through a tray built into the outer portion of the secured door. Mitch quickly stepped aside and stood where he knew Abella could not see him. While her passport was examined and data entered into a secure computer, Mitch examined Abella through the window. Her face was exquisite. Her delicate jawline, full lips, petite nose, and piercingly beautiful blue eyes were captivating.

Taking another step backward in anticipation of her entry, he bumped into three guards who were also staring at her. Mitch pointed to the dirty coffee cups on the table, and a guard quickly gathered them. The sergeant of the guards bellowed in Arabic to the remaining security personnel to stand in respect as the special guest of the colonel entered the building. Then he keyed the microphone and informed Abella, in French, that all her paperwork was in order and he was opening the secured door.

Abella immediately filled the room with radiance and beauty. She walked confidently, her suit clinging to her perfectly proportioned body. Mitch stood watching in silent awe and finally managed to croak, "Abella, I'm here."

She turned and their eyes met. Abella ignored all the others as she embraced him, and he felt the softness of her hair against his face. Then the warmth of her lips touched his.

Although he didn't want this moment to end, Mitch grabbed her hand and headed for the door to avoid putting on a display for the guards. The sergeant of the guards handed him Abella's passport. Mitch thanked him, and the sergeant smiled and whispered, "Well done, *mon colonel.*"

It felt strange walking along the embassy path with Abella. He had dreamed of it, but now it was actually happening. He took her to the rose garden and then near the tennis court and pool.

"Mitch, I often wondered what it was like inside these walls. I felt sorry for the Americans because I knew you were imprisoned inside and could not freely leave. But it seems as though you reside in a secret cabana club within Algiers."

Mitch laughed. "Abella, it might seem like a resort, but after a couple weeks' confinement behind these walls, it quickly turns into a five-star prison."

Before Abella could comment, they arrived at his residence. Mitch opened the door that led to the foyer, and Abella's eyes widened as she surveyed the interior of the house. Her eyes wandered from the staircase to the formal living room, the dining area, the den, and finally the entrance to the kitchen. It had been many years since she had stood inside such a lavishly large home.

"So, what do you think?" he asked.

Without hesitating she uttered, "Nice digs, Colonel!" as she admired a Winslow Homer painting.

He stared at Abella. *How the hell does she know that slang and use it so perfectly?* He was dumbfounded. Yves's comment about being cautious of everyone echoed in his mind, but soft, mellow jazz music began to flow from the living area. *I'll have to wait to ask Abella where and when she learned that slang.*

"Let's follow the music and relax in the living room," he said, leading Abella into the room. "I hope you're in the mood for a little wine before dinner."

"That sounds perfect, and I love American jazz," Abella casually stated as she settled into the corner of his brown, well-creased leather couch.

Mitch handed her a glass of wine and proposed a toast. "To us, to life, and to adventure." He raised his glass and softly touched hers, then sat in a formal leather chair and set his glass on a small table in front of the couch.

He noticed that Abella's demeanor was not as lighthearted as before the toast.

"Is something wrong?" he asked.

Abella looked up from her glass. "Yes, Mitch, there is something wrong. Why aren't you sitting next to me on the couch?"

A flush of embarrassment flowed over his face. What Abella had asked was exactly what he wanted. "I'm sorry. I should—"

Before he could finish, Abella leaned toward him and kissed his open mouth.

"Mitch, please join me here."

He quickly moved to the couch.

"Thanks for making this moment what I wanted. I wasn't sure how fast to go," he said as he looked into her eyes.

She laughed. "Mitch, we have so little time tonight and so much to discuss. Let's enjoy every moment." Abella raised her glass again and smiled. "To us."

"Abella, I hope you don't mind, but I've gotta ask you a question that has been bothering me ever since the hospital. How did you learn to speak American, and where did you pick up all that slang?"

Her face became somber. "It doesn't surprise me that you would ask that question. I would if I was in your shoes. I came to dinner this evening to be with you, but also for you to learn about me. This will take some time, so I hope we have many hours tonight."

"We have all night if that's what it'll take," he said, knowing full well that allowing a foreign guest to spend the entire night at an embassy residence would be a violation of State Department rules.

"What I will tell you I have never told anyone. I will never lie to you, and that is a promise that I make to you and God. Please, I have no problem at any time if you want to corroborate what I am about to say. But I must ask you a question: is your residence secure from listening devices, and can your cook hear us?"

"Every residence is swept electronically once a month, and mine was done last week. Djamila can't hear a thing from the kitchen, especially over the music."

Abella nodded, took a deep breath, and began to speak.

"My father was a major in the Algerian army. Specifically, he was an intelligence and diplomatic officer. At an early age, he realized that learning English would be invaluable to his career. He had noticed that most Algerian officers could speak French and Arabic, and a few knew Russian, but since Algeria had aligned itself with the Soviet Union, speaking English was looked upon as a waste of time. Privately, over many years, he took it upon himself to learn that forbidden language. Somehow he wanted to achieve an almost impossible dream—taking his family to America.

"My father also immersed himself in learning and understanding the Algerian terrorist movement and its organizations. He studied counterterrorism in Moscow and became one of the leading authorities in my country. Becoming an expert in this area was very dangerous, but because of it, he became an extremely valuable officer. This made him unique to our army and government, but also made him and his family a huge terrorist target.

"I will never forget the evening my father came home and informed my mother and me that we would be leaving Algeria. I was seventeen and had lived in Algiers all my life. My friends, school, and all that I knew were here in my community. I didn't want to leave, and I didn't care where our new home would be—even if it was to the beautiful beaches of Cuba. I protested and refused to leave. My father ignored my complaints and directed my mother to plan to move within the month. I was devastated and clutched my mother. I sobbed uncontrollably. My mother stood stoically, almost as if she was in shock. She said nothing but continued to stare at my father. As we each tried to comprehend what was happening, my father continued. He had us sit in our tiny living room and explained that his dream had finally arrived.

"We were to move to America, specifically Washington, DC, and my father would be the assistant defense attaché in the Algerian embassy. I recall turning toward him and yelling, 'No Algerian can go to America! It's impossible! Besides, America is our enemy.' My father stared at me with no emotion other than shaking his head. He then explained to us that the world was changing, and regardless of what we had been taught about America, it would be a strange and exciting country. Then he took my hand and looked at me with soft, compassionate eyes. 'Abella,' he said, 'you will enter a world that is beyond your imagination. It will allow a woman all the opportunities that you have ever dreamed of and perhaps even more. You don't realize how restricted you are, living in an Islamic country.'

"At the time I didn't realize what he meant. But there was one thing that my mother and I shared that was very dangerous. My mother's ancestors were the original French colonists that inhabited Algiers during the 1830s. As the years passed, my mother's family adamantly retained their Catholic religion. It was very difficult initially for my mother and father during their courting. My mother had to pretend that she was Muslim, but my father knew of her Catholic beliefs and swore with all his love that he would never reveal her secret.

"When I was born, my family went through all the Muslim rituals for a newborn. But secretly my mother would take me to the only remaining Christian church in Algiers. It was the beautiful Catholic basilica known as Notre Dame d'Afrique, built by the original French colonists. It is located on the north side of Algiers, on a cliff that overlooks the Bay of Algiers and the Mediterranean Sea. Perhaps you know it? It is absolutely stunning, and my French ancestors helped to build it. The basilica was never converted to a Muslim mosque but retained its Catholic heritage. What saved it was the Vatican. The basilica was designated as the Embassy of the Vatican in Algeria, and the archbishop the ambassador.

"Mitch, what I am trying to say is that I am a Catholic, not a Muslim. My mother and I attended Mass each week but very covertly. During the week, usually Tuesday or Wednesday evening, my father would take us out to dinner so as not to raise suspicion. After dinner, we carefully drove to the basilica without any car lights, taking back roads. Once near the basilica, my mother and I would leave my father and the car as we ran toward the church in the darkness. Nuns were waiting in an adjacent lot, and they quickly threw blankets over our heads to prevent anyone from recognizing us. Then we would enter the basilica, remove the blankets, and join a small group of Algerians, like ourselves, that had retained their ancestors' religion.

"The archbishop always personally welcomed us with warmth and love because he truly understood the danger. During that brief hour of Mass that we were all together as Christians, I felt a genuine fellowship of love and freedom. In the meantime, while we were in church, my father would drive to many different locations throughout Algiers just in case of surveillance. He would return at the end of Mass, and the blankets were again placed over our heads as we ran to the car. A few nuns, hiding in the darkness, would take the blankets and then kiss our hands. Driving home usually took twice as long as normal because of all the different routes we had to take to deceive anyone that may have followed us."

Mitch sat in awe as he drank his wine. Without hesitating, he refilled his glass and rapidly consumed the contents. He had many questions but didn't want to interrupt. Dinner became a distant thought.

"My father said that in America my mother and I would be able to walk to Mass without any danger of persecution. My father also stated that he would attend a local Muslim mosque in DC when we went to Mass. Of all the topics my father discussed that fateful evening when he informed us of our move to America, this was what convinced me America was a place I must discover."

- • - •

Protocol in the diplomatic world was to never interrupt or hasten a meeting, discussion, or before-dinner drinks. But it was already 8:30, and dinner should have been served at 8, so in desperation, Djamila did something that she had never done before. She held a very large silver ladling spoon above her head and dropped it on the tile floor of the kitchen. The sound of the spoon striking the floor reverberated throughout the house, causing Abella to gasp in the living room.

Djamila did not leave the kitchen but spoke loud enough that she knew Mitch would hear.

"I am so sorry to have dropped the dinner serving spoon." Djamila knew that Mitch would then glance at his watch. As soon as he looked, he realized that the time was fleeting and dinner was late.

"Abella, would you please hold your thought for a moment and accompany me to the dining table?"

Abella smiled. "Yikes, I've been talking for over an hour. I'm so sorry."

"No, no, Abella, I want to hear more and more about you. It's so interesting and very surprising. I love it!" Mitch realized that in his haste to reply, he had used *love* in the sentence. He wondered how Abella would react. She leaned slightly and kissed him on the lips.

They sat at the small, intimate table as the lights dimmed, the candles flickered, and soft jazz encircled the room. Djamila served the food as if they were dining at a five-star restaurant in Paris. Everything was superb, and the food was to die for. All was turning out as Mitch had hoped.

"Djamila, everything looks and smells fabulous," Mitch said. "Why don't you leave early this evening and we can take care of the dishes and leftovers."

Although Djamila protested, she knew that it would be much better for all if she departed. So she thanked Mitch, gave a slight nod to Abella, gathered her items, and disappeared into the darkness of the evening.

Mitch waited to hear the security guard bid Djamila good evening, followed by the steel security gate closing with authority. "Please, Abella, I want you to enjoy the dinner and relax," he said.

Abella knew that Mitch wanted to hear more, and she had much more to tell. "Mitch, I want you to know me . . . to know who I really am. So please let me continue."

"If you insist," Mitch said with a smile and a wink.

"Once in America, I became completely immersed in the culture and freedoms. There was so much that I could do that was forbidden for a woman in Algeria. As the days turned into weeks and months and then one year, I regretted the thought of ever returning to my patriarchal, Islamic, terrorist country. America offered so much to a young woman on the cusp of beginning her life. I relished being in an environment where women had an equal say in decisions and were as empowered as a falcon freely flying in boundless skies. It was nothing like Algeria where women are essentially caged canaries.

"Through my father's influence and connections in the DC diplomatic world, I was able to attend Georgetown University. My mother was so proud because she knew how prestigious the university was, and it was Catholic! I had always wanted to dedicate my life to helping others, so it was a perfect match to begin studies in the school of nursing. The years I spent at Georgetown were not only enlightening but a wonderful learning experience in many different ways. The friends I made and the professors that guided me through my studies left an indelible mark on my soul.

"While growing up in Algeria, my home was near an open dirt-and-grass field. Almost every day, the neighborhood boys would gather and play football. Americans call it soccer. As a girl in a Muslim country, I was forbidden from participating. But sometimes they didn't have enough players for two teams. I would wait near the sideline until one of the boys asked me to be a goalie. Because I had watched them play, I had a pretty good idea of the goalie's responsibilities. Their only demand was that I dress more like a boy so others would not get suspicious. I wore trousers, a T-shirt, sneakers, and a cap. I would tuck my hair into the cap. Over time I became quite a good goalie, and the boys always wanted me on their teams.

"You are probably wondering why I am telling you this! At Georgetown, I discovered that they had women's sports, which included a soccer team. I was what you Americans call a walk-on because I showed up one day during their practice. The coaches were initially skeptical, but when I blocked all attempts to score during the practice, I left that day with a Georgetown University soccer uniform. I played on the women's varsity team for four years. My parents were proud, and I felt so lucky.

"While I played, I formed a close bond with the other girls on the team. Over time they asked many questions about life in a Muslim country and the restrictions for women. Many of the players were very active in women's movements, clubs, and organizations on campus. I became interested and joined some of the organizations. Through the fellowship of those clubs, I learned the power and uniqueness of being a woman in the world. I also realized how suppressed women were in my country. I learned that women had so much to contribute and, if allowed, could change the world for the better. I began to despise my country's government, the graft, the corruption, the cheating, the treatment of women, and the suffocating laws. I knew that many Algerian government officials and military officers were linked to the terrorists. I hated the very fabric that made up and symbolized Algeria.

"I had long conversations with my parents, explaining to them that I was not going to return to North Africa but live forever in America. My father would get angry and explain that it was impossible for me to stay because our visas were only valid while he was working in the Algerian embassy. I was heartbroken. I continued being very active in the women's movements on campus and continued to learn. But there was something else that I concentrated on as much as my studies, soccer, and the women's organizations. I worked diligently to lose any trace of my accent while speaking your language. I immersed myself, with the help of my friends, in English, learning to speak as an American. I loved the slang and used profanity whenever I could while socializing, but especially while playing soccer. It was uplifting and something that was forbidden for a woman in my country. Those years at Georgetown were the best of my life, and I will never forget them."

"Abella, as much as I want to hear more of your life in America, I'm concerned that the food is getting cold. Tonight, you must let me be your waiter—please." Mitch stood, draping the cloth napkin over his left forearm and balancing the large bowl of couscous in his right palm.

Abella laughed and nodded as she leaned back in her chair. "I will pretend to be the First Lady having dinner in the White House, and you the head waiter extraordinaire."

Their mutual laughter lightened the mood. Conversation during dinner was more about the fundamentals of playing soccer than serious discussions of world politics—but what Abella was to tell Mitch after dinner would change their relationship forever.

Once the meal was complete, dishes rinsed in the kitchen sink, and the coffee brewing, Mitch took Abella out on the kitchen balcony.

"Oh, Mitch, this is so beautiful. This tiny balcony has one of the loveliest views of the Bay of Algiers that I have ever seen. It is too bad that we couldn't fit a table here and eat dinner under the moon as it reflects on the Mediterranean Sea. From this point, you can see every movement of the ships as they enter and leave the harbor. Also, you have a good vantage point to monitor the activities on the pier and the cargo that is being moved. I know that is very important for you as a military attaché. Although you can see every movement, they can't see you. I hope this doesn't alarm you, Mitch, but my father taught me many things about military espionage. I know that there are many facets of your military profession, and one is to monitor the activities and capabilities of our military. But another is to observe our commerce and our trading partners."

Mitch stood silent. Abella was quite intelligent and very curious. It was no surprise that her father had taught her well about this crazy military diplomatic-surveillance business. He undoubtedly participated in the same activities while serving as the Algerian assistant defense attaché in America.

"Mitch, could we go back into the living room with our coffee? I must tell you something that is very important." Abella looked at Mitch with a trace of pain and sadness in her eyes.

"Why, of course, Abella. Do you take your coffee with sugar and cream?"

"No, actually I prefer mine black. I learned to drink coffee like an American, and I have never lost that habit."

"Black it is!" Mitch said as he poured the coffee and placed the silver coffee pot on a tray with Djamila's homemade cookies.

They walked into the living room and sat together on the couch as they had before. The jazz was still playing, but the candles had burned themselves out, leaving a slight scent of smoke in the air. As Mitch lowered the tray to the table, he picked up the silver serving pot and poured the coffee into their cups, which rested on fine china saucers. The deep coffee aroma replaced the smoky scent of the candles.

"I can tell that this coffee is a rich blend from Africa. It will keep us up into the early hours of the morning," Abella observed before taking a sip of the hot brew. "Mitch, what happened when my family returned to Algeria drastically changed me. During the time my father worked in the Algerian embassy in Washington, he continued his counterintelligence training. Not with the Russians or Cubans, but with your Defense and Central Intelligence Agencies. He didn't discuss the intricacies of what he learned. But from time to time, he mentioned how superior the training was compared to what he received in Moscow. Once he had completed his training, my father received orders to return to Algeria. This really was no surprise, because he had become the Algerian army's most knowledgeable counterintelligence officer. The army and government wanted him to return as soon as possible, not only to use his expertise but also to keep an eye on him.

"My father had learned many things about Algeria and the leaders of my country during his time in America. He mentioned to me that many of the high-ranking officers and important politicians were dangerous people who were being paid off by Osama bin Laden. Bin Laden wanted to spread his influence across North Africa by restoring Sharia law because he believed that was the only way to set things right in the Muslim world. His tools to accomplish this were payoffs, terrorist organizations, and violent jihad. Because of Bin Laden's impact, our generals did not adequately use our army and air force against the terrorist movement. My country's government leaders ignored counterterrorist recommendations made by other countries.

"When we returned to Algeria, I was able to get a nursing position at the People's National Army Hospital. I knew that my family was continually being watched by the authorities, so it was logical that the government wanted me to work in a military environment. The surveillance was much easier to establish than in a civilian hospital. It became difficult for my family to reestablish ourselves in my country. My father was very frustrated because he was being restricted from productively using his counterintelligence skills. Although he had been notified that a promotion would be imminent, it was a falsehood and never happened. This lie gave his superior officers an excuse to assign him to a menial desk job in the Ministry of Defense. They reasoned that someone with his knowledge and ability needed to be closer to the chief of staff of the People's National Army."

Abella abruptly stopped talking and lowered her face into the palms of her hands, softly crying. When her crying became uncontrollable, Mitch wrapped his arms around her and pulled Abella to his chest. Her body quaked as she sobbed and trembled.

"Abella, Abella, it's okay," Mitch softly said as he held her tightly and rocked back and forth as a father with a newborn.

She continued to cry, but the intensity slowly subsided. Mitch felt the moisture of Abella's tears through his shirt and cradled the back of her head with the palm of his hand.

"You're here with me. You're safe. Please don't worry." Mitch lightly stroked her hair, which had a wonderful fresh scent of jasmine.

After what seemed like an hour, Abella asked if she could freshen up in the bathroom. Mitch helped her stand and then walked with her to the small visitor's room near the kitchen. He asked if she needed anything special. She looked away and softly whispered, "No."

Mitch retrieved a box of tissues from the kitchen, then returned to the living room. He sat and worried about Abella. *What is it that caused such emotions? It must have been something tragic.*

Eventually the bathroom door opened, and Abella walked out looking refreshed. Mitch stood as she approached and grasped her hands. She looked into his eyes. "Mitch, I'm ready to continue. I must tell you, and I must be strong."

They sat, and Abella kept her hands in his as she continued.

"Approximately two months after leaving America, my father was to travel to Paris and attend a conference of military representatives from all the Maghreb countries. Perhaps you know that the Maghreb is an ancient term for that region of Mauritania, Morocco, Algeria, Libya, and Tunisia. The conference was initially planned to focus on discussions covering potential training exercises with the French military. But the night before my father's planned departure, a military officer came to our house. I had seen him before and knew that he was a very close friend of my father's. I overheard him say that he had spoken with a French embassy representative and discovered that the actual discussion would involve the terrorist threats in each of the Maghreb countries. Ultimately, the French wanted to send in their special forces to assist in the fight against the jihadist threat. He said that the French were pleased to know that my father would be attending because they had received many positive reports about him from the Americans in Washington, DC.

"After this visit, my father's demeanor changed, and he seemed very nervous. He and my mother went into their bedroom, closing the door, and I heard him telling her of the potential dangers. I could not sleep that night and did not want him to go. The next morning we were all up early, and my mother had made a large breakfast. There was very little talking at the table, and my father seemed to be the only one who ate. After breakfast, he gathered his bags and walked to the front door. He turned toward me, and I noticed tears in his eyes. He said nothing but held me tight. He kissed me on the top of my head and whispered that he loved me. My father then held my mother and kissed her. He picked up his bags and I opened the door. Our car was parked in the driveway, and he walked to the trunk and opened it.

"We didn't notice the two men who had been hiding behind a large hedgerow that separated our front yard and the road. They were as swift as the wind, and in a single moment, one of the men stabbed my father in the back as the other slit his throat. In disbelief I watched my father fall to the pavement. When I reached him, I held him in my arms. He stared at me, trying to speak, and then his body went limp. I collapsed in his pool of blood. My mother had fainted and hit her head. She was unconscious. I sobbed uncontrollably as our neighbors ran to our aid. I didn't want to let go of my father, but my friends pulled me from his lifeless body.

"My mother never recovered from seeing my father's assassination. Within a year after his death, I had her committed to a special home for the insane. Six months later she died, and all my dreams of a happy life with my parents were gone. We had been so happy together in America. And now it had all vanished except for the memories."

Abella began to cry again, but she controlled it. Taking a tissue, she lightly touched her bloodshot eyes and wiped her nose. Her makeup had streaked, yet her natural beauty emanated through her sorrow.

"I'm sorry, Mitch, but I had to tell you. It was very important to me that you know," Abella said softly.

Mitch was stunned and had difficulty replying. "My God, how do you live every day with those thoughts? Where do you find the strength to go on with life?"

"It took time, but I slowly recovered and immersed myself in my work as a nurse. It was difficult because I knew a combination of the government, military, and terrorists had killed my father. Somehow, they had found out that the meetings in Paris were to discuss and plan counterterrorist activities. It was too late for the authorities to tell the French that my father would not be attending; politically it would be too suspicious. So, their solution was to use the GSPC terrorists to kill him before he got to the airport. Of course, the killers were never found."

Mitch still had difficulty comprehending all that he had heard. "Where do you live? How can you continue to work in an environment that represents those that had your father killed?"

"Unlike your country, being Algerian makes it very difficult to leave. Visas must be granted, and each attempt I made to attain a visa to France, America, and the UK were all denied. I later found out that my country's paramilitary police had inserted false information in my records, indicating ties to the GSPC. With that, I could go nowhere.

"But one day, I went to work and discovered a wounded American colonel who had been mistakenly placed in my ward of the hospital. You were supposed to have been placed in another location. But there was a terrorist ambush on a company of soldiers patrolling in the outer security perimeter of Algiers the night before your arrival. They filled most of the beds in the hospital. My area was the only one free when you arrived. It was truly a very fortunate day for me. I hope you feel the same way."

Abella pressed her lips against Mitch's cheek and smiled.

Mitch was happy to see her smile, and to hear how Abella felt about him. "Yes, I definitely feel the same way. It's strange how people can find each other when they are worlds apart yet living in the same location."

"Not everything about living here is terrible. I live in a small apartment not far from the Martyrs' Memorial near the bay. I could see the memorial from your kitchen balcony. The memorial is tall, and regardless of where I am in the city, I can see it. I have a roommate who is also a nurse in the army hospital. I've known her all my life, except for the six years I spent in America. She attended nursing school here in Algiers and is jealous that I had such a superior nursing education at Georgetown.

"We talk about America often, and she dreams of one day visiting and perhaps living there. I told her that when she does live in the States, we'll have to find an apartment together in New York City. We laughed because we know it's only a dream that can never become a reality. Our reality is living in this city, surrounded by Islamic terrorists. Don't get me wrong, Mitch, I love my country. It's the government and the military I despise. They killed my parents, and I will never forgive them."

"Can you trust your roommate?" Mitch asked. "It would be convenient for the government to use her to keep an eye on you."

"While I was living in America, my roommate's brother was abducted by the GSPC while he was traveling to the western coastal city of Oran. Because her family is of the upper middle class, the terrorists publicized his abduction and demanded a ransom from the government and her family. Her father was willing to pay their portion of the ransom, but the government refused. The GSPC then videotaped her brother's beheading and sent copies to all news networks in the Maghreb.

"Unlike your news media, ours are completely controlled by the government, and they decide what is to be shown or printed. Everyone saw the cruel, inhumane beheading. It was not only broadcast on the television news but also pictured on the front page of all our newspapers. My roommate has never completely recovered and is plagued with mental breakdowns when she hears of terrorist abductions. So your question was can I trust her. I'll let you decide, now that you know her pain."

Mitch could tell Abella was emotionally drained.

"Abella, let's not talk about that anymore. I would rather talk about your hobbies, what you got to see in America, and how you stay in such great shape. Would you like something more to drink? Perhaps coffee, wine, or water?"

"Another glass of wine would be wonderful, as long as you'll have one with me."

As Mitch stood, he noticed that Abella had kicked off her heels and reclined on the couch. The tension in the room was replaced with tranquility. He disappeared into the kitchen and shortly after returned with clean wineglasses and another bottle of merlot. Abella had curled up in the corner of the couch and closed her eyes.

He gazed at her. Her toes were delicate, their manicured nails polished with a dark red that matched her fingernails. Her athletic legs complemented her firm buttocks. Abella's suit coat was partially unbuttoned, and the white silk blouse underneath rested loosely on her flat stomach. Her well-proportioned breasts pulled tightly at the seams of the blouse. The rays of the lamp adjacent to the couch reflected off her deep, luxurious black hair as it cascaded over her shoulders. Mitch lowered the glasses to the small table and quietly pulled the cork from the bottle. He poured a small amount into each glass, removed his loafers, and stretched out, resting between Abella and the edge of the couch. Abella felt Mitch's warm body and wrapped her legs around his, her eyes still closed.

"Hold me, Mitch. Hold me as if you never want to let me go."

Mitch pulled Abella to him. They found each other's lips, and as they kissed softly, Mitch tasted the remnants of her tears. Their breathing became heavier, and Abella tugged on her clothing.

"Mitch, please help me with my clothes."

Mitch sat up, and Abella moved from the corner of the couch. He gently removed her jacket as she unbuttoned her blouse and then unfastened her slacks. She removed them and fell back on the couch. Mitch pulled off his shirt and khakis and softly settled on top of her, resting his weight on his arms. Abella placed her right leg over the back of the couch and wrapped her arms around Mitch's naked chest. They kissed and kissed again with a burning, unquenchable passion. Then Mitch gently removed her bra and panties as he slid from his briefs. Their eager bodies became one, moving to the soft rhythm of the jazz playing faintly in the background.

6

Mitch's hand slipped from the edge of the couch and dropped to the carpet, waking him from a deep sleep. Before he opened his eyes, he smelled jasmine and felt the soft, rhythmic breathing of a woman. As the fog of sleep cleared and rays of sunlight brushed his face, reality startled him.

Oh my God, it's 6 a.m. and Abella is still here! Mitch thought as he jumped from the couch, almost falling over the small table that still held the glasses of wine and cups of stale, cold coffee. He knelt next to Abella and whispered, "Abella, please wake up. Djamila will be arriving soon."

Abella stirred and opened her eyes. Seeing Mitch, she smiled and kissed him. "I thought this was all a dream, and what we shared last night was fantasy. Thank God it was reality."

She stretched and sat up. Her naked beauty distracted Mitch momentarily from formulating their getaway. Abella reached out and lightly caressed one of the glasses of leftover Merlot. Her lips touched the glass as she sipped, leaving a fine trace of lipstick on the outer edge. Abella handed the glass to Mitch. Feeling a combination of desire, stress, and a slight headache, he drained the glass with one gulp.

"Abella, we've gotta get going. Help me pick up our clothes and let's run upstairs. We'll take a shower together!" Mitch frantically grabbed clothes, shoes, and anything else that might raise an eyebrow.

He took Abella's hand, and they rushed up the spiraling staircase into the sanctity of his room. Never before had a lady stepped into his room except for a maid. But Abella was no longer just a lady. During the evening she had crossed over and entered his heart.

"Quick, Abella, would you please start the water in the shower as I run a razor over my face? You don't mind using my toothbrush, do you?"

Abella laughed, grabbing the toothpaste and brush. "Hey, when you're living a dream, who cares?"

She stepped into the glass-walled shower and reached out for Mitch. He entered and lathered the soap in his hands, then squatted and slowly washed Abella's legs, working his way up until he completed his duties by kissing her neck. She took the soap and mirrored what he had done, washing Mitch. Once completed, they rushed from the shower and laughed as they danced around, quickly toweling and drying each other. It was Sunday, so Mitch could relax, but before that could happen, he had to come up with a plan to avoid being counseled or reprimanded by the ambassador for Abella's overnight stay. As Abella dressed and examined Mitch's selection of colognes, he grabbed the phone, called the security-guard house, and requested to speak to Jake Davis.

A few seconds passed. "Jake Davis speaking. Can I help you?"

"Jake, it's Colonel Ross. I need a really big favor. Is there any chance that the security paperwork that Abella . . ." Mitch paused, realizing he didn't know her last name. Embarrassed, he turned to her. "I don't know your last name!"

"Well, Colonel, you should have been more attentive. You did have my passport in your hands for a moment." Abella smiled and then said, "Amari."

"Jake, are you still there?"

"Yes, Colonel. Do you have her last name?"

"Yep, it's Amari." Mitch's pulse raced, stress saturating his entire body.

"Got the paperwork right here. What do ya need me to do, Colonel?"

"Could you please indicate that she left my residence at 1 a.m.?" Mitch held his breath as he waited for Jake to respond.

The ensuing pause seemed to last an eternity. By now, Abella was dressed and sitting on the edge of the bed, staring at Mitch with concern. She felt guilty and responsible for the situation he was in.

"Mitch, I'm so sorry for this. It's entirely my fault."

Mitch leaned over and kissed her. "Shh . . . please don't worry. Everything will be okay."

He tried to act relaxed despite the burning pain of acid reflux.

"Colonel, sorry for the delay. I wanted to make sure that in addition to the paperwork, the computer input also indicated a 1 a.m. departure. You're good to go, and yes, you owe me big-time now!" Jake chuckled.

"You've got that right, Jake. The next time we're in the Marine bar, it'll be top-shelf bourbon for you on my nickel. Thanks again, my friend. You are a career saver."

"For all the sacrifices you've made for Uncle Sam, Colonel, it's the least I can do. Take care and enjoy your day off."

Mitch hung up. He felt like an elephant had stepped off his chest. He sat next to Abella on the edge of the bed. "So, Ms. Amari, what's a sweet girl like you doing in a place like this?"

"Falling in love with an American colonel," Abella responded without hesitation.

"Glad we're members of the same team, sweetheart," Mitch said as he kissed her hand.

"Mitch, as much as I would love to stay, I really must get going. My roommate is going to think I've been kidnapped!"

"Hmm, I like the way that lady thinks. Actually, that's not a bad idea."

"Seriously, I should get going."

"Okay, sweetheart, I'll call for a taxi."

Mitch called the security office again and asked to have a taxi wait outside the embassy gate. He slipped into khakis and a polo, then grabbed a pair of sandals. Abella took one last look to make sure she had everything, and then they went downstairs. They had missed breakfast and neither felt hungry, but the aroma coming from the kitchen was marvelous.

Djamila had quietly slipped into the house and cleaned up the living room, which sparkled in the sun after her expert tidying. She was cooking a roast that she would later use to make sandwiches for Mitch's lunches during the week. Mitch put his finger to his lips and tiptoed past the kitchen, pulling Abella along. They quietly opened the door and escaped the house. At the security door, Mitch asked the guard on the wall to check if a taxi was waiting on the road. The guard gave a thumbs-up. Mitch put his arm around Abella's waist and kissed her. She smiled and brushed his cheek with her hand as the security door opened.

"Call me when you get a chance, Mitch," Abella whispered as she stepped out of the security of the embassy and into the taxi. Mitch reached into his pocket and stepped through the door, handing Abella 1,500 Algerian dinar to cover the taxi fare. She shook her head, smiling, and took the money. She mouthed "thank you" as the taxi rapidly accelerated down the avenue.

"Don't worry, I'm okay," Mitch yelled to the security guard on the wall. The guard had raised his automatic weapon to permanently stop anyone who might find Mitch a target of opportunity while standing outside the embassy. After watching the taxi depart, Mitch walked back to his residence, thinking about how quickly the time had passed with Abella. There were definitely moments he wanted to relive. If all went well, he would get those opportunities again.

7

Almost a week had passed since Abella's visit to the embassy, but the scent of jasmine still lingered in the living room. Each morning, Mitch sat on the leather couch with a cup of coffee before heading to the office. It helped clear his mind of the stress continually pounding his thoughts. The ambassador was being hounded by not only the State Department but also the White House and wanted updates from Mitch on the captured American pilot. Mitch's six-day workweek included many twelve-hour days. It seemed to never end, and he lived for that one day off.

Mitch took another sip of his hot coffee as he reread the invitation Yves had sent him the week before. This would be a special night at the French embassy. It was July 14, or as the French called it, *la Fête Nationale*—Bastille Day to the rest of the world, the "French Fourth of July" to Jake. At any rate, it was always one hell of a good time and not to be missed.

In a phone call from Yves during the week, the Frenchman had informed Mitch that they needed to talk during the festivities. Because of the classified nature of the subject, all Yves mentioned was that he had been reading about the Romans in Algeria and their cultural influences. Mitch wasn't exactly sure what that meant, but he didn't ask for clarification, knowing that the Algerians were listening. During their conversation, Mitch asked if he might bring Abella to the festivities. Yves's only comment while he laughed was, "Why, of course, as long as I get to tell her all your deep dark secrets."

Mitch passed along the information needed to allow Abella into the embassy, and then Yves gave his customary, "*Au revoir, mon ami.*"

When Mitch arrived at his office in the embassy chancery building and inserted the code that allowed his entry, Dave was standing by a large, wall-mounted whiteboard inside his cavernous room. The room was littered with an unclassified computer, film-developing equipment, a classified soundproof telephone booth, and a small refrigerator primarily stocked with Dave's sodas. He never stopped drinking them while at the office, but continually complained about not passing his weight check during his annual physical.

"Good morning, sir. I was writing a note to let you know that the embassy military enlisted committee is meeting at eight, and I will be attending."

"Considering it's six thirty in the morning, when did you plan to depart?"

"Sir, I'm the secretary of the committee and need to set up the room before the other members arrive."

Mitch felt his blood pressure rise; this was just another of Dave's ploys to get out of his real military work. "So, tell me, Warrant Officer McQueen, how many active members make up this committee?"

"Well, sir, if you count the Marines that attend, there are four."

Mitch was really getting pissed, and he hadn't had his second cup of coffee.

"So, for that amount of folks, you must leave at least an hour before the meeting begins. Where the hell do you have your meetings?"

"In the cafeteria just outside the chancery building," Dave responded, a little waver in his voice making it clear that he had noticed he was beginning to irritate the colonel.

Mitch had had enough of Dave's bullshit and knew that it would be easier to just let him go.

"What the hell are you telling me? There's no need for preparation if you have the meeting in the cafeteria. All it's going to be is a bullshit session with a bunch of your buddies while you drink coffee or soda. Besides, the embassy rumor mill has it that you're sweet on one of the Algerian girls that work in the café. So that answers my question of why you need to get there early. When you get back, I want your minutes from the last five meetings plus this meeting typed and formally submitted to me so I can report the outcome to the ambassador."

Dave dropped the whiteboard marker, realizing that he would have to concoct minutes for this meeting and five others.

"Yes, sir, but do you really have to talk to the ambassador about our meetings?"

Mitch wasn't telling the truth about reporting to the ambassador, but he wanted to get Dave's pucker factor up.

"Okay, get the hell out of the office and go to your meeting that doesn't start for another hour and fifteen minutes!" Mitch stated with clenched teeth and a pulsing vein on his forehead.

Dave grabbed his notebook and began to leave.

"Hey, Warrant, you might need a pen or pencil to write something down in that notebook," Mitch mentioned, shaking his head. He handed Dave a pen and then walked into his office. It was probably better that Dave be absent when he called Abella to invite her to Bastille Day at the French embassy.

She picked up the phone on the first ring.

"Hello, Abella, sorry to call you so early in the morning, but I wanted to catch you before you left for work."

"Mitch, it's fine. I'm so happy to hear your voice in the morning. Please remember that you can call me anytime."

"I won't keep you long, and I apologize for this being so last minute, but would you like to join me at the French embassy this evening for *la Fête Nationale*?"

"Oh, Mitch, I . . . I'm so flattered that you would ask me. I'm not sure you realize how important this affair is in Algerian society. This is the premier social event for the elite of Algiers. I truly cannot believe that I'm going to attend. As a young girl, I dreamed that one day I would walk the red carpet of the French embassy and enter *la Fête Nationale* just as Cinderella attended the ball. In the past, just knowing a friend of a friend of a friend that had attended gave me bragging rights. This is so special, Mitch. Thank you so, so much.

"Will the president of Algeria actually be in attendance as the news stated? Will all the ambassadors attend and heads of state from the French government? There was even talk that the American secretary of state would be there this year. Is it really true that they will be there and am I really going with you?" Abella choked back tears, unable to conceal her joy and disbelief.

"Yes, Abella, you'll be on my arm as we enter the embassy this evening. And without a doubt, all the major heads of state from many countries will be in attendance, to include your president and the US secretary of state."

"Mitch, will you be in your uniform?"

"Yes, but it's my formal uniform with medals, badges, wings, silver braided cords, and special epaulets identifying my rank as a colonel. I guess to simplify the answer to your question, it's the military's equivalent to a very formal tuxedo."

"Mitch, would it be fine if I wore a midnight-blue formal gown? Do you think it will complement your uniform?"

"Believe me, with your beauty you could wear anything and be the belle of the ball. Abella, that gown sounds perfect. I'll pick you up at seven this evening. Just keep a lookout for the mini-motorcade pulling up into your apartment parking lot. The security guards in the motorcade will not allow me to exit the vehicle to go to your door. I must remain in the bulletproof limo. So just anticipate approximately three vehicles, and I will be sitting in one of them. They tend to change the order of the vehicles and where I am placed for security reasons. A guard will go to your door and escort you to the proper vehicle. Just be flexible, sweetheart."

"Oh God, Mitch, this truly is my Cinderella dream! People in my neighborhood will be stunned to see such opulent vehicles, and then notice the poor, mousy nurse become a butterfly. Sorry, but I must go and begin planning while at work." Abella was beside herself, crying and thanking Mitch again for the invitation.

Mitch smiled as he hung up the phone and thought, *What is routine for me is something out of a storybook for others.* But this night would be very special because of the beautiful woman on his arm—and hopefully some encouraging information from Yves concerning the American pilot. After jotting down notes, Mitch called the ambassador's secretary to claim a few minutes on his calendar. The secretary informed him that if he showed up within the next few seconds, the ambassador could spare ten minutes. Mitch grabbed his notes, ran from the office up two flights of stairs, and stood in front of the secretary.

"Yikes, Colonel, you're fast!" the secretary remarked. "The ambassador is waiting for you."

Mitch didn't waste another second and strode into the ambassador's office.

"Good morning, Mr. Ambassador, and thank you for finding time on your schedule to see me. I just wanted to inform you that I believe the French attaché, Yves Dureau, has information that will help us find the pilot. Yves and I plan to meet at the French embassy this evening during the festivities."

"Great to hear," said the ambassador. "The secretary of state will be at the French embassy this evening and will want an update prior to her meeting with the French ambassador and heads of state from the French government. Is there anything else, Colonel?"

"Just one other item, sir. I'll be escorting a lady this evening. She was my nurse at the hospital during my recovery from the stabbing incident. It's the least I can do to thank her for being my guardian angel during those painful weeks of recovery."

"Well, I'm sure she'll be very impressed with all the festivities. The French ambassador informed me that they are really going over the top this year. Should be a great time for us all. But remember, it's always an opportunity to gather information for Washington."

"Yes sir, I understand completely. See you this evening, sir, and thank you for your time this morning."

Mitch departed the ambassador's office and thanked the secretary for getting him in to see the boss. *Gotta stay in the good graces of that secretary!* Mitch thought as he returned to his office. As the gatekeeper, if she didn't like someone, it would take an act of God to see the ambassador at a moment's notice.

The rest of the day dragged for Mitch while he completed routine work and answered classified emails from Washington. It had been a long, long time since he felt this excited about attending a country's national-day festivities Abella's presence would make this night unique. Although he tried to concentrate on his duties, she continually sauntered through his mind. He finally stepped into Warrant Officer McQueen's office and asked how the reports were coming. Dave had been unusually quiet all day after returning from his morning committee meeting. He was feverishly pounding out meeting minutes on his keyboard and looked startled when Mitch entered his office.

"Sir, you're not here for the minutes, are you? I believe it will take another half day for me to finalize them all."

"Dave, I was under the impression that the previous five meeting minutes were complete, and you only had one to finalize after this morning's meeting."

"Actually, sir, I reviewed my notes of the previous meetings, and realized that I had missed a lot of information, so I am retyping all the minutes."

Dave was obviously stretching the truth, but it didn't matter.

"Well, Dave, I'll cut you some slack and allow you another half day as you requested. But I expect to see all six meeting minutes on my desk tomorrow morning." Dave flinched. "I've got a meeting with the deputy chief of mission at the moment and won't be coming back to the office today. Keep working on those minutes."

There was no meeting scheduled with the deputy chief of mission. Mitch simply needed an excuse to depart and get back to his residence to make sure that his uniform looked respectable. Usually, Dave would depart the office moments after he knew the colonel would not be returning. But this day was different because as far as he knew, he was at risk of looking bad in the eyes of the ambassador. If the minutes were not on Mitch's desk tomorrow morning, Dave thought he would be up shit creek without a paddle.

Mitch departed the office with a slight spring in his step at knowing Dave would be glued to his computer for a good part of the evening.

As Mitch passed the small cafeteria where Dave had his alleged meeting that morning, he noticed a very large senior special agent standing with a group of Algerian gardeners. They all had coffee in one hand and a cigarette in the other, except for the big man, who had what appeared to be an expensive cigar.

"Jake, how the hell are you, my friend?" Mitch said. He patted Jake's shoulder as the man did not have a free hand to shake.

"Colonel, it's an absolutely beautiful day, and I hear tell that this evening is going to be even better for you!" Jake smiled and sipped his coffee, focusing knowing eyes on Mitch.

"Not sure exactly what you've heard, but if it's what I'm thinking, you are completely correct!" Mitch laughed and gave a prolonged wink.

"It's good that we bumped into each other this afternoon, Colonel. While lookin' at the schedule for this evenin's motorcades heading to the French embassy, I noticed somethin' strange. Your Algerian driver that crashed while returnin' with you from your visit with the French attaché specifically volunteered to drive you this evenin'. No drivers ever volunteer; they're assigned vehicles. This guy is ten miles of bad road, and the sooner I can get him outta here, the better for us all. I just need to find more dirt on the son of a bitch, then I'll fire his ass. What I'd really like to do is kick his ass first, then tell him he's fired!

"Colonel, I'll be personally drivin' your limo this evenin'. I'm not certain that you would've made it to the French Embassy this evenin' with that driver. Plus I hear tell that your vehicle driver must escort a lady from her apartment. If rumors are correct and the gate security guards ain't pullin' my leg, this lady is dynamically beautiful. I just want to be lucky enough to inhale her perfume and open the vehicle door for her." Jake smiled through that special Kentucky drawl of his as he took a long drag on his Cuban cigar.

"Thanks for looking after me, my man! Tonight is special, and I really want it to go well. I don't know why that Algerian driver has it out for me," Mitch said with concern and bewilderment. "Maybe because I represent America's military here in Algeria. Or maybe he doesn't like that I'm taking an Algerian lady to the French embassy."

"Don't you worry, Colonel. Everythin' will go as smooth as water off a duck's ass," Jake said. He dropped the butt of the cigar and crushed it with his enormous boot.

"Thanks again, Jake," Mitch said, glancing at his watch. "I gotta get going or I'll be late picking up Cinderella tonight." He smiled and headed for his residence.

When he arrived, he found that Djamila had already ironed his military dress shirt and inspected his uniform for any stains or unwanted creases. The only thing Mitch had to do was take a quick shower and put on his uniform. Everything looked in order as far as his emblems, badges, and buttons. He decided to blow off taking his formal military hat. It would never touch his head over the course of the evening, and he hated to carry it around. He had already misplaced two on previous occasions and felt that they were underused, overpriced, and looked ridiculous.

Mitch now had fifteen minutes to get to the limos inside the main gate of the embassy. Taking one last look in the mirror, he found himself humbled by his success in the military. He had vastly exceeded all his expectations of what constituted a military career—especially considering that he had graduated from a very liberal Bay Area college during the Vietnam era. His initial goal was to serve a few years, complete his commitment, and then get back to California and its beaches. Those few years had turned into almost three decades, and Mitch had no desire to leave the military. It had given him a unique lifestyle of travel, adventure, and memories usually only found in novels or movies.

Mitch checked his watch one more time and ran downstairs to the kitchen.

"Thanks so much, Djamila. You are amazing! I gotta run or I'll miss my departure time."

"Colonel Mitch, you look magnificent in that uniform," Djamila said as he ran out the door. "Have a wonderful time at *la Fête Nationale* this evening."

Mitch practically sprinted to the main gate. Jake was waiting with the other security guards who would be riding in the lead and follow vehicles. Mitch nodded at Jake as one of the guards opened the rear door of the limo. Sliding in, Mitch noticed how detailed and spotless it was. Jake jumped into the driver's seat as a security guard took the front passenger position with his sawed-off shotgun and a shoulder-harnessed pistol under his suit coat. The other two limos filled with security guards and all their respective firepower.

"Colonel, we're taking the middle position in this goat rope this evenin', so hang on tight. We know where your lady resides." Jake spoke with authority but looked in the rearview mirror at Mitch with a smile.

As soon as the embassy gate opened, the lead vehicle shot out onto the main road. Jake gunned the engine, and Mitch was pressed into the back seat.

Abella's apartment complex near the Bay of Algiers was just off a main boulevard that eventually led to the French embassy. Mitch saw the lead vehicle make an aggressive right turn off Boulevard Des

Martyrs onto a small side street. He braced himself in anticipation of a quick turn by Jake, who was following the lead vehicle at an extremely close distance. Although the motorcade seemed to move at the speed of a Formula One race car, the drivers maneuvered the limos with skill and precision.

As they pulled into the apartment complex parking lot, people quickly scattered. It seemed they had been socializing in the middle of the driveway. The limos stopped in formation without a word being spoken by anyone. Jake unfastened his seatbelt, and as he stepped out, he looked at Mitch and laughed.

"Wish me luck, Colonel. I'm not sure this old man's heart can handle the shock of seeing such a lovely lady."

Mitch's excitement was building. The security guards from the lead limo stood next to their vehicle with weapons at the ready. From time to time, the guards would direct individuals to leave the area because they had gotten too close to the motorcade. Approximately twenty people had congregated along the apartment complex fencing, trying to determine who was in the limo and why had it stopped at their location. As the crowd grew, the security guards in the back limo exited their vehicle and formed a semicircle along the rear of the car. Their handguns glistened as the rays of the setting sun sliced through the surrounding buildings and reflected off their nickel-finished barrels.

Finally, Mitch noticed movement on the second floor of the complex. He spotted Jake walking along the exposed side of the exterior walkway leading to the stairs. He knew that Jake would use all proper protective measures while escorting Abella. In fact, Mitch had difficulty spotting Abella because of Jake's massive size. As they finally stepped onto ground level, Jake and Abella turned, allowing anyone who might be watching to see how beautiful she looked. Although Mitch was confined in the limo, he heard the spectators clap and yell with approval. They had recognized Abella and knew that for this evening she was crossing the forbidden societal line to experience the upper-class world.

Mitch could not believe how stunning she looked. Her midnight-blue gown hugged her body elegantly. He regarded her with the same awe as the spectators. Everyone stared while she glided to the limo. Jake opened the rear driver's-side door and helped Abella enter. Mitch sat speechless and wide-eyed, and Abella smiled, reaching out to take his hand. He felt the warmth of her beauty and knew that he would be with the most gorgeous women at *la Fête Nationale*.

"I would kiss you, but I don't want to ruin your makeup." Mitch finally said, still staring.

Abella leaned in and kissed him lightly. "It doesn't matter, Mitch. All I care about is that we're together."

Jake and the security guard strapped themselves in, and Jake once again took the middle position between the two other vehicles. The three cars roared out of the parking lot in a cloud of dust and small stones. Abella squeezed Mitch's hand as the limo accelerated at a speed she had never experienced. Mitch pulled her hand to his lips and softly kissed it.

"Not to worry, sweetheart. These vehicles only know zero and one hundred miles an hour. We'll be at the French embassy faster than the speed of light." Mitch winked, hoping to help her relax.

The grand boulevard leading to the embassy was lined on either side with hundreds of tri-color French flags. The scene was extremely impressive, with the flags waving in the light summer breeze and crowds along the street clapping at each passing motorcade. As Mitch's motorcade turned into the entrance of the embassy, there was an abbreviated security check of the vehicles and confirmation of the occupants. Once that was complete, they slowly rolled into the embassy. As their vehicle stopped, Jake gave Mitch a nod and hopped out, opening Mitch's door. Mitch glanced at Abella.

"Cinderella, are you ready to enter the ball?"

"Oh, Mitch, is this really happening?"

Mitch squeezed her hand, and they left the limo and entered the festivities.

They were instantly overwhelmed by the grandeur. Near the reception line on either side of the entry to the red carpet were four French Republican Guards mounted on magnificent white horses. They appeared as if they had just stepped out of the nineteenth century and Napoleon's personal cavalry. Their uniforms were superbly detailed with metal breastplates, knee-high leather boots, sabers, and highly polished brass helmets adorned with red plumes. Abella was astonished.

She and Mitch continued through gardens of red roses and tri-color carnations resembling the French flag. In the distance, an orchestra played. As they peered through a grove of trees to find the source of the music, they saw many of the guests dancing.

The red carpet was long and grand. Guests slowly moved down the reception line. Per protocol, Mitch went first, followed by Abella. This would allow him to make the introductions.

"Mitch, is that the French ambassador and his wife?" Abella inquired.

"Yes, and there is the deputy chief of mission, and finally my friend Yves, the French defense attaché."

"What should I say to them?" Abella asked nervously.

"Nothing, sweetheart. Your beauty will have them all talking before you get near them. I suspect that all you will be saying is 'thank you,'" Mitch said with confidence as he smiled and admired her.

Finally, they approached a small podium where a French diplomat was taking invitation cards from the guests. The well-dressed man announced the names of the guests just before they moved toward the VIPs. Each announcement was projected throughout the embassy so all would know who was now meeting the French ambassador.

The French diplomat keyed the microphone and announced, "Colonel Ross, the American defense attaché, accompanied by his lady, Abella Amari."

Abella squeezed Mitch's hand tightly and whispered, "Oh my God, for once in my life I truly feel important."

He looked at her. "Here we go, sweetheart. It's showtime!"

Mitch approached the French ambassador and shook his hand. "Good evening, Mr. Ambassador," he said. "This is truly an amazing event."

"Thank you, Colonel Ross. I am always in awe of how many medals you have, and yet you seem to be so young. French colonels tend to be much older!" The ambassador said this loud enough for Yves to hear. Then he turned toward Abella, and Mitch noticed the ambassador's eyebrows rise as he reached for her hand. "Colonel Ross, you must introduce me to this lovely lady that accompanies you this evening!"

"Of course, Mr. Ambassador. This is Abella Amari, the angel that nursed me back to health after my unfortunate incident at the Hungarian embassy earlier this spring."

"My, my, I never have nurses that are this beautiful when I'm in the hospital." The ambassador seemed to speak to everyone but to no one in particular.

"Yes, and you might find yourself in a hospital sooner than you expect, making statements like that as you stand next to me," the ambassador's wife interjected. She broke the tension with a quick laugh, knowing that her husband had embarrassed Abella. "Abella, let the men talk politics. I want to see your beautiful dress. And where did you find those stunning heels?" The ambassador's wife reached out and pulled Abella past Mitch.

As the two ladies began speaking French, Mitch noted that Abella's nervous tension quickly melted away. He was pleased but knew that those waiting in line behind them would be irritated by the delay. Finally, the ambassador turned to his wife.

"Ladies, we have all evening to discuss fashion, and I'm sure Colonel Ross would be much happier to have a glass of champagne than to spend his time talking to an old diplomat."

The ambassador's wife rolled her eyes at her husband and then whispered to Abella, "Let's talk later this evening. Truly, I mean it."

Abella was overwhelmed by the genuine hospitality. Never had she thought that people of this stature would want to spend time with her.

Mitch smiled broadly. "Looks like you found a friend."

Next, they greeted the deputy chief of mission and finally found themselves standing in front of Yves.

"Well, well, Mitch, you never ever disappoint me. But I must add, Abella is much more attractive than what you described!" Yves spoke with his typical French flair. He ignored Mitch and extended his hand to Abella.

Abella flushed as Yves held her hand and gazed at her.

"Okay, my French comrade, let my lady go," Mitch interrupted. "It's time to set our evening rendezvous." He was anxious to hear Yves's information concerning the American pilot.

Without hesitating, Yves responded, "My garden in one hour." Then he turned to Abella. "*Avoir une belle soiree a la fete.*"

"*Merci, Yves, et vous aussi,*" Abella said and reached for Mitch's hand.

Mitch and Abella moved away from the red carpet. After a few moments, a waiter asked if they would like a drink, lowering his platter of multicolored alcohol selections. Abella took a glass of chardonnay as Mitch grabbed bourbon.

They walked to an area of the embassy park that resembled a French carnival of the 1890s. There were jugglers, mimes, fire-breathers, dancers, a squeezebox player, and tall men on stilts and dressed in colorful outfits. They all seemed to move to the beautiful music of the distant orchestra.

"Good evening, Colonel. You're looking splendid this evening." Mitch recognized the British ambassador, who spoke while taking a glass of red wine from a passing waiter. "I'm glad to see that you're enjoying the entertainment. Oh, by the by, the French ambassador's wife mentioned that you are with an exquisite lady."

Abella had been sidetracked by a few ladies who recognized her from a dated news report. They asked whether she was related to the army officer who had been tragically killed several years ago. As much as she despised the painful subject, she maintained her decorum and spoke with them. It would not be diplomatic to accuse the ladies of being rude, much as she wanted to. Just as one of the ladies asked how difficult it was to move on from such an experience, Mitch reached out and touched her arm. She graciously excused herself and turned toward him with a sigh of relief.

The British ambassador continued speaking to Mitch as he gazed at the hundreds of guests surrounding them. "Excuse my language, Colonel, but this is a bloody fine national day if I do say so myself. Everyone is dressed magnificently. Have you sampled the food? It is truly to die for!"

Turning toward Mitch, the ambassador noticed Abella.

"Oh my, the ambassador's wife was spot on! Colonel Ross, your lady is extraordinary! Excuse me for being so bold and direct, but it's the truth," the British ambassador exclaimed, knowing full well that proper introductions had not been made. "I'm terribly sorry," he said, extending his hand to Abella. "I'm Fredrick Parker, British ambassador to Algeria."

"Mr. Ambassador, this is Abella Amari, the finest nurse in all of Algeria!" Mitch knew his statement would embarrass Abella, but it was how he felt.

"Well, I have no doubt that she is. As soon as I find my wife, Sylvia, I must introduce her to you two splendid people. But please don't let me keep you from all the activities, food, and fellowship. Have a wonderful evening! And please allow my wife and I to have you over for dinner sometime soon. Cheers!" Ambassador Parker meandered away, periodically stopping people to ask if they had seen his wife.

"He was such a nice man. I hope he finds his wife," Abella said as she watched the portly, red-nosed ambassador disappear into the crowd.

"Yeah, he's a great guy," Mitch said. "We have about twenty-five minutes before our rendezvous with Yves, so we better head toward the chow line."

"What's a chow line?"

"Sorry, those damn military terms keep slipping out. I mean we should have something to eat before we meet with Yves." They headed toward the long tables, each festooned with flowers and delicacies like those from the finest restaurants in Paris.

Obviously the embassy had flown in some of France's most renowned chefs. Abella was overwhelmed as she admired tantalizing foods from all over the world. Then she spotted the four-foot ice sculptures strategically separating each chef and their specialty dishes.

"Abella, have you noticed that each ice carving resembles a famous piece of sculpture from the Louvre?" Mitch asked, watching a chef fill his plate with fine culinary delicacies.

"I'm in awe!" Abella exclaimed. "I would stand here all night just tasting and examining. This must be the best that Paris can offer. Mitch, why do you think France is going all out for this particular national day?"

"I'm not sure, but Yves seemed to be holding back from telling me. It must be very important for the French because they're really wining and dining the elite of Algerian society. Hey, isn't that your president just a few tables to our right?"

Abella peeked and saw a group of security guards near a shorter man with an extreme combover and a mustache. "Yes, yes, it is my president!" she hissed.

"Do you want to say hello? I'm sure that you could catch his eye, considering his playboy reputation." Mitch laughed as Abella shook her head.

"Actually, Mitch, what I would really like to do is kick him in the balls. He's one of the sons of bitches that I believe conspired to have my father killed!" Abella's jaw clenched angrily.

"Alrighty then, remind me never to piss you off! That could be detrimental to my health, which includes the welfare of my balls," Mitch said, attempting to change the complexion of the discussion.

They found a small table under a tree near the orchestra and shared their plates of delicacies. Mitch requested two glasses of pinot noir from a passing waiter. It was a beautiful, starry evening, complete with a Mediterranean breeze lowering the summer temperature to a perfect seventy degrees. A soloist stepped from the orchestra, took a microphone, and began to sing "Moonlight Serenade" in perfect English.

"I don't ever want this night to end," Abella said as she sipped her wine and then kissed Mitch.

Mitch desired the same but realized that Yves would be waiting for them in a few minutes. "I'm sorry, sweetheart, but we gotta cross over the park and meet with Yves."

"I know, but maybe after the meeting we can listen to the orchestra. It's so beautiful." Abella gazed at the singer.

Mitch nodded and took Abella's hand. The two of them headed toward the darkened housing area on the other side of the park. As they passed through the crowd, a voice rang out.

"Abella dear, do you have a moment?"

The request startled Mitch and Abella, and they turned in the direction of the voice. It was the French ambassador's wife. She was followed by Ambassador Parker and his wife, Sylvia.

"Abella, why don't you stay here and socialize? I won't be long," Mitch said, kissing Abella's hand.

She knew that it was probably better for her to talk with the ladies than stifle any subject areas that Yves needed to relate to Mitch.

"Go, Mitch, I'll be okay. But promise not to forget me when you're done."

"That'll never happen!" Mitch turned toward Yves and waved. Yves raised his hands, acknowledging Mitch, and revealed a bottle of wine and three glasses.

Damn, just what I don't need right now—more booze, Mitch thought as he approached Yves.

"Yves, my friend, how are you?"

"Splendid, Mitch, but where is that lovely lady of yours?" Yves asked.

"Well, if you look carefully in the distance, you can just about see her talking to your ambassador's wife, and the British ambassador and his wife."

"Ah yes, it's easy to pick her out in a crowd. Like a fine diamond in the rough." Yves grinned and began pouring the wine. "I won't keep you long, but the information I have is very important. Unfortunately, it also brings danger." A stern look came over Yves's face as he raised his glass in a toast. "May we find success and live to tell about it."

"On that ominous note, I'm anxious to hear what you have to tell me," Mitch said, glad Abella hadn't heard Yves's words.

Yves sat down on a small bench and motioned for Mitch to take the adjoining chair. He took one last sip of wine and placed the glass on a table between them. "Do you recall the GSPC terrorist Omar Abdul Hamady? As I mentioned before, Hamady confirmed that Captain Hunt is alive and well but could not identify the exact location of the pilot here in Algiers. When asked about the hierarchy of the GSPC, Hamady said there had recently been a change in leadership.

"The terrorist organization, under the new leader, was ordered to be much more aggressive in their activities against the Algerian military and police forces. Specifically, Hamady mentioned that several of his colleagues had received special training in Iran that concentrated on explosive devices and how to assemble them. Also, there has been a push to recruit local city residents to support the terrorist cause. The GSPC has made a concerted effort to convince Algerians working in foreign embassies here in Algiers to take up their cause against the government and infidels. That means people like you and me have become even larger targets.

"Of course, much of this information came out after prolonged torture. At one point in his cross-examination, he was hit on the side of his head by an interrogator and rendered unconscious. Physicians were called into the room and, after examining him, advised that he be taken to a hospital for immediate treatment.

"A security guard accompanied Hamady and the physicians in the ambulance that was to take him to the People's National Army Hospital. If I am not mistaken, that was the same hospital where you recovered after you were stabbed. Unfortunately, Hamady never made it to the hospital. The security guard was a covert member of the GSPC and killed the two physicians and driver of the ambulance. The ambulance was later found with the three dead bodies in the city of Blida, thirty miles southwest of Algiers. It was initially conjectured that Hamady made his way to Cherchell, along the coast. But that was later dismissed by eyewitnesses, who said that they had seen a man with a bandaged head being helped by another dressed as a security guard near the ancient Roman city of Tipasa, thirty-five miles west of Algiers."

Yves paused and put the Chardonnay to his lips.

"So, Yves, other than living in this terrorist-infested country they call Algeria, where is the danger in this story?" Mitch inquired as he sipped his wine and wondered if Abella was still talking fashion with the dignitaries.

"That, my American friend, will now be told!" Yves responded. "You have probably wondered, along with many others, why the French government has gone well beyond what other countries normally spend on their national day festivities. The National Orchestra of France, the finest chefs from Paris, the elite Republican Guard in their Napoleonic uniforms on beautiful white stallions, the 1890s French carnival, the wines and flowers flown in from Bordeaux, the French government dignitaries, your secretary of state, and the president of Algeria.

"The French government did this to show appreciation for the classified agreement made recently with the Algerian government. This agreement allows for French intelligence agents and a limited number of special operations forces to operate in this country. Why is this important to France and the United States? Because our two countries have noted that there are large numbers of North Africans finding their way to Europe, Canada, Mexico, and the United States. They enter

France by hiding on ferries from Algiers, Tangier, and Tunis. A few of them eventually find their way to Canada and Mexico, then cross your porous borders illegally and become small teams of extremists ready to attack. This has already occurred throughout Europe, and it's conjectured that the attacks will increase in magnitude in the next ten to twenty years if nothing is done. I'm talking purely about the terrorists from North Africa. This does not include those extremists from the Mideast! We must stop them now, or we will be fighting them in our cities, towns, and neighborhoods for years to come.

"But I have still not discussed how all of this directly impacts you, my friend! A covert French Algerian operative was recently captured by the GSPC in the Roman city of Tipasa. Instead of us finding his headless body, which is their modus operandi, they cut his heart out and stuck a note in his mouth. They dumped his body in front of the French embassy last night as we were preparing for our national day.

"Mitch, I have that bloodstained note here and will read it to you. The note states that in two days, Omar Abdul Hamady desires an audience with an American representative of the United States embassy. This representative must be of a military nature, have experienced combat, be an officer, and be willing to communicate with the captured American pilot, Captain Hunt. The American will not travel in a secure motorcade but must find alternative means to get to the meeting location. The American can only travel with a driver and have no firearms. It goes on to demand that no other American be told of this event, and if their operatives within the US embassy hear of any talk concerning this meeting, the American representative will be killed.

"The location of the meeting will be in the center of the ancient Roman amphitheater of Tipasa. The meeting time will be at 2 p.m., and only two individuals will stand in the middle grounds of the amphitheater, Omar Abdul Hamady and the American military representative. If there is no American at the appointed time and location or if these instructions are not carried out to the letter,

Captain Seth Hunt's headless naked body will be dragged through the streets of Algiers and then deposited in front of the main gate of the United States embassy. Mitch, you asked about the dangers. I believe you now understand why I made such an ominous toast."

Mitch was stunned. He made no reply other than grabbing his wineglass. He attempted to lift it to his lips but could not control the nervous shaking of his hand.

"Mitch, are you okay?" A soft voice broke the silence, and Mitch felt a tender, warm hand take the glass. Abella noticed his pale face.

Yves quickly grabbed the remaining empty wineglass, poured a little Chardonnay, and gave it to Abella as he took Mitch's glass from her. She could tell that whatever was discussed had unnerved Mitch.

Yves attempted to change the subject. "Abella, how were your discussions with all the dignitaries?"

Abella wasn't going to bite. "I know I shouldn't ask the question, but what the hell have you two been discussing that has caused Mitch to become ill? When he left me to come to your garden, he was on top of the world. Now he looks like death warmed over!"

Mitch finally regained his composure. "Abella, please don't ask because we can't tell you. Just trust me when I say that everything will eventually turn out okay."

Abella turned to Yves and said, "Mitch and I will be leaving now. Thank you for your wine." She set her glass on the small table, took Mitch's arm, and they both walked toward the festivities. The orchestra was playing the theme from *The Godfather*.

Yves whispered to Mitch before he was out of earshot, "I'll be your driver."

"Abella, I need bourbon," Mitch said as they walked to a secluded table away from the crowd.

A waiter appeared. Abella requested tonic water with a slice of lime.

Mitch blurted, "Bourbon, Jim Beam Black, straight up!"

They sat in silence, listening to the orchestra and waiting for their drinks. The waiter eventually returned with their refreshments and then disappeared into the darkness.

"Mitch, I know you can't tell me what was discussed, but is there anything I can do to assist?" Abella pleaded. She reached out and took Mitch's hand as he drained half the glass of the Kentucky liquid.

At this point in the evening, Mitch's give-a-shit level was extremely low. He wasn't in the mood to play around with diplomats and their word games. He just wanted to be with Abella and drink his bourbon. "Did you ever study the Romans and their great empire?" Mitch inquired, taking Abella by surprise.

"Romans? What does that have to do with anything?" Abella replied, bewildered.

Mitch sat silently and took another hit of bourbon.

"Aren't you going to elaborate for me?" Abella asked with a slightly annoyed tone.

"You haven't answered my question about the Romans," Mitch replied.

"I find this conversation extremely odd, but if you must know, my father was a great scholar of the Romans' influence in Algeria. Growing up, not a month passed that my family didn't venture out and play Indiana Jones in the Roman ruins. My father was our personal tour guide. He knew the layout of each city, what they produced, and why they were there. One location became so familiar that I actually felt as though I had lived there as a Roman woman."

"What location might that be?" Mitch inquired.

"It doesn't really matter, does it? All you want to do is play this silly bullshit game about Algerian Roman ruins. You know, Mitch, you're really pissing me off!"

Mitch sat silently, swallowing the last of the bourbon in his glass. Then he broke the silence. "I'm serious, Abella. What Roman location was your favorite?"

Abella glared at him. "Tipasa. Tipasa! Does that make you feel better? I know it like the back of my hand. Every little turn of the streets and paths, where the merchants sold their goods, the temples of their gods, the homes of the elite with their mosaic floors, their theaters, their amphitheater, and the ruts in the stone roads from their chariots.

"My mother and I would sit in the stone seating of the amphitheater as my father ran to the grassy center, acting as if he were a gladiator. We would cheer as he was in the throes of battle with an adversary. When he was victorious, we would stand and give him the ancient Roman thumbs-down signal to finish off his foe. Then we would take our picnic lunch and sit by the beautiful cliffs that overlooked the Mediterranean Sea and imagine what it would have been like to be a Roman in Algeria.

"I would love to take you, but it's too damn dangerous. Every week there are several foolhardy foreigners found beheaded in the ruins. It was not that way growing up in Algeria, but now only a crazy man would venture there."

As Mitch turned to Abella, his hand inadvertently hit her glass of tonic water, spilling it on his uniform. She took the small white cloth covering the table and began to wipe off the liquid. As Abella leaned into Mitch, he took her hand that held the cloth, and then softly kissed her lips. She tasted traces of bourbon on his tongue as their passion rapidly intensified.

"I wish we were at my place," Mitch said between kisses, their uncontrollable cravings for each other building.

"Yes, Mitch. Oh yes. To be on your couch!"

"As much as I would love for this to continue, Abella, we should throttle back and act more like diplomats," Mitch reluctantly said as he straightened his tie and readjusted the badges on his uniform. "So, you know the lay of the land as far as Tipasa is concerned?" He hoped to get more information without sounding too inquisitive.

"What is it that you want to know? I can draw the layout of the town by memory," Abella responded with confidence.

"Come on, let's find Jake and get the hell out of here. The clock is ticking, and I've only got two days," Mitch said. He grabbed Abella's hand, and they headed toward the diplomat parking area.

"Two days? What's that mean?" Abella asked.

"I'll tell you at my place. I shouldn't say a word even there, but at this point I don't give a damn. You might be the only person on this earth who could help me continue breathing after my meeting with a terrorist." Mitch knew he had just crossed the line.

"Meeting with a terrorist? What's this all about? Mitch, you can't meet with extremists. They can't be trusted. Terrorists don't care about you or what's to be discussed. It's a trap to kill you. Please don't do this!"

"We don't have time to argue about this, plus there are too many ears listening right now. There's Jake with a plateful of food. Oh, is he going to be pissed when I tell him we've gotta go."

Mitch gave him the bad news.

"Hey, Jake, it's time to pull chocks and get airborne. I was just notified of some important work that I gotta take care of. Sorry, buddy, but Uncle Sam needs me at the US embassy pronto."

"Damn, Colonel, maybe this is a good thing. I was just grabbing my third plate of all these fine French delicacies. A few more festivities like this and I'll be growing out of my jeans," Jake responded. He took an empty plate and placed it over his food. "Don't wanna waste this fine grub. I'll have it for midnight chow!" He carefully put the covered plate on the dash of the limo and instructed the security guard to keep his paws off it.

While the three embassy vehicles sped through the streets of Algiers, Mitch hesitantly said, "Jake, I have a request, and I know it's out of line."

"Colonel, I already got ya covered. As soon as ya told me that we had to make a beeline back to the embassy, I knew that we wouldn't be stopping at your pretty lady's apartment. I notified the other two vehicles to press on straight to the embassy. I'll also take care of her visitor paperwork and computer entries once we get back home. I believe I'll see her depart your residence around one in the mornin', if that sounds reasonable to you, sir?"

"Jake, there's not enough gold in this world to reward you for all you've done for me. Thanks so much, my friend."

"Not a problem, Colonel. That case of bourbon that magically appears on my doorstep will be a wonderful thing," Jake said with a laugh.

8

The motorcade entered the embassy and abruptly stopped. Jake opened Mitch's door, then ran to Abella's side of the vehicle and helped her out. "Don't worry about the time of your departure. I've got that covered, pretty lady," Jake whispered. "I can tell that you two have more work to do than just sipping wine and looking into each other's eyes. Take care of the colonel. I can see through that false smile of his that he's worried about something." He gave her a wink and yelled at the security guards in the other vehicles to report to the armory and check in their weapons.

Mitch shook Jake's hand and thanked him again.

Once inside Mitch's spacious residence, Abella pulled Mitch toward her. She kissed him with a passion only found deep within someone's heart.

"I know I can't dissuade you from this meeting in Tipasa, but in case it doesn't go well, I want you to understand how much I love you," Abella said as she looked into Mitch's eyes.

"Believe me, sweetheart, I feel the same way about you! But this meeting is very important. I can't avoid it. Let's change out of our formal clothes. I have some sweats that you can wear. They might be a little big, but I guarantee they will be very comfortable!"

They ran upstairs and pulled off their formal attire. Mitch noted the black Chantilly lace on Abella's underwear that barely covered her exquisite backside. Unfortunately, Mitch had to concentrate on the task at hand rather than circumnavigating Abella's beautiful body with his lips. Noticing Mitch's gaze, Abella turned her back to him, slowly bending over as she pulled the sweatpants above her hips. Once changed she said, "Come on, big boy, we have work to do, and it doesn't involve what's on your mind at the moment!" She laughed as she threw a T-shirt in his direction.

After changing, Mitch led Abella along the hallway to a room adjacent to his bedroom. His study, although small, had everything he needed: two computers, classified and unclassified, arranged on a large desk with an expansive flat top; a floor-to-ceiling bookshelf full of files, articles, and books related to the countries of North Africa and their military capabilities. On the walls of the room were maps of Algeria, charts of military airbases and installations, and pictures of all the prominent leaders of Algeria's military and government. It reminded Abella of her father's study while he was the assistant attaché in America.

"Abella, there are some large rolled-up sheets of paper over in the corner. Would you please bring them to the desk? I'll move the keyboards so we have a clear spot, if you wouldn't mind rolling out the paper?" Mitch asked as he pointed to the rolls.

Abella did as he asked, and Mitch put a book on either side of a sheet of paper to keep it firmly in position. He pulled a chair to the desk, opened a drawer, and took out a handful of pencils. Then he invited Abella to sit in front of the blank paper.

"Would you please draw a generalized, God's-eye view of the layout of Tipasa?" he requested. "If you can, include the roads going into and out of the ruins. Also, it would help if I knew where the large wooded areas and rocky hills along the coastline are located. Make sure you identify where the nearest inhabitants live adjacent to the ruins. They could be of major assistance if I really find myself in a bad situation."

Abella looked at him with conviction. "I've got news for you, my love," she said. "You're already in a bad situation, and I'm not sure whether you realize it! Can't you contact your army's special operations folks and have them in place when you arrive in Tipasa?"

"You're completely correct, Abella, but it's too late now. They couldn't get out here and deploy in time."

Abella had been around army operations for much of her life and knew what Mitch was saying was bullshit, but she decided to draw the maps rather than argue. As she sketched the landscape and ruins of Tipasa, Mitch wrote down the fine points of the terrorist's note that Yves had shared. Although he had heard it only briefly that evening, it left a detailed mark on his memory.

It did not take Abella long to complete the first drawing. Mitch stood behind her, pointing at different items she had drawn and asking her to label them.

"So, as far as you are aware, there is only one main road going into and out of the ruins?" he asked. "The other roads and paths within the ruins were built by the Romans. Are they dirt or are any of them paved?"

"There is only one road that goes to the ruins," Abella said, tracing the route with her finger. "Any of the larger roads within the ruins were paved by the Romans, with large slabs of stone and cobblestone. They seem to be in much better condition than our modern roads. Many of them still have the chariot and cart grooves worn into the stones."

"Are the larger Roman roads wide enough for vehicles?"

"They would be except that the Romans built sidewalks and columns along the roadsides that would become major obstacles for any motorized vehicle. Why do you ask?"

"Well, what that tells me is that the terrorists would not be able to bring in large trucks full of equipment, firearms, or men. It sounds like they will only be equipped with what they can haul in on their backs. That limits their capabilities—unless they have access to small boats that could come along the cliffs . . ." He pointed to the cliffs she had drawn. "I suppose equipment could be hauled up by ropes to the ruins."

"That is a possibility," Abella agreed, "but I do remember seeing some fishing boats in the area years ago. They were brutalized by the currents and waves. It made for very difficult fishing, let alone attempting to anchor and off-load heavy equipment. I doubt anything could be brought into the ruins by boat." She leaned back in the chair, thinking about the wonderful days she'd spent with her parents in Tipasa.

"I'm glad to hear that," Mitch said, studying the map. After a moment he spoke again. "Can you draw a detailed sketch of the amphitheater from different angles? God's eye and ground view from each cardinal compass direction?"

"Yikes! You don't want much, do you?" Abella said with a laugh. She grabbed another pencil, leaned over, and began drawing.

"Hey, can I get you a little wine?" Mitch asked, still perusing the initial drawing of Tipasa.

"Ah, now that sounds nice. Do you have Bordeaux?" Abella asked.

"I believe I have a couple bottles in my wine cellar just for you."

By the time Mitch returned, Abella had finished the God's-eye view and was working on the first of the four cardinal compass directions, though she was still confused as to why he wanted such detailed perspectives of the amphitheater. He handed her a glass of Bordeaux and set out a bowlful of mixed nuts he'd brought from the pantry.

"Wow, you're really trying to butter me up with the wine and the nuts. I should come here more often and work for you. The hospital never treats me like this!" She took a sip of wine and looked up at him. "Before we left the French embassy you said you would tell me more about this meeting. I'll make you a deal—I'll continue to draw, and you can talk to me."

"Okay, sweetheart." Mitch nodded. "The meeting is in two days. Monday, July 16 at 2 p.m. in the center of the amphitheater. The terrorist is Omar Abdul Hamady, a member of the GSPC. He was one of two GSPC representatives who paid off a Libyan terrorist organization and gained custody of an American pilot named Seth Hunt. The pilot has been a prisoner of war since 1991—shot down during a bombing mission in Desert Storm.

"Oddly enough, I had something to do with his unfortunate capture by the enemy. I'll tell you that story someday when we are far from here and relaxing on a tropical beach with boat drinks in our hands. But getting back to Tipasa, I've been warned not to inform any American. I will arrive in a nondescript auto without any support or sidearm. It will just be me and the driver of the vehicle. No one is to know where I'm going and who I'm meeting. If word gets out, the terrorists have threatened to drag Captain Hunt's decapitated body through the streets and deposit it in front of the US embassy." Mitch finished off the contents of his wineglass.

"I know I can't stop you from going," Abella said, "but let me say this, and please don't explode: I'm going with you to Tipasa. No ifs, ands, or buts. I know that amphitheater better than anyone, and I'll be able to monitor how many GSPC members are present and where they are. The terrorist note said nothing about a listening device, correct? I'll be able to keep you informed of any others who might be present. It'll help your situational awareness and make it a hell of a lot better for you than standing alone out there."

She paused and took his hand as tears welled in her eyes. "Mitch, I beg you to let me go with you. Please don't say no. I don't believe you'll get out of that amphitheater alive if you go without me! There is definitely a reason why they want you there, and I doubt it has anything to do with the captured American pilot."

"No, Abella, I can't risk it! The thought that you might be in the crosshairs of a terrorist's weapon . . ." He shook his head and shuddered. "It's something that I don't even want to imagine."

"You have never been to the ruins," Abella said firmly. "I heard Yves say he will drive you, but I doubt he knows Tipasa either. Of the three of us, I'm the only one that knows the lay of the land. My family had a game we would play during our visits. My father would drop me off in a wooded area before arriving at the ruins. I would then run through the trees and find different hiding locations amongst the larger Roman structures.

"My favorite spot was always the amphitheater because it had places that I could hide and yet be above most of the other ruins. My parents would try to find me, but I could observe their every movement as they closed in. It was easy to evade them. I would merely move to another hidden location when I felt threatened. They were never able to find me. After a given period, my father would whistle. That was my signal to reveal my location and celebrate my victory. I am telling you this story because I want you to know I can hide from anyone out there. If you drop me off in the wooded area well before arriving at the ruins, the terrorists will not find me."

Mitch looked at her. "I believe you can hide, sweetheart. But how will that benefit me when I'm standing in the middle of the amphitheater with a sniper's crosshairs on my forehead?"

"I would be able to see the sniper and warn you of his location. I will be in the highest position in all of the ruins. If any snipers take up a position, I will see them."

"Let's say I agree with your plan. What if I wasn't wired up with a communication system like you described? Then what?"

"Then I would scream out to warn you," Abella said, knowing that was a weak response.

"Then there would be two of us with bullet holes in our foreheads," Mitch said, shaking his head grimly. "I'm sorry, Abella, but your plan just doesn't seem to work. I can't wear that wire. At 2 p.m., in full daylight, I'm afraid Hamady would easily see the device and I would be a dead man."

"Listen to me, Mitch. You didn't come strolling into my life just so I could see you get blown away by some scum extremist. I'm going with you whether you like it or not. If you won't let me go with you and Yves, then I'll find my own way to Tipasa. I know the time, day, and location. I'll be there, Mitch, and I'll do everything in my power to prevent them from killing you! Do you understand me?"

Mitch walked to a small cupboard beside the desk and withdrew a glass and a flask of bourbon. He poured two fingers' worth of the magical medicine and gulped half of it. He walked back to Abella and placed the glass in front of her. She looked at it, met his gaze again, and then drained the remaining bourbon. She stood to meet him, and they began undressing each other. They realized that this unspoken agreement could prove deadly, but if it was to be, they would die together.

9

They woke early the next morning. After showers and breakfast, Mitch arranged for a taxi pickup. Abella was still wearing his sweat suit as she gave Mitch a quick kiss and jumped in the car. Mitch's planning was a little better during this visit. He made sure that Abella had the taxi fare well before leaving his residence. He also insisted that she leave her formal attire in his closet so she looked less conspicuous when arriving at her apartment. Mitch felt that surviving Monday afternoon was impossible, but he told Abella she could pick up her gown and heels after the meeting with Hamady.

Questions still plagued Mitch, and he needed to finalize the arrangements with Yves. He decided to give the Frenchman a quick call.

"Hello, Yves, this is Mitch. Any chance you can drop by my residence today?"

"Mitch, my American friend, I was hoping you would contact me. I felt bad after our meeting in the garden. I hope everything is well between you and Abella. She is so sweet and beautiful, and it's obvious that she loves you. That's a rare combination in this day and age. Yes, I can be over in your neck of the woods in an hour."

"That's perfect, Yves," Mitch said. "But I must apologize to you now for not having anything prepared for this visit. My cook, Djamila, is off today, so if mixed nuts work for you, then I'm golden."

"As long as there is a cabernet chaser, then it'll be a meal fit for a king!" Yves responded.

"Great, see you soon!" Mitch hung up and ran downstairs to make sure he had a bottle of cabernet. Then he poured a container of mixed nuts into two bowls.

— • — •

Meanwhile, the taxi pulled up to Abella's apartment, and she quickly ran up the stairs. She was surprised to find her roommate sitting on the living room couch.

"Samia, what are you doing here?" Abella said. "I thought you were working the day shift at the hospital?"

"I traded my day shift so I would be here when you got back. I knew you wouldn't return last night, and I wanted to be the first to hear all about the French national day and who you met. By the way, Cinderella, your gown and heels have turned into sweats and flip-flops!" Samia laughed and moved from the center of the couch to give Abella room to sit.

"Before I begin, I need to brew a cup of tea and nibble on a croissant," Abella said.

"That sounds great. I'll brew the tea, and you get two croissants from the pantry," Samia said as she jumped from the couch and grabbed the teapot.

Abella spent several hours talking to Samia about the magnificent evening at the French embassy. She told of the diplomats she had met, the grandeur of the decorations, the food, the music, the fashions, and the elite of the Algerian society who had attended. She attempted to hide her concern about the planned meeting with the terrorist, but Samia could tell something was wrong.

"Was there an issue with you and Mitch last night, Abella?" Samia asked.

"No, not really. Everything was like a dream come true," Abella responded.

"I've known you all my life, Abella, and I know when something is not right. Something is bothering you, and it's serious! Did you and Mitch have a falling-out?"

"No, it's nothing like that. Mitch and I are wonderful—we couldn't be better. Well, maybe if we were on a tropical island on the other side of the world, it would be better." Abella laughed nervously.

"See, I knew it," Samia said. "Something's up, and I'll not stop prodding until you tell me."

"Okay, okay, but I can't tell you everything. Mitch must meet a terrorist on Monday, and it's terribly dangerous. That's all I can say, Samia, so please don't ask for more information."

Samia moved closer, embraced Abella, and then whispered. "I'm sure it's not as bad as you might think. From what you have told me about Mitch, he's a very smart man. By Monday, he'll have a plan, and everything will turn out just fine."

Tears formed in Abella's eyes and streaked her face. "I hope you're correct, Samia. I don't want to lose him."

— • — •

Mitch met Yves at the US embassy security building. There had barely been enough time to complete the paperwork to allow Yves to enter the embassy. As the two attachés walked to Mitch's residence, they planned for the meeting with Hamady.

Inside his residence, Mitch uncorked the cabernet. "Yves, please have some nuts while I pour the wine. I won't detain you too long this morning. I'm sure you have many things to do now that your national day is complete."

"Not a problem, my friend," Yves said, making himself comfortable. "It's a nice respite from all the chaos at the embassy over this past week. First the planning of the national day and then that dead body outside of our gate. It has been nonstop pandemonium.

Anything we plan here, as you Americans say, will be a piece of cake!"
Yves raised his wine and touched Mitch's glass.

Mitch looked at Yves and shook his head. "Well, I'd like to think
that. But I suspect that what I'm going to tell you will not be so pleasant."

Yves looked at him quizzically.

Mitch sipped his wine, then spoke. "First let me say, I'm convinced
that this meeting on Monday will be a one-way trip. I don't expect
us to return from Tipasa. It's an ambush from many different angles.
If we don't go, the American pilot will be killed. If we go and have
a security backup, the pilot will be killed, and I'm sure I'll receive a
few rounds of lead in my forehead. Even if we go and follow all the
rules the GSPC spelled out in their note, I believe they will kill us.
So regardless of how this whole plan transpires, the way I see it, an
American is going to be killed. Also, more than likely, a Frenchman
will be added to the body count for shits and grins." Mitch said all
this in a matter-of-fact, unemotional way.

"And if you didn't like what I just said, well, my friend, hang on!"
Mitch continued. "You know that absolutely beautiful lady who
accompanied me to your national day? When she makes her mind up
to do something, there's nothing on God's sweet earth that will stop
her. Well, she's determined to be at the ruins during my meeting with
Hamady. If she doesn't ride with us, she'll find alternate transportation.

"Abella knows those ruins well. So well, in fact, she was able to
draw detailed sketches from many different angles. I now know the
layout of the amphitheater, where individuals can enter and exit,
hiding locations, and the highest spot in all the Tipasa ruins. Now,
how does that help us? Beats the shit out of me! But as I said before,
if she is not with us, she'll find another way to get there.

"Abella wants us to drop her off well before approaching the ruins.
She's familiar with the wooded areas and knows how to approach
the amphitheater without being seen. My vote is to accommodate
her. Abella is an intelligent woman. I'm convinced that if anyone can
help us out of this deadly situation, she is the one!"

Yves sat in silent contemplation. He stared intently at his wine, then spun the red liquid around several times. Finally, he said, "Yes, I believe you're correct, Mitch. Abella is intelligent and grasps the gravity of the situation. I saw that last night in my garden. I'm sure she heard me tell you that I would be driving. That undoubtedly raised many questions in her mind. And your physical reaction to our discussion must have given her further insight into the dangers at hand." Yves paused for a moment, then continued. "I believe it's probably better if she comes along with us. I wouldn't want her to be alone as she attempts to help out."

With that agreed on, Mitch got back to logistics. "Yves, let's review the plan as far as we know it at this point. I'll go to the French embassy at 11 a.m. on Monday. At your residence, we'll go over everything we know. Around noon we'll take your Peugeot and depart. We'll pick up Abella at her apartment a little after 12. That should give us approximately two hours to get to Tipasa. That's more than enough time. Did I miss anything?"

"Will you be wearing body armor?"

"Yes, under my shirt."

Yves nodded. "Everything else sounds fine, but please bring Abella's drawing of the amphitheater on Monday. I would like to review the entry points to help decide where I'll park the car. It will be critical for our escape route, God willing!" Yves's response wasn't typical for him.

After their discussion, they attempted a little relaxation by watching the last minutes of Manchester United beating Barcelona. But it didn't really help. Mitch kept thinking about Monday and whether he would be waking up on Tuesday morning. Either Djamila would have coffee ready for him in the living room, or the embassy would be making plans to fly his body back to the States.

Yves finally left the US embassy slightly drunk after consuming what remained in the bottle of cabernet. He was still muttering about the American use of the word *football* despite the players using their hands. Mitch thought of Abella, knowing that she had to work the night shift at the hospital. Any communications with her were not possible. He couldn't relax, so he changed into his uniform and went to the office.

10

The early-morning sun streaked through the curtains of Mitch's bedroom. As usual, the call to prayer had served as his alarm clock. But sleep had not been a gift during the previous night. The foreboding doom of Monday had finally arrived, Sunday merely a blur of meaningless tasks to get to Monday. Talking to Abella and confirming her pickup time had been the only bright moment. She was working the night shift and would return to her apartment at around 7 a.m. Her sleep had also been troubled during the weekend, so working nights helped the dark hours pass.

Mitch left for his office well before Djamila's arrival. He told Warrant Officer Dave McQueen that he would be working at the French embassy with his colleague Yves and wouldn't return for the rest of the day. That task complete, he ran up the chancery stairs to the ambassador's office and was fortunate to catch the ambassador between meetings.

"Mr. Ambassador, I won't keep you long," Mitch said. "I just wanted to inform you that there might be new information concerning the American pilot. The French attaché, Colonel Yves Dureau, and I have scheduled a meeting with French Algerian intelligence operatives who claim to have discovered new information on the pilot's whereabouts. I'm anxious to hear what they have to say and where they received the information. This could be the big break we've been waiting for. I know Greg Cain is currently in the States, so I'll inform his assistant of what I'll be doing. Do you have any questions or inputs that you would like me to relay, Mr. Ambassador?"

"No, Colonel, not at this time. The State Department and White House are anxious for any updates, so whatever you learn, please don't hesitate to get back to me as soon as possible. Oh, by the way, I noticed that lovely lady who was with you during the French national day. She was the talk of all the diplomats who saw her. It seems that everyone who spoke to her found that she was fabulous. Don't get me wrong, I love the comfort of married life. But at times when I see an extraordinary woman, I dream of being a single Air Force colonel." The ambassador laughed and slapped Mitch on the back.

"Sir, I'll have that information to you as soon as I return," Mitch said. The ambassador nodded and disappeared into his office.

Mitch ran to the other side of the chancery building and knocked on the embassy CIA office door. A covered peephole opened, and Mitch stood back to be easily seen. Within a few moments the door opened.

"Good morning, Colonel," the assistant chief of station said, motioning for Mitch to have a seat. "What brings you to our office of confusion, misperceptions, and intrigue?"

Mitch chuckled politely before replying. "Can't stay long, but I just wanted to inform you that I might be getting some valuable information concerning the captured American pilot today. I've apprised the ambassador, and upon my return, I will update you both. Please make sure that you relay any of our conversations to Greg. Although he's in the States, I promised him that I would keep him updated. Thanks! Gotta run!" Mitch backed out the door, dashed down the stairs, and headed for the security building to find Jake.

"Jake, how are you, buddy?" Mitch said, spotting Jake smoking under a coconut tree.

"Any day that I'm aboveground is a damn good day, Colonel!" Jake responded as he took a long drag on his cigar. He expelled four perfect smoke rings at a calico-colored cat chasing a small mouse.

"I know I sound like a broken record, but could you drop me off at the French embassy at 11 a.m.? I've already cleared it with the ambassador, and there's no need for you to wait until my meeting is over. In fact, the meeting will probably continue until late in the afternoon." Mitch hoped that Jake wouldn't ask too many questions.

Jake looked at his watch and then motioned to a driver to bring a security car around to the inside of the embassy gate. "Colonel, I'll ride shotgun on this trip and Farid will be doin' the drivin.'"

"Thanks! See you in an hour." Mitch turned and headed back to his residence.

He had to change his clothes and put on his body armor under his shirt. The armor wasn't that thick, and he often wondered whether it was just a formality. *Today, I'll probably find out if this armor really stops bullets,* he thought as he put on his shirt. Grabbing his jacket, he went downstairs. Djamila was busy in the kitchen, preparing his afternoon meal.

"Hey, Djamila, why don't you just make that meal my dinner? I'll most likely not be back this afternoon. Once you've finished preparing the meal, take the rest of the day off. I'll pay you for a full day's work. By the way, remind me if I'm around tomorrow to give you a raise. You deserve it!" Mitch scooped a handful of dates out of a bowl and waved goodbye to Djamila.

His watch showed 10:30 a.m. *That gives me thirty minutes to get to the French embassy,* Mitch thought. *I have Abella's drawings, so there shouldn't be anything else I need. Actually, what I need is the 82nd Airborne Division, but that would just complicate the situation.* As he neared the embassy entrance, he shook his head and noticed Jake standing by the security car.

"Well, Colonel, it's about time to get outta Dodge." Jake grabbed his shotgun and felt for his shoulder holster, which held a .357 Magnum.

Mitch took one last long look at the embassy before getting into the car. More than likely this would be his final view of the place.

The embassy gate opened, and the vehicle flew out onto the boulevard. They were quiet during the ride. Mitch contemplated different scenarios and possible outcomes of today's rendezvous. None of them had a happy ending.

"Colonel, looks as though we've arrived," Jake said. "Too bad the Frenchies aren't having another wingding. That food was the greatest and the price was right! Anyway, give me a call when you want to be picked up this afternoon. It's not like I have anything better to do other than smokin' stogies under a tall tree."

The vehicle cleared the arduous French security procedures, and Mitch jumped out before Jake could open his door. He thought about all he owed Jake and felt guilty that perhaps he wouldn't be around to give his friend that case of bourdon he'd promised. Mitch watched the car depart the embassy, then turned toward Yves's garden.

"Yves, are you in there?" Mitch said as he approached Yves's partially opened back door.

"Come in, Mitch. Although it's still morning, I thought we should start with a little wine."

"No offense, Yves, but do you have any bourbon? If I'm going to have something to drink right now, I'd like a little of that Kentucky magic, please," Mitch said seriously.

"Excellent choice," Yves said, nodding. "A little fire in the belly clears the mind. Bourbon it is!" He pulled a bottle of Evan Williams 23 from the shelf.

"Damn, that's top shelf–quality Kentucky Bourbon you have there," Mitch said, feeling a little relief from his stress.

Yves handed Mitch the bourbon and they both raised their glasses.

"May we never regret this!" Mitch said before draining half the contents.

They moved to the study, where Yves spread Abella's drawings on a large drafting table. Mitch described what he'd learned from

Abella about the layout of the ruins. Specifically, he emphasized the location of the wooded areas, the one main road to the ruins, and the amphitheater entry points. They measured distances from the southern entry of the amphitheater to determine the best parking location. One spot seemed to be partially hidden prior to making the final turn to the theater. It was approximately fifty yards from the wall of the Roman ruin and afforded them what appeared to be a shaded, obscure location. They agreed that if Abella's drawings were somewhat accurate, they would stage out of that location.

Now they had to determine the wooded drop-off point for Abella. As they examined the God's-eye view of all the ruins, they calculated the distance and time required for Abella to enter the amphitheater.

"She's quite the athlete," Mitch observed. "I have no doubt she'll be sprinting through the wooded area once we drop her off. I don't think she will enter the theater in any of the logical locations. Therefore, this particular spot would be perfect." He pointed to an area along the road prior to the final turn toward the ruins. "It seems to be shaded and the woods are very close to the edge of the road. Also, it's approximately half a mile to the theater. She'll be running full out, and I can guarantee no one will be able to track her down."

"You know her much better than I, Mitch," Yves said, finishing off his bourbon. "I have no doubt that she'll do everything in her power to protect you. That spot you've determined looks good, unless Abella objects."

"More than likely, the GSPC will track me as I walk to the amphitheater, so I'll enter the theater by way of the southern portal. Frankly, it's the only location that I'm aware of on that side of the ruins. Abella didn't mention alternate entry points, and it would be too risky to play games with the terrorists if there are other locations. Especially knowing that I will be in their crosshairs the entire time I'm walking and entering the amphitheater."

Yves checked the time and grabbed his jacket and a pair of sunglasses. "Let's get going. I can never anticipate the traffic in this city during the noon call to prayer. You would think that the roads would be empty, and all Muslims would be in their mosques, but like any religion there are heathens causing the traffic jams." Yves laughed but stopped quickly, noticing that Mitch was not in the mood for joking.

Clear roads brought them to Abella's apartment parking lot exactly at noon. She had been waiting and peering through her curtains, anticipating their arrival. Abella gathered her blue Georgetown University cap, a flask of water, and a small pair of binoculars. Wearing tight denim jeans, a sweatshirt, and running shoes, she locked the door and swiftly descended the stairs to the car. Mitch stepped from the auto and opened the rear door for her. She smiled and kissed him before climbing in. As soon as Abella engaged her seat belt, Yves accelerated out of the parking lot and onto the main avenue heading southwest.

Mitch turned to her. "Abella, your drawings really came in handy. We have a good spot to drop you off prior to eyeshot of the ruins. Also, the parking location seems to be strategically located, but we can modify our plan if you determine that a change is needed."

"I'm sure aerial photos would have been optimal," she responded, nodding, "but I gave it my best shot from memory. As I mentioned the other evening, the Roman ruins at Tipasa are like my favorite old sneakers. I know every crack, wrinkle, and tear in them. I just hope that the damn Algerian government didn't bulldoze anything. There was talk that some corrupt politician wanted to build a house along the cliffs overlooking the sea."

Their conversations centered on corrupt politicians rather than the task at hand as they continued southwest. At one point, Yves interrupted to ask Mitch to open the Peugeot's glove compartment. Mitch complied and froze when he saw the pistol inside.

"I believe you should take that for protection," Yves said. "It's the standard French military officer issue, Pamas G1. It resembles a Beretta, which you should be familiar with."

"Yves, the note stated that we weren't to have firearms with us. I'm sure they'll examine me quite closely once I arrive. I'd be endangering myself and Seth Hunt. This is not a good idea, my friend. Thank you, but we should hide this gun." Mitch carefully pulled the pistol out of the glove compartment and shoved it under his front seat.

"You're correct, Mitch," Yves said, eyeing him. "Sorry for not thinking this out completely. I just hate to think that those damn terrorists can dictate all the rules of our meeting. You're essentially walking into the amphitheater with your hands tied behind your back and no protection. As a fighter pilot you would never enter air-to-air combat unarmed. It would be just a matter of time before you were shot down!"

"Let's talk about something else, okay?" Abella pleaded. "I don't want to think about all of the negative aspects of this meeting. I'm already getting a bad case of acid reflux, and this flask of water doesn't help suppress it."

"Sorry, sweetheart, we didn't mean to upset you any worse than we already have," Mitch said as he turned and winked at Abella. She reached out and softly stroked his face.

Yves glanced at his watched. "It seems we're making good time," he said. "I'll slow down our progress somewhat so we don't arrive too early. But we must get there in time to complete the drop-off, Abella, and account for your walking distance into the amphitheater. I suspect if we arrive ten minutes before 2 p.m., that should give us enough time to accomplish all the pre-meeting activities."

They continued driving without much conversation until Yves noticed something odd on the road.

"Not to alarm you two, but there seems to be a major problem ahead," he said as he reduced speed. Mitch and Abella looked up and saw that a car had slammed into a tree and the vehicle was on fire. Yves pulled off on the right shoulder and stopped the car.

"Damn it!" Mitch groaned. "Thirty minutes until the meeting. This can't be happening. Shit! Abella, you stay in the car and watch over our things." Mitch got out and followed Yves to the burning vehicle.

As they got closer, Mitch saw that the flames were primarily coming from the engine compartment but spreading rapidly to the car's interior. Shielding their faces from the heat, they peered through the shattered windshield. A man and woman were inside, unconscious.

Yves opened the driver's door as Mitch ran to the passenger side. Pulling open the door, Mitch saw that the woman's slumped position prevented easy access to her seatbelt. Moving her could result in further injuries, but he didn't have a choice. Flames had nearly engulfed the car, and the heat was becoming unbearable. Mitch carefully moved the woman upright and unfastened her seatbelt, pulling her free of the vehicle just as the fire spread to the front seat where she had been sitting. Yves had the driver out and lying in the grass.

Abella realized that they needed to make the terrorist timetable, but her nursing instincts screamed at her. Yves had left the keys in the car, so she climbed into the front seat and started the engine, then drove to Yves and the driver. Leaving the car running, she grabbed her flask of water and climbed out. She gripped the left sleeve of her sweatshirt and tugged until it ripped off. Pouring water on the fabric, she placed it on the face of the driver, allowing the liquid to moisten his lips. Then she applied it to a large swelling on his forehead.

Abella next ran to Mitch's side. The woman he'd pulled from the car was gaining consciousness and moaning loudly. Abella had Mitch rip her right sleeve off, and then she put the moistened sleeve to the injured woman's mouth. The woman began to suck on the cloth, and Abella poured more water on the sweatshirt material. This seemed to revive her. The woman opened her eyes and spoke rapidly in French. Abella told her to be still and began to evaluate her for injuries. The woman seemed fine except for an intense headache. Mitch carefully moved the woman near a tree and sat her up against its trunk. By then Abella had returned to the driver, who was speaking to Yves. Abella handed her flask to the man and told him to share the contents with the woman.

"Yves, we've gotta leave them now or we'll never make Tipasa by 2 p.m.," Mitch yelled as he grabbed Abella's hand and ran to the Peugeot.

"Okay, Mitch, I'm right behind you two," Yves responded. A moment later he climbed in behind the wheel.

"We'll never make it on time if we stay on this main road," Abella said desperately. "I remember an alternate route that my father would take when he was not concerned about trashing the car. There is a dirt road just to the right of this main route ahead. It was the original trail to Tipasa, and it should lead us back to the main road just before the final turn to the ruins."

Yves wrenched his car off the main road, following Abella's instructions. The dirt road was essentially a wide, overgrown path, and tree limbs and bushes scraped violently against the sides of the Peugeot like claws of an angry beast. At times the car hit large bumps, slamming their heads against the ceiling.

"Yves, we have ten minutes. Step on it!" Mitch yelled. Yves floored the pedal and the engine screamed.

"The main road should be just ahead! It's just beyond that large tree on the right," Abella said as she braced herself for the final turn onto the main paved road.

"Yves, there's the drop-off location on the right," Mitch said moments later. Yves slammed the brakes, and the car ground to a stop. Mitch jumped out as Abella put on her ball cap and grabbed her binoculars. He took her by the waist and pulled her to him.

"Never forget how much I love you, Abella." He kissed her and then let her go.

She looked into his eyes, turned, and ran for the thickly wooded trees. Within a moment she was gone. Mitch leaped back into the car, and it sped to the preplanned parking location. When Yves saw the spot, he slammed on the brakes again and Mitch jumped out. He had two minutes to get to the amphitheater.

"Wish me luck, my friend," Mitch said as he sprinted to the southern entry portal of the theater.

Entering the ancient ruins of the Roman amphitheater, he felt a foreboding that weighed on his soul. In the shadows of the thick walls, the air was cool, but he sensed another coldness that made him shiver. The amphitheater's open arena lay in front of him, and he stepped out into the brilliant sunshine, squinting. It was 2 p.m. exactly.

He saw no movement and absolutely no sign of anyone in the amphitheater. Walked to the center of the arena, he wondered what would happen. *Am I about to be gunned down? Is this all just a trick by the GSPC?* He glanced around the lifeless seating area and wondered if Abella was watching.

Then a voice spoke in French and shattered the silence.

"Colonel, I'm so happy that you have arrived, and right on time."

Mitch's eyes followed the voice to the northern portal. Stepping out of the shadows was a thin man of medium height. He had a full head of black hair, a beard, and olive-colored skin and wore sunglasses, trousers, and a light-blue shirt. He looked like a vacationing tourist sightseeing in the Roman ruins. But of course, Mitch had to assume that this man was deadly.

The man approached. "I am Omar Abdul Hamady, formerly a member of the GSPC. And you are Colonel Mitch Ross of the US embassy. I am extremely happy that you followed my instructions explicitly. At the present time your driver is being entertained by one of my men." Hamady said all of this in a matter-of-fact way, his voice almost monotone.

Entertained? What the hell does that mean? Mitch thought as he examined Hamady for any obvious weapons.

"You must forgive me, Colonel, but I trust no one!" the terrorist said, coming within arm's length of Mitch and beginning to pat him down.

Mitch wanted to push Hamady away, but better judgment took over and he stood there, letting the scum touch him. He knew that if he protested, the result would be a bullet ending his life.

Hamady completed his examination of Mitch and stepped back with an arrogant smile. "Your body armor is quite interesting, Colonel, but useless. We only shoot for the head, and then we cut off what remains. I believe you're familiar with our technique."

Mitch felt a spasm of fear as he tried to maintain a poker face.

Hamady stared into Mitch's eyes and said nothing. Mitch's mind raced. He felt confident that Abella had eluded the terrorists. Had she been caught, Hamady undoubtedly would have either killed or beaten her and displayed the naked broken body in the amphitheater.

Finally, Hamady broke the silence. "Before I give you details concerning Captain Seth Hunt, you must commit to me. I demand that the American, French, and British governments grant me immunity for any crimes that I have falsely been accused of committing. Why do I demand this? Because I have committed no crimes in the eyes of Allah! The American government will provide a private aircraft that will fly me direct to London. This aircraft will be secure. The authorities must make no attempt at any time to prevent me from fulfilling my plans. If I perceive that there are any obstructions, I will destroy the aircraft and many innocent people.

"Did I mention that you, Colonel Ross—or Colonel Dureau—will accompany me on the flight? You seem to be a younger man than Colonel Dureau. You have many years ahead of you. I'm sure you have plans for a happy life, a wife, possibly children. Let's hope you don't do anything unwise today that would end all of your dreams with one well-placed bullet.

"In addition to the aircraft, I demand five hundred thousand in American currency. When I arrive in London I will be allowed to fade away into the fabric of English society. The American and French governments will work out the details of my demands with the British authorities. As I stated earlier, if these demands aren't met, I can guarantee many innocent people will be killed. They will be killed in your embassy, the French embassy, the British embassy, and they will include prominent officials in each of those respective countries. Also, your close female friend that you have gotten to know recently will no longer exist on this earth if you don't abide by what I say."

Mitch was not surprised by these demands, although they were quite extreme. He knew the information he wanted would not be free. But Hamady was taking a big risk by making demands that involved some of the most powerful nations on earth. It was a gamble for Hamady, because his odds of success were extremely low. Mitch also knew that any mistake made at this point would mean that Yves would fly with Hamady to London, and Mitch would no longer be breathing air.

Hamady paused, allowing Mitch to comprehend and memorize what had just been said. Then he continued. "The details that I am to tell you concerning Captain Seth Hunt are quite comprehensive. Therefore, I believe that it would be better if we discussed the specifics in English."

Mitch was startled, unaware that Hamady spoke any languages other than French and Arabic. *But why hasn't he spoken English throughout our conversation?* Mitch wondered.

Hamady stood a few feet away, staring at him intensely. Suddenly he spoke in very loud and rapid Arabic.

What the hell did he just say, and who the fuck is he talking to? Mitch's attention was drawn to the shadows of the northern portal as a man emerged from the darkness. The sunlight revealed his face, and a jolt of remembered pain gave Mitch heart palpitations. It was the US embassy driver who had crashed through the main embassy gate. Mitch realized that someone would be dead at the end of this meeting, and the odds were definitely stacked against him. He was unarmed and helpless, standing in an open arena that had witnessed many deaths stretching from gladiator competitions during the Roman era to present day.

"Good afternoon, Colonel. It's so good to see you again," said the embassy driver. "I'm sure you're surprised to see me. I know that you and Jake were having me watched closely at the embassy. I'm done with that shit job! I have no allegiance to you Americans. I would prefer to rid Algeria permanently of all infidels. Perhaps I'll have an opportunity to start this afternoon."

Hamady raised his right hand at the driver, signaling him to stop talking. Mitch watched both men silently, trying to determine what would happen next.

Hamady spoke rapidly in Arabic, and the driver took a few steps closer to Mitch. Now he stood almost abreast with Hamady. The driver spoke again. "Mr. Hamady will now discuss the American pilot Seth Hunt, his condition, and his whereabouts. But you are to keep in mind that he expects you to carry out his demands! If it is discovered that you are not carrying out his wishes, then my people within your embassy will capture you. I have already informed them that it is my special desire to see you cut open alive and have your entrails devoured by rabid dogs. There will be no escape for you if you do not fulfill Mr. Hamady's desires."

Hamady looked at the driver and spoke slowly. He continued for a moment and then stopped, nodding at the driver.

"The American pilot, Captain Seth Hunt, is in good condition," the driver translated. "He has been a captive for many years and has taken up much of our Bedouin culture. He no longer wears a military flight suit but prefers clothing that he describes as resembling Lawrence of Arabia. In other words, it is a long white tunic, a sleeveless cloak, and a distinctive head cloth known as a kufiyya." The driver turned to Hamady and waited.

Again, Hamady uttered a long monologue in Arabic, then nodded.

The driver said in English, "Captain Hunt can now speak fluent Arabic and French. He very rarely speaks English, and his diet is that of a Bedouin in the desert. This diet consists of sheep, lamb, rice, milk, coffee, figs, and dates. He is allowed to journey for a few hours each week into the marketplace, but only under strict control by GSPC security guards. He speaks to no one other than those within his immediate dwelling. The vast majority of those individuals are the security guards. He spends much of his day playing the rabab, an ancient bowed instrument of the Bedouins. Captain Hunt also writes poetry and reads the Koran. Allah should give us all a life like this!"

Once again, the driver turned to Hamady, and the process continued as before.

"Hunt resides in a two-room dwelling located approximately in the middle of the Casbah of Algiers. It is well guarded and has only one door and no windows. It is attached to many other buildings, and the only approach is by way of narrow steps. The entire Casbah is similar to a large citadel or fortress of connecting buildings on the side of a hill. Most people would get lost in this white jungle of ancient buildings that has existed since well before there was an America!"

The driver stopped talking and looked at Hamady, who then began to give more details and passed the driver a slip of paper.

"The residence of Captain Hunt is adjacent to the Mosque Sidi Abdallah in the Casbah, and the exact latitude and longitude is written on this paper that I am to give to you. Do you understand, Colonel?"

"I understand completely, but I'm still confused why you are betraying the GSPC," Mitch said. "It is extremely dangerous. Were you slighted by them when you completed your mission to acquire Captain Hunt from the Libyans?" He knew that he shouldn't ask questions, but that part of the puzzle was still unresolved.

Hamady grabbed the driver's arm and motioned for him to step back a few feet. Then Hamady moved close to Mitch. The stench of his foul breath made Mitch gag. He slapped Mitch across the face and then said in broken English, "You not question, but listen!" He reached back and spoke in Arabic. The driver handed Hamady the paper with the latitude and longitude written on it. Hamady wadded it into a ball and shoved it violently into Mitch's left ear. Mitch stumbled and almost fell to his knees. Hamady and the driver laughed, and Hamady spat in Mitch's face. He backed off and spoke Arabic to the driver. The driver moved within a few feet of Mitch. Before Mitch could react, the driver pulled a pistol and pointed it at his forehead.

"I thought you were an intelligent man, Colonel. But you're stupid just like all the other infidels. It fills my heart with joy to see you belittled and spat upon. You are no better than a pig that eats its own shit."

Hamady exaggerated his laughter and then screamed in Arabic like a madman. In response to Hamady's order, the driver pulled the gun away and slammed it against Mitch's left eye socket. Mitch crumpled to the dirt, fighting to stay conscious. He felt blood flowing along his eye, and he realized that he could no longer see from that side. He rose to his knees with his head bowed and felt the gun press against the crown of his skull. Hamady screamed in Arabic again while laughing uncontrollably.

"We have grown tired of you. You were to listen and not open your filthy mouth!" the driver seethed as he pushed the gun barrel harder against Mitch's skull.

There was a long pause. Mitch knew that he had pushed them too far with his questions. But Hamady seemed to be losing his grip on reality. The terrorist abruptly stopped laughing and, with a crazed look toward the driver, shrieked a command in Arabic.

11

The echo of the pistol's discharge ricocheted throughout the arena, scattering birds from their lofty heights in the trees. The sound traveled for miles in the late-afternoon stillness. The lifeless body struck the dirt, and blood pooled around him. Then, from the southern portal, Abella screamed as she collapsed to her knees, sobbing uncontrollably.

As the echo faded, tranquility returned to the ruins. Death had once again visited the arena. The motionless body lay as if sleeping, red liquid coursing from the bullet hole. Its glazed, sightless eyes stared into the sun, unblinking. He would never again hear the demands and threats of a crazed terrorist.

Abella's sobbing penetrated the silence, followed by the sound of footsteps pounding the earth like a bass drum as Hamady ran to escape. These sounds finally snapped Mitch from his hypnotic thoughts of death. His eyes opened, and he gazed upon the driver and the cavernous hole ripped in the man's chest, the pistol beside his lifeless foot. Then he saw Hamady nearing the northern portal leading out of the arena.

Still on his knees, Mitch picked up the gun and yelled after Hamady: "Stop now or I'll shoot you dead!"

Hamady halted, then spun around while pulling a gun from his belt and firing. A shot kicked up dirt near Mitch's knee as the colonel fired off two rounds. The first struck the ancient stone wall behind Hamady, but the second ripped into his neck, severing the carotid artery. Hamady screamed and fell to his knees, clutching his throat. Then he stared at Mitch as blood poured from his mouth and he spoke words that only Allah could hear. He collapsed onto his face as life streamed from the mortal wound.

Mitch dropped the gun and ran to Abella, still on her knees, weeping and clutching a gun. Mitch took the pistol from her hand and shoved it in his waistband, then wrapped his arms around Abella, holding her tight against his chest.

"Mitch, hold me! Please hold me!" Abella pleaded as she buried her head into his chest, clutching him as if she were falling.

He kissed the top of her head, and his mind scrambled to understand what had happened. *Abella killed the driver. That was a bullet to the center of his chest from over twenty-five yards. She saved my life as she predicted. But how did she know? And where did she get a pistol?*

Abella's voice brought him back to reality.

"We must leave now before others arrive," she said. Then she looked up and saw his face. "Oh my God, Mitch, your eye is bleeding!" Abella touched the left side of his face.

"Not now, Abella. We've gotta get to the car!"

"Follow me," she said. "I know a hidden passage that'll take us into the wooded area near the main road."

Instead of running through the southern portal, Abella entered a small room to her left. She grabbed Mitch's hand as the light of the room disappeared into obscurity.

"Mitch, there are stone steps on the right that lead to a hidden corridor. Lean on the wall as we descend and don't let go of my hand."

He tightened his grip on her hand in the dark. Just as Abella had said, the stone steps and the wall led them down to a corridor.

"I know you can't see me, but hold on. We'll get to the light soon," Abella said, pulling him through the ancient underground corridor.

In a few moments Mitch saw stone steps ahead and light emanating from above. Abella released his hand and cautiously climbed the staircase, looking in all directions once her head was aboveground. Mitch realized that this must have been the route gladiators took to make their grand appearance into the arena. As they cleared the steps, Mitch saw that they were completely hidden within a thick forest.

"We've gotta head in this direction to get to the main road and the car," Abella said, pointing and then setting off at a run, with Mitch following.

The pain from his left eye began to pulse, and he tasted blood as it streamed into his mouth. A growing ache pounded his head with each step. She came to an abrupt stop before entering the main road and focused her binoculars on Yves's vehicle and the surrounding area.

"I see the car," she said, "but where's Yves?"

Mitch moved around a tree to get a better view. The car was approximately fifty yards from their hidden location and appeared undisturbed, but Yves was nowhere to be found.

"Damn, I hope he's okay," Mitch said, maneuvering between trees. As he gained a different angle, something caught his eye. He turned to Abella and put his finger to his lips. In one smooth motion he pulled the gun from his belt and cocked it. Abella moved close to him and followed his line of sight. Now she could see it too. Lying motionless, facedown near the front right tire, was Yves.

"I pray that Yves is okay," Mitch whispered. "But this could be a trap. We have to assume the terrorists are waiting for us. You stay here, and I'll move to the right in the trees to see if there is any movement or anyone hiding. I'll look back at you periodically to check if you've noticed anything." Abella nodded and he began moving.

As Mitch surveyed the area from his angle, Abella did the same from her vantage point. It seemed that whoever had been with Yves was no longer around. Perhaps they had run toward or away from the amphitheater during the shooting. Mitch suspected they had run away and were still running.

It seemed clear that he and Abella needed to get down there, put Yves in the back seat, find the keys, and make their escape. Mitch rejoined Abella, and they ran to the other side of the road, keeping their exposure to a minimum. Mitch raised the gun into a firing position as he moved swiftly toward the car, with Abella just behind him, keeping watch. They crouched at the front of the vehicle near Yves's body to make less of a target.

"He is breathing," Abella whispered. "I see dust being blown near his mouth."

"Thank God!" Mitch responded as he surveyed the perimeter.

Abella moved closer to Yves and lightly stroked his head, whispering to him. "Yves, Mitch and I are here to take you home," she said. "Everything will be okay. Just hang on and we'll be on the road soon."

As Abella cradled Yves's head in her hands, Mitch found the keys under the driver's seat. He held them up to show Abella. "Let's get Yves into the back seat," he said.

Mitch opened the back door, and Abella continued cradling Yves's head as she lifted his shoulders. Mitch carefully raised Yves's feet and legs. They struggled until Yves began to moan and then coughed.

"Just lower my legs," Yves whispered. "I believe I can drag myself to the seat." His eyes remained closed and his body didn't move.

Mitch did as Yves had requested, but Abella continued to hold his head in her hands. Life gradually entered the tall Frenchman's limbs, and he rose to his knees and pulled himself up on the back seat, where he slumped onto his back. Making sure not to catch his friend's legs, Mitch closed the door. Abella and Mitch scrambled to the front seats, and the engine woke as Mitch turned the key and hit the accelerator, spinning the Peugeot's wheels in the gravel. He wanted to get out of there without delay.

Suddenly Abella yelled for Mitch to stop. "Over to the right of that large tree." She pointed. "Do you see legs protruding from the bushes?"

Mitch strained to see where she pointed through his damaged left eye, but it was too far away.

"Let's go see," he said, opening his door. They left the vehicle running, and Mitch followed Abella.

The lifeless body belonged to an Algerian. He was clutching a pistol, and a knife protruded from the man's chest.

"I believe this was the terrorist who slammed Yves's head with his pistol," Mitch said. "Look at the blood on the barrel of the gun. Still, this camel jockey didn't get too far. I'm amazed Yves was able to bury his knife in that bastard's chest before losing consciousness." He shook his head. "Good riddance, you scum!"

"We need to get out of here, Mitch," Abella said, grabbing his hand. "That's three terrorists who won't see another sunrise, but there might be others around!" He nodded, and they ran back to the car.

Mitch took the vehicle onto the main road and headed northeast. He focused on the road, pushing the Peugeot to an aggressive speed. He leaned forward and blinked continuously, his vision on the left still completely obscured. He could only hope that a quick getaway would help them avoid an ambush.

From the back seat, Yves began to speak. "I won't ask at the moment how the hell you two pulled this off," he said, sounding weak but otherwise like his usual optimistic self. "I won't even ask why we are all still alive. But sometime in the not-too-distant future, over an expensive bottle of cabernet, I would like an explanation."

Yves paused and rubbed his swollen forehead, groaning softly. "I can scarcely remember my name. In all honesty, I recall nothing except showering this morning. And I'm sure there are a few dents in my beloved Peugeot that were not there when we began this journey. My neighbors at the embassy will undoubtedly be talking and wondering, 'What now has the wild bachelor gotten himself into?'"

Mitch and Abella looked at each other and smiled; Yves would be fine. It was the first levity they had experienced all day, mixed with a feeling of being weak and parched and the realization that they had cheated death.

Questions burned in Mitch's mind as he drove. Soon he could no longer repress them. "I need to ask you about what happened in the arena," he said, catching Abella's eye. "Were you watching every movement once I entered the amphitheater? Where did you get the gun, and was it just a lucky shot? Why did you scream after killing the driver?"

He paused for a moment, rubbing blood from his eye. "You saved my life. Those two crazed terrorists may have wanted me alive to carry out Hamady's desires, but they also hated everything I represented in this world. They wanted to kill me, but they also wanted me to live! I believe that their fanaticism was overtaking their logic, and it would have led to my death this afternoon. But you ended it all, and we sent them on a one-way ticket to hell. Perhaps my questions are too much for you to answer now. They can wait for another day."

Abella turned to him, tears welling in her eyes. "This is the right time and place to explain. I arrived at the amphitheater well before you entered and positioned myself where none could see me. I had an excellent view of all the ruins and the arena. Once you entered, I maneuvered to a location that was at ground level but still in the shadows of hidden theater rooms.

"When you pulled Yves's gun from the car glove compartment and pushed it under your seat, I retrieved it from the back seat. In my six years in America, my father had to maintain his expert qualification rating using small arms. Twice a month on Saturdays he would practice at a firing range in Northern Virginia. After a while I gave in to the influence of my Georgetown soccer colleagues and asked my father if I could go along. At first, he was reluctant, but once my mother and I applied the boldness of our newfound American equality, he acquiesced. Twice a month for six years makes for a good marksman—actually, a good markswoman!

"There was no luck in that shot, Mitch. It was one I had practiced for years. As my father taught me—one shot, one kill! I cried out when the bullet hit the terrorist's chest because I realized that I hadn't shot at a fabricated target; I had just killed a man!"

"Abella," Yves said quietly, "perhaps you're the answer to the French Army's long-standing problem. We need someone to teach us how to shoot and consistently hit a target."

The three of them laughed. For the remainder of the journey back to the French embassy, the conversation was light and had nothing to do with what had happened in Tipasa.

Near the embassy, Yves took over as driver, having recovered somewhat. French security procedures would go much more smoothly if he was driving.

The sergeant of the guard recognized Yves's car and abbreviated the normal security procedures. He would personally take care of Colonel Dureau's clearance into the embassy.

"*Bonjour, mon colonel, ça va?*" the sergeant of the guard said as he approached the Peugeot in the adjacent parking lot.

"*Bonjour, Sergeant, bien, mais je suis ici avec mes amis américains,*" Yves responded, telling the sergeant that he was fine and accompanied by his American friends. Yves was not telling the truth by identifying Abella as an American, but it would expedite the sergeant's blessings for their entry.

"*Mon colonel, nous pouvons maintenant parler anglais?*" the sergeant said, asking if it would be okay to speak English.

"Yes, please, because I want my friends to understand everything that we say," Yves responded.

"My colonel, first I would like to contact the embassy hospital and have you all examined by the doctors. Colonel, your head seems twice its normal size, and the gentleman with you has an eye that looks extremely damaged. The lovely lady looks dehydrated and fatigued," the sergeant said. He immediately turned to one of the guards and had him call the hospital. Yves didn't protest because they all needed some form of medical assistance.

"Thank you, Sergeant. That is very kind and considerate," Yves said.

"Also, my colonel, I will contact the embassy vehicle garage and at your convenience have them pick up your Peugeot sedan to repair the damage. In all due respect, it appears that you attempted to use this beautiful automobile as an off-road all-terrain vehicle."

"Yes, the road became quite challenging at times and required us to test the auto's suspension," Yves replied, his mind drifting back to the dirt path and the gouging of the bushes and trees as flashes of his missing memory returned. He left the keys on the dash.

"Excuse me, my colonel, but there is one more item before the hospital transportation arrives. Perhaps your American friend will remove the pistol from his waist belt and hide it in his jacket pocket? It might arouse concern when the three of you enter the hospital," the sergeant diplomatically stated.

Mitch pulled the gun from his belt and shoved it into his jacket pocket. "I'm terribly sorry," he said, embarrassed. "I just finished up with a little target practice and forgot to check the gun into security prior to my departure from the US embassy."

The sergeant of the guard's eyebrows raised and he replied, "Yes, it's such a common mistake."

As the hospital van arrived, the sergeant of the guard escorted them to the vehicle and then winked as he gave Mitch one last glance. The old sergeant knew that what Mitch had said was complete and total bullshit, but he also realized that the three of them had experienced something very traumatic. He would not ask any questions, merely saluting smartly as the van departed for the embassy hospital.

The hospital wasn't large, but it had state-of-the-art equipment. As soon as they arrived, doctors and physician assistants were assigned. A physician assistant had Abella sit in an examination room and brought her two large bottles of water and fluids that would replace her electrolytes. She was also given a warm washcloth and towel to wipe off her face and hands. A physician cleaned and examined Mitch's eye socket; X-rays were taken to determine the extent of the damage to the area. Ice packs were immediately administered to the swelling on Yves's forehead. Further examination was completed, and it was concluded that there was no swelling of the brain, but Yves's eyesight would most likely be blurred for a few days. He was given medication for the swelling and his headache.

A small fracture of Mitch's left eye socket was found, and the doctors decided that surgery was not needed. Mitch's body would eventually repair the fracture. A closer look at Mitch's left eye determined that there was minimal permanent damage, and that within a month his eyesight would be almost 100 percent. Twelve stiches were applied to the gash. Once all the examinations and treatment were complete, Yves, Mitch, and Abella were driven to Yves's residence. Yves contacted the sergeant of the guard and informed him that he could take the Peugeot to the vehicle garage for repairs.

12

nside Yves's residence, Abella and Mitch collapsed on the couch. Abella rested her head on Mitch's shoulder and closed her eyes. Yves went to the kitchen and requested that his cook bring the best bottle of cabernet with three glasses. He also asked that baked brie pastry along with grilled bacon-wrapped figs be warmed and served. The cook immediately got to work, and in the meantime, Yves grabbed shot glasses and the bottle of Evan Williams 23.

"Let's begin this evening of relaxation with a little fire and, if Mitch would be so kind, a toast!" Yves said as he poured three shots and handed Abella and Mitch their glasses of dark Kentucky heaven.

Mitch raised his glass well above his head. "This morning I made a toast of foreboding doom, and now, reflecting on today, I have no regrets. In spite of the fact we really didn't have a plan and we gambled with our lives, all I can think is something that was said many, many years ago: 'Life is not a matter of holding good cards, but sometimes, playing a poor hand well!'"

All three raised their glasses and then drained them with one quick flex of their wrists.

Yves's cook brought in the wine, glasses, napkins, and plates and recovered the shot glasses. He then returned to the living room, pushing a small cart of French hors d'oeuvres, spreading the delectable aroma like wildfire. The freshly baked pastry and the scent of cooked bacon created a delicious atmosphere of blended perfection. Mitch and Abella's cravings were so intense that they found it extremely difficult to remain diplomatic. It was truly a feast for the nose as well as the palate. They wanted to begin but glanced at Yves, waiting for him to say something.

The room had gone silent, and Yves looked up from pouring the wine. He instantly read their expressions and knew that they all shared the same heavy hunger. "Yes, today has been enough to drive anyone crazy," he said. "It makes me recall something that W. Somerset Maugham once said: 'Excess on occasion is exhilarating. It prevents moderation from acquiring the deadening effect of a habit.' Let's not delay; the food is to eat, the wine to drink, and not to be admired!" Then he passed each their wine, napkin, and plate.

They dove in with unabashed zeal.

Yves paused while devouring his third brie pastry and second glass of wine. "By the way, would one of you be so kind as to tell me what happened today? As I mentioned earlier, I really don't remember anything except showering this morning and then the happenings once we returned to the French embassy."

"Well, my French friend, it's a lengthy story, but I'll give you the abbreviated version," Mitch said. "Abella, please don't hesitate to jump in on my narrative to clarify bullshit statements I might make."

"That's not a problem, Mitch, as long as it doesn't interrupt my eating and drinking," Abella said as she stuffed her mouth with another bacon-wrapped fig.

Mitch proceeded to recount what had happened from the time they picked up Abella at her apartment, finishing with their examinations at the French embassy hospital.

Yves sat reflecting in silent disbelief. "It's hard to believe that we all survived!" he said eventually. "Someday, one of us must write a book about all of this. Of course, no reader will ever believe it's true, so it will have to be fiction!"

They all laughed. Mitch leaned forward and removed the pistol from his jacket pocket. He handed it to Yves. "I believe you should treasure this gun. It not only saw action, it saved my life!"

"That's a true statement, but to increase its value we must remember that it was the lovely lady sitting next to you who pulled the trigger!" Yves emphasized as he raised his glass toward Abella.

"Yes, she is one amazing, beautiful woman!" Mitch said, looking at Abella.

Abella blushed. "With all of those compliments, maybe I could get one of you gentlemen to pour me another glass of wine," she said.

The bottle was empty, so Yves dashed to the kitchen for another. Mitch took Abella's hand and kissed it. "Thank you for being you!" he said. "We make a perfect team."

Abella looked into Mitch's eyes and passionately kissed him. "I truly hope that one day we'll be more than just a team," she whispered as Yves reentered the living room.

"Let's have more wine to celebrate life!" Yves said. He poured more cabernet, then sat in a well-used leather recliner. His pant leg rose above his right ankle, and he noticed the empty knife sheath. He put down his glass and leaned forward to touch the leather strapped to his lower leg.

"Is something wrong?" Mitch asked as he noticed his friend's expression of remorse.

Yves looked up. "When you mentioned there was a terrorist lying dead in the bushes near the car, I assumed that I had stabbed him with my mother's knife—although I don't recall doing it." He shook his head. "It might sound odd, but that knife was something I truly treasured."

Abella and Mitch looked at each other, taken aback by Yves's comment.

"Your mother's knife?" Abella questioned.

"It's a long story," Yves said, "but she grew up in Paris and was in her early twenties when the Nazis invaded. She became a member of the French Resistance during the occupation. Her job was to find out Nazi plans and troop movements from drunken German officers at the bars and cabarets. That knife was her only means of protection.

"Now I realize that the knife killed twice. My mother used it to kill a German colonel one evening when he attempted to rape her. I only know because several years ago I researched documents of the French Resistance. I came across an official document dated July 10, 1943, which identified my mother, the German colonel, and the circumstances of his death. Unfortunately, my mother had already passed away when I discovered that information. But nevertheless, it filled my heart with pride, knowing that she was totally committed to the freedom of France and the defeat of its enemies.

"My mother talked very little about the war, but as I got older and began to read and hear about her exploits, I realized that she was quite a hero. In fact, Charles de Gaulle personally awarded her the Cross of War, or as we say in France, the *Croix de Guerre*. It was at a special ceremony in Paris after the liberation of the city in August of 1944.

"I never imagined that the knife would save my life as it had hers. I remember spending hours looking at it, touching it . . . It had a large black cross of Lorraine—the symbol of the Resistance—chiseled into its handle. I always wished it could tell me the stories that it shared with my mother."

As Yves finished his reflection, they all sat in silence and sipped their wine, thinking about the day and thankful they were all alive.

13

A week after the fateful trip to the ruins, Mitch, Abella, and Yves had all fallen back into their usual work routines. Mitch wrote his report regarding the information he had discovered from Hamady, omitting illegally leaving the French embassy without proper security and killing Hamady. His report detailed that he had met with the French attaché, who informed Mitch that French intelligence had discovered that the American pilot was likely being held in the Casbah. He gave no further facts because he knew there would be more questions if he went too far.

He completed the report but did not take it to the ambassador, who was away at a conference in the Bavarian Alps village of Garmisch, Germany. The ambassador's absence gave Mitch time to refine the report and make it as believable as possible. Warrant Officer Dave McQueen, his administrator, had taken leave and was currently back in the States. This left the office very quiet, just as Mitch had hoped it would be.

He wanted to be left alone, but that had become quite difficult. Wherever he went, everyone noticed and commented on his swollen black eye. Considering the embassy was just one big fishbowl, rumors ran rampant around the compound. Nothing went unnoticed! He stuck to his office as much as possible, hiding from those who had yet to see him. The bruise was still dark, and his eyeball had taken on the color of a red rose. Also, the throbbing pain from his eye socket tended to fatigue him during the afternoons, despite the pain pills. Each day since the trip to Tipasa, Mitch would leave the office for a coffee at the embassy cafeteria. The caffeine helped to relieve the weariness. One day as he was about to enter the cafe, a deep voice called out.

"Colonel, how are ya? I haven't seen ya all week, but I've heard a whole lot about that eye of yours," Jake said as he squinted to focus on Mitch's left eye.

"Yes, I've become quite the talk of the embassy these days. It's hard to hide this shiner!" Mitch replied.

"Hope ya haven't had a falling-out with that sweet young lady of yours. I know she's very athletic, but much too sweet to give you a right uppercut." Jake laughed as he repositioned his cigar in the corner of his mouth.

"No, it wasn't Abella. I didn't notice a cupboard door that was opened in the kitchen and walked into it. Looks much worse than it is," Mitch replied, trying to look honest.

Jake stared at Mitch and then looked off for a moment, taking a long draw from his cigar. He then focused back to Mitch and asked, "Any chance I can buy you a cup of mud and borrow a few moments of your time?"

"Sure, Jake, the break will be good, and a little of your Kentucky accent will brighten up my day," Mitch responded as he opened the cafeteria door and motioned for Jake to enter.

The two men grabbed their cups of coffee, and Jake paid the tab. They found seats in a back corner of the cafeteria.

"Colonel, I had been meaning to see you this week," Jake said, "but with the State Department security inspections and transportation requests, it's been a zoo around here. What I wanted to discuss are rumors that I heard from the Algerian paramilitary police about three bodies discovered in and around the Roman ruins in Tipasa.

"I'd wondered why that embassy driver that we disliked had not reported for work this week. I found out that he was one of the three found dead in the ruins, with his chest blown away. Ballistic analysis of the bullet identified it as French military officer issue, a Pamas G1. Within the amphitheater where the driver's body was found was also the body of Omar Abdul Hamady. He had recently escaped arrest, and there was an all-points bulletin sent out to the embassies to be on the lookout for him. I'm sure you know he was a dangerous extremist. It seems that he was killed by a shot to the neck.

"At first the Algerian police thought that the two men had scuffled and killed each other. But there was only one gun, and the gun that killed the driver could not be located. Also, the police said that the driver was lying in a position that would not have been correct had Hamady shot him while standing near the amphitheater's northern portal. The gun found near the driver's foot had quite a lot of blood on it. The blood analysis didn't show a match for the driver or Hamady.

"The third dead man was outside of the amphitheater with a knife stuck in his chest. There were fresh tire marks near the body. The knife had an interesting design on the handle—the cross of Lorraine.

"All three were killed last Monday. That was the day I drove you to the French embassy and you were there for at least ten hours. My buddies at the French embassy vehicle garage informed me that the French attaché's car was quite dented and had deep scratches along the sides. They also said there was blood in the back seat and along the window and door of the driver's side. I'm acquainted with a few of the nurses at the French hospital, and I gave them a quick call today. They told me that the French attaché, along with two American-speaking folks, had been treated and released early Monday evening.

"Colonel, all of this stays with me, and no one will ever hear it from this Kentucky boy's lips. But I brought this up for two reasons. The first is something that I always want you to remember. I've got your back,

Colonel, regardless of whether you're doing something legal or not! Please never forget that. Next time you decide to go on an adventure, let me know. I need the target practice, if you catch my drift! I'm certain those three bastard terrorists deserved to die, but I'm not exactly sure why. Now, the second reason I wanted to talk to you is because of this."

Jake took a small box from his jacket and placed it on the table between their cups of coffee.

"I drove to the paramilitary police station yesterday to take a look at all of their findings. I noticed that there was not much except for the gun, lab results, and the box that's on the table. You know, Colonel, being an old country boy, I know all kinds of sidearms and weapons. I know knives very well, and the knife that killed the terrorist was made in the last half of the 1930s, but the marking on the handle was that of the French Resistance during World War II. The sergeant of the guards at the French embassy informed me a few years ago that he grew up in the same region of Paris as Colonel Dureau. He had heard the stories of the colonel's mother and her involvement with the French Resistance. She was quite a woman!

"Colonel, what I'm trying to say is that the three of you left an easy trail to follow. That's why the next time you take off on one of those escapades, make sure I'm involved. I'd sure like to get my licks in on some of those terrorists before I permanently return to the States. Now, I'm sure that your French colonel friend would like to have the knife returned to its rightful owner. It's not every day ya see an object with such historical significance. While I talked to those Algerian paramilitary folks, I discovered that they love our US Marine Ka-Bars. Call it kismet, but I just happened to have one with me when I paid them a visit. It's amazin' how eager those fellas were to trade anythin' for that Marine knife, even an old French knife."

Mitch looked at Jake, then slowly reached between the cups and grabbed the box. He pulled the lid off and gazed at Yves's mother's knife. Mitch touched the handle, then looked up at Jake with a speechless stare.

"Well, Colonel, it's about time to get back to the salt mines. Can't let those guards sit around too long without Papa Bear looking over their shoulders. Oh, by the way, the Algerian police also had a small wad of paper with numbers written on it. I took a quick look and knew that it was latitude and longitude info. Thought I should take it, so I traded the Ka-Bar sheath for the paper. When you take your trip to the Casbah, make sure I'm tagging along. I hear tell that there are some interesting things to see and do in those old white buildings. Well, that's about it, sir. You have a great embassy day!"

Jake rose and headed out the door. He wasted no time pulling out a fresh cigar. He lit it and took a few quick drags to spark life into the long, thick Cohiba. The fragrance transported Mitch back to the days when his father, long since gone, had worked on their '63 Dodge, a smoldering cigar firmly clenched between his teeth.

That old Kentucky boy is much smarter than he lets on! Mitch marveled. He set the knife back in the box, then noticed bloodstains on the paper Jake had given him. His blood. Only the grace of God and Abella's quick trigger finger had saved his life.

Mitch tossed his cold coffee in the garbage and stuffed the box and small piece of paper into his pocket. Upon returning to his office, he noticed a note taped to the large metal door that allowed access to his workplace. It was from the ambassador's secretary, requesting that he contact her as soon as he returned. Mitch didn't hesitate and went straight to the secretary's desk.

"Colonel Ross, the ambassador has just returned from his conference in Germany and was hoping to see you this afternoon. He didn't say what the topic would be, and lord knows I'm not one to ask questions. By the way, that eye of yours looks painful!"

He thanked her for her concern but didn't elaborate on the cause.

"Colonel, is that you outside my office?" the ambassador asked.

"Yes sir," Mitch promptly replied.

"Come on in. I've got Greg Cain here, and we're anxious to hear any updates on the pilot," the ambassador said.

Sweet mother of God, am I going to get drilled again by those two? Mitch thought. "Good afternoon, Mr. Ambassador. How was your trip to Germany?" Mitch said, hoping to delay the inevitable.

"That region of Germany is absolutely beautiful," the ambassador said. "Small villages nestled amongst the Bavarian Alps. I spent as much time as I could outdoors because the conference was just the same old political mumbo jumbo. When you bring a group of ambassadors together to discuss their unique issues and problems, there are never any concrete resolutions made. But it's always a nice break from this confined lifestyle we have here in Algeria."

"Sorry to butt in, Mr. Ambassador, but I'm extremely curious about any updates that you might have, Colonel," Greg Cain interrupted.

Mitch tried not to look too pissed off at Greg as he responded. "Not a problem," he said. "In fact, I've written a report with my updates, so you'll have it on your desk before you depart this evening."

"Great, but we still would like to hear the verbal rendition," the ambassador said.

"Yes sir," Mitch responded as he began his carefully filtered update. "This information was received from French intelligence authorities approximately one week ago while I was at the French embassy. Captain Seth Hunt is in overall good health. He has immersed himself in the Bedouin culture, which means he consumes their cuisine daily of lamb, goat, rice, dates, and figs. His clothing has changed from a flight suit to robes similar to what Lawrence of Arabia wore. Over the past nine years he has learned to speak French and Arabic fluently, and it was reported that he rarely speaks English. He reads the Koran, plays something similar to a guitar, and writes poetry daily. His location is believed to be in the Casbah. That's the extent of what I know. I hope to receive more updates within the next couple weeks. The French stated that they were not planning any major operations to rescue Captain Hunt at this time. They need further refinement of his location and complete agreement with the US authorities, including this embassy."

"Good concise report, Colonel. Once I get your written version, I'll be able to send the updated information to the State Department and White House staff. Do you have any questions for the colonel, Greg?" the ambassador said.

"Nothing at this time, sir. I'll talk to Mitch later about his report," Greg replied.

"Mr. Ambassador, if there's nothing else, I need to get back to the office and take care of a little business before calling it a day," Mitch said, hoping that was a good enough excuse to leave and distance himself from Greg.

"I'm sure you have better things to do than hang around my office. Take care of that eye! Heard you ran into something in your house. Hope it wasn't a fist." The ambassador chuckled and nodded while Mitch turned to leave.

He tried to expedite his departure, but Greg was too quick.

"Colonel, do you have a minute?" Greg said as he stared down at Mitch from the top of the staircase. "I have a few questions, but I didn't want to take any more of the ambassador's time."

"Sure," said Mitch, realizing he was out of excuses. "Your office or mine?"

"Actually neither. Let's go outside," Greg said. He followed Mitch down the stairs and toward the chancery doors.

Damn, I knew he had more questions! Mitch thought once they were outside.

"Need a cup of coffee?" Greg asked, examining Mitch's damaged eye.

"No, I'm good. Thanks."

"Okay, let's take a walk to the tennis courts." Greg pointed to the path through the embassy garden. "That eye of yours doesn't appear to be something that occurred in your kitchen," Greg said as the two of them walked through the garden. "Years ago, in Iraq I was hit by shrapnel from a rocket-propelled grenade. It slammed into my face and fractured an eye socket. I couldn't focus in that eye for about a year, and the socket never really mended correctly. It actually looked a lot like your eye!"

Mitch wasn't sure how to respond, so he kept silent and let Greg continue.

"Going back to your update," Greg said, clearing his throat, "it seemed rather odd to me that French intel knew everything about Hunt's personal life but didn't have any further refinement of his location in the Casbah area—considering they probably have seen him, from time to time, wandering around the marketplace across from the docks. I truly hope that you told us the complete truth, and that you aren't holding out on us."

Mitch stopped walking and glared at Greg. "Are you accusing me of lying or holding information?"

Greg met his gaze. "There isn't much difference between lying and holding information, is there?"

Mitch pushed back his anger. Of course, what Greg had said was true, but he resented the arrogant delivery. "I believe this conversation is over," Mitch said. "You'll have the written report delivered to your office this afternoon." He turned his back on Greg and continued down the path to his residence.

Shit, Greg knows more than he's letting on, Mitch thought. *I can't fall into his trap of disclosing information he might not know. I'm sure he wouldn't hesitate to tell the ambassador that I'm withholding information, and that's a one-way ticket back to the States and the end of my military career. I'm not ready for that. He can speculate all he wants, but as far as I'm concerned, he can blow it out his ass!*

Mitch waited until he knew there had been enough time for Greg to return to his office before he headed back toward the chancery. He took an alternate path that led to the side of the chancery building, and he slipped in, hoping only the security cameras saw him.

He moved through the Marine security procedures with as much speed as he could and then quickstepped to his office. Picking up copies of the update report from his desk, he headed back to the ambassador's office. He gave one copy to the ambassador's secretary and then, as luck would have it, the other to a CIA field agent coming out of the men's bathroom. Mitch told him to take the report directly to Greg. With that complete, he headed back to his residence.

He entered the house to hear the phone under the staircase ringing. Mitch snatched it and found Yves on the line.

"Hello, my good man," Yves said. "I was wondering if you were planning to attend Alexander's dinner this evening. If so, I believe we must discuss a few items concerning our next step, if you know what I mean."

"Shit, Yves, I completely forgot about it," Mitch said, mentally kicking himself. "I did RSVP last week, so I better get my ass in gear. If I recall correctly, the vodka shots will begin at 8 p.m. I'd better get there at 7:30 to begin lining my stomach with bread. The last dinner I attended at Alexander's house, I believe we toasted every world leader plus all the Russian World War II generals and admirals. My God, they had to pour me into my limo. I barely remember going home and lying in the shower for at least an hour. That's how long it took me to realize I was still wearing my entire uniform.

"Tonight I plan to stand near a large plant during the toasts and dump the vodka when I'm not being watched. That's the only way I'll be able to survive!"

"That's an excellent plan and one that I'll most likely copy," Yves said. "Except for the part about showering with my uniform! But we must stay sober long enough to talk about the Casbah so we'll remember the conversation tomorrow."

"Will do, Yves. See you tonight," Mitch said. He quickly realized that he hadn't made transportation arrangements with embassy security. He dialed Jake, hoping that the big Kentucky boy could work a little magic.

"Jake, this is Mitch. I need a favor. Can you have a car and security for me in an hour? Sorry for the last-minute request, but I completely forgot that I had committed to attend a dinner at the Russian attaché's house."

Jake chuckled as he replied. "The Russian attaché always has great meals sent out to the parking lot for us, so I'm definitely going as your security cover. And Farid is listening and giving me the thumbs-up. We'll be ready to blast out of here in an hour, Colonel. Thanks for covering my dinner for the evening!"

Mitch ran to the kitchen and apologized to Djamila for not informing her about the dinner arrangements.

"Not to worry, Colonel Mitch," Djamila responded. "I'll put everything in the refrigerator. If you don't mind, it'll be your meal tomorrow."

"You're a jewel, Djamila." *Too bad she really doesn't understand the value of that statement,* Mitch thought as he ran up the stairs to his room.

The ride to dinner was uneventful. When they arrived, Mitch entered the large house and attempted to keep a low profile. But that never worked when the Russian attaché, Colonel Alexander Rodzyanko, was nearby.

Rodzyanko was as large as a grizzly bear, and when he applied his welcoming hug, he tended to lift his guest completely off their feet. Men and women alike got the same greeting. It was just his way of showing his appreciation for your presence in his home. Alexander's wife was his opposite in stature. She was barely five feet tall, but her smile and petite shape made for a cover-girl combination. Plus, she could speak English very well. Alexander had asked Mitch on numerous occasions to escort his wife to receptions he was not able to attend. Although Mitch felt awkward, he never declined. In these situations, he knew that she was attending not only to represent the Russian military delegation but also to listen in on anything Mitch might say to other diplomats.

As expected, Alexander spotted Mitch within a few minutes of his arrival. He bellowed a greeting and wrapped Mitch in a crushing embrace. Mitch readjusted his uniform after Alexander's hug and said a few complimentary words to the attaché's wife. Then he headed to their huge, beautiful garden.

The garden was already full of diplomats, military officers, and an army of servants. Russian symphony music floated softly through the air like a flower in a pond. Mitch stuck to his plan and found a vast table covered with Russian delicacies, including the caviar and toast. As he filled a plate with the small pieces of bread covered with black fish eggs, a waiter approached, and Mitch took a glass of tonic and lime. He wanted to postpone the hard stuff as long as he could. He turned and proceeded to an inconspicuous area of the garden somewhat concealed by trees and bushes. Feeling quite discreet and shoveling the food into his mouth, it seemed his plan was coming together. Then he noticed the scent of cigar smoke drifting into the shadows where he was standing.

"Good evening, Colonel Ross," said a voice from the darkness. "How are you?"

Mitch recognized the Cuban ambassador sipping a rum and coke while smoking a cigar just a few feet away. He had become close friends with the ambassador. As far as the State Department was concerned, befriending a Cuban diplomat was crossing the line as that Caribbean island country was considered a pariah state. But Cuba always fascinated Mitch, and in his philosophy, if it was good enough for Hemingway, it was definitely good enough for Mitch Ross.

The smell of the Cohiba was smooth and mellow.

"Good evening, Mr. Ambassador. That cigar smells great!"

"You must join me. I don't take no for an answer, my friend." The ambassador reached into the interior pocket of his leather jacket. "These Cohibas just arrived from Havana—Coronas Especial, Laguito no. 2, the cigar selected by our leader Fidel. *El presidente* no longer smokes, but when he did this was his choice!" the ambassador proudly stated, handing the treasured blend to Mitch.

Mitch dumped his tonic water in the bushes and gave the glass to a passing waiter. He cradled the cigar as if it were a rare gem. "One day I will have the privilege of smoking a Cohiba on the beach of Havana Harbor, and I hope that you will join me on that special day, Mr. Ambassador."

"Yes, Colonel, our countries are ridiculous with their politics that prevent genuine friendship. I and my family would be proud to join you!"

They stood smoking and talking about Key West and the ninety miles separating their countries. The ambassador's cigar began burning unevenly, so he reached into his jacket pocket to withdraw a lighter. As he did, Mitch noticed the manufacturer's label on the interior pocket. In broad letters it read, *BELAIZ OF THE CASBAH, ALGIERS.*

"Mr. Ambassador, that jacket is quite nice," Mitch said. "Did you get it here in Algeria?"

The ambassador nodded as he expertly corrected his cigar's burn. "But it was quite an ordeal. I knew of a small shop that sold quality leather coats in the Casbah, and noticed a few diplomats wearing them. I made arrangements with my security detail and Algerian police to allow me to enter the shop. Many of my security agents were concerned that I might be wounded or killed by terrorists residing in the Casbah. But I insisted and used my ambassadorial leverage to overrule them. At times I like to live on the edge! It was foolhardy, but I did it anyway.

"It's a finely made leather coat, but I'm not sure that I would risk going into the Casbah again. There are too many unsavory individuals within those ancient fortress buildings. The narrow passageways are only large enough for a solitary person to pass from one level on the hill to the next. There were men standing around, watching every movement that I and my security detail made. It was rather unnerving and extremely dangerous, but I now have earned bragging rights of surviving the Casbah. Although my wife thinks that I'm crazy to have risked it all for the jacket."

"Did you have to journey deep into the Casbah, or was the shop within the first few layers?" Mitch asked.

"I would estimate that it was within the second layer, as one climbs the interior steps of the buildings. It was near a mosque that I have heard is the only house of worship within the entire ancient fortress."

"Did you approach the Casbah from the harbor, near the Algerian naval headquarters?"

"Colonel, if you're interested in buying one of these fine jackets, just tell me your size. I will have my security agents pick one up for you."

"Thank you, Mr. Ambassador, that's very kind. But I'm just curious because I've heard that the Casbah is teeming with extremists. I didn't really think that there was any safe entry in or out."

"My security agents researched the area quite extensively and recommended that the safest approach was from the harbor area. One must maintain a low profile and wear clothing of those that reside in the Casbah. Also, it's suggested that minimal time is spent inside, and a secure exit plan should be adhered to. As I said before, it was extremely foolish of me, but I will never let my wife know the real danger. So, Colonel, you must pledge that you will never mention any of this to my wife."

"Sir, you have my word."

"Talking about my wife, there she is across the way, motioning for me to join her. Colonel, it is always an extreme pleasure talking to you over good Cuban cigars. Have an enjoyable evening."

"Thank you, Mr. Ambassador, and please never forget my request that we one day spend time together in Havana."

"I will never forget that request, my good colonel."

The ambassador stepped from the shadows and entered the sea of diplomats in the garden. Mitch was sure that somewhere amid the crowd, Yves was slowly working his way to the caviar table. As Mitch politely said hello or nodded in recognition to the guests he knew, he made sure not to get bogged down in any lengthy political or military discussions. He and Yves needed to talk, especially now that he had new information from the Cuban ambassador. As he neared the table of delicacies, the symphony music stopped. An announcement came over the sound system in French.

"To all my honored guests, it is so wonderful that you are here to share this special evening with me and my family. Please take a shot glass of vodka from a passing waiter and I will lead you all in a toast to begin the dinner."

Mitch didn't have to find a waiter. They spread like ants among the guests, loaded down with trays of that enchanted Russian staple composed primarily of water and ethanol. He took a shot glass and eased back toward a group of rose bushes running along a large wooden fence. He felt quite confident that the roses would enjoy the vodka more than he.

Alexander had positioned himself on an elevated podium in the center of his immense garden. The size of this botanical wonderland was just under that of a baseball field. But it was much more beautiful, decorated with flowers, palm trees, manicured bushes, and sculptured fountains imported from Russia. Alexander raised his glass and bellowed, "Welcome and thank you for taking time out of your life to be here. There is an old Russian saying that there are just two kinds of vodka: good vodka and very good vodka." He quickly put the glass to his lips and the clear liquid disappeared. Then he yelled, "*Budem zdorovy* . . . let's stay healthy!"

Everyone cheered as they raised their empty glasses toward Alexander. Mitch had pitched the contents of his glass over his right shoulder. He quickly scanned the diplomats near him, but none had noticed his unique approach to completing a toast. As he placed the empty shot glass on a waiter's tray, he looked beyond a group of Canadian diplomats and noticed Yves. The tall French colonel was talking to the Vatican's ambassador to Algeria. Mitch sidestepped a Moroccan diplomat who obviously wanted to ask a question and made his way to Yves. The Vatican ambassador was explaining the distance from the Notre Dame d'Afrique Catholic basilica to the Casbah.

"Colonel, what you must understand is that the roads are not direct and quite narrow along the hillside," the Vatican ambassador said. "It would take approximately thirty minutes to travel from the basilica to the Casbah. But I must warn you that the Casbah is not a location that a Frenchman should visit. It is very dangerous, and if you insist on going there, then please come to the basilica for prayer prior to your departure. You will need the added protection!" the ambassador emphasized.

"Good evening, Mr. Ambassador. It's been some time since we last talked," Mitch said as he joined their conversation.

"Colonel Ross, it is so good to see you again. I hope you are feeling well, but your eye seems to have seen better days," the ambassador said.

Mitch responded with his usual reply. "It actually looks worse than it is," he said. "I have no pain."

Mitch looked at Yves and nodded.

"You must assist me in convincing your French military colleague not to visit the Casbah," the ambassador insisted.

"Yes, you are completely correct. Yves shouldn't worry about distances from the basilica. If he wants to get a good panoramic picture of the bay, then he needs to move closer to the water. Perhaps parking near the Algerian naval headquarters would be much better," Mitch said as he looked at Yves and then back to the ambassador.

"So, that's your reason for coming to the basilica, Colonel Dureau. I was hoping that it was for Mass and fellowship. But Colonel Ross is correct. If a panoramic photo of the bay is what you want, then take it near the naval headquarters. Some of those old naval buildings were being used by the Barbary Coast pirates during the early nineteenth century," the ambassador said.

"Well, Mr. Ambassador, it seems as though the guests are moving into Alexander's home for dinner," Yves said. "Perhaps we should join them. We definitely don't want to miss any of the toasts given before, during, and after dinner." He looked behind the ambassador and rolled his eyes at Mitch. The ambassador turned toward the house and quickly disappeared in a large group entering the double doors.

Mitch and Yves waited until only a few diplomats remained in the garden. When the coast was clear, Mitch spoke.

"Yves, earlier this evening I was talking to the Cuban ambassador.

It's a long story, but the bottom line is that of all the entry points into the Casbah, the southern entrance from the Algerian naval headquarters is the best. None of them are really safe, but the southern access allows for a quicker exit. The Cuban ambassador said that it's foolhardy to enter the Casbah. But I really don't have a choice. This will be like reliving Tipasa again, but much more dangerous!"

"I wasn't going to mention this to you, Mitch, but what the hell," Yves said. "One year before your arrival in Algeria, the Bulgarian defense attaché inadvertently entered the Casbah while taking his morning jog along the harbor. His headless body was found stuffed in a round metal container that was picked up by refuse collectors. Later in the week his head was discovered on a twelve-foot pole just outside of the Notre Dame d'Afrique basilica. Bulgarian diplomats have stated that their country refuses to replace the defense attaché, but rumor has it that no one in their military will take the position."

"I know it's dangerous as shit," Mitch replied, "but as I said before, I have no alternative. Let's go in and have dinner. Oh, by the way, you might want to cut your beef with this." He reached into his trouser pocket and handed the small box to Yves.

Yves slowly opened it and stared. Mitch knew that Yves had thought his mother's knife was lost for good. He was not surprised to see a small tear welling up in Yves's eye.

"Come on, let's find a table, my French friend," Mitch said, breaking the silence. "We have to get one that's near a few potted plants. It'll be easier to drown them with vodka rather than drowning our livers!"

The massive house was rather ridiculous, on a scale comparable to a small castle. Alexander, his wife, and his daughter had the choice of three living rooms, six bedrooms, five bathrooms, and two large dining areas that hosted seventy-five guests in each room. The first dining room was full, so Mitch and Yves defaulted to the second. Mitch led the way to a group of large potted plants just behind two open seats. They took their diplomatic positions standing behind the seats, and waited for Alexander to request that all guests be seated.

Alexander stood within the doorway that linked the two dining areas and raised a shot glass, thus beginning what seemed to be a never-ending ritual throughout these dinners. "May you all join me by taking your glass of vodka and welcoming those at your table," he said.

"We might have to down this shot," Yves whispered, leaning toward Mitch. "The couple at our table is staring at us."

Sitting at the table with Mitch and Yves was the Spanish deputy ambassador and his wife. Mitch flashed a quick thumbs-up, and within a few moments everyone at their table had greeted each other and swallowed the contents of their shot glasses.

"My, that eye of yours looks very painful," said the wife of the deputy ambassador as she looked at Mitch.

"I must admit, from time to time it is painful, but I believe that the worst is behind me," Mitch said. He noticed a beautiful jade pendant hanging from a delicate gold chain around her neck. "Your necklace is exquisite. Is it from Spain?" He thought of Abella and a potential gift for her.

The woman glanced at her husband with a somewhat embarrassed look. "Actually, I bought it from a little shop that is owned by my housemaid's father here in Algiers."

"That is absolutely gorgeous. I would love to go to that shop and buy a few items for the special lady in my life," Mitch said in all sincerity.

"That might be a little difficult, Colonel," the Spanish deputy ambassador said, giving his wife a look of disdain. "My fearless wife decided to visit that shop while I was traveling to Madrid for meetings with our *ministerio de gobierno*, or as you might say, the Spanish secretary of state."

"Ernesto, you promised me that you would not say a word," his wife pleaded.

"It is fine, Camila," the deputy ambassador said. "These two gentlemen are military and understand that at times one must take risks for what they truly want."

"Now you have our complete attention," Yves said. "I agree that the necklace is beautiful, and I would love to hear the story of its risky purchase."

"Tell them, Camila," the deputy ambassador said, chuckling. "It is okay. I promise that I will not be angry at you for this ever again. But you must promise me that you will never do it again."

"I will tell them," Camila said with a smile. "But I'm not sure that I can promise never to enter that shop again. Ernesto, there were so many items that caught my eye!" Camila paused to take a sip of her wine, then told her story. "Our housemaid has a habit of coming to work dressed like Spanish royalty. She wears fine dresses and jewelry that would make any woman envious. One day I asked her about the jewelry because I knew it was of high quality. She laughed and said that the jewelry was not hers, but she wore it to advertise. Her father knew that diplomats' wives would notice and want to know where she bought the jewelry. He is a very wise businessman! She mentioned that his shop is in the Casbah."

"Casbah! That's a dangerous location here in the city. Did you go there?" Mitch asked with much more interest than before.

"Yes, she did, Colonel. Continue, Camila," the deputy ambassador flatly said.

"After I talked to my maid, I asked if she would take me there. My husband was away, and I was very curious. The maid said that the only way I could go to the shop would be at night when it is very dark, but she agreed."

"She preferred the night because it would be difficult for others to notice that you are not Algerian?" Mitch asked.

"Exactly, but I'm Spanish, and I look somewhat similar to an Algerian . . . as opposed to your blond hair and blue eyes," Camila said.

"Do you remember where you went while in the Casbah, or had it gotten too dark?" Mitch inquired.

"I really only remember driving along the harbor road and then parking near the dock. My maid asked that I wear a large scarf over my head along with my denim jeans and jacket. She also requested that I not make eye contact with anyone once we entered the Casbah. As we approached the ancient steps that led through the catacomb-looking buildings, I lowered my head and never looked up until we arrived at her father's shop."

"Do you remember how long you walked?" Yves asked.

"I believe it was almost fifteen minutes of walking up those steps. I felt very confined and nervous with the small homes and shops just an arm's length on either side. But once we entered her father's jewelry shop, everything was so nice. I had hot tea and pastries as I looked and shopped. Her father locked the door as soon as I entered."

The waiters came to their table and placed the first course in front of them. It was a large bowl of soup accompanied with bread and wine. After the first course, Alexander stood between the rooms again and began another vodka toast. The deputy ambassador and his wife took their glasses along with Mitch and Yves. But then Mitch noticed that their Spanish companions moved their shots behind their backs. Then they completely covered the shot glasses with their hands when they brought them forward to toast.

"Excuse me, Ernesto, but I believe you are taking a page out of Yves's and my playbook," Mitch said, attempting to stifle his laughter.

"'Playbook?' I don't understand," Ernesto said.

"Watch me. I'll demonstrate for you," Mitch responded. He moved his shot glass behind him and dumped it into the tall plants. Yves copied Mitch.

As Alexander made his toast, all those sitting with Mitch began to laugh and then raised their empty glasses at the appropriate moment and pretended to swallow the vodka.

"Ernesto and I worried about all the vodka. We try to sit near plants and attempt to be discreet when dumping the alcohol. It is so much better than going home feeling ill for the next few days," Camila said.

"I'll drink to that!" Yves said, laughing.

The waiters came and took what remained of their soup and replaced it with large salads and more wine.

"I know this might seem somewhat out of line, but would your maid be interested in taking me to her father's shop or other locations in the Casbah?" Mitch inquired.

"Why in God's name would you risk your life to enter that cesspool?" Ernesto asked.

"I don't have the same opportunity you do to travel freely throughout Algiers," Mitch said. "I'm very much restricted by my government, as you well know. But perhaps I could visit Yves at his embassy and then we could drive and pick up your maid. Yves has his own vehicle, as you do, although his car is currently being repaired because he loves to travel off-road on dirt paths." Mitch chuckled as he looked at Yves, who shook his head and rolled his eyes.

"I have no problem asking my maid. If it means that her father may potentially make a sale, then I'm almost certain she'll do it. I'll call you tomorrow with her answer," Camila said with confidence.

Waiters came and placed another shot of vodka in front of each guest as Alexander toasted the leaders of Russia, the US, the UK, Spain, and France. All four at Mitch's table went through their ritual of dumping the vodka on the plants. This routine continued throughout the evening, generating smiles and laughter among the four.

After the sixth course, which ended the formal dinner, all the guests returned to the garden, and the men were given glasses of cognac and large Cohiba cigars.

"Yves, I believe our work is done for this evening," Mitch said, raising his cognac to his old friend. "We now know that the best Casbah entry is near the docks. Hopefully I'll receive a positive call from Camila tomorrow. If her maid agrees, then we have a personal guided nocturnal tour of the Casbah. If she turns us down, then it'll be the blind leading the blind, at night, in a terrorist-infested location. We won't know where the hell we're going and what the hell we're doing. But other than that, life is good and we're not drunk!"

"Yes, my friend. You speak the truth. But I must admit that I'm a little tipsy. I just couldn't let all that good Russian vodka go to waste. Plus, this cognac is to die for!"

"Well, it's past my bedtime and I'm sure that Jake has had a few plates of that heavy Russian food. I'll bid you adieu and call you tomorrow. Take care, buddy."

As Mitch walked to the garden exit, he glanced at the cigar in his hand. He laughed, thinking how this evening had gone full circle, bookended by Cuban cigars.

14

The next morning, Mitch sat in his living room, sipping coffee and eating a bowl of diced bananas. *Le Monde*, the French daily newspaper that closely monitored the pulse of Algeria, was spread before him. He noticed a small article on page three about Algerian police finding three dead men in the Tipasa ruins. The article mentioned that the Algerian authorities had closed the case due to lack of evidence. There was more than enough evidence to ultimately lead investigators to Yves and the French embassy, but apparently the authorities didn't care and didn't want to expend time and effort on three lowlife extremists.

Mitch was about to close the newspaper when he saw an interesting statistic regarding an upsurge of terrorist activity in and around Algiers. The article mentioned that the increase in violence happened to coincide with a rumored shift in GSPC leadership. Experts perceived the new leadership to be much more active and dangerous, no longer attacking only Algerian military targets but now also including civilians in and around Algiers. French authorities said there had been an increase in the saturation of terrorists through the military protective corridors around the Algerian capital city.

I wonder if that's had an effect on Seth Hunt and his captive situation, Mitch thought after reading the article. *Perhaps they've moved him to a new location, or worse, killed him. That would really be the shit—to make it all the way there just to find out that he is no longer there.* He took his empty coffee cup and bowl to the kitchen, trying not to interrupt Djamila.

"Thanks for the coffee and bananas, Djamila. How are you doing this morning?"

"I'm fine, Colonel Mitch. And you?"

"I'm great! The only downside is that I must go to work. Some days I just hate that. But it is what it is, so I have to face reality."

"True, but for me I really enjoy coming here and preparing your food. I have a very nice kitchen, a radio that plays music, a good salary, and I get to sample the food. Life is good for me. Plus, this afternoon I'm going to visit my father and bring him a few gifts. That always fills me with joy."

"You've never really mentioned your father before," Mitch said. "Does he live in Algiers?"

"Oh yes." Djamila nodded. "When he married my mother in 1954, he bought a small three-room home in the Casbah. I was born in that house many years later. He has lived there all his life. In fact, my mother and father lived there throughout the Algerian War of Independence. My father fought against the French as a member of the Front de Libération Nationale. He was what you would call a guerrilla fighter and escaped death many times throughout the war. Even my mother was involved.

"When my mother died five years ago, I pleaded with my father to move into my apartment near the embassies where it's secure and safe. He's seventy-one years old, and I worry about him living alone. But he tells me that there are too many happy memories of my mother in that house, and he will never leave."

"I've heard that the Casbah is extremely dangerous," Mitch said.

"Yes, it is dangerous," Djamila agreed. "But my father feels he is protected because of what he did during our war against France.

The older terrorists respect him for the sacrifices he made to gain Algerian independence against French colonialism."

"Then I don't completely understand why you want him to move."

"Younger elements of Algerian terrorist organizations don't care about what they consider ancient history. They were born and raised long after the war ended. In their eyes, my father is just a relic with prehistoric stories. I'm beginning to fear for his life."

"How often do you see him?"

"I try to go twice a week with food and little gifts."

"Djamila, when you cook for me, take some of my meals to your father. Please, I insist."

"That is extremely kind of you, but I would feel very guilty," Djamila said, smiling. "Actually, I've told my father about you and your military career. He is honored to know that his daughter works for a military officer who serves and sacrifices for his country, residing thousands of miles from his home. He tells me that most people in this world would never sacrifice as you do. They would never leave their home or their families as you have done. I wish I could introduce you to my father. He would be honored."

"On the contrary, it would be an honor for me."

"Thank you for saying that. I will tell my father what you said."

"Does he ever leave his home or the Casbah?"

"He only leaves during the call to prayer, and then he walks to the mosque near his home."

"His home is within walking distance to the mosque?" Mitch asked.

She nodded. "My father only has to walk a few minutes to reach the mosque, and he walks very slowly."

"You mentioned that you visit twice a week. When you're there, do you ever notice other men walking to the mosque for prayer?"

"Oh yes, many of the older gentlemen that live within his neighborhood walk with him."

"Have you recently noticed any younger men walking to the mosque?"

"Usually it's just the older men," she said thoughtfully. "But in the last month I have noticed a group of younger men attending prayer. About five of them."

"Do they all wear contemporary clothing, or are they dressed in robes as if they were Bedouins from the desert?" Mitch asked.

"It's interesting that you ask," Djamila said with a quizzical look. "Last week, as I was helping my father down the stone steps outside his house, the younger men passed. As they did I noticed that one of them wore robes. In my culture, I'm not permitted to stare at men, so I only took a quick look. But I knew he was gazing at me as I helped my father. And I noticed something else odd about that man. His head and face were covered, but his eyes were the color of yours. They were light blue."

"Did you stay at your father's house until he returned from prayer that day?"

"I always wait for his safe return. Then I prepare his evening meal."

"Did you notice the younger men, especially the one wearing the robes, walking back to their residence?"

"As I waited for my father that day, I looked out his small front window. After prayer the younger men passed my father's house, climbing the steps within the walls of the Casbah. They are younger, so they walk much faster. The one wearing the robes seemed to be surrounded by the four others as if they were protecting him. It was odd because men usually talk politics when they leave the mosque. But there seemed to be no talking amongst these younger men."

"Did you happen to notice where they went?" Mitch asked.

"No, but when my father returned I asked about them. He told me that I should not ask such questions. He believes that they are dangerous. Still, I asked if he has ever looked at the man in the robes. My father said that he had noticed the man's light eyes. He believes that this man might be a Frenchman within the GSPC." She paused before continuing. "Colonel Mitch, why are you so interested in a place and individuals that you will never visit or see?"

"I can't really answer your question, but what I will say is please be careful when you visit your father. I agree with him that those younger men are very dangerous. Now I must get to the office. Thank you for this conversation—it meant a lot to me. I truly appreciate knowing what a loving and kind person you are. But please, take some of the food you prepare here to your father. You must!"

"Colonel Mitch, you're very thoughtful. I'll tell my father that this meal is from you."

"Have a wonderful afternoon with your father."

Mitch departed his residence, reflecting on the conversation. For years he'd wondered why Djamila requested to leave early twice a week. It never occurred to him that she was visiting her father. He wondered when she had time to shop and clean up her apartment.

His thoughts quickly turned to the man in the Bedouin robes. *Blue eyes, face covered. The man must be Captain Seth Hunt.* Hamady had said Hunt had taken up the Bedouin lifestyle. It was interesting that the GSPC allowed him to walk to the mosque but unsurprising that he was surrounded by guards during these trips. Most observers would likely think the guards were his security detail.

Hopefully, I've planted the curiosity seed in Djamila, Mitch thought. *Perhaps now she'll be looking for the young men passing her father's home. It would be great to get weekly updates on Hunt's location and well-being. If he attends the same call to prayer each day and walks the same route, that might be the time to rescue him.*

As Mitch headed to the chancery building, he noticed the ambassador walking from his residence to the cafeteria.

"Mr. Ambassador," he said, "I was planning on seeing you this morning to find out if you had an opportunity to review my written report on Captain Seth Hunt. Any questions?"

"No, Colonel, it was good. I took your information and sent messages to the State Department and White House. I have yet to receive word back from them."

"Sir, I noticed an interesting article in *Le Monde* this morning. It described an increase in terrorist activities in and around Algiers.

This increase coincides with a rumored shift in leadership of the GSPC. Supposedly, the new leadership is much more aggressive and dangerous. They not only target the military but are also going after the civilian populace of Algiers."

"Yes, I was at the French ambassador's residence for dinner last night, along with Fredrick Parker, the British ambassador. We discussed this very same subject. This morning I talked to Jake Davis and informed him that we're increasing our security levels. He and the Marines are to take appropriate measures. What it basically means is that there will be more restrictions on American diplomatic movements outside our walls. Sorry for the news, Colonel, but we can't take any unnecessary risks."

"I understand completely, Mr. Ambassador. The death of an American diplomat in Algeria would set back any progress we've made in the enhancement of the relationship between our two countries."

"I'm glad you understand, but you've had the luxury of visiting many diplomats in their embassies or homes. On the other hand, there are a good number of diplomats here that are at their wits' end with cabin fever. They so infrequently get outside of these walls, and there is only the gym, pool, and tennis courts to use during their free time. They are on two to three-year diplomatic assignments here in Algeria. There's no shopping and going to dinner outside these walls. I believe you put it appropriately the other day: 'Living and working in this embassy is like residing in Fort Apache during the old Western era. It's very dangerous once we leave our protective walls.'

"Well, Colonel, it's time to grab a coffee and say hello to the cafeteria staff."

"Thanks for the update, sir."

Damn it! Mitch thought as he entered the chancery building. *I'm sure that every movement off this embassy compound will now be reviewed by the ambassador. He'll have the final vote on whether I can journey out or not. That means Abella will have to come to the embassy more often, and I'm sure terrorists are watching every movement in and out of these walls. They'll notice her frequent visits, and that will put a bigger target on her forehead.*

After clearing the chancery security, Mitch passed the State Department special agent office and noticed Jake standing near a large whiteboard full of names, rubbing his brow ridge as he attempted to update the embassy guard-posting schedule.

"Hey, Jake, looks like you have your hands full," Mitch said from the doorway.

"You've got that right, Colonel," Jake said. "The ambassador wants double security coverage. This is a real ballbuster. We just don't have the manpower. The Marines are bringing in more troops from the US embassies in Tunisia and Morocco. State takes care of the diplomats, and the Marines watch over the embassy buildings. The ambassador wants to hear my security plan early tomorrow morning. It has to cover all security contingencies in and outside of the embassy . . . *and* evacuation routes to the Port of Algiers, and that involves the US Navy and potential extraction of all Americans by helo and naval ships. Of course, this would be our last resort in the event of an overwhelming terrorist attack."

"I guess that means the ambassador will want to review the travel-request schedule each day," Mitch replied. "And I'm guessing that I won't be priority number one!"

"Well, Colonel, you never can tell unless you submit your travel request. Did you have anything in mind?"

"Not just yet," Mitch said. "But I will most likely schedule a trip to the French embassy in the next couple days."

"Colonel, are you suggestin' that you and Colonel Dureau will be takin' another road trip in his Peugeot? Remember what I said to you the other day. If your plans will take you to places that most intelligent people would avoid like the plague, let me know. I need more target practice. Now, with all due respect, Colonel, this country boy has gotta complete this damn schedule for the ambo." Having said his piece, Jake turned back to his whiteboard.

"I understand completely," Mitch said, nodding. "I'll make sure that you're involved. Now that the ambassador is tightening down the travel, I'll rely on you more than ever to help me get past these embassy walls legally. You have a great State Department day, Jake."

"You take care, Colonel, and remember that today is just another day closer to retirement."

Mitch headed down the stairs to his office, anticipating a quiet afternoon. He opened the secure cypher door and entered his darkened cave. Warrant Officer Dave McQueen was still on leave in the States, so Mitch was free to begin developing a plan and a timetable to rescue Captain Hunt. But what he really wanted to do was call Abella. She had been working the night shift at the hospital, which meant she slept during the day. Although he was reluctant to ring her, he wanted to invite her for dinner—assuming she could fit it in before her next night shift. She answered on the first ring.

"Hello, Abella," Mitch said. "I hope I didn't wake you."

"Mitch, it doesn't matter. This is such a nice surprise," she said, sounding sleepy. "I was hoping you would call. I'm always reluctant to call you because I know that your schedule keeps you on the fast track."

"I won't keep you long, but is there any chance you can join me for dinner this evening before you go to work?"

"Even if I have to walk to the embassy, I'll be there," she replied. "Luckily my schedule is changing to the second shift, so I'll be working tomorrow from 3 in the afternoon until 11 p.m. We won't have to rush dinner this evening."

"Great! Then how about coming over at six for a little wine before we eat?"

"Okay, six it is. I can't wait."

"I'll be at the security building, waiting for your arrival."

"See you soon, Mitch. Bye-bye."

Mitch listened for the sound of a second receiver hanging up, his anxiety about terrorist links to members of the Algerian military staff heightened. Instead of calling Jake, Mitch went in person to interrupt

Jake's embassy-security planning again.

"Sorry to interrupt," Mitch said as Jake turned away from his whiteboard. "Abella will be coming to the embassy today at 6 p.m. for dinner."

"So, your pretty lady will be visiting again." Jake nodded with a sly smile. "She is a breath of fresh air. When she's around, the whole complexion of this embassy gets sweeter! I'll take care of the paperwork and make sure that we clean up the security entry point. Sometimes that place is a shithole, with all the cigarette butts and cups half full of stale coffee."

"Thanks, Jake. Sorry to compound your day with more work."

"Not a problem, Colonel. If it means that I get to feast my eyes on one of God's perfect creations, I don't mind a little more work." He laughed and gave Mitch a thumbs-up.

Back in his office, Mitch called Djamila at his residence. Per their agreement, the phone rang ten times before she picked it up. That amount of ringing indicated to her that it was Mitch.

"Bonjour?" said Djamila after the tenth ring.

"Djamila, it's Colonel Mitch."

"Is there a problem or do you need help?" Djamila asked.

"No problems, but yes, I definitely need assistance. Abella will be coming over around six this evening. I was hoping that you would prepare something simple for us."

"Would you like fish, rice, mixed vegetables, rolls, fruit, and cake, Colonel Mitch?" she asked.

"Wow! In the States that would be considered a big meal. I'll only say yes to your menu if you promise to take some to your father."

"That is very kind of you. Perhaps, if you have the time soon, we can talk about the latest information regarding my father and his neighborhood. Did you want wine?"

"Yes, I believe I have a chardonnay cooling in the refrigerator. It's smooth and light and goes well with fish. Have two glasses and the wine in the living room just prior to six. Thanks so much, Djamila!

Oh, by the way, I definitely want to continue our conversation about your father."

– • – •

Mitch spread a large, detailed chart of the Casbah across his massive desk. Grabbing a magnifying glass, he pulled the desk lamp closer to his position on the map. His first task was to identify all the potential routes in and out of the ancient walled city.

He circled the southern entry point near the Algerian naval headquarters. From the information he had so far, it seemed the best route to take. Next, he highlighted in yellow the latitude and longitude point that Hamady had given him. He put a cross over the site of the mosque near Djamila's father's home and from her description estimated where his house was positioned.

Mitch retrieved a small note bearing the coat of arms of Spain from his desk drawer. Handwritten by the deputy ambassador of Spain, Ernesto, the message had been delivered earlier in the week by a Spanish diplomat attending a business meeting at the US embassy.

He read it again:

I asked my maid whether she would be willing to take you to her father's jewelry shop. Her response was that she would be more than happy to escort the American defense attaché to the shop in the Casbah. Arrangements will be made at your convenience. Sincerely, Ernesto.

Mitch estimated the location of the shop by recalling the details Camila had given. She had described entering near the harbor and then walking up steps for approximately fifteen minutes. That would have placed the jewelry shop north of the latitude and longitude given by Hamady. But it would be roughly in the same Casbah neighborhood.

Once Mitch had finished marking the locations on the map, his thoughts drifted to Djamila. He wondered if she could confirm whether the man wearing the Bedouin robes passed her father's home at approximately the same time each day. *From what Djamila said, it would be the evening call to prayer, when the sun is setting. If he's allowed to attend the evening prayer, then his timing and route would be very predictable.* That aspect troubled Mitch, and he wondered if perhaps there were more terrorist guards lurking along the route who Djamila hadn't noticed. Obviously, she had not been trained to recognize shady individuals skulking in shadows.

Taking Hunt during his walk to the mosque could be a lot riskier than it first appeared. Mitch looked again at the estimated position of Hunt's confinement house and measured the distance to the mosque. The maximum time it would take Hunt to walk to the mosque was five minutes. Maybe less. *Damn, that really reduces the opportunity to snatch Hunt. Also, that doesn't factor in other hidden terrorists in the vicinity.*

Unfortunately, Mitch had to close the door on planning a daylight rescue attempt. To have any chance at all for success, the operation would have to occur under cover of darkness. Mitch rolled the map and placed it inside a cardboard tube leaning against the bookshelf near his desk. He checked his watch and realized that it was time to depart for his residence. He wanted a moment to talk to Djamila before heading to the embassy security building.

Mitch returned to his embassy home and went directly into the kitchen.

"Djamila, that smells delicious," he said. "Do you cook with a special aroma spice that the rest of the world hasn't discovered yet?"

Djamila laughed. "It's just the natural fragrance of food without preservatives and supplements," she replied. "These ancient Bedouin recipes have been passed down through my family for thousands of years."

"Well, whatever you do, it's magic!"

"You're so kind, Colonel Mitch, but I can tell there's something else you want to ask." She turned away from her vegetable cutting and looked directly at him as he grabbed a few dates. "Be careful; I've not pitted those dates."

"I'll be careful, especially since my dentist resides in Northern Virginia. I do have something else to ask. Have you seen the man who wears the Bedouin robes again in your father's neighborhood?"

"Oh yes," she replied. "During the early evening hours. My father and his older friends have said that they've never seen the young man except during the evening prayer."

"Have you or your father noticed the home of the young man?"

"As I have said before, it is forbidden for me to stare or gawk at a man. But I have asked my father and his friends. They laugh and tease me because they think that I find the young man attractive. I must admit that he looks rather dashing. As you say, he resembles Lawrence of Arabia—especially his vivid blue eyes against the white silk. I can only glance quickly at him, but each time I do, he is gazing at me. My father said that his home is only a few minutes above the hill from where my father lives. It is on the opposite side of my father's home."

"If I was at your father's house, could you point out the young man's residence?"

"It would be as easy as identifying the tennis courts from your home here at the embassy. I should not ask, but why are you so interested in this man, Colonel Mitch?"

"Someday I'll tell you. But for now, I'll just say it isn't every day that someone resembling Lawrence of Arabia walks through the Casbah without being accosted."

"My father and I have discussed that issue. But as he says, the young man and his colleagues cause no problems, and it is good that the young ones attend prayer. They need to get right with God."

"I suspect your father is completely correct in that respect," Mitch said. "Well, it's time for me to change and prepare for Abella's arrival."

"Colonel Mitch, I have only seen her for a very short period, but my intuition tells me that she loves you very much. Be kind to her. I feel she has experienced great sorrow in her life."

Mitch looked at Djamila and smiled. "Your insight and intuition are beyond your ability to cook, and you're the greatest cook I have ever met!"

He turned from the kitchen and went upstairs to change. He was amazed how quickly Djamila could analyze a person by briefly observing them.

She could be a tremendous asset, and my eyes in the Casbah, Mitch thought.

15

As Mitch departed his residence, he noticed the increased security along the walls and points of entry into the embassy. The Marines were wearing their full battle gear. Although it made him feel secure, it was also unsettling. The heightened threat loomed more clearly than ever. And if Hamady was correct, the threat was not only surrounding them but also here inside the embassy walls.

Mitch arrived at the embassy security building to find Jake smoking a cigar under the shade of a palm tree.

"Good evening, Colonel. It's another day in paradise. And I suspect your paradise will be much better than mine once your lady arrives." He smiled, then blew out a long stream of smoke through puckered lips.

"Jake, we've got to arrange our calendars so that I can buy you all that bourbon at the Marine bar."

"I don't see that as a problem, Colonel. Cause this old boy knows where you live and where you go. That's unless you pull a fast one on me and slip out of another embassy once I've dropped you off."

"There's no chance of that this evening. I'll be having a nice peaceful dinner with Abella at my place."

"Yes sir, it must be nice having two desserts in one evening.

Lordy, I can only imagine."

The security entry building was surprisingly clean, just as Jake had promised it would be. Even the Algerian security guards' uniforms seemed spotless. Mitch was impressed.

Precisely at six, a taxi pulled up and Abella stepped out. Mitch did a double take, in awe of her beauty once again. Although it had only been one week, it seemed as though months had passed since he was last with her.

She slipped her passport through the slot in the secure metal door. The security guard took it and sat at the computer. Within moments he returned and spoke in Arabic through the microphone speaker. He opened the door, and she entered as the guards stood gazing at her. She quickly spotted Mitch and held out her hand, grasping his as she leaned and kissed him. Jake stood near the back door of the building. He bowed as Abella and Mitch approached him, and then he handed her the passport.

"I must admit, young lady, you have an uncanny ability to turn hell into heaven by your mere presence," Jake said. "Welcome to the US embassy, my dear. Now get along, you two, 'cause you're just wastin' heartbeats standing around in this building. Have a great evenin', and remember that if you have any special requests, I'll be here on duty almost all night." Jake smiled and patted Mitch on the back.

"Thanks, Jake," Mitch said as he and Abella left the building. Jake nodded, and they walked away through the rose garden, heading toward Mitch's home.

At Mitch's residence, they went to the living room. Abella placed her purse on the leather chair and noticed the chardonnay and glasses.

"I love a chilled white wine on these warm summer evenings," she said. "It makes for such a refreshing taste. Mitch, could I please say hello to Djamila? She works so hard to make the most exquisite meals for us."

"I'm sure Djamila would love that. But before you go to the kitchen, let me pour the wine."

He uncorked the bottle and poured the wine into the two glasses.

Setting the bottle aside, he handed Abella her glass.

"To us, to love, and to our future," he said, raising his glass to her.

They both took a sip of the cool wine, and Abella stepped closer and softly kissed him on the lips.

"Yes, to us and to our love," she said as their lips met again and their tongues gently touched.

They put their glasses on the table, and Abella pulled Mitch toward the kitchen. Peeking around the corner, she saw Djamila putting the final touches on the gourmet meal.

"Djamila," Abella said, "*Assalam alaikum, kaifa haalik* ?" She followed up the traditional Arabic greeting by asking how Djamila had been.

Djamila turned with a big smile and embraced Abella. Mitch left them to it as the two women chatted in Arabic. What was happening in the kitchen was obviously a mutual-admiration society.

Abella suddenly rushed past him to the living room and grabbed her purse. She returned to the kitchen and pulled out a little wrapped gift. She handed it to Djamila and hugged her again.

"I want you to have this gift," Abella said. "It is a small token of gratitude for all the work you have done and will do for Mitch. He thinks the world of you, and honestly you are a fabulous cook. Please, the gift is truly from my heart."

Djamila opened the gift, tears welling in her eyes. Inside the small box was a pair of exceedingly rare golden earrings. Her eyes opened wide as her shaking hand carefully took one of the earrings from the box.

"Abella, I cannot accept this gift. These gold earrings are extremely rare and made by the blue people of the Sahara."

"You are a very kind and gentle person, Djamila. I give these earrings to you as a sister. Mitch has told me that you are the only child of your father as I was the only child of my father. Please, take the gift and think of me when you wear them."

"I will proudly wear these earrings the next time I visit my father.

As a young man he journeyed many times to an oasis city in the Sahara. It was called Tamanrasset. There he met many of the blue people, and they taught him the ways of the great desert and how to survive. Over the years he would buy their jewelry, but never could he find such exquisite earrings as these. He will know immediately how rare and valuable they are. Then, when I tell him about you, he will want to meet you. So, I ask of you one favor, Abella. When my father requests to meet you, will you accompany me to the Casbah?"

"It would be an honor to meet your father," Abella said, wiping a tear from Djamila's face.

Mitch tried to puzzle the Arabic together, knowing little of the language. He was not completely sure what had just occurred. Still, he knew that the conversation was touching and heartfelt. There was no mistaking their facial expressions and tears.

Abella and Mitch returned to the living room and sat in silence, sipping their wine. Then Mitch broke the stillness. "Abella, that was so kind of you. Your compassionate heart is larger than life. I hope one day I can give to you as you have given to me."

"Mitch, you've given to me more than any man I have ever known. You just don't realize it, and that is why I love you as I do," Abella said, then kissed him passionately.

In the meantime, Djamila had placed food at the table, lit the candles, and keyed the soft jazz that now floated into the living room. The music snapped Abella and Mitch from their euphoria, and they rose from the couch to sit at the dining table. Without a sound, Djamila slipped from the house and headed to the Casbah with a warm basketful of dinner for her father.

Mitch and Abella sat at the table and shook their heads as they looked at the feast before them.

"It's amazing how Djamila can transform plain food into a sumptuous meal," Abella said. "One would expect to see this dinner on the cover of *Gourmet* magazine."

"I've told her many times that she's a miracle worker," Mitch replied.

"I believe it's because of her tender heart and respect she has for you. I'm so glad she accepted my gift. I will go to the Casbah soon to meet her father."

"Is that what you two discussed after you gave her the gift? Going to the Casbah?"

"I'm so sorry; I forgot that you couldn't understand. Djamila has invited me to visit her father. As a younger man he spent a lot of time in the Sahara amongst the blue people. They made those golden earrings."

"Blue people?" Mitch asked.

"The Tuaregs," Abella explained. "They've been called the blue people because of their indigo-dyed clothes. The dye stains their skin blue. They're nomads and descendants of the Berber tribes of North Africa. Their impact on Africa's history is undeniable. Their nomadic lifestyle allowed them to spread Islam throughout all of North Africa."

"Do you know what amazes me about you?" Mitch asked. "Not only are you a tremendous nurse, but you are a walking encyclopedia. Now I know more about the blue people than ninety-nine percent of all Americans!" He raised his glass to Abella's.

"Let's not let this fabulous food go to waste," Abella said, smiling. "Let's eat first and talk later."

"Okay, but first one more question. How is your roommate doing?"

"She's fine, and continually asks questions concerning you and me."

"What type of questions?" Mitch asked.

"Primarily girl talk about our relationship, but sometimes she asks about your work and if I get involved with your projects. It's strange at times because her questions relate to terrorism and what you do to counter the threat. I try to explain to her that I don't get involved with your work here at the embassy. At least that's the story I tell her."

"What type of terrorist questions does she ask?"

"Last night she asked what I thought was America's next step to put down the rise of the GSPC threat here in Algiers. I told her that I didn't have a clue, but I'm not so sure she believed me. When

I inquired why she seemed to be so interested in the American activities in Algeria, she said that hearing intriguing stories is like listening to an audio adventure novel."

"Be careful what you say to her, sweetheart. She's prying beyond what I would expect a roommate would ask."

As Mitch reached for the chardonnay, he was jolted by a sudden crash outside and the sound of shattering glass and screams. The bottle slipped from his hand, spilling the contents onto the white linen tablecloth. In the same instant Mitch glanced up at Abella, his residence was rocked by a massive explosion. The concussion blew out the front windows, ripped the front door from its hinges, and collapsed a portion of the dining room table. Mitch and Abella were thrown from their chairs and fell amid the food, glass, and rubble covering the thick-carpeted floor.

Dazed, Mitch tried to bring his semiconscious mind back to reality. Flames outside his residence pierced the evening sky and slowly helped him focus. He had no idea how long he'd been lying on the floor, but he was completely covered in debris from the explosion. A distant ringing filled his head and muddled his hearing, making this chaotic, horrifying scene strangely quiet. The sound of automatic weapon fire broke through. The shots sounded close—within the embassy compound.

With a great effort, he pushed himself into a sitting position. Through the hole where his front door had been, he saw flames, people running, chaos, and a gaping crater in place of the security entry building. Mitch's mind sluggishly recovered. His eyes focused on an object positioned awkwardly on the collapsed dining room table. As he squinted to get a better perspective, the object moved. Mitch gasped, and his heart rate leaped. It was Abella's foot.

"Abella! Abella, are you okay?" Mitch yelled, struggling to get to her.

He crawled closer and saw that her body was covered with glass and pieces of the table. Her face, arms, and hands were bleeding. Mitch slowly raised her head and put his head close. He felt her breath. *Please, God, don't take her from me*, Mitch thought as he gently wiped blood from her face with a piece of his torn shirt.

The crackle of automatic weapons and explosions grew more intense. Mitch realized that the threat was just outside his residence.

"Abella, can you hear me?" he pleaded.

Her eyes fluttered open.

"What happened, Mitch? What's going on?" She paused, taking stock of her body. "Why am I covered in blood?" She gripped his arm tighter as reality came into focus. The automatic weapon fire rang out again, even closer this time. The gunshots seemed to snap her awake.

"What's that noise?" She quickly sat up, reached down, and found that her feet were bare. She scanned the room for her shoes.

Mitch held her and they both looked toward the flames and fighting. Just beyond the rose garden, they saw Marines and State Department special agents shooting toward the destroyed security building. Mitch counted at least six bodies lying near the flames. As they watched, terrorists ran into the embassy compound through the flaming rubble, firing and yelling, "Allahu Akbar."

"Can you get up, Abella?" Mitch asked. "We have to get upstairs." Before she could answer, he urgently pulled her to her feet, picking her up so she wouldn't have to walk on the broken glass.

Once inside Mitch's room, Abella said, "I remember a crash and screams. Did a vehicle explode into the embassy?"

Mitch nodded. "I believe there was a car bomb followed by smaller explosives. They're entering the embassy where the security building used to be."

Mitch grabbed a padlock-secured metal toolkit from his closet and unlocked it. Fishing around inside, he found two large-bore, snub-nosed flare guns and eight 25-millimeter flares. Mitch opened one gun, inserted a flare into the rear of the barrel, and then closed the weapon. He handed the second gun to Abella. She copied Mitch's loading and closed the pistol.

"Here, you take three flares and I'll take the rest," he said. "Flare guns aren't accurate, and they don't kill. But they should scare the shit out of anyone trying to do us harm."

As they turned to leave the bedroom, they heard someone downstairs. Mitch put his finger to his lips and pointed to the wall, motioning for Abella to back up against it. He slowly stepped to the doorway and peered beyond the staircase. He saw a terrorist grab an unopened bottle of wine and shove it into his jacket. The bearded extremist looked around and then glanced upstairs as Mitch moved back into the bedroom.

"He's coming upstairs," Mitch whispered with panic in his voice. "Stay away from the door and fire when you have a good body shot. I'll crouch on this side of the room. Remember, these guns aren't accurate."

The barrel of an AK-47 poked through the doorway. Flames leaped from the weapon as the terrorist fired wildly, spraying the back wall and Mitch's dresser. After an initial burst of gunfire, the terrorist slowly entered.

Mitch aimed his flare gun and fired, hitting the terrorist on the side of the head. Abella responded with a shot that hit the extremist in the right eye. The terrorist screamed and dropped his AK-47, clutching at his bleeding face and head. Mitch sprang from his crouched position and bodychecked the terrorist, pushing him out of the bedroom. As Mitch moved away, Abella fired another flare at point-blank range, hitting the man in the forehead. The impact propelled him over the second-floor railing, and he fell headfirst to the floor below. Judging by the awkward position of the terrorist's head, the impact had broken his neck. Abella ran to Mitch's side.

"What should we do now?" she asked.

He paused, listening to the automatic weapons and chaos outside. Flames from the burning car bomb and floodlights along the embassy walls and buildings illuminated the dark night sky. They carefully peeped through the second-story window and spotted Jake directing a group of Marines. The Marines were being overwhelmed by the invaders and had to retreat to a safer firing position behind two embassy vehicles. Mitch could tell that the terrorists were attempting to surround Jake's position and completely take out his group. Several special agents and Marines lay motionless near a charred embassy SUV. Mitch could only speculate how many embassy personnel had been killed in the blast.

Mitch glanced to the left and noticed movement along the tree line and inner wall of the embassy as another group of terrorists scampered through the trees. It appeared that this group had circled behind Mitch's residence under cover of darkness. From their current position, Jake and the Marines wouldn't be able to see the threat.

"We have to warn Jake to cover his flank, or else he and the Marines will be dead men," Mitch said as he picked up the dead man's AK-47 and made sure it was cocked.

Abella grabbed a pair of Mitch's old running shoes and pulled them on. They were a little large, but she laced them up tightly, stood, and gave Mitch a determined nod.

Descending the stairs, they cautiously went into the kitchen, then onto the terrace and into the darkness of night.

"We're going to climb down from the terrace," Mitch whispered. "The backyard looks clear, so we should be okay. I'll climb down first; then hand me the AK and your flare gun. Then you follow."

Abella nodded, and Mitch climbed over the fencing that partially surrounded the terrace. He hung from the bottom railing and released his grip, dropping to the ground. Abella handed down the weapons and then dropped down from the terrace as Mitch had done. He handed her the flare gun and took the AK-47. They crept to the edge of the house, using the back wall as protection. At the corner, they peered through tall bushes and saw the terrorists approximately twenty yards from their position. One of them held a rocket-propelled grenade.

"I wish we had grenades or some form of explosives," Mitch said. "That RPG will blow the shit out of Jake's group. We've gotta take them out or at least distract them."

Abella crouched in one of the bushes. "Why don't you get down into a clear firing position and I'll launch a flare in Jake's direction to get his attention?" she asked.

"If you get hit, I'll never forgive myself for getting you into this."

She winked and raised the flare gun with two hands, waiting for his signal to fire.

Mitch looked back toward the invaders and spotted a terrorist positioning the RPG.

"Fire your flare!" he yelled.

The flare shot through the bushes and exploded to the right of Jake's position. Mitch opened up with the AK-47 just as the terrorist fired. A round struck the extremist in the upper right chest, spinning him to the left and sending the rocket flying erratically into a building just behind Jake. Meanwhile, Abella's flare had accomplished what they had hoped. Jake looked to his right and directed two Marines to fire at the terrorists in the tree line. Mitch continued his pressure on the radicals, knowing that he only had a few more bursts before he was out of ammo.

"Abella, how many flares do you have left?"

"I have one in the gun and that's it."

Mitch fished in his pocket and handed two unused flares to Abella.

"Sweetheart, I'm just about out of ammo. We can't hold this position much longer, so when you fire these flares, fire for effect!"

"Believe me, Mitch, I'll scare the shit out of them."

Mitch fired his last rounds and motioned for Abella to fall back to his house. He hoped the Marines would cover them. Bullets ricocheted off the embassy wall and the house as they ran back to the terrace.

"I'm not so sure going back into the house is a good idea," Mitch said. "They could blow up the second story with that RPG if they know we're there."

Just as they arrived at the terrace, a terrorist emerged from the corner of the house and tackled Mitch. Abella gasped at the flash of a knife blade in the moonlight as the two men wrestled on the ground. The terrorist used his size advantage to pin Mitch down, then raised his knife, ready to thrust it into Mitch's chest.

In a flash, Abella grabbed Mitch's AK-47 from the ground and brought it down on the terrorist's head like an ax. The knife flew out of the attacker's hand as his eyes rolled back into his head, and Mitch threw him off. The terrorist slumped motionless to the ground. Mitch searched through the man's clothing, taking his pistol and ammunition.

"Damn, that was too close for comfort. I'll take his AK-47 ammo and you take his pistol," Mitch said as he handed Abella the man's Beretta M9 and two clips of ammo.

Abella grabbed Mitch's shirt collar and pulled him toward her. "If we keep having close calls like this, I only want to remember the last thing we did together." Then she kissed him, tasting the sweat on his lips and parched mouth.

Mitch clasped his hands together and motioned for Abella to step into them.

"I thought we were going to blow off going into the house?" she asked.

"Now that we have firepower, being able to look down on the bad guys might give us an advantage."

Mitch pushed her up to the terrace railing. She grabbed the lowest rail and swung her leg up onto the balcony. Once up, she took the weapons from Mitch, and he hoisted himself to where she was standing.

"We better be careful entering the house," Mitch said, slipping a new clip into the AK. Abella nodded and made sure that the M9 was cocked.

In the relatively short period of time since the blast, Mitch's kitchen had been ransacked. He and Abella cautiously moved through the debris and toward the kitchen. Mitch looked to the staircase and saw the dead body of the terrorist that had fallen from the second story.

"Wait here and cover me while I pass the dining and living room to the stairs," Mitch said and stepped from the protection of the kitchen, moving to his left.

The house was dark, only illuminated by the fading fire from the blast. He shouldered the AK-47 and ran in a bent, crouching stance. As he approached the stairs, two terrorists emerged from the living room, firing their weapons. Mitch dove under the staircase and behind a large wooden desk.

Abella saw muzzle flashes and instinctively shot at the nearest terrorist. The man fell lifeless into his companion. As the second terrorist struggled to get back on his feet, Mitch crawled from behind the desk and fired a burst from the AK, dropping him.

Silence returned to Mitch's house as he and Abella waited for others to respond. There was nothing—no movement, no sound from within the walls of the room. Mitch rose from his position and signaled for Abella to join him. She ran to him, and they both ascended the steps to his bedroom. Carefully they searched the rooms on the second floor and found them clear. They entered the bedroom, closing and locking the door.

The fighting outside was still ongoing, but Jake and the remaining Marines were moving toward a small building partially protected by sandbags and camouflaged netting.

"What is that building?" Abella asked as she strained to see through the darkness and smoke.

"That, my dear, is the Marine bar. I'm sure they're not going there to grab a quick beer—at least not yet. We've gotta cover them. Stand back."

Mitch used the butt of the AK-47 to break out the glass of the side window.

"I'm almost certain that some of the bad guys are still in the trees and waiting to get a better shot at Jake and company," Mitch said. "Sweetheart, could you fire a flare over the tree line to help with the illumination of that area?"

Abella responded immediately. The flare streaked just above the trees and exploded, revealing six terrorists maneuvering into a better firing position. Firing his weapon would give away their location like a neon sign, but Mitch had no other course of action. He pulled the trigger and took out two of the terrorists. In the meantime, Jake and the Marines rushed into the bar and took up positions behind the sandbags and blown-out windows.

Mitch and Abella continued to fire from their position until Abella screamed, "Mitch, they've got two RPGs!"

Mitch dropped the AK-47 and leaped on Abella, covering her as the rocket slammed into the side of the house. The explosion blew a gaping hole in the second floor, sending flames raging out of the wreckage.

"We gotta get outta here now!" Mitch shouted. "They're going to fire another rocket at us." He picked up Abella and grabbed their weapons.

Just as they reached the front door of the house, another rocket hit the roof. Huge chunks of the second story collapsed into the first. The blast propelled Mitch and Abella out of the house, leaving them exposed. Crawling behind a pile of bricks and debris, they realized that there was nowhere to escape. Even worse, their ammunition was just about gone. They lay prone on the ground, exhausted and out of ideas.

Mitch took Abella's hand as machine gun fire flew over their heads. They tried to bury themselves in the rubble and wait for the inevitable.

But before they could, men in camouflaged military uniforms appeared beside them, throwing grenades at the extremists. Mitch looked toward a charred embassy vehicle and recognized a tall officer directing the military members coming through the remains of the security building.

"I'll be damned; it's Yves and the French embassy security forces," Mitch yelled over the gunfire. He scanned the area and saw more French military swarming into the compound, lobbing grenades at the terrorists along the tree line.

In the meantime, British and Canadian embassy forces had reinforced Jake and the Marines in the Marine bar and secured the

US ambassador's residence. The terrorists began to flee, and many were cut down by Marines and allied forces as they attempted to scale the embassy walls. Those who were not killed threw down their weapons, raising their hands, and pleaded for their lives. Within thirty minutes the US embassy had been secured and the fires extinguished.

Abella and Mitch stumbled toward Yves through the smoke and darkness of the obscured night sky.

"Yves, your timing is always impeccable. I was out of airspeed and ideas just before you showed up," Mitch said, patting Yves on the back. He stepped aside, and Abella gave Yves a hug.

"We heard explosions and saw the smoke from the French embassy," Yves replied. "Then we received the desperate radio calls from your security staff. As our security forces were getting ready to roll, I grabbed my combat equipment and joined them. We arrived just as the Canadians and Brits were forming their strategy. Abella, are you okay? You seem to have a lot of blood all over your clothing."

"Thanks for asking, but I'm alright for now. Maybe tomorrow I'll have quite a few aches and pains," Abella said.

"Let's go to the Marine bar and see how Jake's doing," Mitch said and pointed in the direction of the sandbags. He noticed men gathering there, smoking cigarettes and cigars.

As the three of them approached, they heard Jake and the Marines discussing their actions during the firefight.

"Colonel!" Jake shouted when he spotted them. "Thank the good lord you and your sweet lady covered us as we fell back to this bar. I'm tellin' ya, I'd be pushin' up daisies if you hadn't taken out those bad hombres! I didn't think you flyboys knew how to handle an AK, but I must admit it was the flare that got our attention and our heads down." Jake smiled, his cigar firmly clenched between his teeth.

"We're just happy to see you standing upright and breathing oxygen," Mitch said. "The way those terrorists were moving to surround your position, I wasn't too sure that you and the Marines could have held out much longer."

They briefly stood in silence, relishing being alive.

Mitch considered the personal repercussions of the night's events. "I believe I'll be putting in a request to the ambassador for new quarters. In fact, I should check on the ambassador to make sure he got through this mess."

"I'm thinkin' that won't be necessary, sir. The ambo is headin' our way right as we speak."

"Thank God you're all safe," the ambassador said, looking them up and down as he approached. "I just saw your house, Colonel. What a disaster! My security staff and I did notice the three bodies inside and one in the backyard. Looks like you were quite busy."

"Sir, I can honestly tell you that we were. Abella contributed just as much, if not more than I, in saving American lives this evening."

"Well, that's not hard to believe, considering her clothes are completely covered in blood. How are you, Abella?" the ambassador asked.

"It looks much worse than it is, sir. But to truly answer your question, I'm really thirsty."

"Well, sports fans and Mr. Ambassador, would ya like to join this country boy in the Marine bar? I'm sure my leatherneck companions will be more than happy to serve us anything they have on the top shelf. If it's not on the house, then put it on my tab," Jake said. He opened the door of the bar and motioned for all to enter.

"Thank you, Jake, but I have a few more locations to check before I'll be able to raise a glass. Have the first round on me, please," the ambassador said, rejoining his security staff and heading toward the embassy clinic to examine the wounded and dead.

Once the group entered the bar, they dusted off the dirt, glass, and debris from the countertop. Jake found an ancient bottle of Old Fitzgerald bourbon that had at least sixty years of aging.

"I reckon this one's been kicking around since World War II," Jake said. "Probably liberated by a GI during his swing through Algiers. Whoever the poor bastard was that intended to drink it in '42 never got the chance. Let me find some glasses and we can put a dent in this bottle of hooch." He looked around behind the bar and came up with four glasses.

"Jake, if you don't mind, I would prefer a bottle of water," Abella said. She rubbed her blood-encrusted left arm.

"Absolutely, my lady, but I might slip ya a shot of bourbon to accompany that bottle of H_2O. That is, if ya don't mind."

Abella laughed. "Not a problem, Jake. Wouldn't want to sour the celebration."

As each took the bourbon and raised their glass, Yves cleared his throat and said, "If there are no dissenters amongst us, perhaps this Frenchman will be so bold as to quote Hemingway." He paused and then continued, "'Today is only one day in all the days that will ever be. But what will happen in all the other days that ever come can depend on what you do today.'"

As they all touched glasses and then tasted the sweet brown water of Kentucky, Jake raised his glass again. "I ain't much of a reader, but I do like Hemingway's 'preciation for alcohol and a good cee-gar. When I think of Papa Hemingway, there's only one quote that comes to my mind: 'Never sit at a table when you can stand at the bar!'"

They all laughed, and it felt good, because it was the first moment of genuine laughter for any of them since the attack.

As each told their particular war story of surviving the evening attack, Mitch reflected on the state of his residence. *Damn, I never thought at this stage of my military career I would be considering a tent to live in. I went into the Air Force because fighter pilots don't march, grovel in the dirt, or live in tents. This situation is like trying to handle a piece of shit by the clean end!*

"Mitch, are you okay? It seems as though you are a thousand miles away," Abella asked, tugging on his tattered shirt and looking worried.

"I'm okay, sweetheart, just thinking about my house and where

I'll be staying."

Before she could reply, they all stopped talking and tilted their heads toward the ceiling. A tremendous beating and thrashing noise had erupted above the Marine bar, followed by dust and dirt flying through the open door and broken windows. Then a Marine ran in.

"Jake, there's a MH-60 chopper circling above. Must be from one of our destroyers in the Med," the Marine screamed above all the noise.

Jake dropped his drink on the bar and followed the Marine outside as Mitch, Abella, and Yves trailed behind. Downward wind vectors from the chopper's rotor blades kicked up dirt and made it extremely difficult to see the helicopter. Jake ran to a rise of land near the bar where a Marine was directing the naval chopper to land.

"That's the embassy helipad," Mitch yelled to Abella and Yves. "It appears that the Sixth Fleet is going to give us a helping hand. Too bad they weren't here a few hours ago. We could have used their firepower!"

As the chopper settled on the landing pad, the door opened, and a half dozen Marines jumped out in full battle gear. The blades slowed but did not stop as the Marine directing the landing hooked in to the helicopter communication system with his headset. After a few moments the Marine turned to Jake and yelled something that Mitch couldn't hear.

"Colonel, the pilot wants to start the extraction of the wounded and dead to get them to the destroyer ASAP," Jake shouted with his hand cupped over his mouth and Mitch's ear.

"I'll contact the clinic and the ambassador," Mitch replied. "We'll need to see what type of transportation is available between here and the clinic." He ran into the bar and found the phone. "Hello, Mr. Ambassador, the Navy chopper is here to extract the wounded and dead. I need to set up transportation between the clinic and the helipad."

"Colonel, the plan is to take all the wounded and dead to the USS *Arleigh Burke* and then on to the US Naval Hospital at Sigonella Naval Air Station in Sicily," the ambassador replied. "I'm still at the clinic and we're arranging the transportation. Most of our vehicles were taken out during the attack, but we still have a flatbed truck and three SUVs. They should be ready to go in a few minutes."

"That sounds good, sir. We'll be standing by for the vehicles' arrival here at our end. The chopper can most likely take anywhere from four to six individuals per trip, but that depends on whether they're on stretchers or in body bags." Mitch spoke bluntly.

"Keep me posted on how things are going. And, Colonel, one more thing: I'm extremely grateful for what you did this evening." With that, the ambassador hung up.

Mitch ran outside and informed Jake and the Marines. By the time all the wounded and dead had been evacuated from the embassy, it was 4 a.m. Mitch and Abella had been pounding the Marines' coffee all night while helping the chopper crew and embassy staff with the removal of the wounded and dead. They both felt nauseous from hunger and completely drained of energy. They knew that they were extremely fortunate to have evaded injury and death, but now they felt alone as all the other members, including Yves, departed. There were floodlights and construction workers putting up a temporary wall where the security building had once stood, but that work didn't involve Mitch.

As they sat on stools at the Marine bar, too tired to think, a phone on the wall near one of the shattered windows rang. Abella had laid her head down on the bar and was trying to ignore the noise. Mitch didn't want to answer the phone, but the ringing was too much for his frayed nerves, and he hobbled over and grabbed it.

"Colonel Ross speaking," Mitch answered.

"Colonel, I must apologize because I completely forgot to tell you earlier. There's a small bungalow adjacent to my residence that will be your temporary quarters, if you don't mind. It has a bedroom, living room, small kitchen, and a shower. Nothing compared with what you had before, but at least it's a roof over your head and a place to sleep." The caller paused, and Mitch struggled to comprehend what was being said.

"Who the hell is this?" he responded without thinking.

"This is the ambassador, Mitch. Sorry for the lack of proper introductions, but today has been a day I wish never occurred. We lost a lot of good Americans. I'm being recalled to DC in a few days to testify to a congressional committee on what happened and what went wrong. I suppose we should have fortified and secured the embassy to a greater extent, but who the hell is fortunate enough to have a crystal ball?"

"Mr. Ambassador, I apologize for being so rude," Mitch replied. "Sir, the quarters sound great, and I truly appreciate what you have done. If I can help you in preparing for the congressional inquiry, please don't hesitate. I'll be writing my report for the DIA and I'll make sure you have a copy before your departure to Washington."

"Thank you. I'll need your input. The bungalow door isn't locked, and the key should be in an envelope on the kitchen table. Sleep well, and I don't expect to see you in the chancery building or anyplace tomorrow. Just kick back and relax, as much as that's possible. We all went through hell today." The ambassador hung up, and Mitch stood staring at the shattered window.

"Is the ambassador okay?" Abella asked, her face on the counter angling toward Mitch.

"He's as good as he can be, considering the circumstances," Mitch said. "I have a small bungalow to stay in here at the embassy, near the ambassador's residence. It's not that bad, just small—usually used for State Department folks visiting for a week or longer. Let's go, sweetheart."

Mitch grabbed a bottle of wine from behind the bar as they left. The reddish glow of sunrise was just appearing along the horizon of the sea. The rose garden was now just upturned dirt and bare, thorny stems awkwardly sticking out of the earth. Mitch felt a pang of remorse as he carefully guided Abella through what now appeared as Satan's shrubbery.

The bungalow was nestled among bushes and palm trees and smelled of humid air locked behind the closed door and windows for weeks. The house was small, but it suited Mitch's needs.

Abella went to the kitchen and noticed that the refrigerator had been stocked with food. Finding old coffee in a container on the counter, she brewed a pot. The ambassador's cook had placed a slightly overbaked apple pie in the fridge for them, and Abella pulled it out and cut two slices. The quality of the coffee and the charred edges of the pie made no difference to them; it was a good distraction from the evening's events. Once they had finished their last cup of joe and second piece of pie, they peeled off their clothes and climbed into the double bed that filled the tiny bedroom. They shared the warmth of their grimy, naked bodies and then drifted off to a place much better than reality.

16

As the sun rose in the midday sky, Mitch's mind furiously relived the events of the previous evening. The images awakened him from his deep sleep, and there was no returning to the slumber that he so desperately needed. He quietly slipped out of bed, making sure that he didn't disturb Abella, and took a quick shower, scraping the filth of the attack from his body. He donned a robe hanging behind the door. Enjoying the coolness of the tiled floor under his bare feet, he went to the kitchen and reheated last night's old coffee, then grabbed a cup from the cupboard and sat at the small dining table.

Using the embassy stationary and a pen left in the living room, he jotted down the events of the attack. His blood pressure and stress level rose as the words formed on the paper. The bitter coffee began to burn within his stomach, and he felt nauseated. Putting down the pen, he looked in the refrigerator for something to eat other than apple pie.

Abella peeked into the kitchen. "Hey, you, how long have you been up?"

"Not long. I took a shower and now I'm just looking for something to eat that'll help soak up the rancid coffee from last night," Mitch said, noticing the dried blood on Abella's body as she moved, exposing her nakedness.

"Okay, I'll make you a deal. I'll take a shower and you make a fresh pot of coffee. Once it's done, please bring a cup into the bedroom for me. Also, I get the robe," she said with a mischievous smile and a wink.

"I follow the coffee request, but if I give you the robe, what'll I wear?" Mitch asked.

"I never said that I would wear the robe, did I? I just don't want you to have it on," she said as she entered the shower.

"Oh, the clue bird just landed," Mitch responded, getting a move on to brew a fresh pot.

When Abella finished her shower, Mitch brought two cups of coffee into the bedroom and draped the robe over his shoulder. She smiled as she lay on the bed, raising her arms toward him. Mitch put the cups down on a small dresser. He gently covered Abella with his body, kissing her with all the loving passion that dwelled within his heart. Instinctively her legs wrapped around him, their souls touching as the rhythm of their bodies merged.

— • — •

With the approval of the ambassador and help of a few embassy staff, Mitch returned to his destroyed residence and was able to recover most of his clothes and other artifacts from his bedroom. When he arrived back at the bungalow, he and Abella piled all the items in the living room.

"Mitch, can I sort through your clothes and find something to wear other than this robe?" she asked.

"Not a problem, sweetheart. Although I rather enjoy seeing you wearing that short robe. It's quite entertaining when you bend over." Mitch laughed as he took a bottle of water from the refrigerator and poured two glasses. Abella rolled her eyes and shook her head.

— • — •

Abella eventually departed the embassy wearing a pair of Mitch's khaki shorts, a red polo shirt, and his sandals. Although the ensemble was a little large, it looked rather fashionable on her athletic body. The taxi arrived, and she kissed Mitch before stepping through the embassy gate and entering the cab. She had an hour to report to the hospital for the second shift, and she hoped that no one would notice the small cuts on her forehead, arms, and legs. A few of them were still tender to the touch, but the hospital would have medication for her use.

It seemed as though weeks had passed since Abella had last set foot in her flat. As she opened the door, she noticed a large note taped to a picture on the wall. It was from her roommate, Samia:

Oh my God, the television is inundated with news of the attack at the US embassy. I hope and pray that you are okay and that none of your friends were injured or killed. How is Mitch? The pictures of the attack were terrible and gruesome. Were you near any of it? Oh my God, it's tragic with all those Americans killed and many of the embassy buildings destroyed! I'll keep an eye out for you at the hospital. Meet me in the cafeteria when you arrive. I need to make sure you're okay.

Samia.

Abella changed into her nursing scrubs, combed her hair, changed her shoes, and left the apartment as quickly as she had entered. She hailed a cab and within twenty minutes arrived at the massive army hospital on a large hill within a mile of the Bay of Algiers. She checked into the nurses' station to determine what ward she would be working and then immediately went to the cafeteria. Samira was waiting just inside, sipping a cup of tea. She rose and ran to Abella, hugging her and then examining her face and arms.

"Oh my God, you were in the middle of it all, weren't you?" Samia exclaimed.

"Unfortunately, yes," Abella said, nodding. "The battle was terrible and a complete surprise. I thought at any moment we would be killed. It will take many months, if not years, for the US embassy to be rebuilt."

"Look at these scrapes and bruises!" Samia said, pointing at Abella. "We need to take care of those right now!" She grabbed Abella's hand and led her to the nearest nurses' station. There she began administering disinfectant and flooding Abella with questions: "Was the ambassador's residence hit or destroyed? What is the status of the chancery building, and is it still operational? Were there a lot of US Marines killed in the fighting? How did the other embassy security forces arrive so quickly, and what embassies did they come from?"

"Samia, I appreciate your concern, but actually you ask odd questions," Abella said, becoming slightly annoyed. "There were many loyal Algerians killed while defending the Americans. Also, for every embassy employee wounded or killed, there were at least five terrorists who lost their lives. That means there are quite a few terrorists that will never have the opportunity to kill innocent people ever again. That is the important aspect!"

"I'm sorry, but I have so many questions flying through my mind. I know I should be more empathetic, but the pictures were dreadful. The bodies, burning buildings, gunfire, it was unnerving. I can't imagine what it must have been like being in the middle of all of that."

"It was the most horrendous experience," Abella said matter-of-factly. "What I saw was as shocking as witnessing my father's killing. The terrorists screamed 'Allahu Akbar' as they entered the embassy, but I wondered where God was during all the killing and destruction. It was a living hell on earth!"

Samia realized that she had touched a nerve. "We can talk later," she said. "It's time to get to our wards and attend to our patients."

– • – •

After cleaning up the bungalow, Mitch got back to work on his after-action report to the DIA. But thoughts of items destroyed in his former residence entered his mind. He felt remorse for those pieces that were irreplaceable. His wandering mind was brought back to reality by a knock at the door. He rose and opened it to find Djamila carrying a huge basket of food and wine. She set down the basket and hugged Mitch with heartfelt passion that he had never seen before. She sobbed and kept repeating, "*Oh, mon Dieu! Oh, mon Dieu! Dieu merci tu es vivant!*"

"Yes, we should all thank God that we are alive," Mitch said as he stroked the back of her head.

Regaining her composure, she stepped back and picked up the basket. Speaking French, she said, "Last night I was watching television when the newsbreak occurred. The cameras showed the terrorist attack on the US embassy. I was shocked and screamed out loud when the camera showed the destruction of your house. The Algerian newsman reported that there had been bodies found in the rubble of your residence. I prayed all night that you and Abella were safe. I tried to call the embassy, but all the lines were dead. The embassy security would not allow me to enter the compound, so I have been waiting for hours. Then they selectively allowed a few of us to come inside. Your friend Mr. Jake saw me waiting, and he was the one who allowed me to enter. God bless him!"

"Yes, he's a good man! Please, Djamila, sit in the living room. It's much more relaxing."

"Colonel Mitch, before I ask about what happened here at the embassy, am I to continue working for you?"

"Why of course! Please continue to work for me," Mitch said. "I must apologize for the small kitchen, but I believe it has all the equipment you need. We will have to make do with what we have here."

"I understand. That fills my heart with joy, Colonel Mitch. My father will be so happy to hear that you are safe. But Abella—is she okay?

"Oh yes, actually she spent last night here, and she is currently back at the army hospital, working."

"*Hamdu Lillah.*" Djamila praised Allah for Abella's survival.

"Djamila, let me make us tea," Mitch said, standing and moving to the kitchen.

"No, Colonel Mitch, that's my job. I would like to see all that this little kitchen has for me to use."

Mitch laughed and bowed with a grandiose swinging motion of his arm toward the adjacent kitchen. "It is your new kitchen kingdom, my chef extraordinaire," he said.

Djamila looked in the cabinets and found the tea pot. She pulled fresh tea from her basket and began to brew traditional North African green mint tea. The fresh aroma quickly filled the bungalow. As the tea brewed, she took a small pound cake from the basket and sliced it into delicate portions. Then she put the cake on a plate and decorated it with fresh mint leaves.

Once the tea was ready and served, Mitch exclaimed, "Djamila, you can take such a commonplace item and turn it into Disney World!"

"Colonel Mitch, I don't understand what you said. Disney World?"

"I meant you can take something simple and turn it into something magnificent!"

Djamila smiled at him. "Thank you, that is so kind of you to say."

"You mentioned that you saw the news coverage of the attack on television. Were you at your father's home in the Casbah?" Mitch asked.

"Yes, I was staying with my father and warming the dinner that you had given me to take to him."

"Did you notice any activity outside once the news report concluded?"

"I am embarrassed to say, Colonel Mitch, but there was dancing and yelling throughout portions of the Casbah."

"Do you mean there were celebrations?"

"Yes, as if a great victory had occurred."

"I'm curious—did you happen to notice if the young man wearing the Bedouin robes participated in the celebrations?"

"I did not directly observe because I was too emotional, but my father went outside to witness all the activity. He noticed the men that usually accompany the young man with blue eyes, but the young man was not outside. His companions were shooting their guns in the air to celebrate. My father came back inside quickly because he said that they were all crazy."

"I'm sorry to hear about the celebrations, but it's not surprising," Mitch said.

"You must understand that it was not the old ones celebrating, only younger men," Djamila said. "They have no clue what is right or wrong. My father calls them pigs."

"Let's change the subject," Mitch said. "I want us to enjoy the tea and cake. Thank you for bringing the basket of food. Let's talk about serious topics, like how do you want the kitchen decorated?" They laughed and she proceeded to tell him her thoughts on how to make the bungalow a real home.

Later, after Djamila had left the embassy for the evening, Mitch resumed work on his after-action report. With the increase in GSPC terrorists within Algiers, the attack wasn't surprising. But it was quite bold of the extremists to launch an assault of that magnitude. Perhaps the terrorists had been hoping for a complete takeover as was accomplished in Tehran, Iran, in November of 1979. Whatever the GSPC plan had been, it had failed as far as Mitch was concerned. Still, the celebrations in the Casbah troubled him. *It's the youth that stay up late and will be hanging out in the Casbah when any attempt is made to take Captain Hunt,* he thought. Mitch had hoped to minimize the amount of backup firepower required.

He wondered about Hunt's mental stability. After all, the man had been captive for close to eleven years. Mitch could not even imagine what it was like to be away from the United States for over a decade. He considered what Hunt must be going through. *One's way of life would completely change,* he thought. *Over time, all thought processes would alter as the culture and the language influence everyday life. One's mental language would no longer be in English. An individual would begin to take on the mindset of their captors.* Hunt might have developed a psychological alliance with his captors as a survival strategy during captivity—or a classic version of Stockholm syndrome like Patty Hearst while she was a prisoner of the Symbionese Liberation Army in the mid-1970s.

Of course, unlike Hearst, Seth Hunt was trained to resist by the military, physically and mentally. Many prisoners during the Vietnam War withstood years of physical and mental torture and assimilated back into society once they returned. *I wonder if he's that strong mentally. From what Djamila has said, Hunt doesn't appear to be physically damaged, but what of his mental state?* Considering his staring at Djamila, Hunt at least knew an attractive woman when he saw one. And his lifestyle didn't sound overly stressful, if Mitch was to believe Hamady. In fact, Hunt appeared to have it pretty good as a captive if he was allowed to play instruments, read the Koran, eat what he wanted, wear what he wanted, and go to the daily call to prayer. *Or is he playing the game just to survive day-to-day as a prisoner of war?*

Mitch put the final touches on his report and departed for the chancery to type it up. When he finished, he tracked down the ambassador.

"Mr. Ambassador, sorry to bother you," Mitch said, poking his head into the ambassador's office. "I wanted to get my report to you prior to your departure."

"Thanks, Colonel. You were closer to the explosion than the other Americans that have given me their inputs. How are you and Abella doing now that all the dust has settled, so to speak?"

"We're getting back to normal as best we can. Abella has returned to work, as have I . . . but there are those nagging thoughts that persist. You know: 'What if Abella had arrived late to the security entry building?' or 'What if we had taken a walk during the evening before dinner?' The what-ifs drive me nuts. I guess I should just be thankful that we're all still alive."

"Yes, Colonel, that's the bottom line—we're all still alive. There's no rewriting what occurred yesterday. It is what it is."

"Sir, on that note, I had an interesting conversation with my cook a few hours ago. During the night of the attack, she was preparing dinner for her father at his home in the Casbah. She informed me that shortly after our embassy was hit, many young Algerians were dancing and celebrating there. Some had weapons and were shooting in the air. I suppose that shouldn't be a surprise, but if Captain Seth Hunt is held captive in that environment, then it will compound the problem of extracting him."

"It doesn't surprise me that terrorist elements of the GSPC inhabit that location," the ambassador said. "It has a history of harboring fanatics, dating back to the Barbary Coast pirates. Thomas Jefferson had that same problem to resolve, and it cost many American lives, plus the US warship *Philadelphia*."

"Clearly, any operation within the Casbah will be difficult. I can't guarantee that it will be free of casualties," Mitch warned.

"Colonel, I can't afford any more American deaths in Algeria. I'm walking a political tightrope now, and if there is even a hint of future US casualties, my career as a professional diplomat is over. Be exceedingly careful with any extraction plans for Captain Hunt. I'm sure that while I'm testifying in DC this week, President Bush will want to talk to me about Hunt, among other things. I'm facing a huge dilemma that I see as a lose-lose. If we do nothing now to gain Captain Hunt's freedom, I will most likely be replaced as the ambassador. Which means my career is over. But if there is an attempt to get Hunt and it fails with American lives lost, I'm fired and my career ends. This is one helluva way to end a great career."

The ambassador shook his head with a look of despair.

"Sir, as far as I'm concerned, you've made unbelievable progress in nation-building between the US and Algeria. I would have no qualms testifying on your behalf. I only regret that I don't carry as much weight as a colonel as I would if I were a general officer."

"Thank you for those kind words, Colonel," the ambassador said. "I'm not so certain any military rank could help me now. My career is in the hands of that congressional committee. What matters is their thoughts about the attack. Perhaps I should have fortified the embassy much earlier with more firepower. But then I would have been chastised by the State Department for making this embassy a military fortress and not a bastion of democracy and diplomacy.

"Well, Colonel, I've cried enough on your shoulder. I'm sure you have better things to do than to console a has-been diplomat. If I don't see you again prior to my departure, may your career continue on a high note." The ambassador reached out, patting Mitch on the shoulder and shaking his hand.

On the way out of the chancery building, Mitch stopped at the embassy café for a coffee and then walked to a secluded location with a view of the sandy, deserted shoreline and the Mediterranean Sea. He sat on a large rock and thought about his conversation with the ambassador. *It's a shame that careers can be lost or saved by actions of others who have no real vested interest in the final outcome. The ambassador did as much as he possibly could have to maintain a functioning embassy, not a fortress.* Those in Washington didn't really understand the situation in this bizarre, terrorist-ridden, anti-American environment. Yet they would decide the fate of a man who had devoted his entire life to the service of his country. Mitch finished his coffee and wandered over to his former residence to see if anything else might have survived the attack.

17

As Mitch sifted through the charred remains of his living room, he found a partially burned book of short stories by Jack London. His father, dead at least a decade, had given it to him years before he passed.

Mitch opened the book and read his father's inscription:

Son, always remember that in life you will encounter many ups and downs. So have faith—always have faith. For it is faith that will get you through the despair. Faith is not about everything turning out okay; faith is about being okay no matter how things turn out.

Love Dad

Mitch pondered this prophetic statement. He wondered why this book was the only one to have survived the fire. As a fighter pilot, he was superstitious by nature; there must be a reason why his father's words had endured and revealed themselves at this moment.

"Holy shit, Colonel! All those rumors at DIA headquarters in DC weren't bullcrap. Your house is a pile of shit, with all due respect sir," Warrant Officer Dave McQueen said. He stood just outside the rubble, holding his suitcase.

"So, Dave, you finally decided to come back and work," Mitch responded sarcastically. "See all the fun you've missed?"

Dave dropped his suitcase and climbed over piles of burned furniture to get a better view of the collapsed second story and demolished kitchen.

"It was reported back in the States that you were in quite a firefight. That you personally took out a number of the GSPC terrorists while protecting State Department agents."

"That part is correct, but those State Department agents and Marines were fighting for their lives and did one helluva good job."

"Sir, I regret that I wasn't here to give you guys a hand. It would have taken me back to a time in my military career when I loved what I did."

"What the hell are you talking about, Dave? As far as I know, you've been a shoe clerk your entire career. The most action shoe clerks see in the military are pencil pokes and paper cuts," Mitch said with little sympathy, knowing Dave's objective each day was to escape work.

"Well, sir, unfortunately you only know this Dave McQueen," Dave said as he attempted to step over portions of the collapsed formal dining table. He didn't successfully clear it, and as he dislodged the table, part of the bedframe from the collapsed second story slammed into his left leg. He fell but caught himself to prevent further bodily damage.

"Damn, Dave, are you okay? Is your leg broken?" Mitch yelled. He quickly moved to Dave's side to help him.

"Sir, I'm okay. Just a little embarrassed by my clumsiness," Dave responded, struggling to get up even with Mitch's assistance.

Mitch was astonished that Dave was now standing and brushing ash marks from his trousers. Anyone else would have been hobbling around in pain or waiting for a stretcher. As Dave brushed his hand against the stains on his slacks, Mitch noticed the metal bar attached to his shoe.

"Dave, do you not have a left leg? Are you wearing a prosthesis?" Mitch was stunned.

"Sir, it's five o'clock somewhere. I was wondering if I could buy the first round at the Marine bar. I believe we have a lot to talk about." Dave climbed out of the rubble and grabbed his suitcase.

Mitch looked at his watch. "You know, Dave, I believe you're correct, but I'll take care of the tab."

As they approached the Marine bar, Dave gawked at the bullet holes, broken windows, and general damage to the building.

"Damn, I hope they're still open for business," Dave said. "It appears that nothing escaped the battle."

Inside they found a few off-duty Marines cleaning up debris and the gunny sergeant pulling a couple bottles of beer in anticipation of Mitch and Dave's order.

"Gunny, thanks for the beer, but I believe that we'll be having bourbon straight up," Mitch said. "Don't worry about pouring it. Just give me two glasses and the entire bottle of Jim Beam Black, please."

The gunny didn't hesitate. He pulled the bottle from the shelf and grabbed two glasses.

"Just put it on my tab and add a twenty-dollar tip," Mitch said with a nod. He took the bottle and glasses, then sat with Dave at an undamaged table. Breaking the seal, he poured a healthy portion into each of their glasses.

"Dave, I've known you for a few years, and I thought I knew everything about you. Obviously, I'm mistaken." Mitch raised his glass, toasting Dave. "Now, if you think you're here to listen to me talk about the attack on the embassy, you're mistaken. I want to know everything about your previous military career. It's my dime and your dance floor. Start talkin', and that's an order."

Dave nodded and took a deep breath. "Sir, let me begin by apologizing for not being the best supporting administrator. It's not in my blood, but it was the only way I could stay in the Army." He paused and took a long drink of bourbon. "I won't start at the very beginning because it would take too long. I know that you were in Desert Storm and flew many combat missions. I also was in combat during Storm, but my combat was very different. I was in the 75th Ranger Regiment, 1st Ranger Battalion, conducting raids, and a member of a quick reaction force working with allied forces.

"I returned to the Mideast in December of '91, deploying to Kuwait in a show of force called Operation Iris Gold. My unit performed an airborne assault onto Ali Al Salem airfield, near Kuwait City. We then marched over thirty miles through desert minefields left from the ground campaign of Desert Storm. That was while I still had both legs. I was transferred to the 3rd Ranger Battalion in January of '93 and deployed to Somalia to assist UN forces attempting to bring order to that shit-stained nation.

"In early October of '93, my Ranger unit conducted a daylight raid that became known as the Battle of Mogadishu—or as we call it, the Day of the Rangers. Our mission was to travel from our compound to the center of Mogadishu with the aim of capturing the leaders of the Habr Gidr clan, led by Mohamed Farrah Aidid. Our assault force consisted primarily of Black Hawk choppers, vehicles, and approximately one hundred sixty men. The plan was to take care of business and be out of there within one hour. But shortly after the assault began, the Somali militia and armed civilian fighters shot down two Black Hawks. That completely changed the complexion of the mission.

"Our new objective was to secure and recover the crews of both choppers. This became an overnight standoff and daylight rescue operation on October 4. I was at the first Black Hawk crash and remained near the crash area during the initial evacuation. My buddies and I became isolated on October 3, and the urban fighting continued throughout the night.

"During the early morning of October 4, a task force was sent to rescue us. Thank God they arrived when they did because we were trapped and slowly being killed off. I was one of the fortunate survivors—getting out of there with only my left leg blown off below the knee by an RPG. My buddy saw me fall and wrapped his belt around my thigh as a tourniquet. I would have bled out within moments had he not done that. As he finished saving my life, he turned to pick up his weapon and a bullet pierced his skull. He died instantly."

Dave's voice quivered, and he stopped talking. He grabbed his glass and drained the contents. Mitch poured more Kentucky spirit into Dave's glass.

"Thank you," Dave said and then began where he had left off. "It's estimated that we killed approximately six hundred Somalis and lost eighteen Americans plus two Black Hawk choppers. I was medevac'd out of country and ended up at Landstuhl Regional Medical Center in Germany. After months at Landstuhl, I was transferred to Walter Reed Army Medical Center in DC for extensive physical and mental therapy. I continued my recovery for at least six more months. I was told that I would be discharged from the Army once I was released from Walter Reed.

"The Army was the only life I knew, and being a Ranger was everything to me. Now my world was collapsing around me. I wrote to my congressmen and contacted anyone I thought could help me out. I pleaded with them that I could still contribute to the Army and be a viable soldier. It motivated me to excel in my physical therapy and learn to not only walk but run with specially made prosthetics. Several influential folks supported my cause: one former US president and two state governors, one of whom lost a leg and received the Medal of Honor during action in Vietnam. This support changed the minds of the decision makers in the Army, and I was allowed to stay on active duty. The downside was that I would no longer be in the operational combat units but had to take a support role. That's how I ended up as administrative support working for you, sir, at this embassy."

Dave paused and stared at his bourbon. He was lost in the past until a shard of glass fell from one of the damaged windows and broke on the bar floor. Dave grabbed his glass, pressed it against his lips, and drank until it was empty.

Mitch sat speechless and stunned. Never in his wildest thoughts had he perceived Dave as a combat-hardened veteran, but now he realized why Dave had those scars on his face, head, and neck. His combat experiences in the first Gulf War and the Battle of Mogadishu had left their marks.

As Mitch struggled for words, a thought finally surfaced. "How were you rewarded for your gallantry in combat other than getting to stay on active duty?" he asked.

"Well, sir, I didn't get the vice president as you did. But the secretary of the Army was present during my ceremony, and I was awarded the Bronze Star with Valor and a Purple Heart."

"You should be exceedingly proud of your combat service to your country," Mitch said. "So few Americans enter the military. Less than one percent of the population serves, and of those, only a fragment see combat. Dave, why don't you wear your Ranger badge or your decorations on your uniform?"

"Sir, it brings up too many questions, too much sadness, and then I eventually have to mention my leg. For the short time I have left in the Army before I retire, I would prefer that those here at the embassy are kept in the dark concerning my military background."

"Are you telling me that no one here at the embassy, except for me, knows about your leg?"

"As far as I know, that's correct, sir."

Mitch's thoughts quickly went to his extraction plans for Captain Hunt. *Damn*, he thought, *with all of Dave's Ranger experience in combat, he would be a tremendous asset on a mission into the Casbah!*

"So, I take it that you don't want me to mention anything about our conversation to anyone?" Mitch asked.

"Sir, if you don't mind, can we just keep it between the two of us?"

"Okay, Dave, but I believe there is a deal to be made. In other words, a quid pro quo."

"What are you talking about, sir?"

"I won't mention anything concerning this conversation. But you must promise not to mention anything about what I'm about to tell you."

"I'm not sure I completely follow, but I promise to keep all of our conversations as if they were classified top secret."

"Well, let me just dangle this carrot out in front of your nose, Warrant Officer McQueen. Would you like to see action one more time before you hang up your spurs for good?"

"Sir, if you could make that happen, I'd be the happiest warrant officer in the US Army!"

"Be careful what you wish for, Dave; you might just get it! Okay, then let me fill our glasses. I want you to sit back and listen closely. You'll ask no questions until I'm done. I'm going to start from square one and end with you and me sitting here in the bar. Once I'm done explaining to you, there is no backing out! Do you understand?"

"I understand completely, sir. I'm totally in receive mode."

"Good, so let me begin at the point when I first returned to the embassy after being released from the Algerian army hospital."

Mitch spent the next two and a half hours explaining every detail involving Captain Hunt and his suspected whereabouts. He also described the roles of Yves, Abella, Djamila, and Jake. By the time Mitch was done, he had witnessed a complete metamorphosis of Dave's character. The warrant officer was no longer that administrative pansy Mitch had known. Now Dave had a real mission to accomplish, and he was going to be ready for it.

"Sir, thank you for this opportunity to once again be the soldier I was. I thought that was lost forever. You've now given me a reason and a purpose to get up each morning. I believe it's time for me to accompany the Marines during their weekly target practice. They've teased me for years about being in the Army and only turning paper. Well, it's time for me to take up their offer. I'll have to fight my own demons when I first get back to pulling the trigger, but I held an expert rating on four different weapons in my Ranger life, so I'm sure I can regain some of my skills, even with this peg leg."

Dave raised his glass to toast, and Mitch mirrored his actions.

"Sir, to you, to the mission, and to my rebirth! Hear! Hear!" Dave said and then finished the last of his bourbon, as did Mitch.

"Dave, I'm going to my new residence—the little bungalow near the ambassador's home. I've got a harebrained idea to throw a small—very small—reception there. The house is about the size of a postage stamp, so it'll be tight, but you need to be introduced to the major players who have and will contribute to the rescue of Captain Hunt. The easiest approach is to have them all at my place. There is one major caveat: these folks need to know about your Ranger background. Believe me, they will greatly appreciate your combat experience and knowledge. This is not a violation of our promise to not tell anyone about your background. These folks can be trusted to tell no one. So, why don't you step on over to the bar and arrange with the gunny that trip to the firing range. If there's any pushback, just let me know, but I'm sure there won't be any problems. The gunny is a good man."

Mitch stood, and for the very first time in all the years he had known Dave, he reached out and shook his hand.

Dave stood and said, "Thanks, sir. You have no idea how much this handshake means to me."

- • - •

Mitch entered the bungalow just as Djamila was rearranging the contents of the kitchen cabinets. The aroma of baked bread and roast beef immediately made him ravenous. Mitch attempted to find the right French words to describe both what he smelled and how impressively she was decorating the kitchen.

"Oh, Djamila, the food smells great. Thanks for putting your magical touch to the kitchen. Too bad your pictures and personal effects didn't survive the destruction of the other house. But I'm sure in time you'll have this kitchen looking like something out of *Better Homes & Gardens* magazine."

"Colonel Mitch, I'm glad you're here. I was going to ask if it would be alright if I went to your destroyed residence and looked through the remains. I had put your formal crystal glasses, silverware, and china dishes in strong wooden containers that kept them separate from your daily-use items. Perhaps some of them survived."

"We can go together, but only after I've told you about my plan to host a reception here at the bungalow."

"A reception in this tiny house? How many people were you planning on inviting? Colonel Mitch, I don't want to sound rude, but the limited size means some of the guests will be standing in the kitchen as I prepare the food," Djamila said with a tone of distress.

Mitch laughed. "I appreciate your concern. You're completely correct, of course. Yes, without a doubt there will be guests looking over your shoulder as you put the final touches on the hors d'oeuvres. But please don't worry; you know them all. I'm sure Abella and Yves will help you in preparing the appetizers. The folks attending the reception are Abella, Jake Davis, Colonel Yves Dureau, Warrant Officer Dave McQueen, and you. I'll leave it up to you concerning the hors d'oeuvres that'll be served. I'll work with the Marine bar and buy some wine and booze.

"I believe I'll contact the folks this evening to see if Saturday would be good for them. Normally I would send out written invitations well ahead of the event, but with these friends, a phone call will do. So, Djamila, you are the first person I will ask. Would you like to attend a reception at my bungalow on Saturday? Unfortunately, you'll be working part of the time, but I do want you to socialize with everyone."

"Not a problem, Colonel Mitch. Can we go to your old residence now, before it gets too dark?"

"Sure, let's go."

They left the bungalow and walked through the remnants of the rose garden. Mitch noticed that the work had been completed on the temporary wall where the security building once stood. As they approached the burned ruins of Mitch's former residence, he noticed

Jake and a few security guards looking at the embassy wall behind the destroyed house.

"Colonel, what brings you back to your old stompin' grounds?" Jake asked. "There ain't much to see 'cept for a bunch of burned-up furniture, crushed kitchen appliances, two outer walls missing, and a second story that decided to partially collapse onto the first floor. But other than that, the house is in good shape." Jake laughed as he relit his cigar.

"Hey, this is actually perfect timing. I would like you to come over to my bungalow on Saturday for a reception, and I won't take no for an answer. My new residence isn't much larger than a walk-in closet, but Djamila has assured me that she can work it all out." Mitch quickly looked at Djamila, knowing that she couldn't understand the full conversation in English. But she recognized her name and gave Mitch an inquisitive look.

"Colonel, I don't usually get to go to those types of shindigs unless I'm working to protect a diplomat or two. I would love to attend as long as I can partake in some of Djamila's famous appetizers and sip a little of that bourbon you owe me."

"Great, so why don't you drop by around 7 p.m. on Saturday? By the way, the dress is extreme casual. So, those blue jeans and cowboy boots that you're wearing will be just fine."

"Okay, Colonel, I'll be wearin' these duds and my specially autographed Willie Nelson Western shirt. That should impress the ladies attendin."

"Well, Jake, only two ladies will be attending, and one will be working most of the time. Abella and Djamila will be wedged into the house along with you, me, Warrant McQueen, and Colonel Dureau."

"That's an interestin' group of folks. Kind of transitions my curiosity antenna into the full receive mode. If I consider the attendees, three of 'em went on an interesting trip to the Roman ruins not long ago. I also heard that you and Dave McQueen spent a lot a time talkin' and drinkin' in the Marine bar earlier today. Hmm,

I might be just a good ol' dumb country boy, but I smell somethin', and it might mean that I should visit the firin' range." Jake took a long drag of his cigar.

"You might be a country boy, Jake, but you're definitely not dumb!" Mitch said as he patted Jake's shoulder and then helped Djamila step into the rubble of his former house.

"Be careful as you approach the kitchen area," Mitch said. "I don't trust that second floor. It might entirely collapse at any time."

"I'll keep an eye on it. I think I see one of the wooden boxes, and it appears undamaged."

Djamila carefully stepped over the crushed microwave and examined the contents of the wooden box. The crystal glasses were still intact.

"This is a good sign. I was worried that we would have to serve the drinks in old military coffee mugs and paper cups," Mitch said as he blew dust off one of the crystal wineglasses.

By the time Mitch carried the wooden container out of the ruins, Djamila had found another that was partially crushed. The china within was completely destroyed, and she shook her head in disappointment. "*Maashallah.*"

Jake was still standing near the house and overheard Djamila's Arabic comment. "Yes, the Lord does work in mysterious ways sometimes," he said. "It's difficult to understand, but the man upstairs has a reason to do what he does."

"You've got that right, Jake!" Mitch responded.

18

The next morning, Mitch was up early. After his coffee he headed to the office. It was a much shorter route now that he lived adjacent to the ambassador's residence and could take a shortcut near the ambassador's private pool. As he passed the pool, Mitch shook his head. It was a shame the pool was so infrequently used, with the weather being perfect for swimming year-round. He wondered how the ambassador was doing with the congressional committee in DC.

When Mitch entered the chancery building, the Marine at the security desk informed him that Warrant Officer McQueen was already in the office. Mitch went down the stairs and entered to find Dave waiting near Mitch's cavernous work space with two cups of coffee and wearing a freshly pressed uniform.

"Good morning, sir. Thought you might like a cup of good old Ranger mud, considering we have a lot of planning to do."

Mitch was impressed. A flame burned within Dave that he had never seen before. "Damn, I should have discovered that prosthetic leg of yours years ago. Good mornin', Dave. Yes, we do have a lot of work to do. First thing is that you need to brush the cobwebs off your map reading and analysis. Then we need to find a large blank wall in the office to put up this chart of the Casbah." He pointed out the rolled-up chart leaning against the bookshelf. "I need your expertise to evaluate the distances on the map, strategic locations, entry and exit routes, potential positions for our vehicle, placement of personnel, timetable, and weapons to use."

"Sir, now you're talkin' my language. Hooah!"

Dave took the map from its container and cleared plaques from a large wall adjacent to his office. He grabbed some thumbtacks and put the chart up. The map faced the whiteboard on the opposite wall running along the hall between his office and Mitch's. Dave noticed a circle around the southern entry into the Casbah, yellow highlighted markings over small buildings, a cross pinpointing what appeared to be a mosque, and latitude and longitude points identifying a geographic position just north of the cross.

"Sir, are those the lat-longs that Hamady gave you at the Roman ruins?" he asked.

"Yes, but I wouldn't categorize it as being given to me. The lat-long paper was shoved into my ear," Mitch replied.

"Okay, so that's the geo location where Captain Hunt should be. All our planning must center on that point, sir. Looking at the map, what you told me in the Marine bar makes a lot more sense. The timing is critical and should occur after Hunt's return from the evening call to prayer. Once he's in his quarters, the guards should be in their max-relax mode, getting ready to hit the rack after a little grub. The neighborhood should be quiet—not too many folks outside watching as we move in from the jewelry store. Sir, if I'm stepping over protocol boundaries by taking lead on the planning, please let me know."

"Dave, my combat experiences occurred anywhere from five thousand to fifteen thousand feet in the air. Believe me, I'm all ears. If you get off base, I'll be waving the bullshit flag, but so far, you're right on point. Keep going, Ranger!"

Dave smiled and continued, "Colonel, as I was saying, our position will be at the jewelry shop north of Captain Hunt's location. Abella will be with Djamila at her father's home. Jake and Colonel Dureau will be positioned in the southern entry point near a large SUV for our escape. If we have Hunt, believe me, there'll be a lot of pissed-off terrorists wanting to kick our asses. Those sons of bitches will be chasing us, and most will have weapons. We'll need Jake and the colonel to come up and give us some firepower cover at that critical time. Now, if you're wondering why the two ladies will be standing by in Djamila's father's house, it'll be dark, and I'm hoping that we can duck into that sanctuary with Hunt. Sir, can Abella handle a sidearm?"

"Well, at the Roman ruins she blew out the solar plexus of a terrorist at a range beyond twenty-five yards," Mitch responded.

"Okay, I guess I missed that part of the story yesterday," Dave said. "Note to self, don't get into a duel with Abella!" He gave a thumbs-up, then continued. "Hopefully there's a back door or window in Djamila's father's house. That could buy us time and protection while we get to the SUV. The downside is that if the bad guys feel that Djamila and her father are helping us, they'll be put to death. I need to think about that part of the plan, but it does eliminate our outside exposure as we attempt to escape. Sir, that large church—Notre Dame d'Afrique— is it still a Catholic church? If so, that would be an excellent point to position prior to each group of folks going to their respective positions. Also, if need be, it would be a great rendezvous point after we get Captain Hunt."

Mitch nodded. "It's the only Catholic church in Algiers. Abella is familiar with the clergy and the nuns. She has attended since she was a baby."

"Excellent. I believe we have some homework to do prior to the reception, sir."

"From what you've just said, Dave, we need to find out about Djamila's father's home and whether it has a back exit. Abella needs to schmooze the clergy at the Notre Dame d'Afrique, and I need to contact Colonel Dureau ASAP to find out if he can make the reception on Saturday," Mitch said. Dave went back to studying the map of the Casbah, and Mitch sat back, marveling at how quickly Dave recalled the information they discussed in the Marine bar the day before. They still needed to determine the sequence of events and timetable, and the proper firepower needed. But they had time to define those critical items.

– • – •

As Dave pored over the map, Mitch ran into his office and called Yves. "Hello, my good French friend, *bonjour* and long time no hear," Mitch said as Yves picked up the phone.

"Mitch, my American hero, you sound rested. If I recall correctly, the last time we met you looked like hell, and we both had been fighting terrorists. We have a bad habit of doing that! It could really become detrimental to our health if we don't find a better hobby," Yves said, laughing.

"You're correct, Yves, but the reason I'm calling is to invite you to a small reception at my little embassy bungalow. It'll be on Saturday, beginning at 7 p.m. You'll be one of the guests of honor, so you must come."

"Saturday and the guest of honor . . . I must dress in my formal military uniform," Yves said. "How can I say no? Of course I will be there, and I will expect you in your military finery. But tell me, my fine colonel: is the reception just you and me?" Yves knew full well that Mitch was bullshitting about the guest-of-honor business.

"There will be a total of six folks, and that includes you and me," Mitch said. "Dress is very informal, so please don't come with a sports coat and ascot."

"Okay, I'll be casual, but I do have a question. The people attending, are they part of what I call a most excellent adventure?"

"Absolutely, and that's why we all will be guests of honor at the reception."

"Fabulous, then I'll see you at seven on Saturday. Take care, my friend," Yves said as he hung up the phone. As usual, Mitch heard the second receiver click as the conversation ended.

Mitch speculated whether the Algerian military members listening were able to decipher anything. *The statement about a most excellent adventure shouldn't clue them in to anything. Besides, they know my residence was blown to hell, and it's customary to hold a reception when a diplomat moves into new digs,* he thought. As Mitch daydreamed, the phone rang, startling him into spilling some of his coffee.

"Colonel Ross speaking, can I help you?" he asked, looking around for something to clean up the coffee.

"Mitch, it's Abella. I wanted to talk before I go to work this afternoon. Am I interrupting you?"

"No, actually it's perfect timing, sweetheart," Mitch said. "I was just about to call you. I'll get right to the point. Is there any chance that you can be at my bungalow on Saturday around 7 p.m.? I'm hosting a small reception, and it wouldn't be complete without you." He hoped that Abella's schedule would allow her to attend.

"Absolutely!" she said. "Even if I was scheduled to work, I would have Samia or someone else cover for me. I would never miss going to a reception with you, but this is even better because it's at your place. Can I come earlier than seven to help out in the preparations?"

"Please come as early as you can. Be sure to wear casual clothes, and I truly mean c-a-s-u-a-l. I hope you don't mind, but I already told Djamila that you would help her with the preparation of the hors d'oeuvres. Everything seems to work out better when you're around."

"That's sweet of you to say," she replied. "I hope in the future you'll still want to say that! Let's run away to some distant island in the South Pacific and eat pineapples and drink coconut milk all day. Then when it's time to sleep we'll cuddle on the warm sand and sleep until the sea breezes wake us. No terrorists, no embassies, no cars, no work, just you and me."

"Oh, that's paradise! Now you're making my head spin with ideas of going to the Hawaiian Islands, or the Philippines, or Tahiti, or Bora Bora once I kidnap you. But first we have to prepare for the reception on Saturday."

"Mitch, if kidnapping is defined as already having my bags packed and running away with you, then bring it on! I'm ready now! But as far as the reception, how about if I get to your place at 3 p.m.?"

"Great! I'm sure Djamila will appreciate your help. By the way, how was your first day back at work with all your cuts and bruises?"

"Samia was very concerned and helped with the medication at the hospital. She also was asking a few strange questions, but that's probably because of the news coverage. She said that it showed the destruction inside the embassy and your demolished residence. As for other folks at the hospital who asked about my injuries, I told them that I had fallen off my bicycle. They seemed to buy that excuse."

"Good. I know Samia is caring and concerned, but just be careful what you say around her. Although you trust her, she could accidently mention something to another colleague at the hospital. I do worry about your safety when we're not together."

"I know you worry about me as I worry about you. So, can we talk each day prior to Saturday? My day isn't complete unless I get to hear your voice."

"Okay, that's a deal. But remember when we talk there are other ears," Mitch said, to make sure Abella didn't say anything critical.

"That never leaves my thoughts. But before I leave, just remember that I love you," Abella said. If the military didn't know that already, then they were idiots.

"And I love you too. Let's talk tomorrow. Bye-bye." Mitch followed his usual routine and waited for Abella to hang up. Then he heard the second receiver. As always, it pissed him off. He took the mug of cold coffee and drained it with one big mouthful.

19

The week passed uneventfully, except for a few questions the Marine gunny had for Mitch about the sudden popularity of the firing range. The gunny found it odd that Jake, Dave McQueen, and Mitch seemed to think that they needed practice with shooting tactical targets.

Although Dave had not been to a firing range in years, he was still quite accurate even with his prosthesis. He and Jake put a bet on who would have the best score at the end of the day. The bet began with an agreement that each bullet was worth a dollar. At the end of each round, the gunny would have a Marine gather the targets to evaluate the amount of hits, and the dollar total for each shooter would be written on a chalkboard behind them. At the end of the day, the winner would have the highest dollar amount, and the loser would pay. Mitch decided that he was not at their level and bailed out of the competition.

Dave and Jake were nose to nose going into the final round. The side bets went up to five bucks a bullet, placed by a few of the Marines watching the competition. Dave and Jake decided to raise their stakes to not only cover the dollar amount but also include the best bottle of bourbon in the Marine bar. The last targets were life-size depictions of Osama bin Laden pointing a handgun at the shooter. There were three concentric racetrack rings printed over bin Laden's chest and two rings centered on his face. Each location had a bull's-eye X. Both shooters were given nine bullets in their clip. There was no time limit, and the distance to the target was twenty-five yards.

"Dave, I don't want you to feel any pressure, but the entire Department of Defense is depending on you. You can't let this senior special agent from the Department of State beat you," Mitch said loud enough so all the Marines in the immediate area could hear him.

"Sir, I was feeling rather cool and calm up until now. But my stress meter just pegged out!" Dave wiped the sweat from his forehead and rechecked the sight on his M9 pistol.

"Colonel, don't wanna intrude, but this is how I see it," Jake drawled. "I'm just an ol' country boy who's been around the block a few times and seen a lot of shooters. If'n that good warrant officer here is a prime example of how all US Army support administrators can handle a sidearm, then I'm not worried about any adversary that might think about attackin' the States. I'd keep all our Army sharpshooters and expert marksmen in reserve and let the support administrators take out the bad guys.

"But, Colonel, why does that little voice inside my head keep telling me that I'm bein' set up? It reminds me of an old sayin' that my mama use' to say back in the day. Fool me once, shame on you. Fool me twice, damn you're good!" Jake smiled as everyone laughed at his country humor. But Mitch knew that Jake was no dummy, and he was slowly putting the pieces together concerning Dave.

As the final portion of the competition commenced, Jake and Dave fired at their respective targets. After six shots Jake had a score of five hits in the chest and one bullet in the face. Dave had all six shots in the chest. With three bullets left, the pressure was on; Dave had to put all three remaining shots in the face.

"Come on, Dave, be the bullet! Feel it and squeeze the trigger softly," Mitch whispered as Dave concentrated on the target and then fired rapidly. Two bullets drilled the head of bin Laden.

"Damn, Warrant, that's some good shootin'. I bet you could hit a rat's butt at fifty yards," Jake said, shaking his head in admiration.

Dave stepped back from the firing line with one bullet left.

Jake stepped up to the line, raised his M9, focused on the target, held his breath, and slowly fired two shots. His first bullet hit Osama's mouth below the bull's-eye. The second drilled a hole just below the chin and through bin Laden's beard.

"Dang, this be the first time in my life that I scored a deadly shot to the neck and it's not good enough to win the competition. Mr. Dave, I believe we're tied again," Jake said, stepping back from the firing line.

"Well, gentlemen, I hate to inform you, but the sun is setting, and the Algerian military didn't provide us with lights here on the range," the gunny sergeant announced. "We can't go beyond 6 p.m., and that means you two have five minutes to end this. I would hate to think that it ended in a tie because we ran out of time."

The gunny had two new targets raised at forty yards. Each was a basic traditional round target with four concentric circles and an X in the center. He pulled a coin from his pocket and had Jake call the flip.

"I reckon that large Algerian coin is weighted more on the head side, so I'll be pickin' tails," Jake said.

The gunny flipped the coin, and as it bounced twice on the ground, it showed heads.

"Well, so much for my analytical reasonin'. You're up first, Dave, if you so desire."

Dave nodded and stepped to the firing line. With a slight crosswind and the distance increased by fifteen yards, he had to compensate for each new factor. He raised his pistol, held his breath, and lightly applied pressure on the trigger. His last bullet streaked toward the target and blew out the center X.

The gunny raised a scope to his right eye and then yelled, "It's a bull dead-on. Completely blew the center from the target."

Dave stepped back from the line and didn't look at Jake.

"Damn, Warrant, I need to take some lessons from ya," Jake said as he stepped to the line. Even his best shot would result in only a tie. The range fell silent and everyone stared at him. It was only getting darker, so he raised his M9, revealing a slight tremble in his arm. He lowered the pistol and focused on the target, clearly factoring in all the elements that would affect his shot. He slowly raised the gun once again as the Marines and Mitch watched and waited. Squinting his right eye to eliminate peripheral distractions, he slowly squeezed the trigger. The bullet sang through the humid, hazy air, and, a second later, the target reverberated as it ripped apart. The gunny raised the scope to his eye and waited until he was absolutely certain.

"Just to the right of the bull's-eye. Warrant Officer McQueen wins!"

All the Marines immediately started yelling, "Oorah-oorah-oorah," as Dave stood and walked to Jake. The big man was still staring at the target as Dave patted his shoulder and shook his hand.

The handshake seemed to snap Jake from his thoughts, and he smiled at Dave. Then he whispered, "Maybe at the colonel's reception you can tell me who you really are. I know shootin' like that is either special ops, snipers, or Rangers, and snipers like the M24 rifle. Not to worry, Dave. I can tell you don't want folks to know, so I won't mention anythin' about that leg of yours. But I sure would like to talk to ya about your past. Should be quite interestin', my man."

Jake winked and then turned to Mitch and the Marines. He handed his pistol to the gunny and said, "*No más, no más.* Dave wins, and now he's a rich man!"

When they got back to the embassy, Jake, Dave, and Mitch went to the Marine bar in search of the bottle of bourbon.

"That was quite the shooting competition you two put on, so I'll buy the Kentucky magic," Mitch said as he pointed to a few different bottles of bourbon. The bartender pulled the bottles from the shelf and lined them up on the bar. Mitch, Dave, and Jake examined each and determined that it would take a taste test to select a winner. They broke the seals on the bottles and lined up three shots each. After the final shot was downed, they were ready to vote.

"Well, even though we've tasted, I'm not certain there's a clear winner," Mitch said. "I can think of two possible approaches. The first and possibly the best is that we reevaluate all three bottles. But the easiest is that I stop being a cheap shit and buy them all! So, bartender, pour three more shots for my friends, and I'll buy all three bottles."

Mitch flashed a thumbs-up, and his two drinking compatriots began to laugh.

— • — •

Mitch asked Djamila not to rush making the hors d'oeuvres. "Abella should be arriving soon, and she wanted to help in the preparation."

"Don't worry, Colonel Mitch. I still have a lot more to do besides the food. I'll keep Abella busy once she arrives."

Mitch left the house and proceeded to the main gate where the temporary entry had been set up. Just before 3 p.m., Mitch entered the small building, and a taxi pulled up outside the gate. Abella stepped out of the car dressed in skintight jeans, black boots that extended to just below her knees, and a short-sleeve turquoise blouse, partially unbuttoned to reveal a delicate gold necklace. Her luxurious black hair cascaded onto her shoulders and back as she walked. Once she cleared the security procedures and entered the embassy, Mitch gazed at her and shook his head.

"Abella, if I didn't know better, I would swear that you just arrived from Tucson, Arizona. Wow, you look dynamic!" Mitch said as she blushed and kissed him.

They left the temporary building and walked toward the bungalow.

"This is really strange," Abella said. "The last time we walked like this, the embassy was untouched. Now it has scars. I'm not sure we will ever feel the same again as we did prior to the violence." She looked around, taking in the bullet holes, destroyed buildings, charred vehicles, and uprooted foliage. Although much of the destruction had been removed, the embassy still resembled an urban war zone.

"You're right, sweetheart. It'll never be the same in our eyes, but at least our scars are healing, and someday they will fade away."

"I'm not so certain that our internal wounds will ever leave our memories," she responded, squeezing Mitch's hand and looking into his eyes. "Someday I want to leave Algeria with you and never return. I want to make memories with you in America or anywhere but here. I love Algeria, but my wounds are deep and painful. I can never forget all the sorrow that my country has given me." Abella stopped walking, and Mitch put his arms around her. As he held her, she continued, "You're the only one who completes me. You're the only one who truly makes me so very happy."

"Don't worry, Abella. I will forever be with you."

As they approached the bungalow, they noticed Djamila near a coconut palm tree, picking up two coconuts that had fallen. She turned and saw Abella and Mitch coming her way.

"*Assalam alaikum*," Djamila said as she juggled and almost dropped the coconuts.

Smiling, Abella replied, "*Wa alaikum assalam*, Djamila."

Djamila handed Mitch the coconuts and hugged Abella.

"*Kaifa haalik*?" Abella said, asking how she was doing.

"*Al hamdu lillah*." Djamila replied that she was fine and praised Allah.

Djamila and Abella walked arm in arm toward the house as Mitch held the coconuts to his chest. Inside the bungalow the two women began to laugh, pointing at Mitch and continuing in Arabic. Mitch stood bemused. Then Abella wiped a tear of laughter from her face.

"Mitch, I wish I had a camera right now because it's so funny the way you're holding those coconuts. You remind me of Dolly Parton and her forty double Ds!"

Mitch looked down and saw what she meant.

"Yikes, it's a good thing my old fighter-pilot buds aren't here," he said. "They'd give me so much shit for this." Mitch laughed as Djamila took the coconuts from him and placed them on the kitchen counter.

Mitch and Djamila took the coconuts outside to break them open while Abella examined the refrigerator to see what had been prepared. What she found was a bounty of hors d'oeuvres, from dried fruits to the finest French items. The dishes consisted of figs, dates, apricots, mixed nuts, rectangular tarts with sliced eggplant, zucchini, tomatoes, and shaved cheese in a flaky crust. There were also cheddar gougères, resembling muffins stuffed with goat cheese, ready to be heated in the oven, buttery flatbread that resembled a pizza with dates and figs, tarte flambé with small diced cubes of lamb and onions on small crackers, salmon tartare with pressed caviar and tomatoes, tartlets of buttery puff pastry and mushrooms, French canapé with small discs of bread, herb-flavored butter, and foie gras, tarte Tatin with its upside-down tart and sliced apples caramelized in butter and sugar, and finally crème brûlée with a rich custard base topped with a layer of hard caramel.

Abella was in awe and wondered what Djamila would do with the coconuts. As Mitch and Djamila entered the house, holding four halves of coconuts, Abella couldn't hold back her curiosity, speaking in French so Mitch would understand.

"Djamila, you've gone over the top with all the amazing hors d'oeuvres. I'm not sure what army you plan to feed, but it's impressive. What are the coconuts for?"

"That is very kind of you to say," Djamila responded, smiling. "I plan to sprinkle diced coconuts over my last dessert. I thought it would be nice to serve lemon mousse with the shredded coconut on top."

"Okay, so at least there's one appetizer I can help you make," Abella said, taking the extra apron from inside the pantry door. "What else do we need besides lemons and coconut?"

"Ladies, while you make the mousse, I'll walk over to the Marine bar and get the wine and booze," Mitch said, slipping an arm around Abella and quickly kissing her.

Abella whispered, "Of all the desserts in this bungalow, that kiss was la pièce de résistance."

On the way to the bar, Mitch noticed the old Algerian gardener planting rose bushes where the others had been destroyed. He still wore the Dodger cap.

"*Bonjour, mon ami,*" Mitch said, patting the old man on the shoulder. "I have not seen you in a while. I hope you are well. It was a shame that the roses were ruined in the attack."

"*Qui,* Colonel, it was terrible. But fortunately, the roses can be replaced, and they will be better than ever, inshallah."

"Yes, my friend, if Allah wishes." Mitch smiled and continued on to the Marine bar.

Music and laughter filtered from the bar as he entered. Inside he found Dave McQueen standing among off-duty Marines and State Department diplomats. Mitch noted that Dave no longer cowered in the corner of the bar but was encircled by those having a late-afternoon beer on their day off.

The gunny sergeant was shaking his head in amazement. "Dave, how the hell did you beat Jake?" he asked. "He's one of the best shots at the embassy. Our administrators in the Marines are good shots, but nothing like what you displayed. That was quite a show you put on!"

"Well, Gunny, a lot of it was pure luck, and the other half was divine providence," Dave laughed and patted the gunny's back.

"So, the Cinderella story continues about the anonymous Army admin who comes out of nowhere to win the biggest shooting competition of the year," Mitch said as he approached.

"I don't know if I'm anonymous, sir. Been around these parts just about as long as you have. And I surprised myself more than anyone else during the competition." Dave winked at Mitch discreetly.

"Call it what you want, Warrant, but that shooting was impressive," Mitch said. He turned to the bartender. "Hey, Carl, I need two bottles each of merlot, zinfandel, cabernet sauvignon, chardonnay, and pinot gris. You can follow that lineup with Jim Beam Black Label, Jack Daniels, and Jameson whiskey, your best vodka and gin, and Bailey's Irish Cream. Make sure I get two bottles of the bourbon, whiskies, and vodka and gin. Then a large bottle of orange juice, a six-pack of Coke, and finally 7 Up. That should do it!" Mitch reached into his pocket and retrieved a wad of twenties.

"Sir, that sounds like one hell of a party! Do you need help carrying these back to your house?" Carl asked as he packed Mitch's order into cardboard wine boxes.

"Well, perhaps. But I've got this strong warrant officer standing right next to me, and I believe he can give me a hand with the boxes. Thanks for the offer, but we're good." When he hefted one of them, Mitch wondered if he had been premature with his answer.

"Sir, I'll take the wine and you can grab the booze," Dave said. "Or a better idea would be to convince a few of these young, strapping Marines to help us out!"

"You know, that's actually a great idea. How about I buy a round of beer for you Marines if you help us carry these boxes?" Mitch announced as he settled his tab.

Before he could turn around, all the boxes, sodas, and orange juice had been hauled out of the bar by Marines. The only thing that Dave needed to do was lead the entourage of leathernecks toward Mitch's bungalow.

"Okay, barkeep, how much for a round of beers for those hardworkin' Marines?" Mitch asked.

"Sir, beers are only two bucks for Marines, but don't let that out of the bag," Carl whispered, eyeing a few of the nonmilitary bar patrons. "Could cause some bad blood with these State Department diplomats. We charge nonmilitary a little more for each brewskie because they always have access to beer. When we're out in the field or in combat there's no beer to be had. At least, that's the excuse we give to charge them an additional dollar. They also make more money than we do."

"I understand completely. So there were three Marines carrying all my stuff. Now, I wasn't a math major in college, but at two bucks a beer, that should be six dollars. Here's a twenty and keep the change.

I appreciate the support. In fact, why don't you have a beer and take it out of the twenty," Mitch said, giving Carl a thumbs-up.

"Thank you, sir. I believe I'll take you up on that offer!"

As Mitch left the bar, the three Marines returned from the bungalow.

"Hey, Marines, thanks for the help. I believe Carl has just opened a round of cold ones for the work you just performed. I do genuinely appreciate the support," Mitch said. The men nodded and went directly to the bar where their cold, fresh bottles awaited them.

Mitch hurried back to the bungalow where he found that Dave was already helping the ladies out. They had wrapped a tablecloth around his waist and had him shaving the coconut meat. The boxes of wine and booze were on the kitchen table.

"Mitch, I hope you don't mind, but as soon as Dave entered the house we put him to work," Abella said. Dave looked at Mitch with a little embarrassment.

"Great idea!" Mitch laughed. "He looks marvelous in that white miniskirt!"

Dave smiled. "Sir, in my defense, I was going to leave the bar and change clothes for the reception. But then you came in and my plans were immediately altered. So that's why I'm wearing these faded jeans and a T-shirt under my miniskirt."

"You're dressed perfectly for this reception," Mitch replied. "I said it would be max relax this evening."

When Dave finished his coconut work, he helped Mitch put the wine and booze away. Dave followed as Mitch headed into the bedroom to find a spot for the wine since the wine rack had been destroyed.

"Sir, I hope you won't think that I'm out of line to ask this question, but I'm going to fire away," Dave said once they were out of earshot of the kitchen. "Djamila seems to be a very nice lady, and her cooking is beyond belief. So is she married or seeing someone?" Dave sounded like a high schooler asking about a prom date.

"Well, I'm glad to know that you appreciate attributes beyond just beauty," Mitch replied. "I agree that Djamila is very attractive, cooks food that is out of this world, and has a heart of gold. She's the total package, without a doubt. She spends a lot of time with her father in the Casbah, and I can guarantee that she's not married or dating. But that doesn't mean that she wants to date. This is my philosophy on this touchy subject that crosses cultural and religious lines: Be very careful, but remember, nothing ventured nothing gained. Just go slow with her and show her the new Dave that I have recently discovered. Then slowly let her in on your leg. She is the type of woman who would understand why you are reluctant to disclose that secret. But she would also be happy to know that she knew about it before others. Does this make sense?"

"Yes sir, I understand completely," Dave responded. He returned to the kitchen with a wide smile.

When the final dessert was complete, the foursome rearranged the few pieces of furniture cluttering the living room. As Djamila directed the two men on where to move the couch, Abella heard a slight tap at the door. Jake's huge body filled the doorframe. As promised, he wore jeans, cowboy boots, and a Western shirt signed diagonally across the chest in black felt marker by Willie Nelson.

"Jake, come on in and help us decide where to place the couch," Mitch said. "By the way, I thought you were going to wear your signed cowboy shirt?" The others looked at Jake and then back at Mitch with questioning looks. Mitch laughed and shook his head. "Can't say I've ever seen anything like that in my life. That shirt is definitely unique!"

"Well, now that we have that squared away, perhaps someone can pour me a little of that Kentucky libation sitting yonder on the table," Jake said, pointing to the bourbon.

"Considering all I owe you, let me break the seal and pour you a couple fingers' worth," Mitch responded.

As Mitch poured, Jake moved next to him and whispered, "Colonel, are my eyes deceivin' me or is Dave bird-doggin' Djamila?"

"If you're asking whether Dave is attracted to her, the answer is yes. But please keep that classified. He doesn't want anyone to know."

"Sir, my lips are sealed, but it's as obvious as the pope being Catholic," Jake said. He raised his glass toward Dave and Djamila before downing half the contents.

After everyone except Jake had given their inputs on where the furniture should be placed, he finally laid a little of his Kentucky wisdom on the group.

"The way I see it, y'all have good ideas, but none are the same. How 'bout if'n we push all the furniture against the walls to give the livin' room a small ballroom appearance."

Abella looked at Jake and then at Mitch.

"That's brilliant," she said. "It gives us maximum space."

Jake patted Dave's shoulder and whispered, "You and I should take care of the furniture while they pour the wine."

The two men maneuvered the coach against the wall and then moved on to other items. While the others concentrated on which bottles of wine to open and what appetizers to pre-taste, Jake pulled Dave outside.

"Now that we're out of earshot, where the hell did you learn how to shoot? That type of shootin' I saw the other day was either special ops or Rangers," Jake asked, squinting an eye at Dave.

"It's a long story, Jake," Dave responded.

"Well then, give me the *Reader's Digest* version."

"For most of my career I was an Army Ranger. I prided myself in being one helluva an expert marksman. I've experienced combat numerous times and at one point was almost killed."

"Almost killed? Is that how you lost your leg?"

"Of all the people here at the embassy, I figured you'd be the first person to notice. But then I tripped in the ruins of Colonel Ross's former residence and he spotted it."

"It's amazin' how well you can maneuver around. You have no limping or issues that would give away your secret."

"I worked hard during my extended rehabilitation because I thought there might be a remote chance I could get back in the Rangers. But the Army wanted to medically retire me. So, I pulled some political strings, and that's how I ended up here as an administrative specialist."

"Hey, you two, come back into the house and join the party," Mitch bellowed, snapping Jake and Dave from their conversation.

"Thanks for bein' straight up with me, Dave. I do appreciate it!" Jake said. He clapped Dave on the shoulder as they entered the bungalow.

Djamila had carefully cut small portions of the appetizers to ensure she didn't destroy their appearance. Jake went back to his glass of bourbon, and Djamila offered Dave a glass of white or red wine.

"I'll take the white, please, and thanks for being so kind and thoughtful."

Djamila beamed as she offered the wine to Dave.

A security guard appeared at the bungalow doorway and announced that a French colonel was waiting to be escorted into the embassy. Mitch walked with the guard to the temporary entry point. Just as Mitch had suspected, Yves's casual and Mitch's casual were completely different. Yves looked as if he had just returned from the French Riviera. He wore a navy-blue long-sleeve shirt with the sleeves rolled up to mid forearm. Light-tan slacks complemented the soft brown Italian loafers and tan belt. But what really took Mitch aback was the paisley ascot in burnt orange, brown, green, and blue silk.

"Yves, you look splendid and somewhat casual," Mitch said, feeling underdressed.

"Yes, I was having a rather difficult time deciding how casual I should be at your reception. I defaulted to what I usually wear when I go on holiday," Yves stated in all seriousness.

Mitch wondered what the others might think when the dapper Frenchman walked into the bungalow. "Alrighty then, let's not waste time. The folks couldn't hold back—they've started on the wine and are nibbling the hors d'oeuvres."

"We mustn't linger. I missed lunch and want to make sure that I get my fair share of Djamila's special delicacies," Yves said as he and Mitch walked toward the house.

While they walked through the newly planted rose garden, Yves glanced at Mitch. "You know, my friend, Ramadan begins at the end of November. If we're to attempt a rescue of Captain Hunt, it must be soon. For a month the Casbah will be filled with people feasting and partying throughout the night. Using night as a cloak to cover our ingress and egress would never work during Ramadan."

"Those concerns did pass through my mind. The reception isn't really for a housewarming party; it's to get all the major players together and have Dave give a quick brief of the plan."

"Do you have buy-in from all the folks?" Yves asked, looking concerned.

"All except Djamila. She hasn't been briefed in. Abella and I will talk to her prior to Dave's presentation. I believe she has the biggest potential loss in this entire scenario. I need her commitment prior to Dave stepping to the podium."

Jimmy Buffett's "Margaritaville" drifted from the wide-open door of the bungalow. Accompanying Jimmy was Jake, Dave, and Abella singing at the tops of their voices as Yves entered, waving his arms like a choir director. Mitch quickly joined in the singing and drinking.

"Yves, what color wine would you like?" Abella asked.

"I'll take the cool white wine on this late summer evening." Yves responded. "Now, where are those award-winning hors d'oeuvres of Djamila's?"

Abella handed Yves a glass of chardonnay and turned to Djamila. "It's time to bring out those luscious hors d'oeuvres, if Allah wills," she said in Arabic.

While Djamila took the appetizers out of the refrigerator, Mitch whispered to Abella, "We need to pull Djamila away from the feeding frenzy and ask if she and her father would be willing to assist our cause."

Once everything was placed on the kitchen counter, Abella got Djamila's attention, and the two of them stepped out the front door. Mitch turned to Dave. "You've got the controls while Abella and I talk to Djamila. Keep them all singing."

Dave nodded in acknowledgment, then asked who needed their drinks recharged. Mitch quickly slipped out and found Abella and Djamila standing under the coconut tree.

He asked Abella to translate, knowing her French was more reliable than his and not wanting Djamila's non-native understanding of English to prevent complete comprehension of the dangers he was asking her to undertake.

"Not a problem."

Mitch turned to Djamila and spoke slowly in English as Abella translated.

"Djamila, over the past six months, I'm sure you would agree, many strange and violent things have happened to Abella and me. On top of that, the attack on the embassy wasn't a coincidence. It was planned by the new leadership of the GSPC to send a message. They specifically attacked the US embassy to broadcast to all other countries that even a superpower doesn't scare them. I wanted you to be a part of this reception because you and your father have given me a lot of useful information concerning the blue-eyed man who wears Bedouin robes and walks past your father's home each day for prayer. Information from other sources leads me to believe the blue-eyed man is an American prisoner of war.

"I have been ordered by important American officials to find the American prisoner and rescue him. He is being held by the GSPC near your father's home. The men who accompany him to and from the mosque are security guards of that terrorist organization. Djamila, I won't force you into doing anything, and I especially don't want your father hurt or possibly killed. But I must ask if you and your father would be willing to open his home for our cause, the rescue of the American prisoner? What I specifically mean is that during a particular evening, prior to Ramadan, you would take Abella to meet your father. I will make sure that you and Abella have not only transportation but also food for you two and your father. The transportation will not enter the Casbah but will drop you off. Then you would walk with the food to your father's home. This should not arouse suspicion among individuals residing within the Casbah. Up to this point, am I making sense? Do you understand?"

Djamila stared at Mitch. She said nothing but nodded in agreement.

"Good, then I have a question to ask. Does your father's home have a back door or exit?"

Djamila collected her thoughts before speaking. Still looking directly into Mitch's eyes, she said, "Yes, my father's home has a very small back exit. It is only three feet tall and was made to escape fire or French soldiers during our fight for independence. The GSPC has killed and injured many of my father's old friends who fought with him against the French. My father despises the GSPC and would fight them to the death. It is the terrorists who sent the message to the world that Algeria should be left alone. It is the terrorists who have destroyed everything that is good for Algeria. Like my father, I loathe the GSPC and would give all to witness their destruction.

"I will mention this conversation to my father, but I can tell you how he will respond. First, he will allow his home to be used for your cause. Then he will request that I get his pistol that he used during the war of independence. My father will request a cup of tea and sit quietly in thought, his gun resting in his lap as he consumes his warm beverage. Each day he will patiently wait with his weapon and his tea until that specific day of reckoning. His only interruption will be to attend the call to prayer. Colonel Mitch, have no fear. My father will tell no one."

Mitch expressed his immense gratitude for her bravery.

"We should return to the reception," Mitch said as the music inside transitioned from Jimmy Buffett to the Beach Boys. In a few moments the laughter and singing would end as they discussed a sobering topic.

Dave and Jake were comparing notes on which handguns were the best for close urban combat. Yves was still grazing on the hors d'oeuvres and sizing up an unopened bottle of chardonnay.

"Okay, sports fans, grab your beverage of choice because it's time for Dave to make his special presentation," Mitch announced, flashing a thumbs-up to Dave that confirmed Djamila's buy-in.

Mitch quietly asked Abella to close the front door, leaving a small gap no larger than an inch. Then she took Mitch's CD player and positioned the speakers toward the gap so the music would project outward and drown out any conversation occurring within. The bungalow had been swept for bugs a few days prior to the reception.

Mitch helped Dave attach the map of the Casbah to the largest living room wall, and Abella closed the curtains. As each member of the team found a comfortable seat, Mitch stood in front to explain the real reason for the gathering. Abella sat close to Djamila, quietly translating into French.

"I hope you're enjoying the evening," Mitch said. "I don't think I have to go into great detail as to why we're actually here. Dave and I have put together a basic plan of what our team needs to do in the Casbah and how we think the rescue operation of Captain Hunt should be accomplished. If at any time you have questions, please don't hesitate to ask. As the old saying goes, 'There are no stupid questions.' So, with that said, let me turn the presentation over to my expert, Warrant Officer Dave McQueen, combat-tested Army Ranger."

Dave rose from his stool and moved to the map on the wall. "First let me explain the chart and the markings from a general perspective," he said. "Obviously, this is a detailed map of the Casbah with all its narrow passageways, old walls, and ancient steps that have protected its inhabitants for hundreds of years. Since the nineteenth century, it's withstood attacks by the French, Americans, British, and Germans, just to name a few. But let's look closer and concentrate on the area of the map that has been highlighted in yellow."

Dave used a pointer to identify the spot on the chart. "As I continue," he said, "if there is something that seems off base or ridiculous, please don't hesitate to ask a question."

Dave resumed his presentation. "There are latitude and longitude coordinates written on the map. This location was provided to Colonel Ross by the terrorist Hamady and verified by our very own Djamila. The coordinates identify the home in which Captain Seth Hunt is currently being held prisoner. That location is the center point of all our planning. Almost directly across from Hunt's position, slightly to the south, is a yellow marking that indicates Djamila's father's home. This is critical to our egress because we'll take Captain Hunt through this site and exit through a rear door onto an adjacent Casbah passageway.

"Now, let's transition back to our focal point, the latitude and longitude position. On the opposite side of the passageway and just north of Captain Hunt's present location is a jewelry shop, which is highlighted in light blue. That is where Colonel Ross and I will be positioned. Colonel Ross has received approval from the Spanish deputy ambassador's maid, who will escort us to her father's shop.

"We need to shift slightly south of the latitude and longitude position. Please note there is a cross over the site of an important mosque in the Casbah. Why is this mosque so significant? This is where Captain Hunt attends evening prayers each day. The captain and his guards pass Djamila's father's home while going to and from the mosque. They pass so close that although the captain is dressed in robes and his face is covered, Djamila has noticed his vivid blue eyes.

"Now, as you follow my pointer moving south of the mosque, you will notice a yellow highlighted circle that identifies the southern entry point of the Casbah near the Algerian naval headquarters. This is where Yves and Jake will position the embassy SUV so as not to raise as much suspicion. Embassy vehicles frequent the naval base on a weekly basis, as foreign military attachés coordinate business with the Algerian Navy.

"Finally, I've put a red cross over the Notre Dame d'Afrique, which we all know as the only Catholic basilica in all of Algeria. This will be our safe haven. We will gather at this position prior to each group's ingress to their respective locations within the Casbah. Abella has already contacted the archbishop, a personal acquaintance of hers, to make him aware that she will bring a group to the basilica within the next few weeks. The archbishop is eager to show us the beauty of Notre Dame d'Afrique and impart a blessing on us all. I believe that wouldn't be a bad idea, but it's up to you. If all goes well with the liberation of Captain Hunt, we'll rendezvous back at the basilica before piling into the SUV and heading to the US embassy. Any questions at this point?"

Jake raised his bourbon glass and said, "Dave, I'm sure you'll brief us on contingency plans in case things go the way of the outhouse. But don't ya think that once we get Hunt, we should throw his butt in the SUV at the southern entry point and haul ass direct to the US embassy? I'm just saying that once they realize we have the good captain, there will be a whole lotta angry hornets out to sting us."

"That's a very good point, Jake," Mitch said, staring at the map. "Perhaps we should scrap the post-mission rendezvous at the basilica and press straight to the US embassy. The SUV is an enlarged, hardened Chevy Suburban. It can easily take six to seven folks. Worst case, I can sit in the cargo area on the way back."

"Okay, any other questions?" Dave scanned the group. "Then I'll get into the nuts and bolts of the plan. Two hours prior to the commencement of our rescue operation, we will all gather at the basilica. Djamila and Abella will arrive together in a taxi. This is a common practice by parishioners of the church, so it shouldn't raise any eyebrows. Yves will be dropped off by French security, who will remain in their vehicle in the basilica's parking lot. This will add additional firepower if there is trouble during our time at the church. Jake, Colonel Ross, and I will arrive in a large embassy SUV. Having embassy vehicles parked outside the Notre Dame d'Afrique is not unusual, and many embassies leave their security waiting outside the church. Again, this should not raise any suspicions.

"The sun sets at approximately 7 p.m. at this time of year. The first twosome, Djamila and Abella, will be driven by taxi from the basilica to the southern entry point prior to sunset. Why a taxi and not the SUV? Less suspicion, and Djamila usually walks from that entry point to her father's home. The only difference is that she will have a companion, Abella. Djamila, you'll take dinner that will be prepared here at the bungalow prior to all of us departing to the basilica. Thirty minutes after their departure, Colonel Ross and I will be dropped off by the French security vehicle that brought Colonel Dureau to the basilica. The French security will continue on to their embassy.

"We will rendezvous with the Spanish deputy ambassador's maid at the southern entry at 7:35 p.m. Then the three of us will minimize our exposure and hasten our route through the Casbah to the jewelry shop. Our walk with the maid should take less than fifteen minutes. If any communications are required while traversing through the passageways en route to the jewelry shop, they will be in Spanish. The maid speaks Spanish and so do I. The maid knows nothing of our mission, and it's better that she is kept in the dark. I believe the colonel plans to buy a few items from the jewelry shop to legitimize our visit."

Abella glanced at Mitch.

"Dave, that was supposed to be classified top secret!" Mitch said, noticing Abella's gaze and winking at her.

Dave smiled and then continued, "At 8 p.m. Colonel Dureau and Jake will position the embassy SUV at the southern entry point near the naval headquarters. At 8:30 p.m. Jake and the colonel will begin their trek to the back exit of Djamila's father's house. That should put them in position to add firepower coverage if needed during the egress to the SUV. At that same time, 8:30 p.m., Colonel Ross and I will depart the jewelry shop, heading south to Captain Hunt's location. It should take us no longer than a few minutes to arrive. Although Hunt is imprisoned, no external guards have ever been seen, and this fact has been confirmed by Djamila. At 8:30 p.m., the guards within the house should be resting or asleep.

"At this point, Abella and Djamila will be standing ready near the door of her father's home. Abella will watch for any movement from Captain Hunt's location. If need be, Colonel Ross and I will force our way into the site where Hunt is being held. What we are hoping for is a fast extraction and then direct to Djamila's father's home. I will cover Colonel Ross, Abella, and Captain Hunt as they egress to the exit point of the house. Colonel Dureau and Jake should be there to add additional cover as Captain Hunt is led to the southern exit and the waiting embassy SUV. Colonel Ross, Captain Hunt, and Abella will lead the exodus as Jake, Colonel Dureau, and I become the rear guard.

"Djamila will remain with her father at his home. If there are guards chasing and attacking us, Djamila should inform the bad guys that the Americans forced their entry into her father's home. Hopefully that will convince the terrorists that Djamila and her father are innocent, though I have heard that Djamila's father is not a fan of the GSPC and he can still handle his old military pistol. Now, if things really go south into the outhouse as Jake previously stated, Colonel Ross and I will exit Hunt's location and beeline straight to Djamila's father's home. We will pick up the same egress plan minus Captain Hunt. In this scenario there will undoubtedly be more firepower required. If we can't find Hunt within the first moments of entry, then our planning will rapidly disintegrate, and we will have to think of our survival and forget about the captain.

"If Jake and Colonel Dureau encounter resistance while heading to the exit point of Djamila's father's home, we'll undoubtedly hear the gunfire. Our alternate plan will ignore Djamila's location, and we'll continue south on the passageway toward the mosque. Abella, be ready to immediately join us as we'll be running outside your position. Hopefully, we'll have Captain Hunt and we'll continue until the passageway turns a shallow left toward the southern entry/exit point. We'll go directly to the SUV and wait momentarily for Jake and Colonel Dureau. There will be two sets of SUV keys. Jake and

Colonel Ross will be the key holders. If after a few minutes we have not seen Jake or Colonel Dureau—"

Jake interrupted Dave, "At that point, y'all haul ass and get the hell out of Dodge. Do ya understand? The good French colonel here and I have already discussed this situation. We both agree that if our house of cards is implodin', then y'all put the pedal to the metal and burn rubber direct to the US embassy. *Comprende?*"

"The amazing thing about Senior Special Agent Jake Davis is that one never has to question what he says," Yves said as he raised his glass of wine toward Jake. "Even as a Frenchman, I completely understood what he meant and how little he had to say to get his point across. Bravo, my good man, bravo!"

"Well, with that said, let me complete this briefing," Dave continued. "What will be our firepower and who will carry weapons? Colonel Ross, Jake, Abella, and I will carry M9 Berettas. We will have two clips each, one in the pistol and the reserve in a quick-access pocket. Colonel Dureau will carry his Pamas G1 with two clips available. Djamila's father, from my understanding, has a 1950s-era French pistol that he used in the Algerian War of Independence. At his age he can possess as many magazines or clips as he desires.

"That wraps up my presentation today. Colonel Ross and I will be reviewing this plan right up to the final day. Stay flexible, and we'll definitely be in touch. Unless there are any questions, I believe you should all recharge your drinks, and let's turn the music up a few notches."

Everyone gravitated to the kitchen. Once everyone's glass had been refilled, people paired off. Mitch took Abella's hand and slipped out the front door. Once in the dark he pulled her close and softly kissed her. "I don't know your schedule, but is there any chance you can spend the night with me?"

"But, Mitch, I brought nothing to wear for this evening," Abella quipped.

"Exactly my thoughts, sweetheart." Mitch kissed her again. "But what about your work at the hospital?"

"I told Samia today that I would be very late returning home this evening. She informed me that she would take my morning shift tomorrow so I would not have to worry about meeting my early schedule. It was very kind of her, and I, of course, will take her late-afternoon shift."

"Fantastic! Let's go back inside and join the party."

As they entered, Mitch and Abella noticed Dave and Djamila sitting together on the couch. Jake had just handed a huge Cuban cigar to Yves, and they were headed outside to finish the evening off with a great smoke and a little bourbon.

"Well, it appears that everyone seems to be relaxing and enjoying themselves," Mitch said, satisfied. "I'm glad that folks are kicking back and putting our plan in their back pocket for the moment."

Abella looked up with a quizzical glance. "So, you plan to do a little jewelry shopping in the not-too-distant future? Interesting . . . Anybody I know that'll be the lucky recipient?"

"Hey now, you're not supposed to ruin a surprise." Mitch laughed as he squeezed Abella's hand. He noticed that Dave and Djamila had moved from the couch and were now putting together a plate of hors d'oeuvres for her father.

Dave caught Mitch's eye, turned, and spoke softly so others wouldn't hear. "Sir, I'll be escorting Djamila to the embassy security exit gate to make sure she safely gets her taxi. It's a little later than she normally departs. Colonel, thanks again for allowing me to be the man I thought would never return. It's an honor to serve under your command."

"Dave, you're an American hero, and never forget that. Don't ever shortchange yourself—very few receive the Bronze Star with Valor and a Purple Heart fighting for their life in a desperate situation as you did!" Mitch shook his hand. "I'm damn glad you're on my team!"

Dave lowered his head and smiled as he turned to help Djamila carry the plate of food and her shopping bag. He looked at her and with the best French he could put together said, "*Aller maintenant?*"

Djamila smiled and touched his hand. "*Oui,* time to go." She thanked Abella and Mitch for a wonderfully unique evening.

Dave and Djamila briefly stopped to say their goodbyes to Jake and Yves before departing, snapping the two men out of their intense conversation. They had nearly taken their last draws on their cigars as they debated whether the French Vichy government had any impact or influence over the French Resistance during World War II. Dave and Djamila faded into the darkness, and Jake and Yves dropped what was left of their cigars and turned to Mitch and Abella.

"Well, Colonel," Jake said, "it's never a dull moment when we get together, and tonight has been a damn fine evenin'. Thanks for the grub and bourbon, but especially thanks for includin' me in on your wild ride. It's gonna be one helluva venture." He nodded at Abella and shook Yves's hand. Thankfully, he didn't have far to walk to his residence; Mitch noticed that Jake had put quite a dent in the bottle of bourbon and wasn't quite following a straight line as he disappeared into the moonless evening. Then out of the darkness Jake bellowed, "Not to worry, Colonel! I'll take care of your sweet lady's security paperwork for tonight."

Mitch shook his head in amazement. Yves, the consummate gentleman, took Abella's hand and bowed. "*Bon nuit, mademoiselle.*" He then turned to Mitch with a slight mischievous smile and quietly said, "You, sir, are a very lucky man. I don't have to bid you a good evening because you have been blessed with the love of an angel." Yves patted Mitch on the shoulder before heading off.

"What did Yves say that made you smile so broadly?" Abella asked.

"Basically, he said that you're my special angel to love," Mitch replied. "Let's go into the bungalow and forget about cleaning it up. I believe there's a nice warm shower waiting for both of us to squeeze into. But with two major caveats: I get to slowly lather your body from head to toe, and then you can lather mine. Once we step out and gently dry each other off . . . well, that's when dessert will be served."

Abella cradled Mitch's face with her hands and kissed him slowly with all the love and passion that her heart reserved only for him. Then they entered the bungalow, closed the door, and started the shower.

20

It was midafternoon, and Abella had left after eating a late breakfast. She had insisted on helping Mitch clean the bungalow after the previous evening's reception.

As Mitch grabbed a coffee from the embassy café, the chargé d'affaires, John Anderson, noticed him stepping back into the chancery building. Anderson was actually the deputy ambassador but changed titles when the ambassador was out of country. In the diplomatic world, this title change sent a message to all other foreign diplomats that he or she was handling all the embassy business on a temporary basis in the absence of the ambassador. In this case, the US ambassador was still being grilled by the congressional committee in DC in the aftermath of the embassy attack.

Unfortunately for the embassy staff, this chargé d'affaires was quite arrogant and full of himself. Rumor had it that Anderson was hoping the US ambassador would be fired and he would be elevated to the ambassadorial position in Algeria. In the period since the ambassador's departure, Mitch had discussed with numerous diplomats their impressions of the chargé d'affaires. Without exception they loathed him. So, when he called out to Mitch to report to his office immediately, Mitch knew this would not be a pleasant experience.

Mitch also recognized that it made for an interesting dilemma. Mitch worked for the Department of Defense, and Anderson worked for the Department of State. Sometimes that meant trying to mix oil and water. In this case, Mitch would show respect for the office of the chargé d'affaires but could question any orders directed toward him.

As Mitch entered Anderson's office, he was instructed to close the door. Although smoking in a government building was prohibited, the chargé d'affaires had his back to Mitch and was lighting a cigarette with an old zippo lighter from the Riviera Hotel in Vegas. A small fan secured to his large wooden desk softly blew the smoke toward an open window. Mitch's anger rose as he watched the arrogance of this narcissistic ass.

"Good afternoon, Colonel. Please take a seat."

"Thank you, but I would prefer to stand."

"As you wish," Anderson replied, exhaling a large amount of smoke that temporarily obscured his face.

"With all due respect, sir, smoking is prohibited in government buildings." Mitch threw the comment in for effect.

"I'm well aware of federal rules and regulations, but it's good to be king!" the chargé d'affaires countered. "Now let's get down to business, Colonel. Before the ambassador left for DC he briefed me on a few very important subject areas. The one I found most intriguing was your Indiana Jones adventure to find an American POW and rescue him.

"Regardless of how much you have planned or what your timetable might be, it is not going to happen under my watch. This pilot has been a POW for almost ten years, and you suspect that he might be held here in Algiers? What drugs have you been taking, Colonel? I can almost assure you that the pilot has been dead for many years. An American enemy aviator, an infidel, would last moments before his body would be vivisected and thrown to the dogs. What you're ultimately going to discover is your own dead body and those of any others that might be dumb enough to go with you on this ill-fated escapade. Listen closely,

Colonel. I forbid you from taking any more actions concerning this matter. Do you understand me?" Anderson smashed the cigarette butt in a glass ashtray near the fan and stared at Mitch.

"I understand everything that you said," Mitch replied, "and I also understand that you don't give a damn about our country's laws. You just care about your own ass and how to cover it. Let me explain the chain of command to you in very simple terms. The president of the United States, our ultimate boss, sits on top of this command structure, making him the overall boss of everything! Then there are a number of other folks under the president, including the secretaries of defense and state—my boss and your boss. Finally, there is the US ambassador to Algeria. He's been given the authority, by formal diplomatic credentials, to represent the United States in Algeria. You, sir, have never been given that authority. You're just sitting in while the ambassador is out of country. That's why you're called the chargé d'affaires and not Mr. Ambassador.

"By the way, did I mention that the president of the United States has directed this rescue operation? Did the ambassador mention that to you, or did you conveniently forget? If you have any heartburn about what I'm planning to do, then perhaps we can get on a telecom to the White House and discuss this with President Bush. I have no reservations about doing that, and I'm sure he would want to hear the latest plans that I've made.

"In conclusion, John, you know where I work and where I live. If you want to discuss this any further, I will be more than happy to do it, but not while I'm jeopardizing the health of my lungs standing in this fucking illegal smoke-filled room. Have a great State Department day, sir!"

Without waiting for Anderson to reply, Mitch strode out of the room, slamming the door behind him. He bid the chargé d'affaires's secretary a nice day and continued out of the chancery building and into the gardens. He found a large stone and sat near his Algerian gardener friend with the Dodger cap.

"*Bonjour, mon ami, les roses sont magnifiques!*" Mitch said. He marveled at how quickly the roses had grown and the beauty of their colors and fragrance.

"*Merci beaucoup, mon colonel,*" the elderly gentleman replied, nurturing the roses like a newborn grandchild.

As Mitch gazed at God's beautiful creations, a familiar voice interrupted his thoughts.

"I kinda thought you might be hangin' out in these parts of the embassy, Colonel. It's amazin' how this embassy fishbowl can't keep anything hidden too long," Jake said. He smiled and took a deep breath of the rose fragrance. "Just after I got back from the Spanish embassy a few minutes ago, I ran into my good friend who works for that SOB Anderson. She informed me that you verbally kicked his ass. She has this special talent for listening in on his conversations when he's about to get his ass handed to him. I reckon it had been a long time since that happened, but she suspected you had balls enough to do it. You, Colonel, just became her personal hero. I guess the chargé d'affaires stormed out of his office and went directly to his residence. He told her that he didn't want to be interrupted, which basically means he'll spend the rest of the day drinking wine until he passes out. What a loser! Colonel, you're a damn good man."

Mitch smiled but couldn't shake a slight anxiety. "Jake, I need to ask you a question about last night. You've been around the block many times and have been in quite a few tight situations. Honestly, what do you think of the plan?"

"Like I said last night, I think we'll be walkin' into the middle of a hornets' nest," Jake said. "Then we'll stir things up even more. Swatting hornets inside their nest is not the healthiest thing to do. I can guaran-damn-tee hornets will be comin' from places we never anticipated. All I can say, Colonel, is that some of us will be stung. Unfortunately, it's unavoidable in this type of situation."

"Jake, are you suggesting that we stand down until I get more help?"

"Nope, ya must keep this operation as you have it. Callin' in more folks like the 101st Airborne Division would only result in more deaths and casualties on both sides. Plus, the political fallout would be too hot. Let's go with what we have, and the sooner the better. Think of it this way, Colonel. Out of our six participants, five have actually been in combat or been involved in a firefight. I'm thinkin' we're goin' into that hornets' nest with a lot of expertise. Ramadan is just around the corner, and that means approximately thirty days of nighttime partying for all Muslims. During that time the bad guys could very well move Captain Hunt to a different location. Sir, we need to execute the plan ASAP."

"Thanks, Jake, I value your inputs. I should be getting back to the office. Dave is probably wondering where the hell I am."

"Sir, Dave is probably working on the rescue timetable and specific dates to execute the plan. When the chargé d'affaires's secretary told me what you had done, there were a few Marines lingerin' by, and I'm sure they overheard what she said. I'd bet a dime to a dollar that Dave has already heard of the verbal beatdown you gave John Anderson. That will motivate him even more to put the final touches on the plan. Sir, I have a stogie in my shirt pocket that's callin' me, so I'll wander over to the cafeteria and grab a cup of joe before gettin' back to work. You have a great afternoon, and I'm sure we'll be talkin'." With that, Jake turned and headed toward the embassy café.

Mitch returned to the chancery building. Just as Jake had predicted, Dave was reviewing the plan and identifying potential dates for the rescue.

"Sir, heard about your meeting with the chargé d'affaires," Dave said. "I wish I could have been a fly on the wall in that office."

"Bottom line is that John Anderson is not a team player," Mitch replied. "Never has been and never will be. He just doesn't think when he engages his mouth. Plus, the arrogance of smoking in a government office pisses me off. It amazes me that he's eluded the State Department ax. If I recall correctly, Anderson has a relative in

Congress who watches over him. Either way, we've gotta keep an eye on that guy. I don't trust him. Do you have updates for me?"

"Colonel, we know that the Muslim weekly holy day begins at sundown on Thursday and lasts until sundown on Friday. Looking at potential days to implement our plan, I suggest either Tuesday or Wednesday. From what I could understand from Djamila, Captain Hunt's only activity on either of those days would be his attendance at prayer. It shouldn't raise eyebrows if we were to reserve a large SUV for transportation on either of those days. If all looks good for next week, then I recommend either the evening of the twenty-sixth or twenty-seventh of September. Ultimately, Colonel, that would be your call."

"Either of those days would work for you, me, and Jake. But I'll have to check with the other three players and make sure they can clear their calendars. Good job, Dave! I'm leaning toward Wednesday the twenty-seventh. Djamila has mentioned that the evening before the weekly holy day is generally laid back. More than likely, Hunt's guards will not be at the top of their game."

"Sir, that sounds good to me. While we are on the subject of Djamila, I do have one request. If I brought a dessert, would it be okay to drop by your bungalow this evening after dinner?"

"Let me get this straight. What you're actually saying, Dave, is that you want to drop by and see Djamila after dinner? I have a better plan—why don't you bring the dessert, and we both can walk to the bungalow and have dinner with Djamila. Then you two can attempt to communicate while having dessert."

"Colonel, I would hate to impose on your dinner."

"It's no imposition. I'm sure Djamila has made a meal fit for a king and his army. Please, just come along. Djamila will be more than happy to see you."

"Great, sir. Thanks a lot. Is there any chance I can leave the office a little early so I can shower and change my clothes? Plus, I need to pick up a dessert."

"Dave, why don't you blast off now and come to the bungalow around six."

"Thanks, sir. See you then." Dave was out the office door before Mitch had time to tell him that Djamila had undoubtedly made a dessert.

21

Dave was getting nervous. "Damn, there's only two more days till we visit the Casbah," he said, staring at the large calendar just outside Mitch's office.

"The pucker factor's becoming intense alright," Mitch said. "My acid reflux is killing me. But in spite of all that, everyone on the team has confirmed that they're ready for the evening of the twenty-seventh. By the way, I've gotta talk to Jake about the four Berettas, ammunition, and the SUV."

"Not to worry, sir," Dave replied. "I've already touched base with the big man, and he's personally secured everything on the list. Jake is one of those guys you wish would be your neighbor for the rest of your life. He's always there when you need him."

"You're right, Dave. You don't find those types very often. I feel fortunate that his path crossed mine here at the embassy."

"Colonel, I hope you don't mind me asking—and I'm not trying to sound negative—but do you really think we'll succeed?"

"I guess that all depends on a number of factors," Mitch said. "Is Hunt really in the Casbah? What's his mental state? How many GSPC guards are there? Will they be tipped off that we're coming? Can we all get out alive? And is this really worth it? As military members, you and I salute smartly when the commander in chief orders us to accomplish a mission. But I guess the bottom line in everything we do in life is to give it our all. I read a quote many years ago, and I've forgotten who said it, but the quote has never left me: 'Always make a total effort, even when the odds are against you.'"

"Sir, do you think the odds are against us?"

"Perhaps—" The phone rang on Mitch's desk, cutting him off. He lifted it to his ear.

"Colonel Ross speaking."

Abella's voice came over the line. "Mitch, it's me."

"Is everything okay?"

"Everything is fine. I just wanted to ask if you would like a roommate tomorrow night? I thought it would be easier if I was with you at the embassy on the twenty-sixth. Then the next evening Djamila and I can depart together for the basilica. But to be honest with you, I just wanted an excuse to be with you."

"Sweetheart, you never need an excuse. You spending the night makes my thoughts a reality. And my thoughts are about your sexy athletic body and the warmth of your love rubbing up against me. But if we must discuss our adventure, yes, it does make more sense if you're here at the embassy, departing with Djamila."

"Great!" she said. "I'll see you tomorrow, late afternoon. I love you."

"Without a doubt, life is great when we're together—as long as bad guys aren't shooting at us. I love you too. See you tomorrow."

Abella hung up, and Mitch heard the second phone, as usual. He mentally reviewed their conversation and decided that the only concern was when she mentioned departing with Djamila to the basilica. But at this point, the words were now water under the bridge.

"Colonel, I hope you don't mind, but I overheard that Abella will be coming to the embassy tomorrow afternoon," Dave said. "I contacted Jake and asked if he could work his magic concerning her clearance to enter the embassy for the twenty-sixth and twenty-seventh. Sir, it's all been taken care of."

"Thanks, Dave. I do appreciate you taking care of that. Hopefully you didn't hear too much more of our conversation."

"No sir, I heard nothing else."

"Okay, that sounds convincing, and I'm the pope," Mitch said, trying to stifle his laughter. "Dave, let's call it a day and get the hell out of the office."

"You don't have to ask me twice, sir. I'm outta here!" Dave said. He grabbed his small backpack and headed for the office door.

Mitch was close behind as he ran the office checklist to make sure all the desks and tables were cleared of classified materials, the safes were locked, the office had a somewhat neat appearance, and the lights were turned off. As he closed the door and ran up the steps, he noticed a large suitcase in the chancery lobby. The luggage still had all its flight tags. Mitch took a quick look at the tags—Washington Dulles and Madrid International airports.

Why would the ambassador have his bag dropped off here at the chancery building? Normally it would go direct to his residence, Mitch thought.

"Colonel, it's been quite a while since I saw you last," a voice bellowed from the second story of the building.

Mitch spun around and looked up to see the embassy chief of station standing just outside a large secured door. "So, I've often wondered, does the CIA get to fly first class or at least business?" he asked.

"No, Colonel, Uncle Sugar is a little stingy when it comes to flying across the pond. It's economy all the way, and that means stiff knees and a sore back," Greg Cain said, rubbing his back and flexing his knees. "Hey, do you happen to have a few minutes? I'd like to fill you in on what's been going on with the ambassador in DC and also what the chargé d'affaires said to me when I was picked up at the airport."

Shit, that weasel Anderson must have filled Greg's ear with tales of how disrespectful I was in his smoke-filled office. "I'll be right up, Greg."

Greg held the secure door open until Mitch entered the office, and then they shook hands.

"It's been some time, Greg. The last word I received was that you were with the ambassador in the hot seat, being grilled by the congressional committee. That must have been a garden party with the committee serving shit sandwiches." Mitch knew that it was probably hell having to testify in front of that committee of angry members of Congress.

"Believe me, I would have preferred the shit sandwiches over what they served," Greg replied. "I doubt the ambassador will survive this inquiry. They want a scapegoat, and they're willing to throw him under the bus. Don't anticipate his return to the embassy. Unfortunately, I believe his career is over."

"That's a damn shame," Mitch said, shaking his head. "The ambassador is a good man. There wasn't much more he could have done here to prepare for an attack. Perhaps he could have closed down the embassy and sent all the Americans back home, but the State Department wanted it left open. I'd say he was damned if he did and damned if he didn't. Greg, this topic makes me ill. Let's change subjects. What did John Anderson say while you two rode back from the airport?"

"First, let me say that I've never enjoyed that guy's company. He can't be trusted and, basically, he's an asshole. Now let me tell you how I really feel about him!" Greg smiled as he turned, poured two cups of coffee, and handed one to Mitch. "Anderson didn't come to the airport to see me but because he wanted to get the latest on the ambassador's situation. John mentioned that he felt your attempt to rescue Captain Hunt was getting close. He believes you'll go after the captured pilot within the month.

"Colonel, you do know that he will do everything in his power to stop you, correct? Anderson wants absolutely no mistakes while he's sitting on the embassy throne. In his feeble mind he believes that he'll become the next US ambassador to Algeria. Hell, there are members of the congressional committee talking to the secretary of state and recommending names of diplomats from their districts or states. John Anderson's name was never mentioned. If he honestly thinks that he'll be elevated to the position of ambassador, it's just a wet dream. He'll wake up one of these mornings, and the only thing he'll discover are dirty sheets!

"But again, he plans to stop you from attempting the rescue of Captain Hunt. If you're going to try, you better do it now! I heard that Anderson talked to his uncle, a US senator from New Jersey who has the president's ear. I believe he and his uncle will levy enough influence at least to convince the president to delay the rescue attempt. Mitch, I don't know what you have planned, but if there is any assistance needed, please don't hesitate to ask."

"It's happening in the next few days," Mitch said. "My plan is to minimize the number of players involved. I do appreciate your offer to help out, but . . ." He paused, thinking over the plan details. "Actually, there's one aspect where you might be able to assist. I could use one of those covert communication systems similar to what the Secret Service uses. You know, the small earpiece and wire running down under the shirt. I only need two, one for me and one for Jake Davis."

"So, Big Jake will be part of your team? Glad to hear that. I definitely would have him at the top of my list. Concerning the com system you need, not a problem. I'll get that to you before we finish our coffee. Are you sure you don't need any backup firepower? I've got the manpower, and I don't give a damn about the chargé d'affaires and his political aspirations."

"Thanks, Greg, but I think my team is good to go."

Greg opened the top drawer of a nearby safe and pulled out two com units.

"There isn't much to them," Greg said. "Most of the unit ends up hidden under your shirt. But they pay off in spades when you're in a tight situation. Let's hope you don't find yourself in that type of situation, but if you do, being able to communicate can buy you valuable moments."

"Greg, I really appreciate your support and being open kimono with me about the ambassador and that damn Anderson. Who knows how far he'll go to stop me. I guess all I can do is try to keep a low profile until it's time to blast to the Casbah."

"Take care, Colonel. And remember, my offer of support still stands."

"Thanks again, and welcome back to the land of dates and couscous," Mitch said as he juggled the coffee cup and com systems while opening the heavy secured door. He descended the stairs and left the chancery building at a good clip. The last person he wanted to run into was Anderson, so he headed to a group of trees near the ambassador's residence and then walked between a tall hedge grove and a large wall surrounding the ambassador's pool.

"Sir, are you practicing a little escape and evasion while cutting through the ambo's surroundings?"

Mitch spun around to see the Marine gunny sergeant looking through a portal of the wall along the pool. The gunny was smiling and drenched from swimming.

"Sorry to startle you, Colonel. I just found it odd that you were taking this unusual route to your bungalow."

"Gunny, I didn't expect anyone to be around here since the ambassador's in DC and his residence is locked up," Mitch replied. "Did you sneak into the pool?"

"No sir, the chargé d'affaires knows that I like to swim laps, so he told me that I could use the ambo's pool once a day. But unfortunately, it came with a price. That man is out to get you and is spreading the word that you are violating his direct orders to stand down. He didn't disclose what you're planning on doing, but he requested that if any Marine sees you and other embassy staff attempting to depart the embassy in an SUV, we are to stop you immediately. At gunpoint, if necessary! Sir, this puts me and the other Marines in a difficult position. I'm not exactly sure what I should do, but I did want to get my laps in before I'm told the pool is off limits."

"Gunny, what I can tell you is that President Bush and the ambassador have directed me to accomplish a very dangerous mission. I can't go into details, but Jake Davis and Warrant Officer Dave McQueen will confirm the importance of our task. John Anderson has this wild idea that he'll take over the embassy as the ambassador. He doesn't want any hiccups here while he's calling the shots. And he definitely thinks that I'm a roadblock to his success and my mission is a threat to his future plans. Gunny, I will not stand in your way and order you to disobey Anderson's wishes. I have never lied to you, but I will remind you that the commander in chief has directed my mission. You take care and think about this conversation."

With that, Mitch headed toward his bungalow.

22

The next day Mitch spent most of his morning away from the office to avoid the chargé d'affaires. He wanted no issues encumbering the plan in the final hours before it could be executed. At the same time, Mitch looked forward to Abella's arrival. There was a special aura about her. She had an uncanny ability to find that ripened berry in a thorny briar patch, no matter how dark a situation might be. That was one of many reasons he loved her so much.

"Colonel Mitch, I've left your dinner in the oven," Djamila said, gathering her bags and food for her father. "You just need to heat it up when Abella arrives. Thank you for letting me leave early today."

"No need to thank me," Mitch replied. "You'll be making up this time tomorrow. Our special team will be working overtime into the late evening. Let's hope it's all for the good." Mitch struggled to find the right French terms as he responded, a slight tone of despair in his voice.

Djamila immediately picked up on his feeling of remorse and reached out, taking his hand in hers. "Colonel Mitch, what we're doing tomorrow is just and noble. Rescuing a person who has been imprisoned and away from home and family for all those years—it is something I can't imagine." Djamila squeezed his hand and gently touched his face. She looked into his eyes with determination. "Tomorrow night will reveal Allah's wishes, inshallah."

"You are correct, Djamila. It is now completely in the hands of God," Mitch said as he helped her gather her bags.

Mitch stood at the door of his bungalow, watching Djamila walk to the embassy security exit point. During the past few months, he had grown closer and truly gotten to know the hearts and souls of those who were assisting in the rescue attempt. *They are willing to risk all for this cause,* Mitch marveled. As Djamila disappeared from view, his thoughts drifted to each of the team members. He turned and closed the door, looking at his watch. Within the hour, his entire world would change for the better with Abella's arrival.

Later, Mitch anxiously waited in the security building as Abella's taxi came to an abrupt stop outside the embassy, kicking up dust and debris. He peered through the bulletproof window. She stepped out of the cab, carrying a small travel bag and looking as if she could be modeling for *Vogue* magazine.

After the standard exchange of Arabic with the embassy security sergeant, Abella pushed her passport through the small slot of the secured door. Within moments she was granted entry. She immediately greeted Mitch with a kiss and whispered how much she loved him. After the security sergeant returned Abella's passport, Mitch took her hand and her bag, and they left the building, headed toward the rose garden.

"Damn, are you working on building up your biceps?" Mitch asked. "This bag is heavy!"

"Hey, I've brought a few surprises for us," she laughed.

"You know that drives me nuts when you have a surprise and you won't tell me," Mitch replied. "Now I've got to pick up the pace to make it to the bungalow before my arm gives out. And the sooner we arrive, the sooner I can find out what items you've stuck in this bag."

"Okay, but you must promise me that you'll just sit and watch without grabbing anything."

"I can't guarantee that. There might be items that I'll have to examine closely."

"Sorry, Casanova. That's not the deal."

The negotiations were getting quite interesting by the time they arrived at the bungalow.

"You sit on the couch and I'll stand by the window," Abella said as she moved to the living room window and closed the curtains. "Then I'll slowly disclose what is hidden in the bag."

She smiled and winked, placing her bag on a small stool. After a moment she said, "But perhaps before I begin we should have a little wine." With that, Abella pulled two bottles of Algerian red wine from the bag and took them to the kitchen. She returned and gave one to Mitch, then raised her glass. "May we always love and laugh together."

"Hear, hear!" Mitch replied, touching Abella's glass with his, and then kissed her. "Okay, let's get back to the surprises."

Abella took a long draw from her glass and placed it on an end table. "Now for the rest of the mystery items," she said, pulling out a change of clothing. She dug into the bag again and withdrew a homemade apple pie. Mitch stood, ready to carry it to the kitchen, but Abella pointed at his seat on the couch. "No, no, no! Remember, you can't touch any item that comes from this bag."

She placed the pie on the kitchen table and returned to the bag to withdraw a large container of couscous with raisins and almonds. Then came a large bottle of honey. Mitch assumed it would be poured on the couscous once it was heated and ready to be eaten.

"This couscous dessert is always a crowd-pleaser in Algeria," Abella said as she placed the container and honey next to the pie. She sipped her wine again. Mitch watched the red liquid magic dance and swirl in the long-stemmed glass. She smiled at him and reached into the bag once more. Taking her time, she revealed a slender, dark bottle of oil, turning the label so Mitch could read it: *Huile Corps Sensual d'Afrique du Nord*. He nearly choked on his wine as he mentally translated the label: *North African Sensual Body Oil.*

He quickly looked up at Abella as she stepped over to the kitchen table and put the bottle next to the couscous. Then she grabbed the bag and said nothing other than raising her index finger for silence before disappearing into the bathroom. Moments later the door opened, and she stepped out wearing only a burgundy laced teddy that barely covered her buttocks and plunged seductively between her breasts. Mitch's glass fell from his hand, sending wine snaking along a groove in the wooden floor, but he didn't notice. He was stunned by the sheer beauty before him. As Abella delicately reclaimed her wineglass, the teddy swayed and revealed portions of her feminine secrets. Mitch stood and took a step toward her.

"Remember, you can't touch anything from the bag," she reminded him, perching in a nearby chair and smoothly crossing her tanned legs. Her new position revealed the toned thighs leading to her attractively firm derrière. She raised her glass to her lips and slowly sipped. The wine was the same color as her teddy and the polish of her toenails.

Mitch was unable to formulate words in his mind.

"Well, Colonel Ross, do you want to heat up the dinner?" Abella asked.

Mitch stuttered, "I . . . I . . . I think you already have!"

Abella seductively uncrossed her legs and stood. Mitch caught the scent of her exquisitely perfumed body, and he felt intense desire to make love to her. Setting her glass on the kitchen table, she leaned slightly to grab the bottle of body oil, knowing full well that it revealed more of her nakedness. She walked toward the bedroom and paused, then looked over her left shoulder at Mitch and winked.

"Remember, Colonel, the words of a very intelligent American actress: 'If you obey all the rules, you miss all the fun.'" She disappeared into the bedroom.

Mitch sat paralyzed. His mind screamed at him to get up—nirvana was just a few steps away. Finally, he came to his senses, stood, and stumbled to the bedroom. Just before entering he grabbed a bottle of bourbon and two shot glasses. The dinner in the oven was forgotten, as was the pie and couscous. What Abella and Mitch were to share only God could provide.

23

bella decided that the apple pie and couscous dessert would make for a perfect breakfast to be consumed in bed. She grabbed Mitch's oversized robe and shoved on an old ball cap to keep her hair out of her face. Soon the coffee was brewing and she was putting the final touches on their morning meal.

Mitch stirred when he heard the final perking of the coffee pot and smelled the aroma of warm pie. As he sat up, Abella carried a breakfast tray into the bedroom.

"Good morning, sexy!" Mitch said. He moved to one side of the bed to make room for her to slip in next to him. "Hope you're having as great a morning as I am."

"Yes, I am," she replied. "But yesterday evening will be hard to beat!"

Mitch laughed as Abella shed the robe and slipped into bed, still wearing the ball cap. They kissed as she passed the tray of food and coffee.

"You know, I almost thought that this day would never arrive," Mitch said. "All our planning and preparation hasn't been easy. Not to mention the close calls we've had just trying to get information that would assist in finding Hunt. He'd damn well better be there and appreciate what we've done!"

"Please don't get all stressed during breakfast," Abella replied. "Let's try not to think about what we must do this evening. Let's discuss what we did last night." As she spoke, she took a spoonful of the warm, honey-covered couscous and gently fed it to Mitch.

"You're right, that couscous makes for a fabulous dessert," Mitch said. "But as much as I like it, I have to leave room for a large slice of apple pie and a few cups of coffee. By the way, have you greased the skids lately with the archbishop concerning our rendezvous at the basilica this evening?"

"I'm not sure what you mean," Abella exclaimed. "Greasing skids with an archbishop sounds like an unnatural sex act! But if you mean have I talked to the archbishop recently? The answer is yes, yesterday morning. He's anxiously awaiting our arrival."

"Great, just wanted to reconfirm, sweetheart. As you can tell, the needle on my stress meter is nearly pegged out in the red zone. Maybe I need to cut down on caffeine or take another couple shots of bourbon."

"Why don't we finish our breakfast and then jump in the shower together? I would be embarrassed if Djamila arrived and we were still in bed."

"Okay, that sounds like a plan," Mitch replied as he grabbed a large slice of pie and shoved half of it in his mouth. He attempted to continue speaking, but it was impossible with all the crust and apple fragments bulging his cheeks and falling from his pursed lips. He placed the breakfast tray on a nightstand, threw off the bed covers, grabbed Abella's hand, and the two of them raced naked to the shower.

"I love taking showers with you. It's like being on a fantasy vacation without ever leaving the house," Abella said, standing on her toes and massaging shampoo into Mitch's scalp.

"I've gotta agree," Mitch responded. "And the scenery is definitely spectacular from my perspective." A moment later, he went rigid and grabbed Abella's forearms to stop all movement in the shower except for the spraying water.

"What is it?" Abella asked, staring at him.

"I heard knocking at the front door. Djamila has a key, so it's not her," Mitch said. He quickly left the shower, threw on his robe, and sprinted to the door. A young Marine was walking away from the bungalow when Mitch yanked the door open.

"Marine, what's up?" Mitch inquired, his wet hair dripping soapy water onto the wooden floor.

The Marine immediately spun around and stood at attention. "Sir, the embassy operator has been trying to reach you. It appears that the ambassador has been calling from Washington, DC, and wanted to talk to you."

Mitch thanked the Marine and closed the door. In the meantime, Abella had dried off and gotten dressed. Having heard what the Marine said, her mind was spinning with questions.

"What do you think the ambassador wants to tell you?" she asked.

"It could be a number of things. I need to call him pronto." Mitch reached for the secure phone in the cabinet just above the sink and dialed the embassy operator. "Hello, this is Colonel Ross. I understand that the ambassador has been trying to reach me. I'm hoping that he can talk secure from his end."

"Yes, Colonel, the ambassador seems rather anxious to get ahold of you. He stated that you could call him now because he will be at the State Department for the next few hours. He did call from a secure phone."

"Thank you for the information. Would you please connect me to the ambassador?"

"Absolutely, Colonel."

There was a long pause, and then Mitch heard ringing on the other line.

The ambassador's voice came through. "Hello?"

Mitch was shocked by how meek he sounded.

"Mr. Ambassador, this is Colonel Ross. I understand you've been trying to reach me."

"Yes, Mitch, I needed to inform you of a number of issues. Can you talk secure?"

"Yes sir," Mitch responded.

The ambassador continued, "The first item is that I will not be returning to Algeria. In fact, my career has ended, and I'm being forced into retirement. Unfortunately, you will have to contend with that bastard Chargé D'Affaires Anderson until President Bush confirms the State Department nominee as the next ambassador.

"President Bush invited me to the Oval Office and thanked me for my dedication and service to America. But I could tell the president wanted to discuss something much more important than my career. He stated that the chairman of the Armed Services Committee, Senator Carl Levin, had been giving him a lot of pressure concerning progress in finding Captain Hunt. Evidently Hunt's family is wealthy and comes from Detroit, Michigan. They're very close to the good senator. Hunt's father donated heavily to Levin's reelection campaign in '96. Therefore, Levin has personal stakes in this matter.

"Colonel, although I'm no longer in the game, I wanted to make sure you were aware of my conversation with the president. You must move out as soon as possible concerning Hunt. Senator Levin told the president that if no action is taken to find Hunt soon, he will have no other recourse but to take the matter to the press. Good luck, Mitch, and the next time you happen to be near Santa Fe, please look me up. Take care."

Mitch put the phone down and turned to Abella, who was sitting on the couch.

"The ambassador is never coming back. But he told me that President Bush is being pressured by the Armed Services Committee chairman to find Hunt," Mitch said in a monotone. "So much for attempting not to think about the rescue. My pulse rate just tripled. Is that bottle of bourbon still in the bedroom? I might have a liquid lunch today with my good buddy Jim Beam."

Just as Mitch finished his sentence, Djamila tapped on the front door and entered. She smiled at the image of Mitch, still in his robe and bare feet, looking like a drowned rat with soapy wet hair lying limp over his face and ears.

"*Sabah al khair,*" Abella said, wishing Djamila a good morning in Arabic.

While the ladies continued in Arabic, Mitch ducked into the bedroom. Soon the three would need to be ready for their departure. It was 3 p.m. Abella and Djamila would be leaving the embassy at 3:30 and taking a taxi to the Notre Dame d'Afrique Catholic basilica. At that same time, Mitch would walk to the embassy front gate and rendezvous with Jake and Dave at their SUV.

Abella was not her happy-go-lucky self as she helped Djamila clean up the bungalow.

"Are you feeling okay?" Mitch whispered so Djamila couldn't hear.

"I'm not sure. I've got this foreboding feeling that our plan will fall apart. I don't want anything to happen to you. I want us! I want our future to be as we have dreamed it would be. I have lost too much in my life, and if I lose you, there will be nothing left for me." Abella began to sob as Mitch reached out and held her to his chest.

"Don't worry, we'll get through this and be together regardless of the outcome. I love you, and that will never change!"

Abella looked up at Mitch and kissed him. Djamila had been cleaning the bedroom and returned to the kitchen as Mitch and Abella picked up items left on the couch and end table from their previous night of magic.

"Ladies, departure time is in twenty minutes. Grab what you must, and I'll get the taxi for you," Mitch slowly stated in French.

Mitch called embassy security to request a 3:30 taxi pickup as Abella and Djamila grabbed items from the kitchen. After firmly closing and locking the bungalow door, Mitch joined the ladies, and the three of them walked to the embassy security exit where the taxi was waiting. He kissed Abella and pressed the taxi fare into the palm of her hand. Abella and Djamila left the confines of the embassy, and as the vehicle departed to the basilica, Mitch turned and headed for the SUV. An unmistakable cigar aroma floated toward him on the warm Mediterranean breeze rustling the palm leaves of a nearby coconut tree. As Mitch approached the vehicle, he spotted Jake and Dave leaning against the vehicle, talking. They looked in his direction.

"Afternoon, Colonel," Jake said. "Got this SUV packed with all our firepower, com gear, water bottles, and a flask of sweet Kentucky bourbon. I believe we're ready to rock and roll, unless the good warrant officer wants to add a few items to the list." Jake's cigar was clenched tightly between his teeth, and a slight tone of stress slipped through his Kentucky accent.

"No additional stuff from me," Dave said. "I'm carrying my hoodie to slip on for our trek to the jewelry shop and then to Hunt's place." He slowly saluted Mitch and then reached out and shook his hand.

Mitch smiled. "Let's roll, guys. The ladies are already heading toward the basilica, and I'm sure our good French colonel will be there waiting for us."

"Sir, if you don't mind, I'll take shotgun and you can sit in the VIP position in the back seat," Dave said as they climbed in the vehicle. "If we encounter trouble, it's an easier shot for me here in the front."

As Jake closed the driver's door and started the engine, a voice yelled out. It was the chargé d'affaires, screaming from the steps near the security-guard house that led to the chancery building.

"Stop them! Stop them now!" Anderson shouted, rushing toward the vehicle while pointing at three Marines. "If they continue, then shoot them. I'm ordering you Marines to do what I say! I will not allow any of this Indiana Jones mentality to exist while I'm in charge at this embassy. Arrest those three scum bastards!"

The three young Marines instinctively reacted to the orders and ran toward the SUV. Anderson continued to scream like a psychotic madman.

"Stop them! Shoot them! I want those three traitors thrown in the embassy detention chamber."

As the Marines raised their weapons, an authoritative voice echoed loud and strong from behind a cluster of palm trees near the motor pool.

"Marines, stand down!"

Immediately the three Marines lowered their weapons and stood at attention. Then another order echoed out from the trees.

"Marines, about-face!"

The Marines pivoted in unison and stood motionless like steel rods. From the cluster of trees, the Marine gunny sergeant stepped out and moved toward the chargé d'affaires.

"You, sir, have no authority to order US Marines to accomplish your dirty work," the gunny said. "I'm sure had they fired on that vehicle, you would have eventually accused them of murder or attempted murder and ruined their lives. Marines, return to the chancery."

The Marines immediately climbed the steps leading to the embassy's main building. As the gunny walked past the idling SUV, he stopped, stood at attention, and saluted Mitch in the back seat.

Anderson looked stunned. But then he appeared to snap out of it. In a flash, he ran up to an Algerian security guard standing near the vehicle and yanked the nine-millimeter pistol from the man's hand. He moved in front of the SUV and pointed the weapon at Jake.

"Get out of the vehicle now. Do you hear me?" Anderson yelled. Jake squinted and stared at him, unflinchingly calm.

Jake said nothing as he slowly opened the door, stepped out of the vehicle, and forcefully spit the remnants of his cigar toward Anderson. He walked toward the crazed diplomat with cool determination. Anderson kept the pistol trained directly at Jake's head, but the big man continued his approach, looming over Anderson. The nearby security guards froze as the drama unfolded. It was as if all movement and sound had ceased except for Jake's footsteps.

"Stop, you fucking idiot, or I'll blow your head off!" Anderson yelled, holding the pistol in his trembling hands.

Jake stopped just in front of him. Still without a word, he grabbed the gun with his left hand and then drove his massive right fist into Anderson's jaw and throat. The force of the blow lifted the madman off his feet and sent him falling hard on the dirt, unconscious, blood trickling from the corner of his mouth.

Jake glanced at his fist and brushed off his knuckles on his pant leg. Then he finally spoke.

"You two, drag this sorry piece a shit out of the path of the truck. Get a couple ice packs. That poor bastard will need 'em when he comes to." Jake's order snapped the stunned guards back to reality. They hustled over and pulled the chargé d'affaires to an adjacent palm tree and then opened the gate to allow the vehicle to depart the embassy. Jake reentered the SUV, slammed the vehicle into gear, and mashed the accelerator, sending a hail of dirt and stones flying behind them as the rear tires clawed for traction.

Nothing was said during the ride to the basilica. The three men reflected on what had just happened and what might occur in the Casbah. As Jake pulled the SUV into the parking area near the large, beautiful church, Dave handed Mitch an M9 pistol and spare clip. Jake turned off the engine and looked in the rearview mirror at Mitch.

"Colonel, sorry 'bout the commotion just prior to our departure, but that sonuvabitch Anderson was well over the line. No man points a gun at me and gets away with it. Yep, I reckon I sealed the deal on my State Department career, but it was worth it. Oh, I hope you don't mind, but I brought my good luck charm with me. I always like to carry it when I'm operatin' in close quarters." Jake turned toward Mitch and opened his jacket. Just below his armpit was an extended holster holding an Uzi pistol.

"This sweet thang comes with a twenty-round magazine. Don't get me wrong, Colonel, I do like the M9, but for peace of mind, give me my lucky charm." Jake laughed and then pointed at an SUV parked near the entrance of the basilica. "It appears that our friend Colonel Dureau has arrived. Those two French security agents sittin' in the vehicle over yonder are good ol' boys. With them around I feel quite secure. To be honest, those Frenchies make me look small, and I tip the scale at 275 on a good day. There's no fat on them; they're all muscle. Wish they were comin' with us into the Casbah, but tryin' to hide them might be a challenge." Jake stepped out of the vehicle and slowly withdrew his Uzi as he scanned the area.

Dave and Mitch exited the SUV and bolted to the basilica's huge wooden doors. Jake followed closely after acknowledging his French security friends with a wave. From a darkened area near one of the huge entries, a hooded nun appeared and welcomed the men.

"*Que Dieu te bénisse.*"

"*Et vous avez aussi,*" Mitch replied. They all needed the blessing of God this evening.

Dave opened the large wooden door, and the beauty of the old basilica revealed itself. The pews were highly polished but seemed to be of the original lumber of the mid-1800s, complete with nicks and scars. The surrounding walls were engraved with the names of French colonists from that early era. As the three men carefully stepped upon the stone-slab floor, they noticed that they were walking on the colonists' tombs. They focused on the exquisite but simple altar and smelled the burning candles that had been lit by worshippers earlier in the day. Finally, they looked up and took in the magnificence of the painting inside the dome, depicting the Madonna holding baby Jesus in the clouds while ancient worshippers knelt in the heavens and on earth. The beauty and vivid colors were breathtaking.

"Isn't it amazing that this beautiful Christian treasure has survived?" Abella whispered to Mitch as she stepped from a shadowy corner of the sanctuary and reached out to hold his hand. "As a young girl I would gaze up at the dome in awe of its beauty."

"Without a doubt, it's truly a hidden treasure."

As they all gathered under the dome, the silence was broken by a warm voice.

"*Bonsoir, bonsoir, mes amis. Je suis Archbishop Jacques Durand.*" Switching into halting English, he said, "I am so happy you are here."

As the archbishop greeted the group, Mitch made sure his M9 was well hidden. Yves noticed and reached into his jacket to push his pistol grip farther into its hidden holster.

"So, it's finally come to this, my good man," Yves whispered to Mitch. "We tour God's house before we enter Satan's den of iniquity."

"Ironic, isn't it?" Mitch responded philosophically. "We're carrying out the desires of politicians as we pray to God for a successful outcome. At the same time, those who we'll confront tonight are praying to Allah. So which side will God bless and protect during our attempt to rescue Hunt?" He glanced at Yves and noticed Abella making the sign of the cross.

The archbishop proudly continued the tour of the basilica in English, pointing out historical aspects of the sanctuary. The only member of the group who seemed to be ignoring the archbishop was Djamila. She was captivated by the beauty of the statues and paintings, the likes of which she had never seen in a mosque.

Eventually, Djamila and Dave broke off from the main group, and a nun who spoke English and French took them on their own private tour.

As the archbishop finished his presentation, Abella quietly asked if he would make a special blessing. The entire group sat and then knelt in the front pews of the church as the blessing was given.

Mitch glanced at his watch. It was 7 p.m. He gently squeezed Abella's hand and whispered, "Sweetheart, your taxi should be waiting outside. It's time for you and Djamila to depart."

Abella gazed at him with tears in her eyes and attempted to say something, but her emotions prevented her. Each member of the group thanked the archbishop and then proceeded to the doors of the basilica. Mitch pulled Abella behind a large column and held her tightly in his arms.

"Always remember my love for you," Mitch said, kissing her one last time. Abella was still too emotional to respond and held on to him as she buried her head into his chest, crying softly. "Sweetheart, it's time." Mitch walked with her to the door and placed his M9 in her purse. He stood at the top of the sanctuary steps to make sure that the two women safely entered the taxi. Soon the taillights disappeared in the distance as the vehicle headed toward the Casbah.

From just behind Mitch, in the shadows, Jake also watched the women depart. He placed his big hand on Mitch's shoulder.

"Colonel, don't you worry about that pretty little thang. She'll be alright. Abella's a jewel in the rough and can take care of herself in a tight situation. By the way, here's your com gear. I already have mine on. I'm feelin' like a real Secret Service agent lookin' out for the president."

"Regardless of the outcome tonight, Jake, I hope we'll always be close."

"You can count on it, Colonel. That'll never change."

Jake reentered the basilica as Mitch gazed into the darkness toward the Casbah. Eventually Mitch walked back into the sanctuary and noticed Dave sitting alone in the pews.

"Dave, I was wondering if you might have brought another M9. I gave mine to Abella just before she departed."

"Ah shit, sir, I gave Djamila the other M9 to give to Abella once they were in the taxi. The women will have a lot of firepower, and we'll be suckin' hind tit for protection during our hike through the Casbah."

"Not to worry, Dave," Mitch said. "With the way you handle a gun, I'm feeling rather confident that anyone trying to stop us will be taken out." He hooked the com gear to his belt, running the thin wire under his shirt and finally placing the earpiece.

"Jake, how do you read me?"

"I read you loud and clear, Colonel. Hope it works this well when we're running through the Casbah."

"It's just about time for Dave and me to shove off. Our French security guards will chauffeur us to a rendezvous with the Spanish deputy ambassador's maid at the southern entry. I'll see you outside."

"Roger that, Colonel," Jake responded.

Mitch turned to Dave, gave him the thumbs-up, and they headed out the door. Jake was taking in the beautiful view of the moon reflecting off the Mediterranean as he smoked.

"Good luck, Colonel. I'll see you and Dave on the other side," Jake said. He shook their hands and took a long drag on his cigar.

"Take care, Jake," Mitch said. He and Dave walked to the French security vehicle waiting for them in the parking lot.

"*Bonsoir, mes amis*," Mitch said as he entered the French SUV.

"*Bonsoir, Colonel*," the senior security guard responded. A moment later he added, "Would it be okay to practice our English while we drive to your drop-off point?"

Mitch responded, "That would be great, considering the two of us cannot speak French as well as you speak English."

The two Frenchmen laughed. The laughter pleased Mitch; it was the first light moment he and Dave had experienced in many hours.

A short time later, the driver stopped in the Algerian naval headquarters parking area, concealing the SUV in the shadow of a tall tree that blocked the adjacent streetlamp. No one would question the embassy vehicle stopping there, even though it was later in the evening. Dave pulled on his hooded sweatshirt as Mitch slid his arms into a worn, brown leather jacket. To cover his blond hair, Mitch donned an old, unmarked, khaki-colored ball cap that showed years of dried sweat along the headband. Dave tightened the drawstrings of his hood, leaving only his nose and eyes exposed.

"*Merci, mes amis*," Mitch said to the French security guards as he and Dave left the vehicle and stepped into the darkness.

"*Bon chance, Colonel*," the driver responded. Then the two guards drove the SUV back onto the main road, heading for the French embassy.

Mitch felt a cool shiver from the evening breeze, which carried a slight salty taste of the sea and the smell of oil from the large ships anchored in the port, waiting to be unloaded of their freight.

"Colonel, what did the guard just say to you? It didn't seem to put a smile on your face," Dave whispered with a tone of concern.

Mitch tugged on the old cap, pulling it as far over his face as possible. "The sergeant wished us good luck, but in a very ominous manner," he said. Then he zipped up his jacket and readjusted his com cord.

Dave glanced across the street and noticed a young woman standing near the ancient portal arch that led to the steps of the Casbah. She was shifting nervously back and forth.

"Sir, I believe our guide is waiting," Dave said, pointing with his thumb to conceal the movement.

"Let's go, but slowly because I don't want to spook her," Mitch replied as he approached. "She's obviously nervous. Can't blame her. We're strangers to her. All she knows is that she is to meet two Americans at 7:35 p.m. at the southern entry. I would be nervous too, seeing a couple guys approach me, looking like they're ready to rob a bank."

The deputy ambassador's maid immediately noticed the two men approaching. She took a few steps back and weakly raised her right hand to waist level, giving them a nervous wave. Mitch acknowledged with a corresponding wave to reduce any unusual movements that others might detect.

"*Bonsoir, je suis* Mitch, *et* Dave *est mon ami*," Mitch said quietly as he approached the young woman.

She smiled, and her nerves seemed to calm as she heard Mitch's American accent. "*Bonsoir, je suis* Kahina. *Je travaille dans l'ambassade d'Espagne*," she said.

"*Enchanter, Mademoiselle* Kahina. *Pouvez-vous parlez en espagnol pour mon ami?*" Mitch asked if she would speak in Spanish so Dave would understand.

"*Bien sûr, pas un problème*," Kahina responded and then turned to Dave. "*Buenas noches*."

"Kahina, *gracias por hablar en español*," Dave responded, smiling. The two of them started up the narrow steps as Mitch followed closely behind, looking for any unusual silhouettes in the darkness of the Casbah.

Damn, wish I had that M9, he thought as he climbed.

As the three progressed, Mitch noticed no one along the narrow passageway. He wasn't sure whether that was normal, but from what he remembered of Djamila's descriptions, after prayer most returned to their homes for an evening meal. The scent of lamb, melted butter, cinnamon, and baked bread filled the closed-in spaces of their ancient surroundings and relaxed Mitch; most of the inhabitants of the Casbah were concentrating on their meal and not the three strangers walking the steps.

They continued to climb in the silent night as Mitch experienced a contradictory feeling of security and fear.

24

Jake took a last pull on his cigar. "Colonel Dureau, it's just about time to mount up and head out to naval headquarters. I believe a quick pick-me-up is in order, if you care to join me?" Jake wrapped his big hand around the silver flask from his inner vest pocket and slowly unscrewed the top to reveal the dark-golden fluid.

He noticed Yves's smile and handed over the flask. "Take a hefty swig of that enchanted liquid. It might be the last you'll taste for some time," Jake said. In the darkness of the evening, the waves of the Med beat like bass drums on the rocks below the cliff near the basilica.

Yves raised the flask. "My good man, I would like to say a few words. May we succeed in our endeavor and one day rejoice in my Paris abode beneath the shadow of the Eiffel Tower."

Jake shook his head in amazement. "Well, Colonel, that beats the shit out of anythang I was gonna say. Let's drink up and head out."

Yves took a healthy mouthful and handed the flask back to Jake. The remaining booze was quickly consumed by the Kentuckian, and he returned the empty vessel to his inner vest pocket.

- • - •

Abella looked at her watch. At any moment, Mitch, Dave, and the maid would be walking past Djamila's father's home. She carefully parted the curtains of the front window, allowing herself a view of the darkened steps. The stillness of the Casbah frightened her, as if the ancient structures concealed impending doom. Djamila sat near her father on the couch, waiting for Abella to indicate that Mitch and Dave were passing. Abella strained to look in the direction of the mosque but took care not to open the curtains more than necessary.

"*Ils devraient passer bientôt*," Abella whispered to Djamila. Their men should pass soon.

Djamila moved from the couch and stood behind Abella, quietly hoping that all was well with them. "*J'espère que tout va bien*," she said.

Then, from a dark corner near the steps leading up from the mosque, a cat sprang out and howled in fear. The noise startled Abella, and she quickly looked to her left, opening the curtain a few more inches. She barely made out three silhouettes in the darkness as they ascended the steps.

"Djamila, *ils sont ici*," Abella said and moved slightly so Djamila could also look through the slight opening in the curtain.

As Mitch, Dave, and Kahina passed Djamila's father's house, Dave glanced at Mitch, and they both quickly looked at the sliver of light coming from the parted curtains. No special movements or signals were made as they continued their climb.

Abella checked her watch. It was 7:45, and all seemed to be going as planned. Djamila's father was having his dinner, and water for tea was boiling on the stove.

– • – •

The jewelry shop was dark and seemed securely locked when they approached. Kahina tapped on the door a few times and whispered her name. Quickly the door opened, and the three of them were temporarily blinded by the light emanating from within.

"*Veuillez entrer, s'il vous plaît.*" An old, thin, white-bearded man who was slightly hunched beckoned for them to enter. The scent of hot mint tea permeated the interior of the shop. Mitch quickly glanced around the large room as he entered, noticing glass-encased gold and diamond jewelry. He was amazed at the jeweled treasures. They seemed endless.

The glass countertops had been prepared with special displays of rings, necklaces, and bracelets. The large gold pieces caught Dave's eye, pulling him toward the hundreds of necklaces and bracelets. But for Mitch it was the delicate rings that he wanted to examine. He hoped one would reach out to him. It had to be unique, beautiful, robust, yet feminine like Abella. It would represent the love and the future he wanted to share with her. Mitch knew that time was his enemy, but he was not going to settle for second best.

As the old man laid rings on cushions of velvet that rested on the glass countertop, Mitch grew disappointed that no ring spoke to him. In the meantime, Dave had found and purchased a gold necklace and bracelet for Djamila.

"Sir, any luck?" Dave said as he stepped closer to Mitch.

"Nothing seems to jump out and grab me. I'm getting a little disheartened because it's almost time to depart," Mitch responded gloomily.

Kahina poured the mint tea and served it to the men. Then she looked at Mitch and asked, *"Pourquoi es-tu triste?"*

I must wear my feelings on my sleeve. She can tell I'm disappointed, Mitch thought.

Before Mitch responded, Kahina touched her father's arm and whispered in his ear. The old man nodded, then turned and disappeared behind a blanket curtain covering a small room. Kahina reached out and held Mitch's hand. She looked at him without saying a word. A few moments passed, and her father reappeared, placing an aged silk bag on the glass counter. He cleared all the jewelry from the countertop and then slowly and carefully opened the bag and placed its contents on a small velvet pillow. He stood back and looked up at Mitch. Kahina moved to where her father was standing and waited in silence.

Mitch stared at what the old man had placed on the pillow. It was exquisite and rare. Mitch had never seen such a beautiful ring.

"Mon père a toujours visé à l'anneau comme une dame." Kahina explained that her father had always thought of the ring as a lady, and that it had been part of the family for hundreds of years.

Mitch was speechless and overwhelmed. The ring was an ancient Bedouin treasure that undoubtedly had belonged to a Sultan. It was gold, and the band was engraved with old Bedouin symbols and designs. Diamonds encircled the center stone. Rising from the diamonds was a large, dark-blue, oval-cut sapphire that defiantly glistened beyond the fire of the diamonds. The ring mesmerized all of Mitch's senses and far exceeded his expectations. This was truly the ring he had been seeking.

But Mitch knew that he couldn't take it. It was part of their family and could never be replaced. *"Je ne peux pas prendre ce à partir de votre famille. C'est un héritage qui ne pourrait jamais être remplacé."*

Kahina's father picked up the ring and placed it in Mitch's palm. *"Il est temps pour elle de retourner à un Américain. Elle a été prise par un célèbre officier de la marine américaine quand il a tué un ennemi dans la bataille au large de la côte de l'Afrique du Nord. Elle a été renvoyée des années plus tard à mes ancêtres après l'officier américain est mort au cours d'un affaire d'honneur."*

Apparently the ring had been taken by a famous American naval officer when he killed an enemy in battle off the coast of North Africa, and the ring had been returned to the old man's ancestors when the American officer was killed in a duel. Mitch was somewhat confused by the old man's statement that it was time for the ring to return to an American.

"Je ne comprends pas," Mitch responded in bewilderment.

The old man held Mitch's hand with both of his. He smiled and looked into Mitch's eyes.

"*L'Américain, l'officier de marine, le jeune héros, son nom a été Lieutenant Stephan Decatur.*"

A chill raced down Mitch's spin as he opened his hand and stared at the ring. *Stephen Decatur*, he thought in wonder. *The hero of the Barbary Coast War. He fought pirates and helped to make our navy the greatest in the world. A man who lived and died during the formative years of America.*

The old man insisted that Mitch take the ring because the soul of Decatur lived within the fire of the diamonds and the spirit of rebellion within the sapphire.

Dave laid his hand on Mitch's shoulder. "Sir, we must go. It's 8:30."

Mitch turned to Kahina and hugged her, then whispered, "*Votre père n'accepte pas l'argent pour l'anneau, mais vous ne pouvez pas refuser ce même si l'anneau est inestimable.*" He knew that the old man would never accept money for the ring, but Kahina couldn't refuse what Mitch gave her, in spite of the ring being priceless. Mitch pulled an envelope from the interior pocket of his jacket and placed it in Kahina's hand. He quickly turned to the old man, taking the thin wrinkled hand into his two strong hands and kissing it. Mitch put the ring back into the old silk bag and placed it carefully into the interior jacket pocket, over his heart. He looked at Dave.

"Let's go!"

Dave pulled his hood up over his head as Mitch tugged the cap down to cover the tops of his ears. Then they reentered the darkness of the Casbah.

"Jake, how do you read?" Mitch whispered over his com system. Out of the silence of the night, Mitch immediately heard Jake's voice.

"Got ya loud and clear, sir. Colonel D and I are headin' out toward the back door of Djamila's father's house."

"Great, will keep you updated on our progress," Mitch responded. "Likewise, Colonel."

Mitch gave Dave a thumbs-up. Dave nodded, and the two continued to Captain Hunt's location.

— • — •

Djamila asked if Abella wanted more tea.

"*Non, merci. Il est presque l'heure de* Mitch *et* Dave *pour entrer* Hunt's *maison. Je dois continuer à surveiller. Je suis très nerveux.*" Abella would continue to watch in the direction of Hunt's house for Mitch and Dave—despite her nerves.

— • — •

Dave elbowed Mitch and stared at the shadowy door a few steps away. Mitch's pulse rapidly increased, and bile rose from his stomach, flowing into his mouth. He turned from Dave and spit the acid-laced vomit onto the ancient stone steps. The reaction actually settled Mitch's nerves as the acid burned from his throat down to the pit of his stomach. Now was the time of reckoning.

"Jake, we're going in," Mitch quietly said into the small microphone and heard a double-click reply from Jake acknowledging the call.

— • — •

"Djamila, *Ils sont à la porte.* Oh my God. *Ils sont d'entrer!*" Abella cried nervously to Djamila, telling her that Mitch and Dave were entering Hunt's house. Everything Abella and Mitch had experienced, from their initial meeting in the hospital to the last kiss in the basilica, had led to this moment. Tears streaked her face as she watched the two shadows disappear into the house.

— • — •

Intense light once again temporarily blinded them as Mitch released the door handle and Dave steadied himself, slowly pushing the door closed. Both men had instinctively crouched after entering, and Dave had his M9 in a firing position. They quickly surveyed the room once their eyesight returned, and were stunned at what they saw.

25

L ying on pillows in the corner of the cavernous, empty living room was a man of medium build with a great amount of dark facial hair. He was reading the Koran and eating fruit and dressed in the white robes of a Bedouin sheikh. A beautiful young Algerian woman stood by his side, fanning him to provide relief from the humid air. She had midnight-dark hair, angelic olive skin, and wore transparent, lime-green silk veils and nothing else.

"Welcome, Colonel Ross. I have been expecting you," the man said in perfect American English. "It has been so many years since I have spoken my native tongue with those that I hardly know. I find it odd that before I speak I must translate in my mind to French and Arabic. Please, lower your weapon and join me in a relaxing cup of mint tea. Take in the wonderful aroma of the flower-scented incense. My ladies will be more than happy to serve you in any way you desire." The man spoke with a glimmer in his eye and a sinister smile.

"Where's Hunt?" Mitch demanded as he analyzed his surroundings for something to use as a weapon if needed. The Bedouin man began to laugh hysterically.

"I thought you were much more brilliant than that. Colonel, I believe you are an imbecile!" The man continued laughing. "Please forgive me for what I just said. It was rather rude, but true. I should have made proper introductions when you first entered. But you entered my abode without proper decorum. Am I not correct?" The bearded man's jaw tightened, and his hands momentarily formed into fists. "I am Captain Seth Hunt—or that is what I was called before converting to Islam. My real name is Ahmad Muhammad, but please call me by the name with which you are familiar. Colonel Ross, I assume your companion is Warrant Officer David McQueen. Am I correct?"

Mitch didn't respond. His mind spun as he tried to process what was unfolding before him. *What the fuck? Why is Hunt acting like some Bedouin nobleman? Damn it! It's gotta be Stockholm syndrome.*

Mitch finally snapped out of it. "Hunt, get your ass up, and that's an order!" he hissed. "We only have seconds before your prison guards figure out we're here."

"Oh, my good colonel, you are so naïve," Hunt replied. "Please sit down and relax. The guards know that you are here. In fact, let me call another of my wives so she can finally meet you. She has told me many times that she hoped one day to meet the man that she has heard so much about. She is brewing tea for all of us in the adjacent room."

Hunt paused and sat up, crossing his legs under his robe. He made sure not to expose the soles of his feet—an insulting gesture in the Islamic world. "Samia, would you please meet our visitors?" he called.

"*Oui, je vais venir,*" a voice answered immediately. A moment later, a woman appeared from around the corner. Mitch felt a pain in his chest that seemed to travel down his spine. He had seen many photographs of her.

"Colonel Ross, finally I get to meet you," she said in English. "I have heard so, so much about you. Over the years, Abella has taught me English. It has been wonderful because I can talk to my husband in his native language, although he prefers to speak French and Arabic. Abella has told me about all the trials and tribulations you have experienced to be here. I can honestly say that she loves you very much. Yes, I'm Abella's roommate, and we have been the best of friends. Please let me get tea for you two gentlemen." She bustled off.

Oh my God, Samia has been spying for Hunt. I know Abella is very careful about what she discloses, but how could she not know that Samia was married to Hunt? What game is being played here? Mitch was reeling. This was not at all what he had anticipated.

"Sir, let's get the hell outta here!" Dave pleaded, his M9 still aimed at Hunt. "It's obvious that he doesn't want to go with us."

"Now, now, Warrant Officer McQueen, please lower your weapon. You are my guest, and I desire that you stay here until I decide when and how you and Colonel Ross will depart," Hunt stated with a deep monotone as his eyebrows furrowed.

When Samia returned, the room had grown silent, the heightened tension obvious. "Warm mint tea with cake and fruit. It is an old Algerian cure for anything that ails you," Samia said.

"Take and drink the wholesome warm liquid. I beseech you. It will relax your concerns and open your mind to what I have to say," Hunt said as Samia served the tea and cake. "Ladies, please depart to the other room while I talk to these gentlemen." Hunt motioned with his hand. The two women bowed their heads and departed.

"You must be very confused at the moment," Hunt said, turning to Mitch and Dave. "Why am I not running away with you? If I am a prisoner, why am I living so well? Where are the guards, and why have they not revealed themselves? How was I able to have four wives, including Samia, but yet be a prisoner? How did I know that you were arriving? Let me first answer the last question. Cats make for wonderful guards. They howl when frightened. When the cat howled as you were walking to the jewelry shop, it confirmed to us exactly where you were.

"Now let me help you understand and answer the other questions. It was once stated by a US president—I believe it was William Henry Harrison—while discussing democracies and capitalism that 'the rich get richer and the poor get poorer.' Over my years of liberation from the scum of capitalism, I have learned many things. Above all, I have learned that happiness cannot be bought as the capitalist would have you believe.

"In your world, Colonel Ross, the fortunate are not restrained in their exercise of oppression over the unfortunate. Your world is structured on greed, envy, and the pursuit of money. It is wrong that people like you, Colonel Ross, should be comfortable and well fed while all around you people are starving. From an early age you are taught that capitalism, which flourishes within your so-called democracy, is the best way of life. But ultimately, who teaches you that? It is those who have the most to gain from such a claim, most notably those on Wall Street. I must warn you that the predatory corporate capitalism that defines and dominates your life will be your death if you don't escape it. Capitalism is the height of hypocrisy. Why? Because it is a system that is fundamentally inhuman, antidemocratic, and unsustainable.

"When I lived in America, everywhere I traveled I saw greed and the pursuit of self-interest. I realized that the wealthy dictated the basic outline of public policies. Concentrated wealth continues to call the shots in America. Ordinary people do not have a meaningful way to form public policy. All they do is support the decisions made by the wealthy and powerful. One person, one vote is a joke. Yes, it is true that when I voted in America, my vote was equal to a wealthy man's vote. Take for instance Mr. Warren Buffett. My vote, in theory, is equal to his. But is it really the same? When I voted, no one cared. When Warren Buffett voted, all the rich Americans and half the world wanted to know how he voted and why. So, who really has more influence and opportunities in America? Not the ordinary citizen.

"In greed-infested, capitalistic America, the vast majority work at jobs that are not rewarding, not enjoyable, and fundamentally not worth doing. Basically, what I have learned since escaping from America is that the United States is a nation of unhappy people consuming huge quantities of cheap consumer goods, hoping to dull the pain of an unfulfilling life. Your American society steals your soul, enslaves you to the powerful, wealthy few, and eventually will destroy you.

"After looking from the opposite side of the world, I realized that resisting the predatory corporate capitalistic America was the right thing to do. Wealthy Americans live in their opulent castles, driving their two-hundred-thousand-dollar automobiles, and ignore the fact that most of the world's population lives on less than two dollars a day. They don't care that poverty-related diseases claim the lives of five hundred children an hour here in Africa.

"I have everything that I desire in life: a comfortable lifestyle playing music, reading the Koran, eating healthy food, having four wives, and being blessed by Allah. You must think that I am crazy, but if you knew all that I have experienced since the first Gulf War, you would understand. Am I a prisoner? Absolutely not! I have guards, but they are to protect me. I could go with you now, but to return to your greed, lust, and money-centric American society would be the death of my soul. Oh no, I would never return to that hypocrisy you call democracy for all.

"Over the years of my supposed captivity, I was watched, observed, and tested. Once I converted to Islam, I had the great privilege to meet the magnificent Osama bin Laden. We discussed many things, but the one aspect that he emphasized was that I would be evaluated and tested over the next few years.

"The testing began almost immediately after our meeting. They tested my loyalty to Islam and al-Qaeda, my military abilities, and leadership skills. I was directed to plan and lead attacks on Iraqi government officials, Iraqi installations, and US military targets. I was not allowed weapons, but my team members were directed to carry weapons. They were ordered to carry out any plan that I conceived. At any time, if they thought that I was not genuine to Allah and al-Qaeda, they were to kill me immediately. Obviously, I have fulfilled their desires brilliantly and have been rewarded beyond my wildest dreams."

"Colonel, let's get the hell out now while we're still alive!" Dave said as he reached for the door handle with his free hand.

"You are beginning to anger me, Warrant Officer McQueen! I will tell you now that you do not want to persist down that avenue. As I stated earlier, I will decide when and how you leave my home. Shut up and listen to me, or else I will have you put to death immediately!"

"Dave, stand down for the moment. It'll be better for all of us," Mitch said nervously, keeping his eyes on Hunt.

"Yes, Colonel Ross, that is a very wise thing to say. Now I will continue after that rude interruption," Hunt calmly said. He readjusted his sitting position and sipped his tea. "You undoubtedly have heard from your Algerian military colleagues and CIA scum that there has been a leadership change in the Algerian GSPC. Osama bin Laden determined that this al-Qaeda-affiliated organization needed to increase its activities in Algeria to disrupt oil and gas output, destroy military installations, kill government officials that oppose al-Qaeda's cause, and increase attacks on infidel embassies in Algiers.

"So, how have I done so far? Yes, it was I who directed the attack on the US embassy that destroyed and killed so much American filth residing and working within the devil's walls. I was proud when I heard that we had been fortunate enough to demolish your residence, Colonel. My only regret was that you and Abella were not killed. I was informed by Samia that you had invited Abella to dinner that evening. Although Samia thinks the world of Abella, your lady is Algerian scum who was brainwashed by Americans while she lived in the States with her father and mother."

Mitch took a step toward Hunt, but Dave grabbed his arm and held him back.

"You learn very quickly, Warrant Officer McQueen," Hunt said. "The good colonel would have been killed had he taken one more step."

Hunt began to laugh, and his calm expression shifted to that of a deranged madman. Alarmingly wide-eyed, he drooled tea into his beard, mucus drained from his right nostril, he began to shake, and his chest heaved with rapid breaths.

"Over the years since my initial captivity, and after convincing my Islamic brethren that I was truly a warrior for Allah and al-Qaeda, I began to take on more responsibilities and leadership positions." His volume surged. "*I* AM NOW THE LEADER OF THE GSPC!!" Hunt screamed. He now stood with his fists clenched, face red, and sweat beading on his forehead. It looked as though he was attempting to control himself, but his voice remained an unhinged scream. "I AM CURIOUS, COLONEL! WHAT ARE YOUR THOUGHTS AFTER HEARING ALL OF THIS?!"

Mitch took a deep breath. Keeping as calm as he possibly could, considering the circumstances, he said, "My thoughts? I'm not sure you really want to hear them."

Hunt took a step closer to Mitch and began to raise his clenched hand, but then slowly controlled his anger. "Oh yes," he hissed, "I would be honored to hear your truthful feelings about what I said!"

Mitch looked at Dave and nodded, then turned back to Hunt. "Okay, Hunt, here are my true feelings, and I'm sure the good warrant officer on my right will agree with me." Mitch cleared his throat and stared into the eyes of this crazed terrorist traitor. "Fuck you and the camel you rode in on. I don't give a flying fuck about your philosophies of life! As far as I'm concerned, you're full of shit and can shove your thoughts and opinions up your royal ass with pig oil.

"That's the problem with assholes like you and Osama bin Laden—you're so busy stroking each other's egos that you end up blinded by your fanatical beliefs. May the two of you drown in pig fat after you've been castrated! I'm sure that I've sealed my fate and my partner's, but at least I'll leave this planet knowing that my good friend Dave planted a lead sedative between your eyeballs and splattered your brains on the wall behind you!" Mitch braced himself for his impending death as Dave quickly raised his M9 and put Hunt's forehead in his sights.

"STOP!" Hunt screamed. "I demand that you stop immediately! There will be no killing in my house." He took a few steps back, standing among the pillows near the wall. "I will let you depart my residence, but you will have only seconds before my security rises up out of the cracks, the shadows, and every corner of the Casbah and guns you two infidels down. Yes, you will be standing in front of Allah tonight, begging for forgiveness! I recommend that you say your prayers and leave my residence—NOW! ALLAHU AKBAR! ALLAHU AKBAR! ALLAHU AKBAR!"

26

Abella and Djamila were getting nervous. It had been far too long since Mitch and Dave entered the house that supposedly held Captain Hunt. Abella tried to take comfort in the fact that she had not heard any gunshots, but suddenly she caught the faint sound of a screaming voice.

Abella asked Djamila if she had heard something.

"*Oui, j'ai entendu* Allahu Akbar!" Djamila nervously replied, saying that she had heard someone screaming "Allahu Akbar."

Abella insisted that Djamila stand near the door. She knew that the screaming was not good and something unfortunate was about to happen. Seconds later, they heard a gunshot, and the door of Captain Hunt's home flew open, sending a beacon of light into the darkened Casbah.

"Jake, everything went belly up!" Mitch yelled into the mic as he and Dave bolted out of the house.

- • - •

It only confirmed what Jake already knew. He had heard gunfire and immediately realized that things were not going well for Mitch and Dave. "Colonel D, I reckon that this here mission is a bust," he said. "That was Colonel Ross on the radio. Get ready to rock and roll with that French pistol of yours, cause we're gonna see some action real soon."

- • - •

Abella screamed for Djamila to open the door; everything seemed to be going wrong. She pulled one of the M9s from her purse and ran to the open door. Kneeling in a firing position, she spotted two shadows running full out toward Djamila's father's house. As Mitch and Dave neared, she saw the flicker of muzzle flashes coming from Hunt's residence. Bullets ricocheted off the stone wall near Abella and Djamila, spraying them with sharp fragments. Both women instinctively ducked.

Abella knew that she had to cover Mitch and Dave, so she raised her pistol and fired two quick shots in the direction of the muzzle flashes. A scream rang out, and a robe-clad body rolled wildly down the steps. *That's one less slime to worry about*, Abella thought.

More shots exploded from Hunt's residence, and Abella and Djamila moved back from the open door. Then they heard something terrible.

"Oh God, I'm hit!" Dave screamed, falling hard on the stone steps just before the open door. Mitch flung his body next to Dave as bullets skipped along the steps. He reached for Dave's M9 and returned fire.

"Get the hell out of here, sir," Dave grimaced. He coughed and rolled into a fetal position.

"I'm not leaving your side until I can get your ass into the house!" Mitch yelled over the gunfire.

"Sir, if you don't get out of here, there'll be two dead Americans on these steps."

"Damn it, Dave! Okay, but I'm going to get Jake and Yves to help us. Hang in there—I'll be back soon."

As Mitch stood to a crouch and darted toward Abella, a shadow passed him, running into the line of fire. Djamila threw her body over Dave and held him with all her strength, knowing that the next round of bullets might hit her. Mitch dove through the open door. As he crashed to the floor, he lost his grip on the M9 and watched it bounce off an adjacent wall. Mitch rolled across the floor, striking an old dining table and collapsing it and the pot of tea on it, spraying the contents of the teapot throughout the small kitchen.

Briefly distracted by Mitch, Abella didn't notice a man approaching from the right until he began firing at Djamila and Dave. Djamila screamed, and Abella spun and instinctively raise her M9. Her bullet ripped through the terrorist's chest, spraying blood over his white robes and splattering Djamila and Dave as his lifeless body fell beside them.

Djamila tried to drag Dave to her father's door. Seeing Djamila struggle, Abella fired two rounds for effect in the direction of Hunt's residence. Then she helped pull Dave as Mitch took Djamila's father's old pistol and fired at a shadow only a few feet from the door. The body of the terrorist dropped, and his head fell near the entrance of the house. Mitch pushed the dead man's head out of the way with his foot, then bent to grab Dave's shirt collar and help pull him into the living room.

"Close the door!" Mitch yelled as he dragged the couch from the living room. He pushed the couch against the door to prevent it from being forced open. Then he wedged parts of the broken dining table under the couch to prevent it from being moved.

"*La fenêtre!*" Djamila's father yelled, pointing at the front window while he gathered rags to help stem Dave's bleeding.

Abella spotted a terrorist aiming a pistol at Mitch through the window and raised her weapon, firing just as the terrorist's pistol flashed.

Mitch felt a searing pain in his right shoulder. His body spun, and he crumpled onto the tea-splattered floor. Abella's bullet was much more accurate, ripping into the throat of Hunt's guard. The terrorist fell through the shattered front window, his lifeless body slumping half in the living room and half out on the steps. Abella ran to Mitch as he struggled to get off the floor.

"Mitch, Mitch, are you badly hurt?" Abella screamed, her face wet with tears.

"I'm okay, I think. That damn bullet took a chunk out of my shoulder. It hurts like hell, but I'll survive. All I need is a piece of the kitchen towel and duct tape to stop the bleeding."

Abella handed her pistol to Djamila's father and treated Mitch's wound. In the meantime, intense gunfire continued in the back of the house.

"That's gotta be Jake and Yves," Mitch said as Abella placed the last strip of duct tape to hold the towel on his wound. "We've gotta get out of here and help them."

"What about Dave and Djamila?" Abella asked. Djamila was attempting to stop the fierce bleeding of Dave's leg wound.

Dave's eyes flickered and opened. Then in a whisper that could barely be heard above the gunfire, he said, "Get the hell out of here, Colonel. Get the hell out now and don't worry about us!"

Abella grabbed Mitch's shirtsleeve and pleaded, "Let's go, or we'll all be killed."

"We'll go, but only to get Jake and Yves," Mitch insisted. "We need their firepower to help protect us all in this house. I promised Dave that I would not leave him, and I won't!"

Mitch took one last look at Dave and Djamila and gave them a quick salute. Without another word, he grabbed Abella and ran to the small exit door in the back of the house. "Jake, we're coming your way," Mitch said over the com unit.

"Okay, Colonel, but be advised, you stirred up a pack full of them hornets. The bad guys are comin' out like termites in rotten wood on this side of the Casbah. Keep your head down, and we'll cover you when we see the small door open."

Mitch held the old French pistol tight as Abella clutched the other M9 from her purse. Mitch pushed the door open and saw a body slumped against a house across from the steps. Covering gunfire from the right indicated the location of Jake and Yves.

"Keep a low profile, sweetheart, and try to stay close to the walls. If all else fails, follow my shadow." Mitch took one last quick look at Abella before running out the door.

Abella readied herself as she squeezed the grip of the M9 with her right hand. She lowered her head and held her breath, then followed Mitch.

Mitch knew that leaving the protection of the house was extremely risky. Hugging the wall on his right, he followed the muzzle flashes from Jake and Yves, who were crouched behind a large pile of stones and rubble that had fallen from an adjacent building. Abella was practically on Mitch's heels on the approach. As bullets pocked the stones around them, Mitch and Abella scrambled over the debris and squatted near Yves.

Yves turned toward them, smiling, and wiped his brow with his sleeve. "Welcome to my humble abode," he said. "It's a pity I have no wine to serve or French pastries to offer, but if you're looking for gut-wrenching excitement, you've come to the right place." In spite of their situation, Yves's comment momentarily lightened the atmosphere.

"Colonel, it's damn good to see you two, but where the hell is Dave?" Jake asked between bursts from his Uzi.

"I've got some bad news!" Mitch replied. "Dave was hit running from Hunt's house. He told Abella and me to get the hell out, but I refuse to leave him. On top of that, that bastard Hunt has turned—he claims to be the leader of the GSPC. I need all of us to return to Djamila's house. God, I pray Dave doesn't bleed out. Djamila and her father have their hands full trying to keep the terrorists at bay until we get back to help them."

"Holy shit, Colonel, what we need is the cavalry to save our asses," Jake said. "Barring that, I guess Colonel D and me better mount up! I believe the bad guys have some sort of a com network; there seems to be more coming in our direction on this side of the Casbah. Word must have been passed that you and the pretty lady have joined up with us. That'll take the pressure off Dave and Djamila for the time bein'. If you want all of us back at Djamila's house, I reckon we need to move out now. Those slimy critters are swarmin' to the back door of the house you just left. It's not lookin' good, Colonel."

Mitch peeked over the protective stones and rubble. Large numbers of terrorists took positions against the walls on the right and left of the stairs. A few had climbed on roofs overlooking the piles of rubble, and now bullets were hitting dangerously close.

"Mitch, I hate to be the bearer of bad news, but I believe some of those shots came from behind us," Yves whispered, resting his hand on Mitch's shoulder.

Mitch turned and spotted muzzle flashes lighting the darkness down the steps, in the direction of their SUV. Raising the old French pistol, he took a few shots back. Jake noticed Mitch's hand shake as he fired. The wound to the colonel's shoulder was taking its toll.

"Colonel, let me send a few of those bastards to the land of milk, honey, and a handful of virgins!" Jake yelled as he spun around and fired his Uzi in the direction of the gunfire. For a moment the muzzle flashes faded from the rear, but there was an increase of fire from the rooftops and forward positions.

They were slowly being surrounded. Mitch looked at Abella as she fired at the terrorists and thought, *I can't let anything happen to her. She deserves to live a good life. Oh God, help me! You know how much I love her.*

He leaned toward Yves and grabbed his arm. "Yves, it's too late to get back to Djamila's house. The backdoor area is blocked off. The only way to save us all is to fight our way down to the SUV."

"Unfortunately, you're correct. If we stay here, we all die!" Yves yelled, looking over the rubble. In a flash he grimaced and shot a terrorist in the face just as the man reached their protective piles of stone.

Mitch shouted to the group while bullets ricocheted along the rubble wall. "We gotta get to the SUV. Can't help Dave and Djamila now! Just try to stay together and fire on the run." Mitch grabbed Abella and took off running down the steps of the Casbah, firing at muzzle flashes. Mitch heard Abella crying as she ran and fired her pistol.

"This is not how I wanted our lives to end. We barely had time to enjoy our love," Abella said, clutching Mitch's jacket sleeve when she stumbled on a broken step.

Yves and Jake had taken up rearguard action. Jake sprayed an Uzi burst, and three terrorists fell hard on the stone steps, screaming in pain as bullets tore through their bodies. Mitch saw the harbor and knew that they were getting closer to the naval headquarters. That meant the freedom and safety of their SUV, now just forty meters away. *I hope to God that the SUV isn't going to be an ambush and our killing field*, Mitch thought. He pulled Abella closer to him, his pulse racing.

Another rapid exchange of gunfire erupted, followed by an odd silence. Mitch and Abella froze as Jake grunted loudly and fell forward on the steps. His Uzi clattered on the hard surface and skidded out of sight into the darkness. Mitch and Abella ran to Jake's side while Yves fired cover. Jake clutched his stomach with his left hand, attempting to stem the bleeding wound. He grimaced in pain as he reached inside his jacket for the M9, but he was rapidly losing strength and couldn't pull the gun out of its holster.

Jake finally looked up and noticed Mitch by his side. With a blank look in his eyes, he began to wheeze and reached out to grasp Mitch's jacket collar. Then he whispered, "Sorry, Colonel . . . I kinda screwed up . . . I wasn't supposed t'get shot. Damn it hurts." He paused, breathing heavily. "I never thought . . . it would end like this—dyin' in this shit-stained place . . ." Jake's voice trailed off as he closed his eyes and clenched his teeth, the pain overwhelming him as blood flowed from his stomach.

Abella was doing all she could for Jake by ripping portions of her shirt and stuffing it into the wound. Blood covered her hands and arms as she struggled to keep him alive. She pushed hair from her face, leaving a large, bloody streak along her forehead and cheek. Abella felt helpless without the proper medical gear. To make matters worse, the terrorist gunfire only increased as Mitch and Yves fired back in the direction of the oncoming threat.

"Mitch, we've got to continue to the SUV!" Yves yelled.

Shit, I can't leave Jake, Mitch thought. *But Yves is correct—it's just a matter of time before we're all hit if we stay.*

"Abella, help me drag Jake to that area where the two walls merge. It's better protection," Mitch desperately yelled while bullets slammed into the walls and stones, shards slicing into their exposed flesh.

After they propped Jake up between the walls, Mitch pulled the M9 from Jake's jacket and placed it in the palm of his hand. Jake struggled to turn to Mitch and wheezed, "With all due respect, please get the hell outta here. Our house o' cards is fallin' down."

Abella leaned over Jake and caressed his face with her hand.

"Mitch, we're about to be overrun. I can't hold them off much longer!" Yves yelled.

Mitch turned to Jake and cradled his head with genuine brotherly love. "Jake, we'll meet again someday," Mitch whispered. Then he gently repositioned the big man between the two walls. Mitch took Abella's hand, and the two of them dashed toward Yves.

They had only a few steps to go before reaching the gate of the Casbah and the SUV. They periodically turned and fired at their pursuers. On the main boulevard, a single faded streetlamp illuminated the vehicle. The three of them paused under the ancient walled gate where they had entered hours earlier.

"Let me run to the SUV while you two cover me," Mitch said. "If this is an ambush, at least we won't all be taken out." Without waiting for a response, he dashed across the road.

Shots rang out from the darkness as the terrorists continued their onslaught. The extremists seemed to have broken off their attack in the immediate area, so the shots were either coming from

Jake's or Dave's position in the Casbah. But the SUV seemed to be clear of danger. Mitch turned toward Abella and Yves and waved for them to run to the vehicle.

When Abella jumped into the back seat, Mitch pulled Yves aside and whispered, "I'm not going with you. I can't leave Dave and Jake to die here in this godforsaken place. Please take Abella to the French embassy. Her roommate is one of Hunt's wives and is very dangerous. I'm sure terrorists will be waiting at her apartment. She can never return to the army hospital or she'll be arrested and killed. Please, please take care of her for me, my good friend!"

Yves knew that time was running out. He hugged Mitch, then jumped into the driver's seat and started the SUV. Abella was confused, but when reality struck her, she attempted to get out of the vehicle.

"No, no, sweetheart, you must stay! I promise we'll be together again. I'll never stop loving you!" Mitch said, failing to hold back tears.

Abella reached out to him through the open window as the vehicle began to move. Mitch quickly pulled the small silk pouch from his jacket pocket and placed it in her hand, and the vehicle sped away.

27

*D*amn it, what the hell am I going to do now? Mitch wondered as he moved back into the Casbah and toward the enemy. He slunk from shadow to shadow, hiding behind walls and debris as extremists dashed down the steps in the direction he'd come from. Mitch watched them go, then made his way back to Jake. As he got closer, he turned and crouched in an alley adjacent to the steps . He was concentrating on his next move when a voice startled him from behind.

"Colonel, good evening. I thought you might need a little help."

Mitch froze as the speaker placed a hand on his shoulder. He jerked his head around. There, crouching just behind him, was Greg Cain with a big smile on his face. Even better, four CIA officers loaded with high-tech weapons and medical gear flanked Greg.

"Hey, you're welcome!" Greg said. "You can thank me later at the bar. Although, I'm breaking all the rules we made with the ambassador and the White House . . . so actually, don't say a damn word. I won't if you won't!"

Mitch stared at Greg and his companions, trying to form a question.

"I knew that you had stayed behind because we were watching

your SUV from the Algerian naval headquarters." Greg gave Mitch a thumbs-up and then signaled the CIA members to move out.

"But how the hell did you know we were here? I kept a tight lid on this operation," Mitch said.

"Let's talk about it later over bourbon. After all, you owe Jake a big bottle of Kentucky magic," Greg said. "We have things to do here."

Nearing Jake's location, Mitch and Greg saw that three dead terrorists had fallen almost on top of him. Jake was slumped over, bloodstains covering his shirt and face.

"Let's wait a moment," Greg whispered. "The terrorists might be waiting to catch us in an ambush."

But Mitch couldn't take seeing Jake suffer. "Sorry, Greg," Mitch whispered as he ran to Jake from their position. He pulled off the dead bodies and then held Jake with one arm as he aimed his pistol with the other. Mitch desperately searched for a pulse. The big man was limp in his arms. As Mitch looked down at Jake's face, looking for a sign of life, a shriek rang out just above him.

"*Allahu Akbar!*"

Mitch's head snapped violently backward, and he felt an intense pain. The last thing he saw before passing out was the wooden butt of an AK-47.

- • - •

Mitch awoke in agony, his head pounding with the force of several migraines. He lay semiconscious without a sense of reality. Oddly, it was the smell of cigarette smoke that triggered his mind to focus on the muffled ranting of a madman.

"I don't give a damn what condition that bastard colonel is in. That son of a bitch is going on the next military flight to the States! He violated direct orders from the White House, and I'm making arrangements to have the Supreme Allied Commander Europe fly into Algiers and pick up this piece of shit." Mitch recognized the speaker as Chargé D'Affaires Anderson.

"All the newspapers in North Africa and Europe have pictures and articles on their front pages of the disaster that Colonel Ross caused," Anderson continued. "Not to mention the horrendous body count! I contacted my uncle, the US senator, and he's just about guaranteed that Ross will be stripped of his rank and thrown in jail. I will not lose my opportunity to become the US ambassador to Algeria because of what he did. I want him in the SACEUR's jet as soon as possible. It will be a glorious day for me seeing Ross's life destroyed! That's all I've got to report. Goodbye."

Anderson arrogantly slammed the phone down, hanging up on the representatives from the State Department. His face was still swollen and bruised from Jake's punch. He took a long drag on what remained of his cigarette as he leaned back in his leather chair.

Mitch's pain became overwhelming, and his mind slowly closed the door on the world as he drifted back into the abyss of unconsciousness.

- • •

Yves and Abella entered the French embassy as the sergeant of the guard saluted. The sergeant couldn't help but notice that Yves was driving an American embassy vehicle without an American.

"*Excusez moi, Colonel, mais c'est un véhicule de l'ambassade américaine?*" the sergeant of the guard asked about the vehicle.

"*Oui, je vous expliquerai plus tard. Je suis trop fatigué et j'ai besoin de vin,*" Yves responded, telling the sergeant that he would explain later. For now he was tired and wanted wine.

Abella was still sobbing in the back seat, blood on her face, arms, and hands.

The sergeant inquired about medical treatment for Abella. Thinking about the evening's tragic events and wondering if Mitch, Jake, Dave, and Djamila had survived, Yves sadly responded that Abella just needed a hot shower and wine.

Yves parked the SUV near his embassy residence and helped Abella out.

Without thinking, she spoke in English. "Why didn't you take me to my apartment? Why are we here at the French embassy?" she asked, bewildered. Her mind, heart, and soul were still with Mitch.

Yves realized that she was extremely traumatized. "Abella, let's go into the house," he said, thinking it best to continue speaking in English. "I have things I must tell you that Mitch said just before our departure from the Casbah."

As Abella walked into Yves's living room, she reached into her pocket and pulled out the small silk bag Mitch had given her. She sat on the couch before opening it. Gently separating the drawstrings, Abella took the ring from its silken container. She gasped as the large blue sapphire came to life and radiated a bluish glow; the fire of the diamonds seemed to dance. Abella was stunned by its beauty. Yves entered the room, carrying wine.

"My God, the ring is exquisite!" Yves said as he stood over her and gazed at the magnificent treasure. "Something that rare and beautiful can only mean that Mitch wanted you not just for the present, but for the rest of his life."

At this, Abella burst into tears. Realizing he had spoken without thinking, Yves set down the glasses and tried to console Abella. She clutched the ring to her heart as tears streaked through the crusted bloodstains on her face.

"Please, have a little wine while I attempt to explain why you're here," Yves said, handing her a glass. Without any formalities, he sipped a large mouthful of merlot. Abella drank some wine and clutched the ring in her hand, still sobbing.

"This is very difficult for me to say, but your world has completely and totally changed this evening," Yves said, still speaking English. "Everything that you know and have grown accustomed to is either gone or no longer a part of you. You can never return to your apartment—it's too dangerous. All your belongings in your apartment will most likely be lost. Your roommate, Samia, is one of Seth Hunt's wives. This makes her very dangerous because Hunt is now the leader of the GSPC in Algeria. You can never return to the army hospital because of the military link to the GSPC. You must remain in hiding for as long as you stay in Algeria."

Abella placed her glass on the adjacent table and wiped her face with her shirt. "I will never be able to leave Algeria," she said. "I will never again be able to walk freely amongst my people in the marketplace. I will never be able to work and earn a living. I will never see Mitch again. More than likely he was killed going back into the Casbah. I have lost everything. I have no reason or desire to continue on in this world." Abella glanced at Yves's pistol on the table near her wine. Before Yves could react, Abella grabbed the Pamas G1 and held it to her head.

"No, Abella, you can't do this," Yves pleaded. "We don't know if Mitch is dead. I'll do everything I can to get a French visa for you. Please, please, stop and listen to me!" He stood and held out a hand. "You must not end it this way. When I get the visa and you depart Algeria, you can stay in my apartment in Paris. Please listen to me and put down the gun. I beg you!"

"You don't understand, Yves," she sobbed. "The GSPC has inundated my records with falsehoods. They have placed documents in my files indicating my affiliation with them and al-Qaeda. Ever since I returned to Algeria from America, they have been attempting to destroy my life as they destroyed my parents' lives. I have tried to gain a visa to France many times, but my attempts have been futile. I can never leave this country, and eventually I will be hunted down and killed."

Yves knew that every movement he made and word he said was potentially dangerous. "Please don't pull the trigger," he said softly. "Let's contact the US embassy and find out about Mitch. I'm sure there is news about him." As Yves spoke, he gently grasped Abella's hand and carefully removed the pistol, shoving it into his trouser pocket. "Abella, I will do everything in my power to get you out of this country. Do you hear me? You will stay in my extra room here in the embassy for a few days until we can find a location that will guarantee your safety. More than likely there are GSPC working in this embassy, and they will eventually report that you are here with me. I have an idea where we might find lodging for you while I arrange for your departure. Just remember, finding ways for you to leave this country can be very difficult and won't happen overnight."

28

Mitch felt the warmth of the sun on his face. The room was stark white, with no television or pictures on the walls—just his elevated medical bed with side rails, monitoring equipment with the accompanying obnoxious beeping, and the stand that supported his IV. He felt imprisoned under the sheets and blanket, firmly pulled as they were around his entire body. The corners of the bed linen had been squared off and tucked in proper military fashion.

As he eased his right eye open, he noticed a few nurses holding clipboards, monitoring and taking notes on his vital signs. The bandage covering his head was wrapped across his left eye, preventing him from seeing anything on that side of the room. One nurse was communicating the instrument readings from the monitoring machine. In his semiconscious state he said to the nurse, "You speak English extremely well."

The nurse laughed and replied, "Well, Colonel, good afternoon. You've been sleeping for quite a while—almost thirty-six hours! As to your statement concerning my language skills, I'll let you in on a little secret. Being born in Denver helps a lot. And being a nurse at Andrews Air Force Base helps me practice." The nurse continued to laugh as she recorded the time and date that Mitch had awoken and verbally responded.

What did she say? Andrews Air Force Base? How the hell did I get back to the DC area?

"Excuse me, but how did I get back home?"

The nurse lowered her clipboard and stared at Mitch for a moment before answering.

"Colonel, from what I've heard through the hospital grapevine, you were escorted by the Supreme Allied Commander Europe in his personal jet. You landed here at Andrews and were immediately admitted into this medical center. Not only do you have a huge, swollen knot just above your forehead, but a bullet appears to have passed completely through your shoulder. That was some interesting medical treatment: a small kitchen towel and duct tape. As they say, one should never be without duct tape! I know that I can't ask personal questions, but wherever you were and whatever you were doing must have been very dangerous and important." The nurse turned from Mitch and quietly talked to the others in the room.

Mitch was somewhat confused by her response. "Why do you think it was important?"

The nurse turned back to Mitch and leaned over to whisper, "There are two armed military guards standing outside your door. That does not happen here."

ACKNOWLEDGMENTS

A debt of gratitude to my family for their enthusiasm, suggestions, and patience. I will never be able to repay you for all your contributions while writing this adventure.

Also, a special thank-you to Abella. You don't realize that you are changing this world for the better. Without your help, this book would not have been written.

ABOUT THE AUTHOR

T ed Kissel grew up in California. After graduating college in the early seventies, he entered the military and spent twenty-eight years as an officer in the US Air Force, retiring as a colonel. The majority of his military career was spent in the cockpit, flying F-4 Phantoms, and he was awarded the Distinguished Flying Cross for heroism in the First Gulf War. Following his flying duties, he served as a base commander in Europe and then as a deputy division chief in the Pentagon, assigned to the secretary of the Air Force and the Office of the Secretary of Defense. His final assignment was as a defense attaché, building relations and cooperation between the US and Algerian militaries at the US Embassy in Algiers. Since retiring from the military, Ted has worked for a major defense contractor as a manager and director. Currently, he is employed by Harley Davidson as a manager and riding instructor. *Betrayal in the Cashbah* is Ted's first novel, and he is currently working on a new action adventure, continuing the exploits of Mitch Ross and Abella.

TO BE CONTINUED IN ...
ESCAPE FROM ALGIERS

I n the failed rescue attempt that left our courageous group scattered, no one remains unscathed. Mitch finds himself in the spotlight on Capitol Hill, facing an investigation at the highest level that may end his career. Abella is scared for her safety and life as she tries everything to flee Algeria and the constant threat of al-Qaeda. The others have been left injured, traumatized and worse.

Escape from Algiers is the adrenaline-packed action sequel that follows our star-crossed heroes as they attempt to pick up the pieces of their lives. They will face new nemeses and tribulations while undertaking yet another dangerous mission.

Follow Ted on social media for sneak previews of the new book and updates on the publication date. www.trkissel.com

CPSIA information can be obtained
at www.ICGtesting.com
Printed in the USA
BVHW031028040322
630566BV00024B/331/J